The Water Garden

ABIGAIL FRITH lives in Yorkshire dividing
her spare time between gardening and working in the 'peace' and 'conservation'
movements.

She says that writing stories about times
when people lived closer to the earth, and
their horizons were nearer, gives her a respite
from the present beleaguered state of our
planet. *The Water Garden* is her first novel and
she is now at work upon another.

ABIGAIL FRITH

The Water Garden

Fontana Paperbacks

The author would like to acknowledge her
gratitude to William Hodgson (1900–84) who
began work as an apprentice carpenter on the
Leeds–Liverpool Canal in 1914 and who forgot
nothing of interest that happened on the 'cut' for
many years before and after that time.

British Library Cataloguing in Publication Data

Frith, Abigail
  The water garden.
  I. Title
  823'.914[F]   PR6056.R5/

  ISBN 0-00-617382-9

First published by Fontana Paperbacks 1987

Copyright © Abigail Frith 1987

Made and printed in Great Britain by
William Collins Sons and Co. Ltd, Glasgow

Conditions of Sale
This book is sold subject to the condition
that it shall not, by way of trade or otherwise,
be lent, re-sold, hired out or otherwise circulated
without the publisher's prior consent in any form of
binding or cover other than that in which it is
published and without a similar condition
including this condition being imposed
on the subsequent purchaser

PART I

The Garden

CHAPTER ONE

Effie Barrett was born in the large stone house on September sixth, 1864. Her grandfather, Jack, had built it a decade earlier of hard millstone grit from the Bramley Fall quarries just the other side of the River Aire. Even today, blackened by a century of mill smog, the battlements surmounting its low tower and the crisply chiselled architraves around windows and doors are a monument to Victorian confidence and the sturdy pride of its builder.

Jack Barrett also laid out the grounds in neat formality, kitchen garden, rose beds, shrubbery and orchard. His short, broad form had surged through house and grounds as his flat voice commanded builders and gardeners in the directness of their own dialect but with the masterfulness of a lord. They accepted this with Yorkshire fortitude. He had made the brass and it was his right to spend it as he pleased, but their independence of spirit and love of correct values always prompted them to point out his occasional misjudgement (which he would usually amend in the same spirit).

'He may be a stubborn man but he's commonly raight and middlin' fair,' they would mutter to each other. Jim Woodgate, the resident gardener, was more complicated. He was a dalesman bred way up at Airton just below the Malham Cove cradle of the Aire and, though they tend to be 'close' up there, Jim was closer than most. He would be a bachelor of about forty at the time Effie was born, of medium height and build but already with a slight stoop about the shoulders. Maybe this had been with him since boyhood, to shelter the privacy of his irregular rugged features, although 'boyhood' was a difficult state to associate with Jim. He emanated a feeling of absolute neutrality which extended to time as well as to his surroundings. He preferred to be considered as one with the stone wall against which he leant and the soil on which his boot rested. In fact, he was more neutral and less associated with human intervention than the spade he held. He might pass an informed opinion upon the qualities of the spade, if asked soberly and given time to consider, but under no circumstances would he venture to comment upon himself. Jack Barrett never consciously raised his voice to Jim and when carried beyond the short limits of his patience there was always the mutual knowledge that Jim would in no way be influenced. The relationship of master to employee might require lip service – the touching of a cap, the muttered 'sir' occasionally to end a remark and acquiescence in the general layout of the garden but the season-to-season and plant-to-plant gardening was entirely Jim's concern and, as far as one could judge, his *raison d'être*.

Within a mere two years Effie had a good measure of these two men who were to influence her life more deeply than any others, and it only took a little longer for her to gauge her power to influence them.

Jack's wife had been dead for nine years and since there had not been more than a convenient convention connecting them she had left no permanent scar. His daughter-in-law looked after the house, the inside of which did not interest him in any way. So long as there was minimal interference with his study and none while he was in it, she could do as she pleased. The outside of the house gave him great satisfaction. The proud ostentation of the style, the elegance of the detail and the sheer durability never failed to please him.

This era of the garden was an ode in colour to order and precision. Its summer claim to beauty lay in the vivid masses of scarlet, blue and yellow in the annual beds, neatly bordered and offset by the velvet green of the box hedges. The extensive rose beds carried a variety of clear coloured blooms floating above the dark green foliage and well-tilled soil. In the herbaceous borders, spring masses of crocus, daffodils, scyllas, tulips and narcissi were succeeded by spires of tree-lupin, red lychnis, blue and white delphiniums and dahlias in the zenith splendours of the striped fancies or laced varieties like Lucina, and the tousled sun of Crawley Beauty, larger than a child's head.

In the kitchen garden stood two feathery rows of Early Horn carrots, three rows of dwarf peas, two rows of later main-crop and broad beans with their stiff fat pods all standardized in height and shape. The flourishing plants with pods and tubers and names evocative of continental adventure or erotic fertility, could transport a connoisseur of kitchen gardens into a blissful waking dream.

In the air above the garden and house flew, tumbled and rolled the elite of pigeonhood in a swirl of grey and white, circling and settling in continuous alternation on house roof and cote. Against the stone roof gleamed the whitest of doves and the plumpest of pouters soothing the summer afternoons with their mildly garrulous cooing.

In short, the house and garden throbbed complacently with well-ordered life and, at the nub of this life, was Effie. Six years old, she paused meditatively in the great door arch. Her ash-blonde hair was long and untidy, her figure now suddenly slight and leggy bore the last appealing trace of babyhood about the rounded arms and shoulders, while her cheeks and hands were still quite chubby. Her chin was raised, the small nose neatly curved and lips firm. Her posture announced self-assurance verging on hauteur while her large grey-blue eyes, dark-lashed, were, at the moment, pale and remote. Her grandfather strolled towards her, smiling as he wondered again at the strange genetic quirk which had borne this proud slight elf into a long line of stocky, coarse-featured, Yorkshire yeomen. This is what they were: he had no pretensions but, however wide one's girth, short one's neck and homely one's features, one could still appreciate and aspire to beauty. He had carried this dream of beauty with him all his life and had found the reality now, in his garden and greenhouse. Most folk seemed to strive for little but material comfort and maybe it was this difference which accounted for the loneliness which he had felt as a small, barely significant unease behind his confident façade. It was at this moment as he walked towards Effie, anticipating the change in her eyes as she noticed him, that it struck him that this niggling unease had eeased. The little chink in his armour of independence was at last filled. A slip of a grandchild was the soul-mate that neither wife nor son had been and it was she who would share his dream.

Jack had cherished hopes for his son – higher education; perhaps even university; the chance to work in beautiful surroundings with clean hands and stimulating companions. John had done his best, he had worked hard and tried to please but his was not the stuff that scholars are made of. Such momentum as he had was only reflected from his father; his own were the commonplace aspirations to have a comfortable job and marry a comfortable stout local girl and, why not, propagate stolid stout children. In fact, old Jack sometimes believed that was just what his son and daughter-in-law believed they had done. They had never even noticed how different Effie was.

'Well, what are we doing today, my little elf?'

Her eyes fired to a clear, blue awareness. 'You said you'd help me make my garden, Grandpa.'

'Aye, so I did, lass. I bought some seeds for you and Jim says we can use a bit of the side bed.'

She was down the steps in a bound, caught his hand in passing and dragged him along at a slow trot, protesting mildly. Her mother came round the corner of the house in a print pinafore resembling nothing so much as a stout pillar splashed with large blooms; her face was reddened with exertion and framed by wispy ginger hair.

'Effie, don't you pull Grandpa along like that. I can't think why you let her, Faither. *You* ought to be able to make the bairn behave proper.'

There was an emphasis on the 'you' which did not escape

10

Jack. He knew full well that Mary regarded him as a tyrant and lost no opportunity to tell her relatives and friends as much. She devoted some of the more significant moments of her life to prompting her husband to 'put Faither in his place' but young John had placidly accepted the unequalness of such a struggle at a tender age. He now found his mild disposition forming a buffer between father and wife and had conceded his father the victory as far as strength of character was concerned. His wife's claim to superiority was mainly verbal and she had only to needle the old man too far to find herself well outpaced on that score too. Anyway, they had their own part of the big house and so long as Mary kept out of the old man's way as much as she could while carrying out the duties of house-keeper, things went along reasonably smoothly. This situation suited Effie well. She frequented the kitchen as little as necessary to supply her material needs and spent the rest of the time in the garden or study, usually with her grandfather. John and Mary were beginning to learn that if they needed the old man's approbation for anything, the surest way of getting it was through Effie. Her cooperation could not be depended upon, of course. She was a strange wayward girl – spoiled, they supposed, by an old man whose authority had humbled many a strong man.

Jack merely nodded to his daughter-in-law and slackened his pace a little. Effie danced along before him.

'What sort of seeds, Grandpa? Things to eat or flowers?'

'Some of each, lass. Mainly flowers.'

'Are there any of those monkey flowers with the big pouches? Like the ones in the conservatory?'

'N-no. I don't think they grow out of doors here.'

'Are there any daffodils or those enormous poppies that look like crumpled paper?'

'Nay – we'll plant bulbs in the autumn for daffodils. They only come in the spring, you know. I thought you'd want flowers this year. You'd have to wait two years for them poppies of yours.'

11

Effie's face clouded a little. 'Can we grow any really nice ones soon or do all the nice ones take a long time?'

'Aye, cheer up, lass. I've got them Shirley poppies. They aren't quite so big but they're all colours – pinks, whites, reds.'

'Blue?'

'Nay' – sighing – 'not blue. But we've got lobelia. Them's a lovely blue in the summer. Does tha remember the borders with the French marigolds last year?'

She nodded solemnly, still dubious about the absence of her favourites. He drew a brown paper bag from his pocket, opened it and handed each packet to her after he had examined it.

'An' there's cornflowers. They be a grand deep blue for you. Clarkia – that's pretty. Eschsholtzia – John-go-to-beds. You'll love those, lass. The buds look like little pointed candles sitting in their sticks and as soon as a little split shows between the candle and its drip-guard, you just pull the tip and off it comes like a little night-cap!'

Effie's face was aglow. There was only an ink drawing of interlacing foliage and flowers bordering one edge of the buff envelope but in Effie's mind the tiny seeds were already a mass of blooms overspilling from her first garden. She remembered the candytuft – pretty and feminine in its shades of purple and pink. It reminded her strongly of Aunt Rosalie. Effie already suspected that she was alone in her admiration of her aunt's dress taste but when one is miserable, querulous and immensely fat surely one may make some amends by supporting a display of large masses of pretty colours. After all, it afforded something for everyone to rest their eyes on and cushion the impact of the incessant, strident voice that issued from the top of the floral mound.

They were soon on hands and knees making drills in the ready-prepared beds. Jack thought they should stand back and plan where each line should go, considering the colour and height and overall effect. Effie was convinced of the desirability to get them all planted quickly so that they should start to grow at once, and since they were all so beautiful it didn't really matter just where they went, she said. In fact, she was against lines at all! Jack managed to plant a row of cornflower and larkspur towards the back of the bed and intended to put vegetables behind these but he was not fast enough and, within a remarkably short time, Effie had prevailed and the packets had been emptied in wandering little sweeps – some thickly planted and some thinly.

They stood back to survey their work. Jack pictured the inappropriate juxtaposition of spinach and lobelia, carrot and cornflower, which he suspected would rise out of this apparently barren piece of earth. His rueful eye was caught and held by Effie's ecstatic blue ones. There was no longer a hint of the hazy grey as she crouched on the path, unscrumpling each soiled buff packet, spreading it out with her palm and working along the inscription with a small earthy finger, visualizing her summer garden.

They watered vigorously, so vigorously in fact, that even Jack's cornflowers and larkspur ended in unruly confusion. Each morning the first pleasant duty of the day was to go, hand in hand, to search for signs of life in Effie's garden. The radishes came up first and then the lettuces. It was not long before a haze of green seedlings covered the ground and as they grew they were carefully identified to confirm the worst of Jack's anticipations but the best of Effie's – that they were, indeed, all going to grow.

Jack was amazed at the rate they did grow, each plant luxuriating despite its overcrowding. Jim must have prepared and fed that bit of ground mighty well, he thought. He did his best to override his inherent love of order and to share Effie's pleasure to the full. As the summer progressed no piece of the garden was watered or watched more. The weeds were a problem; not that there were many of them in such a well-tended garden, but Effie was morally opposed to pulling them up.

'After all,' she would point out firmly, 'they are plants and they have flowers. Even you told me, Grandpa, that most of the flowers we planted would certainly grow wild in some part of the world. What *is* the difference between "wild flowers" and "weeds"?'

'The difference, lass, is that they are in the wrong place. Do you know what "dirt" is, eh? "Dirt" is matter in the wrong place. Might just be "earth" to us but if it's on the floor in your mama's kitchen it is "dirt", see? Now weeds are wild flowers in the wrong place. We didn't plant them – they just got there and since it's our garden and we don't want them they have to go. They would stop our plants growing properly if they stayed because they'd use up all the light and food!' Reluctantly she helped him pull them out.

'After all, they've got all the space in the world to grow,' he assured her.

'Not these ones, because we're killing them.'

'It doesn't matter. This bit of groundsel doesn't care because it knows there are other little groundsel seedlings growing all over the place – waste ground, sides of roads and such – and they will survive and seed. There will always be groundsel.'

CHAPTER TWO

Three springs later found the garden noticeably more mature. The trees and ornamental shrubs were larger and some of the less conspicuous formal borders were looking a little more as nature decreed and less as a regiment of gardeners imposed. Jim still lived in his lodge-gate cottage and had a lad to help full time with another to hand for busy seasons, but even in 1874 it was becoming less easy to find good gardeners in the outskirts of Leeds. The trade in mass-produced, ready-made clothing was beginning to take off and new tailoring factories were opening. The boards at their gates had vacancies for women sewing machinists and cutters.

'There be a good steady indoor job without t'awful rattle o' weaving looms,' parents would say.

The value of the shares in Barrett's engineering works was increasing apace.

'Tha stands t' be quite a wealthy young woman one o' these days, my lass,' said Jack playfully to Effie. They stood together on the front steps, his hand resting on her shoulder. She was taller, and a shade slenderer but the years had mainly enhanced the ethereal, elfin quality of her face which contrasted strongly with the ruddy corrugated lines of the old man's. He had undoubtedly aged. The blue eyes twinkled with activity but the frame was frailer and lacked the old impetuous vigour. Her eyes were a veiled grey and there was only a hint of the latent ebullience hovering about her parted lips.

'You mean your money – when you die?' she responded.

'Aye, lass.' Jack was a little disconcerted by the expressionless voice for such a direct statement.

The young face changed with the rapidity of a ray of sunshine piercing a cloud. The eyes flashed blue as she turned to smile affectionately at him before drawing him down the steps.

'I don't care tuppence for your money, Grandpa,' she laughed.

His gratitude was mitigated by the challenge to his innermost Yorkshire scruples.

'Eh? But tha should! It's allus useful stuff, is brass. It makes life easier. It makes it possible to live how you want and do what you want, an' don't you ivver believe them as says health an' happiness is worth more than money because that's just plain cantin' hypocrisy on the part of them as 'as plenty and don't nowhere intend to find out how it would be without.

'Nay, there's no need to flash it about but you just see that you've allus got enough to make you independent of others.'

Her bowed head implied careful consideration of this advice

15

as they walked towards Effie's garden. The bed was three or four times as large as the original one with a wide border of bulbs. Effie could never quite bring herself to pull up the annuals at the 'back-end' so, as soon as the first frost had laid low most of them, Jim unobtrusively pulled them out, dug and manured so that now, at the beginning of April, the centre of the bed lay newly raked and inviting.

'Look at these pheasant eyes. Aren't they lovely?' Effie was squatting down, sniffing and examining the orange-red eye encircling the powdery yellow stamens of the white narcissus.

'Aye, I can smell the perfume of them from here,' replied Jack. 'What are we going to plant this year, lass?'

She rose meditatively.

'You know, Grandpa, a pond would be nice.'

'What, here?'

'Yes; it's the only spot, really.'

'Mean digging a hole. I don't know how Jim'd feel.'

'We want a big pond.'

'*Do* we?'

'Oh yes – so we can have lilies and great big goldfish and that gigantic rhubarb stuff – like in that park at Harrogate … Perhaps some ducks, even … Oh – just think of two swans!'

'It's expensive digging and concreting holes *that* size, my girl. Maybe we should start small and just make a little one ourselves, eh?'

'I don't think *you* should dig, Grandpa. Not after being ill at Christmas time. Mama would never hear of it.'

Old Jack's fancy slowly rose to the occasion. Yes, why not think big? Something, say, twenty to thirty feet long with bog beds outside that. No swans; too much for an ornamental garden pond – but maybe a pair of Mandarins? – and a pair of Carolinas. Such superb painted-toys of birds. And yet … even four years ago there would have been a ten-strong team of Irish navvies (nothing to touch an Irishman when it comes to digging holes) the day after next and the lot would be done in three weeks. But now … He felt tired.

'It's too big a job for an old man like me to face, Effie my dear. You shall have your big pond but not raight now. We shall make a little one this year and plan how our big one will be. Don't say anything to yer mama and papa just yet. Let's keep it our secret, eh?'

John and Mary were off to stay with Rosalie in Cheshire the following week. Effie should have gone but her parents didn't like leaving the old man alone.

'Jim will be around during the day,' John said, 'I guess he'll be all right. He certainly won't mind about being on his own.'

'Oh, we can't. Look how bad he was with that turn at Christmas. Dr Smith said he had to go careful or there might be another, and who can tell what he mightn't get up to?'

'He don't get up to much now, Mary. Ee seems to 'ave slowed down a lot this last couple of years.'

Effie lifted her head from a book at the kitchen table and pushed some hair back from her eyes.

'Well *I* certainly don't want to stay at Aunt Rosalie's. I should much rather stay at home with Grandpa; an' you're always saying I can make him do anything I want. I'll see he's all right.'

Her mother shook her head dubiously.

'Well, I can't say as how I wouldn't like a change – even with Rosalie. This house is getting me down. It's too big by half. A vast too much to follow comfortable.'

'I dare say Mrs Wadsworth wouldn't mind coming in each day to do their dinners and teas. I could offer her two shilling a day. That should do it.'

This arrangement was made and Mary reassured herself and John that after all, Rosalie and Effie never had agreed; they seemed to bring out the worst in each other.

'You're lettin' that faither of yourn thoroughly spoil that child, John. I've watched her go from bad to worse these many years. And such a self-willed bairn, too,' Rosalie would complain.

'Do you know, Mama, I almost saw Aunt Rosalie *smile* this morning? Well, it were a peculiar sort of smile. It were when Dr Smith said Grandpa was a bloody-minded old bastard!'

'Dr Smith *never* said that!'

'He did! He said it quietly to Papa in the kitchen. Aunt Rosalie were listening by the door.'

'I'm sure she weren't. An' where was you, madam, may I ask?'

'I were in the corner cupboard because I heard Aunt Rosalie coming, and when I peeped out she were right by me listening at the door with that twisted sort of smile on her face.'

Effie always cherished the memory of that week. It was a time of revelation and made an irreversible change in the nature of her life. The irksome trivialities like washing, brushing one's hair, going to bed and feeding regularly, which accounted for her entire relationship with her parents, just vanished. She and old Jack sat and chatted uninterrupted for hours at a time. Even the following week she couldn't recall exactly what they discussed except that it had often been life's priorities – what it might be worth 'selling one's soul for' and what it definitely was not. She remembered clearly that their thoughts ran along such similar lines that it was often only necessary to exchange half a sentence occasionally to establish their train. It was probably something akin to an initiation ceremony whereby the accumulated truths of human experience are passed from one generation to the next.

During the afternoon they sat in the study and devoted themselves to the plans for the pond. The study was the large square reception room on the right-hand side of the front hall. Its ample bay window faced south across the front lawns and its side window east, so even in early April the sun flooded in from early morning until nearly teatime, almost every day of that week. The new season's warmth enticed out the rich odours of old print and musky leather binding from the book-lined walls to mingle with the aroma of Jack's pipe tobacco and the tarry smell peculiar to the seven or eight pipes which rested in their rack on the windowsill. Effie lay on her back on the old Indian carpet, legs crossed, gazing idly at the elaborately undercut acanthus moulding around the chandelier boss and wrinkled her nose to better savour the odoriferous delights. Jack rested in his elm carver beside the table, gazing complacently out of the window as he smoked. He moved his pipe to the side of his mouth.

'Backhouse's at York have got a fine collection o' alpines in their catalogue. I'd like to make t'rockery a bit larger to take some of them afore we start digging the garden up for ponds,' he murmured meditatively.

'Plenty of room for both,' smiled Effie. 'What are alpines, anyhow?'

'Little rock plants. Mainly spring-flowering, I think. These collector fellows have been bringing them back from the Alps and the Himalayas and what have you. They all sound very pretty. How about some more gentians, lass? They're offering about twelve different species of them now!'

'They're a lovely blue and very big bells on such a small plant. They'd look well with some yellow flowers nearby,' she responded.

'Aye; these "Drabas" might be the job – or there's no end o' saxifrages; some of them is a pleasing pale yellow.' Effie rolled over and bounced up to look at the catalogue.

'Ugh! They may *look* pretty but most of them have dreadfully ugly long names. Let's get on with the pond plans.' She pulled the large ledger across the table and opened it at yesterday's design. She pored over it, running a grubby finger thoughtfully along the pencil marks. Having successfully fired the old man's enthusiasm it was now she who was beginning to doubt that the latest design could be reasonably fitted into the side garden without encroaching on the shrubbery.

'I reckon we shall have to make three ponds to do it, Grandpa.'

'*Three* ponds?'

19

'Yes, if we want the bog garden as big as that, we just can't fit it in. Look at the measurements Jim paced out this morning.

'See, if we put our big pond here with its deep place for lilies in the middle and shallow bit around it and then each side we have smaller ponds with curved ends and join them up with the bog garden. And our bridge goes across there so that we can stand and look down at the fish.'

'Y…yes – I could see better if tha hair weren't all over the page' – then with increasing conviction, 'aye lass. That will be grand because we can have the carp and orfe in the middle and the small stuff like shubunkins and fantails in one side, and the other for those wild fish of yourn. Jack Prescott is the chap to ask about the fish we need. There's nowt worth knowing about fish as Jack don't know.'

They redrew the plans together, carefully measuring each feature and labelling it – partly in Jack's shaky scrawl and partly in Effie's large round lettering. Then Effie began to draw and Jack smoked thoughtfully. He identified the mild anxiety which niggled in the recesses of his mind as the problem of telling Mary and John about the pond plan. He sighed, irritably. Five years back – no, even three – he would never have granted this the status of a problem, but he was ageing fast. He attempted to push it away but the relentless Yorkshire peasant honesty retrieved it. It was fine for Effie; the momentum of youthful determination that had once been his brooked no minor obstacles and somehow surmounted the major ones. He remembered his disappointment that young John seemed to have inherited none of this – that he, like many other people, had had the misfortune to be born middle-aged. He would never know the exhilarating confidence that almost anything is possible. Still, the disappointment was not total. John *had* inherited a share of life's fire albeit latent and now, in Effie, it burnt well.

The following day it rained heavily for a couple of hours before dawn, but a brisk southerly sprang up and scattered the clouds so that the sun rose red and watery. Effie crouched at her window, wrapped in a coarse fawn blanket, and watched the rose and grey cloud wisps speed urgently towards the horizon. A wave of happy expectancy surged through her and flinging away the blanket she pulled on her bodice, petticoat and old pinafore. 'Dirty old pinafore, but there's nobody here cares,' she chuckled to herself. She grabbed a black leather boot from beneath the dressing table, looked round impatiently for the other, and then remembered her garden clogs downstairs. She took some thick black stockings out of the drawer, pulled them on and ran out – stairs, hall, kitchen, scullery – paused to slip into her clogs and out into the rain-drenched garden. She ran round the house, slipping on the wet green flags, down the drive, back along the shrubbery walk – twice round the orchard and into the kitchen garden where she suddenly stopped and leaned against the wall, gasping for breath and wiping the hair out of her flushed face. In a second or so she had noted the line of droplets which hung from the sprouting apple branch near her shoulder, the cordoned pears in small leaf and fat blossom buds; the neat lines of early pea shoots, the invigorating aroma of wet spring earth and the cascade of bird song all around her. A more imperious warbling came from a lusty robin on the water tap post. Her lips remained parted ecstatically as she whispered audibly:

'It's all so beautiful ...'

After she and Jack had breakfasted in the kitchen off some slightly burnt porridge they joined Jim and began pacing out the side garden with constant reference to the ledger. Their exuberant excitement even infected the taciturn dalesman.

'Ah can't think why I troubled meself to dig an' rake this bit o' ground. If we've tramped o'er it once we've tramped o'er it a doozen times.'

'But it will be grand when it's done, Jim,' cried Effie. 'Just think; the whole lot of the ponds will stretch from near the walnut tree right over to this Daphne bush!'

'Aye? Ah allus thought as gardens was for walkin' in, not swimming.'

Jack broke in to mollify him.

'Oh, Jim, just think o' the plants. There's rare things you can have in a bog garden. There's that tall primula wi' the tiers of flowers – candelabra they call it – came from Japan; and there's other primulas do well in the damp … and irises – not just the yellow flag; there's purple and white ones in the nurseries now.'

Effie proffered her support. 'We *could* have a mossery, like the one you was reading to me about from that journal. You have a little sort of mountain, with a small fountain on top and the water trickles down over the burrs with big pads of different sorts of moss on them!'

Jim surveyed her coldly. 'There's more moss than ivver in t'lawn this spring. It fair wears me down.'

Jack shook his head warningly at Effie before she could wax eloquent upon the merits of ferneries, too.

CHAPTER THREE

Jack ordered a long list of alpines from Backhouse's at York and asked them to give him detailed instructions for planting. He wanted to know their preferences for soil and which he could risk out on the rockery. Even though he was one of their best customers he was surprised when his order was delivered by one of the firm's partners accompanied by his twenty-year-old son.

'Well, Mr Barrett,' explained Parker, 'I had to come over this way to get some equipment for the lad, here. He's off to Liverpool Monday next on his first collecting trip. And I've always been curious to see this grand garden of yours.'

'I don't know as how it's that grand but we try hard, don't

we, lass?' Jack squeezed Effie's shoulders. 'And we *do* enjoy showing folks around.'

'This is my son William.'

'How do you do, Mr Parker. Where are you off to from Liverpool, then?'

The young man smiled shyly.

'I'm sailing to Calcutta and then overland to the Himalyas, sir.'

'Should be grand. I wish I were young enough to join you,' said Jack heartily.

'He'll join a couple from Veitch's all being well, and they should show him the ropes. Let's hope he brings us some good stuff back.' Mr Parker clapped his son's shoulder encouragingly then set off with Jack. Effie and William followed.

'What's your name, then?' asked William making an effort to be sociable.

'Effie.'

'Your grandfather's got a very fine garden.'

'Yes, he's very fond of it and me as well – I mean – I like the garden. Do you know the names of all the plants?'

'Oh, goodness, no. At least not as many as my father does.'

'How will you know which to bring back?'

'Ah, well, I shall know ones we haven't got and ones that look good. And there will be the other collectors with me for advice. One's got to start somewhere, hasn't one? Do you know the names of all the plants in your garden?' He was trying to tease Effie but she looked at him gravely.

'Most of them – at least the first name.'

'Really! How about those orange ones with the bronze leaves, then?'

'Sileni ... no I can't remember the next name – I did know it the other day, though.'

'My goodness – what a little plantswoman! I wasn't sure of that one myself.'

Effie smiled at him complacently.

'You have got nice-coloured eyes,' she said, by way of a

23

mutual compliment. 'They remind me of the new violets that Grandpa's got.'

William looked confused and turned away to survey the length of the herbaceous border while he composed himself.

'I suppose you help your grandfather in the garden?' he asked after a pause.

'Oh, yes. I spend nearly all my time here when I'm not at school.'

'Don't you like school?'

'Like school?' repeated Effie incredulously. 'No, of course not. Did you like it?'

'Not much,' grinned William. 'It seemed a bit of a waste of time. I wish I knew exactly where the Himalyas are now, though, but I don't think they ever taught us that.'

'How will you get there, then?' asked Effie in concern.

'Well, I'll have to trust the captain of the boat to get me to Calcutta and I should meet the other fellows there. If I don't, I shall just have to ask the way, won't I?'

Effie laughed. 'Grandpa says they are very high mountains, so you should be able to see them a long way off. However will you carry all the plants you collect?'

'I shall collect seed as much as I can and Father's getting a lot of small glass plates that I can tape together to make little travelling boxes, but they'll be so heavy I shall have to keep them at the base camp. I think I shall only be able to carry a vasculum or two with me, what with the axe and spade and the gun.'

'What do you need a gun for?'

'Well, unfriendly natives, perhaps, but that isn't likely because we'll have a guide with us who'll know the local lingo and customs. One might have to shoot a snake, and there are tigers but they are actually as frightened of people as we are of them, I'm told.'

Effie surveyed him in wide-eyed admiration. 'It sounds awfully dangerous!'

'I hope so. I'm looking forward to that, but I expect catching tropical diseases is the most dangerous thing I'll do,' laughed William.

Mr Parker and Jack were waiting for them.

'You two seem to be getting along well. Hast tha had time to notice the garden, lad?'

'Yes, of course, Father. It's beautiful. I like the way the big herbaceous border's laid out and the rockery should be very fine when it's extended.'

'You haven't seen my garden yet,' said Effie.

'No – please show us,' rejoined Mr Parker.

'It won't be like this much longer because we're going to make three big ponds.'

'Yes?'

'Aye,' confirmed Jack. 'You must come over when we've finished and tell us what to plant in them. There'll be a deep lily pond and bog gardens.'

'It's a date!' said Mr Parker. 'We'll make it high summer next time, eh Will? I should like to see this garden then.'

Jack shook hands with the visitors. Mr Parker patted Effie's head and William shook her hand gravely.

'I shall bring you a special Himalayan rhododendron which no-one else has, to plant by your new pond.'

'Thank you very much,' said Effie. 'I do hope the trip won't turn out to be too dangerous.'

CHAPTER FOUR

John and Mary were returning Saturday. Only one day remained and Effie's face was clouded as she looked out of her window that morning. They must make the most of this last day together. It would take a long time to organize the building of the big ponds but Grandpa had promised her a little one to be going on with. They must make it today. She dressed and ran to find Jack.

'We'll make just a tiny pond for this summer, Grandpa. Just here, by the side of where the big one will be – so as not to be in the workmen's way.' She took up a stick and drew a circle in the earth about one and a half yards across.

'There's that pile of clay up on the canal bank that I saw the other day. We can take up two buckets and get enough to seal it and we can ask Jack Prescott for some small goldfish.'

'My, what an impatient little elf we've got! I suppose a worn-out old feller like me mun't get in your road.'

'You mustn't dig,' said Effie firmly. 'I'll get the wicker chair out and put it just here in this patch of sun and you can watch. Perhaps Jim can help later if he's got time.'

Jack complied placidly. Yesterday he had regained some of the old exhilarating vigour but today he felt so tired that even the alertness of his mind seemed turned in on itself, so he sat and brooded.

Aye, that was it; that kernel-of-being imprisoned somewhere in this unenduring shell – the 'soul'?, the 'mind's eye'? – call it what you will, it projects itself into the surroundings of that human life and becomes one with ideas, plans or cherished objects. When the body fails, though, be it toothache, indigestion or this worn-out tiredness of old age, back that consciousness comes, recoiling from the outer world to beam inwards, toning up each fibre of pain so that it oppresses the more, relentlessly dissecting each frustration and failure. Introspective, self-absorbed and irritable; there is a veritable picture of pain and age.

With an effort he turned that eye and forced it out into the world; the young spring world with the low sun whose slanting beams passed through the bronze fleur-de-lys shapes of the new walnut leaves. Patches of yellow light played about Effie making her lithe form luminescent. As she stooped to scoop out a spadeful of earth her pale hair flew about her in a scurry of light. As she paused to regain her breath there was a transient gold outline of curved shoulder and bare round arms. At those moments Jack was deeply aware of the quick gay smile which accompanied *her* consciousness as it sped out to him. In fact, that smile was completely obscured by the backlighting and the dimness of his eyes.

If only this could continue for ever. If only time would stop and me and Effie could spend eternity together in the spring-lit garden; no Saturday; no Mary and John.

Jim came to help. They finished the hole at a depth of about fifteen inches and contoured the surprisingly large mound of dug-out earth in a crescent behind the hole.

'Landscape gardening,' pronounced Effie complacently and trotted off to get the buckets and trowel.

'Will you come up to the canal, Grandpa?' That was all she said but the concealed note of wistfulness said, 'Please do, Grandpa. I want you.'

'Aye lass. Get me a bucket.'

'Should you? I can easily manage two. That will be enough.'

'Nay, I'm not that useless yet. Get me one.'

They paused on the footbridge above the weir to watch the frothing churn of water beneath them and admire the decorative arch of the old iron road bridge a little higher up. Then they passed on over the railway and up the hill to the canal.

'Shall we walk along to the locks?'

'Aye, we may as well.'

They stood back to let an angular, coarse-headed boat-horse pass and then accompanied its floating load along, at a comfortable walking pace. The bewhiskered boatman reclined against the rudder bar in his blue jersey and wide blue serge trousers. Effie was intrigued by the down-turned clay pipe that hung from his mouth.

'I guess it smokes satisfactorily any way up and he don't need to grip it in his teeth that way,' Jack replied quietly.

The man noticed their interest, and smiled.

'Good afternoon, maister. It be a grand one, though don't it.' Effie noticed that his dialect was not local.

'Aye, grand. Where's tha come from?'

'All t' way from Wigan.'

'Ah! What have you aboard, then – iron?'

'Aye, and some Craven rock from Skipton. None of the seaside sort, I fear, lass,' he teased Effie.

She smiled brightly. 'I like your boat; it's painted beautiful.' He nodded. 'What's the name o' your horse?'

''E's called Retriever – well, 'e's a mare, really, like.'

'Why do you call it "he" then?'

'Ah, habit, I s'pose. We usually call 'em "he". Like cats, you know; tha allus calls them "she", don't tha?'

'Er, yes,' said Effie, a little doubtful of the logic in this biological justice.

''E – that is she – mayn't be much to look at but 'e be a most unusual horse.'

'Oh, why?'

''E jumps in t' canal an' swims in t' summer, when it's hot.'

'What – with the boat behind her?'

'Aye. 'E can pull it along grand. Not quite as fast as walkin', mind you, but nowt so bad – just a short way – till we git to one o' them concrete horse-ramps, and out he clambers and shakes 'isself like a big dog!'

Effie was enthralled and patted the shaggy back admiringly as the boatman unhitched the beast at the lock.

'There, lass, you walk 'im down to the bottom lock and let 'im graze a bit o' grass till we joins you.' He winked reassuringly at old Jack. 'That 'oss knows as well as me. 'E allus walks straight down on 'is own and starts eating!'

Jack helped to close the upper gates and sat on the beam to watch the boat sink lower and lower in the lock. She was certainly a well turned-out craft with the square-cut 'transomed' stern finely painted in a symmetrical foliage design, red and light green on the dark green ground. The short square tapered chimney was painted in red and green panels.

Effie appeared on the steps from the lower lock.

'Have you anything for Retriever to eat, Grandpa?' He felt in his pockets.

'Nay, lass. Try Joe Sugden at the lock-keeper's cottage. He'll likely have an old apple or something.'

Effie's tap brought out the affable Mrs Sugden who waved to the boatman pushing the beam of the middle gates.

'Hallo there, Jethro. 'Ow's Ella?'

'She are fine, Mrs Sugden. She'll probably be over on t' next trip. T' new bairn's a bit mangy so she bided this time.'

'We'll look for'ard to seeing them.' She disappeared into the house and returned with a thick slice of bread and a small apple.

'There, the apple's a deal wrinkled but it's firm inside – you have that, lass, an' give the horse the bread.' Effie thanked her and ran off down the steep bank to the Bramley Fall reach. She fed Retriever the bread and, glancing guiltily over her shoulder, twisted the apple in two halves and proffered one on her flat palm – as Jim had taught her. The prehensile lips lifted it daintily and a succulent crunch announced the release of the delicacy for savouring which was carried out with nose tucked well in and ponderous nodding movements. After a polite pause the bristly upper lips caressed Effie's bare wrist. Effie giggled and produced the other half of the apple, happy to watch its leisurely dispatch in identical manner to the first.

She helped Jethro with the lower lock gates, dashing from side to side across the footbridges, and she and Jack waved them off.

'I'll be back full t'day after tomorrer,' called the boatman cheerfully.

'Where's Wigan?' Effie asked Jack.

'Way o'er in Lancashire – t'other side of the Pennines beyond Skipton.'

'How do they get the boat over the Pennines?'

'They go through!' laughed Jack.

'Through?'

'Aye – t'canal twists and turns about to get to the lowest part and then there's a tunnel. The boatman will pick up a legger to help and they push the boat through – lying on their backs and walking like, with their feet on t'tunnel wall.'

'All in the dark?'

'Well, I think there's a glimmering bit of light, but it's near a mile long.'

'How about Retriever?'

'Oh, a lad will walk her over the top. There's a special horse road.'

'Does the boatman come from there – his talk sounded different?'

'Aye, as different as chalk from cheese,' chuckled the old man, 'Yorkshire is the cheese, of course. Mind, they're not a bad lot, these Lancashire boatmen. Most of them in the blue shirts and trousers and with the nice painted boats are Lankys. The Yorkshire boatmen are a right rough crowd; best left to themselves, lass!' His voice finished in a tone of solemn warning.

'Well, where's this pile of clay o'yours? We'd best be filling our buckets and getting back.'

They walked back to near the humped road bridge and half-filled the three buckets. Effie purposely put somewhat less in Jack's but he noticed and picked up one of the heavier ones. The canal was barely a quarter of a mile from the house but it seemed a long, long way home to old Jack. Effie walked very slowly. She glanced at his face as his breathing became louder. It looked greyish. She yearned to make him give her the bucket but he beamed bravely back at her and she knew that his pride was too precious to risk so there was nothing she could do. They reached the drive gates.

'Put the bucket down here and I'll fetch it when I've emptied mine,' she said lightly.

'Nay, I've got it this far, I'll get it to the pond.'

Their progress along the drive was very slow but at last the pond was reached. Jack put down his bucket and, with back still bent, made his way to the wicker chair.

'Are you all right, Grandpa?' The sharpness of Effie's voice revealed the depth of her anxiety even to her own surprise. His face was a dirty purplish-grey and his breathing was laboured.

'Get me a drink of water, lass. I've got a pain.'

Effie sped off and was back in a moment with a cup of water. Consternation emanated from her face.

'Is it bad?'

'Aye, bad to middling. It will go off in a bit. I've had it before. You just stay here and talk to me, lass.'

His gnarled, discoloured hand clutched the wicker arm of the chair and she placed her small pale one over it, urging herself to think of something trivial to say. It was difficult at first but somehow she started and the chatter began to flow on its own, soothingly.

'...it's been such a sunny, warm spring. There's two dunnocks' nests in the orchard hedge with young in already and a thrush's in the big pink early rhododendron. Jim says he knows of five blackbird nests in the garden. I know where three of them are but he won't tell me the others. He says I must find them myself and I'll only lead cats in if I keep looking. I don't, you know, I only look once a day and I always make sure there's no cats in sight. Mrs Jenkin's Tib kept following me around the other day. I'm sure she was wanting me to visit a nest – but I didn't. Hasn't this week been grand, Grandpa? The weather, and us being on our own...'

She felt him stiffen; his face was darker, although the end of his nose was quite white.

'It's getting worse, Grandpa!'

'Aye.'

'Wait, I'll be back in a moment.'

She fled round the corner of the house. She didn't shout for fear of him hearing.

'Jim,' she muttered, 'Jim! Where are you?' She found him in the potting shed.

'Quick, get Dr Smith. Run, Jim – fast as you can. Grandpa's very poorly.'

When she got back he was relaxed and looking better.

'Where have you been, lass?'

'I asked Jim to fetch Dr Smith.' A fleeting look of annoyance passed over his face and he began to speak urgently.

'There's nowt he can do, Effie. You'll be quite a rich woman, you know. You'll make good use of that, won't you? Money is to buy things you want. Things as give you pleasure. You'll do that, won't you? Whatever folks say, you do as you want.

'These ponds, now; they are worthwhile. If they're made proper they will give you and Jim a deal o' pleasure and then your children and grandchildren.'

'And you, silly.' There were tears in her eyes as she crouched, grasping his hand.

'And me, maybe. I'm not sure, lass. This pain's coming back.'

He stiffened, his face went even darker than before and he drew back his head to get breath, but only an obscene guttural sound came and the body in the chair sank, smaller and smaller...

Effie released his hand. She suddenly felt utterly detached. This withered heap of clothing on which rested a shrunken bald head was not Grandpa. He hadn't ceased being, of course. He had just ... spread out! She glanced round quickly, half-expecting to see a trace of him hovering by the pond hole, and then recalled herself sharply. The crunch of hurrying footsteps on the paved path brought Dr Smith and Jim round the corner. Effie stood up in embarrassment. Smith shot her a searching look.

'He's dead!' she said and, turning, she walked firmly away. She did not care to watch them manipulating the clothing in the wicker chair.

Jack Barrett was buried at St Stephen's, Kirkstall, on

Tuesday April the tenth. The cortège was large – a lot larger than John and Mary had expected.

'Amazing how many people thought well enough of him to come!' said Mary to John.

They were sitting in the kitchen over a cup of tea after everyone had left. They both looked red-eyed and Mary's face was blotched and puffy with emotion as she recalled the day's events to John.

'Did you see Mrs Wadsworth? She were really crying. An' there were all those people with Mr Jowett from the works. They all looked really well dressed in proper mourning, didn't they? An' Jack an' Mrs Prescott from Outwood Lane. I didn't expect them. There was even Joe and Mrs Sugden from up at t'lock. I suppose he must have talked to them when he's been up at t'canal with Effie.

'But I can't for the life of me understand that child. We know she haven't much time for us but at least we thought she were fond of her grandpa.'

'You know – Dr Smith said she didn't shed a tear when he died, and she were the only one with him! He said she just turned and walked off when he came, as if she didn't care and when he went to look for her – after he'd done whativer he had to do to the old man, you know – she were in the study just looking at some notebooks and carrying on as if nothing had happened. He said he were sorry he didn't get there in time and she said – cool as a cucumber – that it were better that he didn't because there were nothing he could have done. Fancy a slip of a wench of twelve saying that to a doctor – and then, too!'

'She didn't seem raight upset this afternoon, neither,' said John thoughtfully. 'But she must have cared. She's just the sort that don't show it.'

'Why shouldn't she show it?' rejoined Mary peevishly. 'It's nothing to be ashamed of. She's too proud by half, like Rosalie says. And we all knows what comes after pride!'

'Where is t'bairn, anyhow?'

33

'She walked back with Jim Woodgate. He said he'd rather not come to the house for the food, so I expect she's with him.'

Effie was sitting by Jim's range in his tiny living room, chin in hand, brooding as she gazed unseeing at the red coals. The strange detachment had not left her. She had carried on mechanically in a waking limbo since Friday. Some sort of emotion had seeped back during the funeral this afternoon, but it had been one of bitter resentment at the sentimental nonsense the vicar had spoken. Grandpa did not go to church; the vicar did not know him and it was presumptuous of him to imply an intimate concern. Her other regret had been the prodigious mass of superbly beautiful flowers which were even now lying out in that churchyard to wilt and die. *He* would have disapproved of both. However, it didn't really matter because this charade had little to do with Grandpa. He was not there and it comforted all these people to be able to acknowledge that his life was a loss to theirs.

Jim touched her shoulder and passed a cup of tea into her hands.

'Tha musn't pine, lass. He wouldn't have wanted it, would he now?' His deep voice was very gentle.

'No.' She swallowed a mouthful of tea and a hot tear ran down each cheek, closely followed by many more. The first real tears she had allowed herself.

'He wouldn't have liked that funeral, either,' she muttered brokenly.

'Nay. But it weren't for him – it were for all of us.'

'Yes, Jim. That's just what I told myself.' She smiled slightly as she dried her eyes. At least there *was* Jim here still.

Effie began to feel real bereavement later that week and the feeling grew steadily deeper over the following summer months. She was glad that they hadn't seeded her garden that year, since the daily inspection would have been unbearable on her own. Jim must have spoken to Jack Prestcott at the funeral since he ambled in shyly the week after and the three of them puddled the pond and planted it with pondweed. A few days later he returned with four small goldfish and two orfe in a bucket.

'Keeps those lazy old goldfish on the move, them orfe does,' said Jack.

He would take no payment for the fish and told Jim that they were instead of flowers for old Jack because he knew he would have preferred that. Jim did not tell Effie but she guessed and appreciated the gesture.

The pond became very important to the child and she spent hours lying on her tummy gazing into the tranquil world where gleaming goldfish glided through olive green stalks, so complacent with their fishy lot. She became familiar with each contoured hill and each rocky cleft and cavern; the groves of *Potamagetum* stalk and radiant clumps of *Elodea*. As she watched, each fish became a personality, their behaviour and the expressions on their faces were quite different as they moved through their enchanted landscape.

She was very grateful that the side garden was the farthest removed from her parents' part of the house. She could not bear her mother's vocal preoccupation with domestic trivialities. It rankled with Effie that four days of concentrated and conspicious mourning had not only appeased her parents in the eyes of the world – it had actually allowed them to come to terms with Father's death; to have felt bereavement, rallied and forgotten. He was now no more and his influence on their lives finished except, perhaps, for the occasional affectionate anecdote. Such is the purpose of mourning and if the aim of human consciousness is complacent self-sufficiency then it is a very valuable rite. Personally Effie despised such comfortable amnesia.

Jack Barrett's will had been committed to the care of his solicitor, Samuel Jenkins of Jenkins, Bailey and Jenkins, Albion Street, Leeds, some two years before his death. Despite what he had spent on the house and garden there was still a tidy fifty-six thousand pounds of which twelve were shares in the engineering works and left to John; the rest, including the house and land, was Effie's. Most was to be invested in the works and some anywhere that Jenkins deemed best until she was eighteen, and the house and the land could not be sold before that time. Five thousand pounds were to be set aside for her education and personal needs between the time of his death and her eighteenth birthday. An additional six thousand were divided into ten incremental annuities for the upkeep of the house and garden under the direction of John, while any residue could be spent by the chief beneficiary in any way she saw fit regardless of her minor age!

John and Mary were contemptuous of these arrangements. They were not avaricious since their horizons were close and they were well satisfied with their twelve thousand pounds – but why not make them the guardians and executors of the rest? It looked as if the old man didn't trust them to decide Effie's best interests, and why oblige them to keep up the huge house and garden for her? It would be so much better sold and a new detached four-bedroomed house bought in a really *nice* part of Leeds, said Mary.

'So much easier to follow with new small furniture in. All this antique stuff may be all right for some folks, but I like them new suites in Denby & Spinks with the silver fittings.'

'Aye, an' there's all that silver cutlery and stuff. I suppose we aren't obliged to keep *that* for her, are we? We aren't ever going to use it and it's just begging to be burgled,' added John.

Mr Jenkins called to see them after dinner one day. Mary showed him into the study with Effie 'to chat' while she went to find John.

Mr Jenkins's elongated, folded face of indeterminate age and his spare frame looked dry to Effie; in fact, positively drought-stricken. He grimaced nervously and played with his black silk hat. He was obviously ill at ease with children – maybe with adults too. Effie surveyed him coldly.

'Eh, now – you're a lucky young lady, aren't you.' He spoke with the exaggerated joviality he deemed suitable for children.

36

'You mean about Grandpa leaving me the house, do you?' she asked coolly.

'Er – yes. He was most particular that should have it as you wanted it, too.'

'Ah … I like it just as it is – except for the pond.' She scrutinized her folded hands.

He became sufficiently intrigued to forget that she was a child.

'What's wrong with the pond?'

'Well, just that there aren't one, really. Not a proper one, you know. We had made all the plans for three big ones just before he died. I'm sure he wants it done.'

Jenkins noted the present tense with mild surprise.

'How about you – do you want it done?'

'Oh, *yes*, certainly. It would be lovely.'

Jenkins was even more surprised to note the swift change from an inscrutable and probably difficult child to the radiant blue-eyed angel that answered his last question.

Mary had her reasons for fetching John herself rather than sending Effie. Mr Jenkins awkwardly offered his condolences. A firm glance from Mary prompted John to ask about selling the silver and perhaps some other small items like the two Chinese vases and the Japanese tea service and lacquered cabinets.

'After all, we have to consider keeping the place secure. We don't want the stuff but there's allus others as do and it's a temptation to burglars. It'll be better to put the money away for the bairn and she can sell the house and furniture when she comes of age.'

Jenkins shot a glance at Effie. She was now seated, elbows on knees and chin on hands, with indignation written over her frowning brow and compressed lips.

'Well, Mr and Mrs Barrett. The will is quite explicit. Allow me to read a bit.' He fluttered through the pages. 'Ah, here … "My house and grounds of Oakroyd I leave inclusive of all the contents to my granddaughter, Elspeth Mary Barrett, to be *preserved intact* until she is eighteen years of age. I set aside the sum of six thousand pounds to maintain the said property until this time". I really don't see how we can dispose of anything yet. Of course, if the young lady wants to dispose of it when she comes of age, there is nothing to stop her.' He cast a furtive glance at Effie. Her attitude had not changed but her face seemed softened by a glimmer of triumph.

'It seems a rare funny carry-on to me,' Mary huffed. 'Fancy leaving a child to cope with all this when she's got a mother and father.'

'Well, she can't make any decision for a few years yet, can she, Mrs Barrett?' The masterly expression of mollification raised Effie's estimation of Mr Jenkins. 'And I'm sure she'll be guided by you when she can.'

'I'm not that sure,' muttered Mary.

'Why not put these things you mentioned into a bank vault, Mr Barrett? I can arrange that for you quite simply, and they would be out of harm's way there!'

John agreed to this and they went on to speak about the upkeep of the house. Mary undertook to keep the inside clean by herself providing most of the upstairs and all but two of the downstairs rooms were enshrouded in covers and shut up.

'Mrs Wadsworth can come in twice a year, in spring and back end for us to give it a thorough do through.'

'How about the garden, Mr Barrett?'

'Oh, old Jim Woodgate will carry on doing that, I suppose.'

'Have you asked him?'

'Oh, of course he will,' cried Effie, a note of horror in her voice. 'He couldn't leave us.'

'Well, things will be different now,' said John.

Effie was standing stiffly. She felt inexplicably shocked. Jim was part of the garden – part of her. Until that moment she had never contemplated the garden without Jim, but now she abjectly realized that 'us' meant Grandpa and her. The confidence in her statement was gone once she substituted 'me'.

38

Only a few weeks before, one of the part-time gardeners had left for a job at the Forge. Effie had overheard his farewell speech to Jim.

'Well, Mr Woodgate,' he had said. 'I can't think why tha stays here. It were bad enough in t'old maister's time, but now it's a petticoat government tha's got, an' all for a pittance, too. Does tha know how much I'll get at t'Forge?' He spoke the figure too quietly for even Effie's sharp ears.

'Tha ought to skip before tha gets too old.'

Effie glanced uneasily from Mr Jenkins to her mother.

'Perhaps we ought to pay him more,' she said.

'Why, child, do you know what he gets?' asked Mary sharply.

'N..no, but I heard young Jo say it weren't much!'

'Ho, young Jo. He may live to regret moving into t'Forge. He nivver thought o' all the hard work he'd have to do to keep hold o' that job when he went so ready.'

'Well, she may be right. I wonder how much he does get, Mr Barrett? It's not easy to keep good fellows on the land when there are so many vacancies in the mills and works. Shall we speak to him?'

Effie was dismissed firmly as Jim edged in, twisting his cap nervously in his big rough hands. He could never have received a look of such penetrating appeal as he did at that moment, but he was probably too upset by finding himself actually standing, not only within the house, but in the sanctity of the study, even to see Effie pass him.

CHAPTER FIVE

Effie spent most of the weekdays at school. The sacrilege of sitting inside doing 'book work' as the golden autumn sunshine fell on the disfigured desk tops grieved her. Miss Robinson was firm but kind and had been particularly lenient with her in the summer after Grandpa's death, but she was now pressing for more 'application' again.

'Elspeth!' she called sharply. 'Elspeth Barrett – do *wake up*, child. There *is nothing* that upsets me as much as seeing a child with ability like you wasting your and my time. I want some hard work and application out of you, my girl, and then I think you might surprise us all.'

Effie gave the traditional flat response. 'Yes, Miss … Robinson.' That lady shot her a withering glance which provoked the blue eyes to fire momentarily in amusement.

That child has more in her than all these affable suet puddings rolled together. If only I could find a way to get it out, she thought.

Effie returned in spirit to the garden. The golden sunshine would be making luminous the late flush of grass and roses. It would be glinting on the golden fish as they sauntered through their elodean glades. The apples were hanging heavily in the orchard, green and red, golden and russet, scenting the still air with their fragrance. And, most important of all, Jim was there and always would be – she had his word – but still a shadowy doubt troubled her as she ran wildly along the lane home, skirt billowing, long black legs pounding. She raced through the gate and along the shrubbery path – turned sharp right and straight to the potting shed. There he was, sitting on his bench – mug of tea in hand. The muscles of his face didn't quiver and he spoke with slow deliberation.

'Ah reckon Miss Robinson be just a'finishing pushing open that classroom door when you arrives here, lass. Ah bet she nivver even sees you leave at that pace.' Effie laughed happily. How different from a few weeks ago. After Mr Jenkins' visit she could not bring herself to face Jim. Her parents didn't mention him and she shrank from doing so. She surveyed the garden from the kitchen window and from her room upstairs but she hadn't seen him working. She promised herself to look for him when she got home from school but somehow went straight to her room instead. She hadn't even gone to the pond. On the third day, as she walked slowly along the lane with downcast eyes, she upbraided herself. Would Grandpa have behaved like this, feebly prostrating himself before a blow which may never have been struck? No, of course not. She quickened her pace, through the shrubbery, right down the perennial border – she could see the edge of the shed – quick, get it over with – she broke into a trot. Another step and she would be able to see inside the open door. There it was – empty! She stopped, utterly dejected – and then, round the corner, mug in hand, stepped Jim. This time he grinned broadly at her.

'Well, here she be! Ah thought as 'ow you'd not forgive me for walking into your study t'other afternoon!'

'Jim – silly.' She flung her arms round him in utter relief, then stepped back awkwardly.

'Will you be staying with us, Jim?'

'Aye. Why shouldn't I?' His surprised face slowly relaxed as he realized her anxiety.

Effie spoke offhandedly as she watched the toe of her best boot excavate a hole in the earth.

'Oh, I just remember Jo saying you could get more money at the Forge.'

'Well, Ah don't fancy working in the Forge, do I? An' anyways, the young maister has arranged to pay me more, so I reckon I've no call to go leavin' at all, have I?' His grey eyes twinkled through their corrugated brown lids.

Effie lifted her eyes and beamed at him delightedly.

'I'm so glad, Jim. You'll stay for always, won't you? I couldn't manage without you – not now.'

'Nay, no more you couldn't with that pond o' yours.'

'What pond?'

'Something Mr Jenkins said when 'e walked down the drive with me.'

'What did he say?'

''E wanted t' know what you meant about the big ponds you'd planned with your grandfaither.'

'What did you say?' Jim made a courageous attempt to revert to his usual taciturnity by turning impatiently away from her. She took a firm hold of his hand.

'Jim, tell me. What – did – you – tell – him?'

'Oh, Ah only showed him the small pond and said you'd made plans in a notebook for a big one and two middling-sized ones.'

'What did he say?'

'Said it would cost a mint o' money, he did.'

'What did you say?'

'Oh, Ah don't know as how Ah said anything!' responded Jim irritably.

'Not even that "gardens was for walkin' in and not swimmin' in"?' teased Effie.

'Aye, Ah *should* have said that!'

'Did he say anything else?'

''E said – if you really want it you must take the plans along to his office and show him.'

'Oh, Jim – why didn't you tell me before?'

'Tha's too full o' questions by half this afternoon. Why this? What that? You go away this minute. I've got things to do!'

Effie suppressed the urge to hug him once more. She couldn't imagine how she came to do it the first time and, laughing happily to herself, she ran off to the pond.

Friday evening found Effie sitting restlessly at the kitchen table, a book before her. The first cold snap of the winter had come. Jim had looked up at the clear sky at dusk and forecast ground frost. The dark evenings were getting longer and Effie's bedroom getting chillier – so there was no alternative but to be in the kitchen. In the old days there would have been a fire in the study and Grandpa sitting smoking his pipe with a gardening journal open on his knee. Effie would tap on the door and creep in when she heard his grunt. She would curl up on the sheepskin hearthrug and watch the blazing coals, without saying a word to disturb his thoughts.

'Eh,' he would eventually murmur. 'You know, gardening be very nice raight through the winter, too. Do ye know what tha calls this sort o' gardening, lass?'

'No.'

'Tha calls it "armchair gardening" – an' it's some of the best. Tha can sit comfortable and warm reading aboot new plants that them collector fellows have just brought back from all corners of the globe. You can imagine what they look like growing there in, say, the foothills of a Japanese mountain or them Himalayas – with t'bamboo tall as trees and orchids and succulents all round. Then you can decide to order them and imagine how grand they'll look in t' conservatory or the herbaceous beds next spring or summer, and that leads you to thinking of all the other flowers you decided to have a try with next season. All you need is some journals and nurserymen's catalogues and a middlin' allocation of imagination up here.' He would tap his forehead and then ruffle Effie's hair.

'Luckily for you, you've got enough o' that commodity, lass.'

Those winter evenings were over. She studied the kitchen trying to register consciously its contents that she was so familiar with. There was the large pegged rug on the floor that she had helped cut the strips of cloth for, from cast-off clothing. That had slightly bad associations in that her favourite old woollen pinafore was in there, and she could remember the painful way the scissors cut into the base of her thumb so vividly that she had to rub it. There was the fire, burning warmly through the basket bars of the range – that was fine but not so interesting to watch as the open fire in the study. The black-leaded range was quite another matter, however. As it gleamed silkily it seemed to be mocking her, from its oven doors on either side of the fire basket to its polished brass knobs on the corners of the steel fender guard. Some of her earliest memories were her mother's wailing complaints of the iniquity of a device 'that needed leading every live-long day of a body's life to keep it raight, so that one needn't hang one's head in shame when anyone called in unexpected-like'. The toddling Effie would be straddled in a large apron to 'help' – which she enjoyed enormously until it came to the part of removing the black lead from the creases round her eyes and nose and her ears. But later, as she got older, the Saturday morning leading fell to her lot alone, and the polishing of the steel fire-irons, the tall dogs that supported them, the fender bar and lastly the shining brass knobs, took two solid hours from her precious Saturday. She winced visibly. There were the two Windsor-back chairs each side of the hearth that her parents sat in – floral-patterned cushions on their seats and backs – quite neutral in associations. There were the heavy cotton curtains hung on mahogany rings from the heavy mahogany curtain rail. They were floral-printed too but in such clumsy swathes of vulgar roses and indeterminate bells – bright yellow, crimson, green and blue – that Effie averted her eyes to the table-top. This was not associated with such tyranny as the range, but bad enough. The pine top was scrubbed white and had been for so long that each hardwood growth ring was separated from its neighbour by a deepish gully. Each mug or plate one placed on it risked leaving a brown ringed tea stain which had to be purged immediately after the meal. At the root of these discomforts which made her abhor the kitchen was her mother and, far worse than the inconveniences themselves, there was her unremitting voice. High-pitched, peevish, almost always complaining, it sawed through anyone's composure. Effie didn't have to listen to the words, but the sheer physical abrasion shattered her peace of mind.

'I wish tha'd stop fidgeting with that book, child. 'Tis clear tha aren't enjoying reading it – books is a waste of a girl's time, anyhow. You don't have time to read when you've growed up, you know. Women's work is niver done and doesn't allow of reading. You'd best be helping me with these pots, an' then I could get on with that vast amount o' mending in the box.'

John glanced up from his pamphlet.

'Let the bairn be, Mary. It's surely best that she reads now while she has got some time, ain't it?'

Effie decided that this slight advantage was the best she could expect and should be pushed home.

'May I go into Leeds tomorrow, Mama?'

'What for, may I ask?'

'I just wanted to look at some shops. Jim needs a new spade so I thought I would get that. The shaft of his old un broke while we was trying to split a big clump of delphiniums.' (She knew her mother wasn't interested but it seemed best to keep talking and prevent her from delivering an immediate prohibition.) 'I could get anything you want, Mam, too.'

'What shops do *you* want to look in?'

'Oh, just general. Betty Grant at school said it were great looking in the big shop windows.'

'Indeed! Is she goin' wi' you?'

'N-no.'

'Who is then? You can't go walking round Leeds on your own and I've got too much to do tomorrow to go traipsing off winder-gazing!'

Effie rose from the table.

'Here – you haven't had your tea-cake.'

'I've had enough, Mama, thanks – honest.'

'It be a long time to breakfast.'

Effie edged out of the kitchen as inconspicuously as she could and, when clear, set off at a run to Jim's cottage.

45

She heard the scrape of the chair legs on the flags as he got up in response to her tap – two steps and the door opened slowly to let out a band of greenish-yellow oil-lamp light.

'Well?' he asked gruffly.

'Jim, could you come into Leeds with me tomorrow to see Mr Jenkins?'

'I'm sure tha can explain tha-sen.'

'Yes, but Mama won't let me go by myself. She keeps wanting to know where I'm going and I aren't going to tell her.'

'They'll have to know sooner or later!'

'Yes – later. They'd only make trouble about it. You need a new spade. Why don't we go and get that as well?'

'Ah was going to dig over the beds ready for the wallflowers.'

'It will keep. You can do it next week.'

He shook his head stolidly.

'Oh, Ah don't know. I don't like doing things behind folks' backs. They find out sooner or later an' it looks bad then.'

'Please, Jim, please. We will get your spade. Perhaps there's other things we need for the garden? You'd have to go to Leeds sometime.'

'Yer Grandpa were raight. There's no winning wi' thee!'

Effie cavorted about in the flagged porch.

'We'll set off early. Eight o'clock. An' p'raps we can take some sandwiches for lunch. It will be grand! You come across and tell Mama early tomorrow.' Jim sighed and stepped back to shut the door. His head was still shaking as he sat down again.

'Oh. How I wish her grandpa were still 'ere.'

He was standing at the back door of the house just after seven in the morning.

'I only hope the bairn's not been a-nagging at you to go with her,' grumbled Mary.

'Nay,' said Jim stoutly. 'Ah've been needing some gardening

46

stuff for a while an' I thought she might like to come. She don't get out much, do she?'

Mary acquiesced grudgingly and a smile of satisfaction crept across Effie's face as she stood listening in the scullery. She was swathed in a coarse cotton apron liberally smudged with black lead as were her hands and face.

'I guessed there were summat afoot when you started that job at half past six in t'morning,' scolded Mary. 'You best hurry up and get it done and then you'll have to have a proper clean-up. You can't go traipsing round Leeds looking like a sweep's apprentice. I'll do a few sandwiches for you both.'

CHAPTER SIX

It was a fine sunny morning with a heavy dew and the horse-chestnuts turning red or gold. Cartwheel cobwebs glistened white in the bushes. They stopped to admire one.

'Isn't it wonderful how they do them, Jim.'

'Aye. An' it don't take long. I've watched one do it in less than four hours. It's only the female that makes those fine ones they say.'

'Is it? Doesn't the male have to eat flies?'

'Oh aye, I suppose so, but they make untidy ones and they be smaller in t'body. Don't need so much to eat perhaps.'

They trudged along the top road through Kirkstall. Jim wore his best 'black' suit which actually had a distinct greenish cast to it. He had an old buff cravat – clean but creased – and a thin gold watch chain across his spare waistcoat. On his head was the better of his two caps – he did have a dark hat because Effie remembered that he wore it at the funeral, but he found caps more comfortable. Effie's soft-cloth bonnet was crammed into her pocket. She had snatched it off as soon as they turned into the lane and grinned nonchalantly at Jim's disapproving head shake. She had on her best long blue coat and her best high button-up black boots, but there was nothing to be done about that. She glanced enviously at Jim's Sunday clogs – smart black leather uppers secured to the wood soles by a neat row of brass-headed nails. They'd be comfortable!

'There's St Stephen's spire,' she pointed. 'I heard them say there were someone important buried there, at the funeral.'

'Aye. There's Richard Oastler, the "Factory King" they called him.'

'Why?'

''E did a deal o' good work for the mill workers. Spent a lot of his life holding meetings and telling Parliament how bad treated they was and how long hours the bairns had to work.'

'How old were the children?'

'Oh, they started in t' mill when they were six or seven years old.'

Effie's eyes opened wide. 'Why did their parents let them?'

'Because their small fingers could do the work, when the threads broke or twisted on t' looms, better than grown-ups could, and jobs was so scarce and bad paid that their faither couldn't earn enough to feed them!

'Anyway – a lot of them 'adn't got no parents – they was orphans from the workhouses – even brought some up from the south, they did.'

Effie was horrified. She had never heard Jim speak so fast and show such emotion before, either.

'It doesn't happen now, does it?'

'Nay – thanks to Oastler and his ilk it's a deal better – but there's still bairns not much older than you working.'

'When did he die?'

'Oh, Ah reckon it were about twelve years ago. I went to that funeral too and it were a sight. I got there just as the pallbearers came and you couldn't get into the churchyard at all, it were that packed with mill-working people. Come from all over the

48

West Riding, they had.' They walked slower as they neared the church.

'Well, Grandpa's weren't that big. Did you think it were all right though, Jim?'

'I didn't go to enjoy it, lass.'

'No – but did you think the vicar should have said all that?'

'They allus do.'

'Just the same for everyone?'

'I guess so. Much the same.'

'Grandpa wouldn't have liked it,' she said shaking her head.

'Nay, but I don't think he'd have cared much.'

'No. That's just what I was trying to make myself think on the day. It just weren't important. It weren't anything really to do with Grandpa at all.'

They had reached the churchyard gate and Jim stopped.

'Does tha want to go in and look at the grave?' His voice was perfectly even and he eyed her steadily. Effie cast her eyes down.

'I don't know … Yes – since you're here, Jim. Just a quick look.' They walked up the path and looked: 'In loving memory of John Arthur Barrett who departed this life on 6th April 1876 aged 72 years.'

The carved headstone was unostentatiously similar to the surrounding ones – large, thick and well masoned – just somewhat newer. Effie looked up to the broken marble pillars and draped urns clustered at the upper edge of the churchyard. She felt glad his mortal remains had not been put up there. She half-smiled at Jim and they walked slowly back down the path.

'I'm glad I looked, Jim. I don't care about it now. It's not even as if he's there – not really.' After a thoughtful pause she asked, 'Do you know where I think he is?'

Jim shook his head doubtfully.

'I think he's in my bit o' garden – by the pond. Not just where he … you know … Not just *there* but sort of all over.' Her eager face fell for the final confidence.

'Sometimes, when I'm looking at the pond, I'm raight sure he's there.'

Jim said nothing and Effie raised her eyes challengingly to his.

'Aye – I know what you mean, lass.'

'After all, you could reckon it was a sort of heaven, couldn't you? I'd be happy with a heaven like that.' She adjusted the ledger in its brown paper bag to hold it more firmly under her arm. They had reached the top of Kirkstall hill now and they strode on through Burley in silence.

When they reached Leeds they made their way straight to Albion Street.

''E may not be in, you know. 'E weren't expectin' us.' Jim's voice sounded hopefully pessimistic and Effie cast him a suspicious glance. They found the polished brass plate beside an open door – 'Jenkins, Bailey and Jenkins. Solicitors, Accountants and Executors.' Effie led the way firmly up the steps into the hall and knocked at the huge polished mahogany door.

'Come in,' called a female voice.

'We want to see Mr Jenkins, please.' Effie's voice was almost aggressive.

'Have you an appointment?' asked the secretary resentfully, addressing herself to Jim.

'Nay.'

'Who shall I say?'

'Elspeth Barrett,' said Effie loudly.

The woman walked over, knocked on a door to the left of her desk, opened it and said 'Mr and Miss Barrett to see you,' in a precise, neutral tone.

'You may come in,' she called condescendingly over her shoulder.

Mr Jenkins looked over his spectacles with a fleeting expression of confused embarrassment as they entered, but he quickly summoned up a front of joviality.

'Good morning Mr ... er ...'

'Woodgate,' supplied Jim. 'Mr Woodgate and Miss Barrett.'

'What can I do for you?'

Jim became utterly tongue-tied.

Effie drew out the brown paper bag and laid it deliberately on the desk with both palms pressed on top of it.

'Well, sit down, won't you?' The awkwardness and silence advanced together. Mr Jenkins tried to smile reassuringly.

'You know t' pond?' blurted out Effie. 'We want it done. I've brought the plans to show you.' She appealed to Jim for support but he was completely absorbed in his best cap which he held clamped between his knees and hands. A feeling of intense exasperation welled up in Effie's breast and furnished her with the momentum she needed to command the situation.

'Look.' She unpacked the ledger and opened it at the final draft, turning it so that she and Mr Jenkins could see. Her confidence increased as she conducted him through the general outline and the detailed construction.

'Well,' he said finally. 'It's a big project. It's going to cost a tidy sum, is that.'

'There's enough, isn't there?' inquired Effie earnestly.

'Y...yes. What do your parents think about it?'

Effie looked at Jim who immediately showed signs of becoming absorbed in his cap again, but seeing how threateningly her brow darkened he made an effort to rally himself.

'Ah reckon as how they don't raightly know about it, do they, lass?' The ball was back in her court.

'Well, they won't approve of it, Mr Jenkins. But then they never approved of anything Grandpa did, really, you know. They just couldn't say "no" to him and he wants that pond."

Mr Jenkins looked at her curiously.

'At least, if he were here,' she corrected herself with care, 'if he was here. He definitely intended to make that pond, and I sort of feel that we owe it to him.'

'Aye.' Jim at last added the full weight of his support.

They discussed what to build the walls of. Jim and Mr Jenkins decided that the pebble-dash rendered brickwork would be adequate and easier to fit to the pond shapes. Effie was worried that Grandpa would have preferred stone.

'It aren't really necessary for a job like this and brick will be easier to waterproof. You can line it all with mortar, you see,' reassured Jim.

They discussed builders and short-listed two local ones whom Jim would approach for quotations.

'You send me the estimates when you have them, Mr Woodgate, and then we really will have to tell Mr and Mrs Barrett won't we, young lady?'

Effie surveyed her feet thoughtfully. 'I'll explain to them, then,' she said firmly.

Mr Jenkins took the opportunity of giving Jim the first instalment of the garden maintenance money allocated for tools and plants, since they had agreed at Oakroyd that he should take charge of this.

Effie and Jim ate their sandwiches in a park up North Street. Effie's heart was singing. The ordeal was over, the decision to build the big pond made amazingly easily, and now a holiday gaiety took over. She danced around the bench where Jim sat stolidly, tossing up and catching her rolled-up bonnet.

'It be a good thing yer ma's not here,' he smiled.

'Let's go and get the tools!' They sauntered happily down to Green's. The heavy door set with cut-glass panes closed behind them, accompanied by a noisy ringing, and Effie sniffed the ironmongery odour appreciatively.

'It's big. I shouldn't think there's anything they haven't got. Just look at all them different spades and forks in that rack.'

'These sickles have a fine edge and feel well,' said Jim balancing one expertly in his hand.

'What's in these big bags with the smell?'

'Bone meal, miss. Three grades,' smiled a young man proudly.

'Oooh – there's bulbs!'

'Yes, miss. Only came in last week. Species crocus; daffs – some of them new white ones; five different narcissus; jonquils and tulips – all guaranteed heights and colours for bedding.' He indicated each basket.

'Should we have some, Jim?'

'Aye. The bedding tulips would be good for the front. It's three years back since we had some and it's awkward to keep them apart when you lifts them in t' summer.'

'Ah, yes,' said the assistant sympathetically. 'They does tend to get all mixed up, don't they.'

'I'd like some crocuses and daffodils and narcissus round the pond – but they'd be in the way, I suppose?'

'We won't get started till spring at earliest. Early crocus and daffs would be near over before we wanted to start,' said Jim.

The young man eyed them, curious to know on what they would be starting.

'What we really be needing are a spade,' Jim confessed gravely.

'Ah!' He bustled over triumphantly to the long rack.

'What sort o' work do you need it for, sir?'

Jim scowled slightly at the 'sir'. He felt it might be sarcastic, but the innocent interrogative face of the lad reassured him, so he stepped over to select one for himself.

'That be a grand job and this un's good for lighter jobs, but it seems a bit dear; an' I shouldn't mind one o' these broad-tined forks. They be fine for general work in our soil, but no good in a heavy one.'

'Oh no, sir. There's new places going up Roundhay way and some of that soil's raight cloying they say.'

'The price don't matter, Jim. There's plenty of money isn't there? You just have which you like best.' There was something very satisfying about being able to buy pleasure for someone special, thought Effie. She caught Jim's eye and saw the merry twinkle. He was going to remind her that she was only a little girl. Her eyes fell and a quick flush suffused her cheeks, but no:

he had complacently set the fork on one side and was picking out the two spades. They also bought a Dutch hoe and then a light fork and a trowel especially for Effie's use. They were all the best in stock. Jim paid and asked for string to tie them together.

'But let us deliver them, sir!'

'Really?' said Effie. 'We live five miles out!'

'Of course. No trouble; they'll be there by Tuesday afternoon. Will that be soon enough?'

'Oh, thank you,' said Effie fervently. Money did seem to smooth one's way wonderfully.

'How about the bulbs?' he asked.

'Oh yes. We'd nearly forgotten. Which ones shall we have, Jim?'

'I suppose that's all right about delivering?' asked Jim doubtfully outside the door. 'I'd be happier carrying them home mesen. We'd have them for certain then.'

'I'm sure they're a very respectable firm. They couldn't let anyone down,' replied Effie confidently. 'What shall we do now?'

'Go home, I suppose. We done what we came for – what else do ye want, eh?' He smiled mischievously as he drew out his large turnip watch. 'It's a quarter past three.'

'Let's just look round a bit. There's all them big shops. Do they sell flowers anywhere, do you think?'

'Ah don't raightly know. Ah, yes, I seem to remember a shop along Briggate and there's the market, o' course.'

They found a florist's. Effie was enchanted by the superb greenhouse blooms. There were red rosebuds that looked like the ones on her bedroom wallpaper; lilies – huge and pure white with crimson spots beneath their graceful stamens and an oppressively heavy scent; and clove-scented carnations in multicoloured tulle. Jim stood awkwardly by the door, twisting his cap as the sales matron eyed them disdainfully. Effie was too transported to notice. The withering sarcasm of 'Can I help you, miss?' roused her suddenly. 'Aren't those lilies beautiful!' said Effie with a timid smile that Jim thought would disarm an angel. The stout matron was not quite disarmed but she softened a little.

'They're rather expensive,' she said.

'How much?' Effie was gazing fixedly up into the trumpet of one.

'One and sixpence each!'

'Oh.' She turned to examine the mimulus and gloxinias. They were undeniably coarse and blousey beside the ethereal beauty of the lilies.

'I suppose we had better get on, Jim.'

'The lilies keep well. They'd stay fresh nigh on two weeks,' said Jim. 'And there's plenty of money,' he added quietly, eyes twinkling.

'Oh, Jim, really ... have you got that much left?'

'Aye. You have two, lass.'

The four-foot-high blooms were ceremoniously wrapped up.

'Could you perhaps put some more paper round them because we've a long way to walk.'

The flower lady melted suddenly.

'Of course, love. I hope you get a lot of pleasure from them.'

They made their way on along the street with Effie clasping her outsized bouquet protectively to her among the jostling crowd. They found a pet shop which was irresistible, but the lilies became a definite encumbrance. A large red and green macaw chained to a perch caught hold of the edge of the wrapping and eyed Effie malevolently as she struggled to wrest her lilies from its pitiless beak. Jim came to her rescue and offered to take the flowers so that she could look round properly. There were some magnificent golden carp and rudd.

'Oh, we must have some o' those really big ones in the new pond.'

'These 'ud be grand in one o' the side ponds.' Jim was watching some plump brown fish which puttered along the surface blowing bubbles through their pursed lips.

There were young rabbits and guinea pigs which Effie squatted down to admire and in a pitifully small cage were two puppies and three kittens. The smaller puppy was black with a white front and white tips to its forepaws. It sat quietly against the wire cage front, its head slightly on one side and a heart-rendingly doleful expression on its baby face. Effie was entranced by the wrinkled velvety folds between its dark eyes and above its tiny black nose. She whispered words of love and it responded by rising uncertainly on its big fat paws, wriggling, and then sat down suddenly again. She turned back to the guinea pigs.

'These baby ones are ever so sweet, Jim. Do you think Mama would mind me having one? They don't make a noise, do they? At least only that soft burble which couldn't disturb anyone and such a tiny thing couldn't eat much.'

'It would eat a lot o' your lettuces if it got the chance.'

'Oh, I wouldn't mind that.'

Jim ponderously withdrew the coins from his pocket and counted them.

'They be sixpence each,' said the shopgirl eagerly. Jim glanced round at Effie, but she was back nose-to-nose with the puppy.

'I'll have that ginger and white one,' said Jim quietly. It was boxed up and slipped into his greatcoat pocket.

'Jim, I'm sure this little pup's unhappy.'

'He be too young to be 'ere. Can't be a day over five weeks.'

'Oh, what a shame … Jim?' Jim inwardly cursed his ill-considered comment. 'He's very small. Do you think Mama and Papa …'

'Nay. Ah reckon yer mam and pa would not entertain the thought o' that pup for a moment. 'E might be small noo – but look at the size o' his feet. He'll grow into a raight labrador, he will.' Jim spoke quite vehemently and Effie's tragic face gazed up palely from the floor.

'Furthermore,' stated Jim firmly, battling against his weakness, 'that puppy is likely to get sick an' die from being chilled an' not fed proper away from its mother.'

'Die – oh! What if he were put somewhere cosy and given warm milk tonight?' A large tear welled up over each eyelid and began coursing down her cheek. Jim muttered darkly beneath his breath. Why did he not keep his mouth shut? At his age he should have learnt that words rarely served him well unless used sparingly and with great care.

'That pup ought to go to a good home tonight. I don't like leaving' them 'ere all Sunday on their own,' said the shopgirl.

'Doesn't anyone come in to feed them Sunday?' demanded Effie indignantly.

'Well, I gives them a lot o' food before I goes, an' makes sure the water's all right. It's only these very young ones as I worries about.'

The world seemed to be conspiring against Jim.

'How much be it?' He enunciated the words carefully.

'You can 'ave it for two shillings and sixpence, mister,' said the girl warmly. 'An' save me if t' maister finds out.'

Effie's eyes were fixed on Jim's face.

'Two shillings and sixpence is all we 'ave bar a copper or two.'

'We don't need no more.'

'Yer ma and pa won't like it one bit. They'll grieve at me and 'appen it'll be me what gets a dog.'

'If that did happen, I would pay for its keep, Jim, but I'll try to keep it myself.'

The money was laid on the counter. The pup was wrapped in a piece of cloth and put in Effie's arms. There was a trace of anxiety on the shopgirl's face. Jim looked questioningly at her.

'It be a bitch, yer know, mister,' she whispered.

'I'll be damned,' muttered Jim viciously, and he bundled Effie and her burden out of the shop.

'An' Ah look a raight saight carrying these rare flowers,' he grumbled as they trudged past the closing shops in the gas-lit dusk.

CHAPTER SEVEN

Effie came downstairs late next morning and crept inconspic-uously into the kitchen, but both her parents looked up darkly. She had hoped they wouldn't be there so she could have warmed some milk for the puppy but she now decided it would be tactful to just sit down and eat her own breakfast. The porridge was cold but uncomplaining she filled her bowl and began to eat.

The silence was broken by Mrs Barrett's strident voice. 'You can't keep that dog, Effie.'

'Why not, Mama? It's only small – I'll look after it completely. You shan't even know it's here.'

'Ha – it might only be small now but it'll grow and you'll be at school all day, remember? And your bedroom is no place to keep animals. I 'spect there's a raight mess up there now. Just because your father was soft on you last night with all that blethering ...'

'Well it were too late ter go sortin' it all out then weren't it?' rejoined her father defensively.

'It should have been put in the shed, like I said, an' taken raight back on Monday morning.'

'It would have died of cold in the shed last night, Mama. You know it would – it's too young.' Tears began to stream down Effie's face.

'It only be a dog, lass,' said her father soothingly. 'No need to get yourself all worked up like.'

'I don't know what Jim Woodgate were thinking of. Fancy letting the child bring that puppy 'ome!'

'Maybe it could live in the shed when it's grown up, Mama?'

'It aren't growing up. Not here it aren't. An' that's final.'

Effie rose from the table tipping over her chair. She caught it up and flung it against the table edge, and flew from the room pushing the door shut hard.

'An' tantrums won't help,' shouted her mother. 'I'm afraid Rosalie's right, John. That child's spoilt. She's that wayward and she seems to be getting worse rather than better now Faither's gone.'

'I don't know ... Maybe we shouldn't get any harder on her. I mean, maybe we are a bit hard and she'd get better if we softened up; she must be very lonely since her grandpa died because they was always together.'

'If she be lonely maybe she could spend a bit more time with me. She's down in the garden or the potting shed all her time at home. A man like Jim Woodgate is no company for a girl of her age. She ought to be learning how to look after a house else it will come hard later on.'

'Well that's what I mean. Maybe if we let her keep that dog it would keep her here a bit more.'

'I don't want a big black dog in an' out of my kitchen. It'll probably get all shaggy and think of the dirt it'll carry in on its feet and all the hairs on the carpet. It's easy for you – you don't do the cleaning. And there's the rest of the house. *That's* waiting for cleaning this back-end. I don't know when we're going to get started on that. Mrs Wadsworth's husband's sick and she can't come in to help till he's back at work.'

'Perhaps we could keep it for a bit and see how it shaped up? Maybe it wouldn't be that large and if it were we could find someone to have it.'

Mary merely grunted, which John interpreted as a sign of weakening, and got on with his newspaper.

Meanwhile Effie had wrapped up the pup and, holding it tightly against her, she ran down the main staircase and through the hall. Sobbing convulsively she struggled with the bolts on the big front door. She had to put the pup down and stand on tiptoe to reach the top one. Eventually it gave. The pup had trailed its shawl a few yards up the hall and was now squatting down gazing back apologetically. She gathered it up in the damp cloth and gave the puddle no more than a guilty glance before she passed through the front door and closed it quietly behind her.

She had almost mastered herself by the time she knocked on Jim's cottage door, but her pink-rimmed eyes and pale smudged face told their own story.

'Ah, lass. I were sort of expecting you two. Come on in.' He sat her by the range, poked up the fire and swung the kettle over the hob.

'Jim, can I please make something for Lily's breakfast? I couldn't do it at home.'

'Lily, eh!'

'Mm. After the flowers we got. Oh, don't they look lovely?' She jumped up to gaze in admiration at the blooms which rose out of a preserving jar on the floor to grace the window of Jim's tiny living room. Their thick cloying perfume filled the room.

'I thought it were best not to mention them last night with all the carry on, and you can ask your mother if you can have them up in your room today.'

'No, let them stay here, Jim. I don't think I'm going back there and I'm certainly not going asking Mama for anything.'

Jim put a bowl of warm bread and milk on the hearthrug and Effie tenderly lifted Lily down to it.

'I've got a bit o' meat off an old chicken carcase for her after that. But, where be tha going, eh?'

'I've not had time to think it out straight, but if I can stay here for a little while, Jim, I'll think of something. Do you think we could live in the potting shed for a few days? Could I keep Lily warm enough there?' Two large tears were burning their way up through her lids, do what she might to keep them down.

'Nay, lass – I don't think that's a good idea.'

Effie told of the encounter over breakfast.

'Your mam may think better of it yet, you know. Maybe your pa *is* on your side and he'll manage to persuade her.' Effie shook her head, brushed away a tear and gazed mournfully into the fire.

'Then if the worst came to the worst maybe I could look after your Lily dog here as well as your lily flowers, eh? An' you could come to see her each day.'

'Oh, thanks, Jim. That would certainly be better than not having her at all but I've got terribly fond of her already and I do want to live with her. I've never had any sort of pet – except the fish, of course.'

'Nay – but you be making up for lost time now, what with pups and guinea pigs ...'

'Guinea pigs! What do you mean?'

'Well, that were something else as I thought it tactful not to sort out last night. You come and look in the scullery.'

He led the way into the tiny lean-to and there, circling happily round a lettuce in the shallow stone sink, was a young ginger and white guinea pig. It paused and looked up at Effie, its dark eyes beady-bright, then with a little burble ran under the shelter of a lettuce leaf.

'But how ever did you bring that home? I never saw it.'

Jim smiled.

Effie laughed gaily, her troubles banished for the moment.

'Well, what's the name of this one going to be?'

'Is it a boy or a girl?'

'Well, Ah don't rightly know.' He picked it up and surveyed its belly thoughtfully. 'I reckon as it's not that easy to tell at this age.'

'It sort of looks like a girl one ... I think "Letitia" because she likes lettuces – and "Lettie" for short.'

Sometime later Jim reminded Effie about her lunch.

'I can't go back, Jim,' she pleaded. 'I can't. They're always on at me about something and now Lily ... Jim, suppose I came to live with you for a bit, to help you look after Lily and Lettie,' she explained.

'Nay, lass, it wouldn't be proper.'

'What do you mean, "proper"?'

'Well, firstly you're a young lady with a big house and quite a fortune, and this little cottage aren't grand enough.'

Her eyes narrowed. 'And what else?'

'Well, there aren't room, are there?' he rejoined feebly. 'Not for me and Lily, like ... and Lettie ... and then you.'

Effie looked downcast.

'Not that I wouldn't like it, see. It would be grand, because I'm a lonely fellow – but – folks wouldn't approve, see, lass?'

'Not really. I mean – it's just what makes one happy that is important, isn't it? You'd be happy and I'd be terribly happy – even if it's small – I shouldn't mind a bit.' She noticed his despairing expression. 'But I suppose you're right, Jim. You understand because you're grown up. It still seems silly to me that people can't be happy in their own way without other folks interfering.'

'Aye, that's right, but it's the way of the world and I can tell ye that if tha try running agin it, it will certainly end in unhappiness whatever it seemed to start like.' His tone became firmer.

'An' the way of the world is that tha has to go home and have tha Sunday dinner as if nothing had happened. You leave Lily here and come back to see her this afternoon.'

Effie's jaw muscles tightened and her head rose defiantly.

'Nay, lass,' warned Jim. 'Just think on what I said. You aren't giving way to no-one. I knows that and you know that. But if you seem to be toeing the line, so to speak, and try to behave just a little friendly to yer mam, I think as 'ow she might come round and then you've won – haven't you?'

Effie gazed into the fire for a few moments and then rose slowly and left the cottage without a word. She walked back to the big house, eyes downcast but without noticing a single plant. There was a turmoil of feeling in her breast, none of which she could distinguish or name, but if she had been able to, the names of two would have been pride and love, each suffering suppression in the name of social convention. This is a mean, sordid oppressor, spawned and fed by timid small-mindedness, but so powerful. She could just perceive its power in the glimpse of futile loneliness stretching ahead of her and in the humiliation and bitterness which she felt.

The Yorkshire pudding had risen particularly well and its golden crispness gleamed through the glutinous gravy as they ate it, local fashion, before the meat and vegetables. John remarked upon it with relish. Mary pursed her lips complacently and looked at Effie. Effie smiled wanly and despised them for their sensuality. Fortunately Mary could only detect the smile and when Effie followed it up two courses later with an offer to wash up, she warmed towards her child considerably. Effie now despised herself as she slowly wiped the suds from each plate and placed it on the board for her mother to dry.

'Your father and I've been talking over this matter of t' dog, lass. If you were to promise me to be a sight more help in t' house and mend your manners, you might keep that pup – but mind – it mustn't go into t'living room because I don't want hairs and dirt in there. And if it grows up very big you'll have to find another place for it – and any misbehaviour from you, and away it goes, *prompt*, miss!' This sentence had begun good-naturedly enough but the tone had become increasingly strident and threatening. Effie swallowed hard and concentrated upon suppressing the temptation to fling the dishcloth into the suds with a satisfying splash and then walk disdainfully out of the room and house for ever. She forced herself to consider throwing her arms round her mother in an abandoned gesture of gratitude but could not bring herself to such hypocrisy.

She merely said, 'Thanks, Mama. I will try,' and fixed her downcast eyes upon the suds.

As soon as Mary carried the tea tray out to the sitting room Effie took her coat and slipped out of the back door. The bitterness of her thoughts gradually gave way to the sense of qualified victory and as it did her pace quickened until she burst into Jim's living room flushed and breathless. The rugged face looked up and dissolved into wreaths of smiles.

'Well, what's t' news?'

'I can keep her.'

'What did I tell thee?'

'Aye, Jim. I guess it were the best thing to do but I don't feel proud of myself,' she answered gravely.

'Nay, lass, but it's life I'm afraid. It won't be the last time you have to dissemble, as they say.'

'When I grow up I'm going to live on my own and please myself, like Grandpa. I'm never going to have anyone around that I have to answer to.'

'He didn't just please himself, Effie.' His use of her name was so unusual that she gave him her full attention. 'He tried to and he managed partly but there were your grandmother and then yer father and mother, and the men as worked for him. He had to consider all o' them.' He drew on his pipe for a bit.

'Mind you, in later years, he had a bit o' brass and that helps greatly when it comes to arranging things as you want them.'

'I can't see why one needs money. You please yourself.'

He half turned to look at her and the furrowed cheeks creased slowly in a bitter smile as he shook his head 'Nay, only a bit. I've·always had to do as my maister wanted in order to earn my bit o' money and if I'd married there'd 'ave been so little to go round that I should have been hard pressed to please a wife. But I should 'ave married. Nay, don't look like that, lass,' he interjected reprovingly. 'I've paid hard for my bit of independence.'

'How, Jim?'

'You'll understand when you're older.' He shook his head irritably and knocked out his pipe. Effie knew better than to interrupt the exacting and protracted business of repacking it so she went to make sure Lettie was happy, looked up the ample speckled trumpet of each lily and then settled into the rocking chair with the dozing puppy in her lap. As she smelt the heavy odour of the lilies and gazed into the cavernous vistas of the fire she was aware of yet another feeling. This was a rapidly deepening happiness which grew into an overwhelming tranquillity and sense of wellbeing against which the pleasures of childhood absorptions seemed quite pale.

CHAPTER EIGHT

The autumn passed wet and dreary to merge imperceptibly with a damp cold winter. Outside, nature seemed to be running down. Sometimes, as Effie sat on an upturned wooden box in the potting shed, she wondered what proof she had that spring and summer *would* come again. They always had, but supposing this period of cold quiescence could not be revitalized? Imagine life as one long unremitting winter, in which birds and insects and people gradually cooled and congealed until they too joined the plants in an interminable suspension of vitality. That is surely how the earth will end, thought Effie – each winter longer and colder and each summer shorter. But such morbid thoughts did not eat into her as deeply as they might since, pressed against her side, warm and intensely alive, was Lily. She had not followed the plants' example one bit. She ate, romped and, above all, grew. Each week Effie's maternal satisfaction with Lily's robust growth rate conflicted with her anxiety about the final size of this boisterous but endearingly dependent companion. Effie did her best to keep Lily out of her mother's sight but each time Mary encountered the pup she shook her head meaningfully. Unfortunately such encounters were not always innocent on Lily's part. She always took a keen interest in the antics of washing drying on the line and spent a large part of Monday mornings sitting, head on one side, watching the play of the sheets, pillow cases and garments. The autumn rain had taken its toll of the well-worn line and one morning, in an early winter wind, it snapped, fully loaded. No sooner had its animated burden reached the ground than Lily was in the midst of it and ten minutes later when Mary appeared it was difficult to discern the natural divisions between linen, puppy and mud. Effie returned from school to find Lily howling in the dog kennel and a foreboding silence in the kitchen.

There was also the case of the missing silk stockings. Effie did not mention the dismembered welt in Lily's basket, nor the partially digested remnant in the garden which she discreetly buried. There was also the time Lily was inadvertently shut in the dog-forbidden sanctuary of the sitting room and chewed up the corner of the carpet by the door in her frustration. On each occasion Mary delivered the ultimatum that Lily must go and the household was plunged into gloom, conflict and pleading for several days. So far Effie had achieved a remittance but there was no security.

In the potting shed on this dank February day, Lily's brown eyes gazed up devotedly into Effie's rueful blue. Perhaps it was the glimmer of the late afternoon sun peeping through the clouds and glistening on the rainwashed window which clouded the proud clarity of her face; or perhaps that elfin charm of childhood had been replaced by another. Her eyes seemed of a violet hue and had a more pensive quality. Pride there was still but the uncompromising set of the chin was softened by the vicissitudes of hard-won battles. The slight, almost etiolated frame had suddenly acquired a pubescent charm as well.

A spray of winter jasmine tossed gently against the drop-bespangled panes, the faded flowers were tinted by the sudden yellow gleam of sunlight. Lily nudged Effie's arm affectionately so she began to fondle her velvet ears as she surveyed the dusty shelves stacked neatly with phosphate, chalk and salt. A thin skein of raffia hung from the cobwebbed ceiling like unkempt hair. Effie sniffed deeply at the comfortable aroma

66

which owed a little to creosote, fertilizer and earth, but seemed an intangible essence of permanency, reassurance and companionship. It was as deeply associated with the happiness of her childhood as the smell of the study had been, but sadly that had passed with Grandpa and she was shocked to consider that this place was not hers either. It was Jim's ... Supposing ... Her heart filled with the irrational fear of last summer and she clutched Lily close, but at that moment the metallic rasp of Jim's iron-shod clogs sounded on the flagged path.

'Ah, so it's you two!'

'Who else might it be?' Jim shook his head and grinned.

'How's Lettie, Jim?' Effie's voice held a forced casualness to disguise the emotional turmoil of her thoughts. Jim surveyed her narrowly through his lower lids.

'She be fine. Go and see her, if you like. Put t' kettle on, lass. I'll just tidy up in here then we'll mash some tea.'

They sat each side of the range, mugs in hand, gazing silently at the coals. Effie was still trying to establish her anchorage. The cosy little room was undoubtedly Jim's and she was occasionally honoured to be invited there. On the other hand, the potting shed was more common ground. There had always been the tacit arrangement that she could go there any time she liked providing there was 'no meddlin'.' So be it. Jim emanated as stolid a permanent presence as a stone wall or gnarled ash trunk. She could not bring herself to imagine life without Jim and so she forced a comforting oblivion on her uneasiness which made it possible to consider the other disquieting news.

'Jim, do you know what Mr Jenkins said to Mother? I think she must have been telling him about me not behaving well and not helping her. He said, why didn't they send me to boarding school and use that money Grandpa set by for my education! They didn't tell *me* of course,' she added bitterly. 'I just happened to hear them talking and Papa said he didn't think I'd like it much and Mama said "it weren't so much a matter of pleasing me as educating me so that I grew up nice and ladylike".'

Jim smiled at the imitation of Mary's high harsh voice and imagined he knew the reason for Effie's confusion when he entered the potting shed.

'Tha seems to make a habit o' listening at doors.'

'Not really. I just like to make sure what's going on before I go into t' room. Especially with Lily – just to save trouble, you know. They never tell me anything – even when it's something important about me – like this!'

'Would you want to go?'

'Of course not. What, leave you and Lily? And there's the water garden. It would be terrible at boarding school – all those girls and nowhere to go on your own.'

'Aye – steady – there, lass. They was only just chewin' it over, I expect. I don't s'pose it will come to anything, anyways.'

'We must get on with the water garden this summer. Just in case they send me away somewhere. We must get it done. You haven't been to see Mr Grinley yet, have you?' she asked reproachfully.

'Nay,' Jim sighed. 'All right, I'll go this week. We ain't told yer mam and pa yet.'

'Leave that to me, Jim. I'll try to be good and helpful for a bit to put them in a good mood. I wonder if Lil can keep out of trouble for a bit. That 'ud help.' Effie eyed the innocent face doubtfully.

'Not that she ever *means* to make trouble. She's just unfortunate, like.' She caressed the silky ears lovingly.

'Aye; it's in the nature of puppies … and bairns.' He added the last very quietly but Effie shot him a searching glance.

Effie shut herself in the study the next Sunday morning. Although the potting shed never changed, this room certainly had. She stood in the centre of the Indian carpet and looked round sadly. It was the room in which Grandpa had spent

68

most of his time. She remembered it, warm and welcoming; the scent of old books, cherished and read, the smell of Grandpa – his clothes, pipe and tobacco – so cruelly evocative. The warmth, welcome and smell had utterly vanished. She couldn't distinguish even a trace of it in the dark, musty odour that filled the cold room. His personal trifles, pipes, pens and their accoutrements, which had littered the desk were tidied away. With a small shudder of dismissal she walked rapidly to the bookshelves and, removing four substantial books, she pulled from behind them the brown paper parcel containing the ledger. She laid it open on the desk and searched the drawer for a pencil and sheet of paper. A familiar red and yellow object caught her eye and she picked it up. It was the crude figure of a quadruped made out of sticks tied together with raffia and bound round with a fragment of red and yellow cotton print. It was the horse Effie had made for his birthday when she was four. She was deeply touched that he had treasured this for so long and her lips quivered; but one lesson she had learnt was not to indulge in self-pity. Although Grandpa was irrevocably gone from the study he was out there, by her garden, waiting for their pond. She was happily aware of that whenever she stood or lay there to watch the fish, and Jim was too. She knew that by the way he had lowered his eyes and nodded when she confided her secret to him in the churchyard.

The plans spread before her looked unconvincing – just black markings on cream paper – but as she began to decipher the side notes and measurements in her grandfather's small crabby hand and the bold thick pencil detail in her large childish one, the pond began to take shape again. Olive green *Elodea* began to spread and bronze lily leaves thrust up through the fish-filled water. The bog garden became luxuriant with kingcups, water flag and buttercup. The newt efts and sticklebacks explored the stems of the bulrush and potamogetum in the side ponds. Undoing two buttons of her blouse she pushed the envelope in and ran eagerly out to her garden. There the feeling of urgency became even more compelling.

She suddenly had so vivid a recollection of her grandfather's impatient voice that she froze and turned her head – lips parted and eyes expectant.

'Well, *come on*, lass – get on with it. Tha must begin before tha can finish.' And then another gentler voice continued.

'Ah, Effie. Looking at your garden then, lass?' She turned sharply the other way to find her father smiling at her. The studied friendship of his manner made her apprehensive and she guiltily fumbled to do up her blouse buttons.

'How would you like to go to a big school on the edge of the moors?'

'Why, Papa?'

'Well …' he looked at his feet uncomfortably, 'just that your mam and me thought you should be better schooled there and your grandpa left the money for it, you know.'

'What about Lily?' she asked dully.

'You couldn't take a dog, lass.' He spoke kindly, almost pleadingly. She knew he had been sent to smooth the passage of the arrangement. A feeling of sinking inevitability overwhelmed her.

'When?' She looked fixedly at the toes of her clogs.

'September, I suppose. That's when they start the new year at schools.' There was a long pause.

'Well, do you think you would like it?'

Effie eyed him sorrowfully. What was the point of saying 'no'. It would happen, like it or not. Inwardly she despised her own lack of spirit but she had learnt some hard lessons recently.

'Perhaps Jim would have Lily,' was all she said.

'Aye, perhaps. You could see her in the holidays.'

'Papa, there is something I must get done before I go. There is this big pond that Grandpa and me planned. It must be made this summer.'

'But what does tha want with a big pond? It just aren't practical and your grandpa's not here any more.'

Her eyes widened into a blazing blue. Her body tautened and her head rose by a full three inches.

'He's left the money. I do want it. It must be done.'

Her father quailed. His stature seemed to have diminished as hers grew.

'What will yer mother say?' he asked helplessly.

'I will get Jim to make the arrangements. It needn't bother her,' said Effie firmly. Now she felt her old self-confidence return. She would not fail Grandpa. The pond would be made and she would survive school and separation from Lily and Jim. She still had a spirit he could be proud of.

CHAPTER NINE

Jim had not yet been to see George Grinley about estimates for the pond work. Effie suspected that even he was hoping that the idea would die quietly if ignored long enough. She dragged him up the hill that afternoon and they searched out George in his end-terrace home. His work yard occupied the garden area which abutted on to an old stone-built barn. The depressingly regimented brick terraces had advanced across the fields to engulf the old farm house and outbuildings, but their obituary could still be read in the time-worn barn. It stood proudly huge, the large stone blocks in its walls as sound and straight as the day they were mortared in place although no-one had repointed them since. The traditional high gabled porch stood forward in the centre of the building, large enough to allow a laden haywain to pass in and imposing a T-shaped junction on the roof ridge. This ridge was sadly ravaged by years of neglect. Its line was undulating and the stone roof slabs it supported had sagged into mossy concavities between the rib beams. The slabs were still miraculously overlapped in the main, with the neat small scale-like ones at the ridge grading evenly into the massive two and a half feet by three feet ones above the grass-grown gutter. Time and decay had given the building an organic, natural aspect which Effie admired despite Jim's muttered condemnation.

'He ought ter get up an'd do summat about that roof. It won't be sheltering his tools and stones much longer.'

'It's so high!'

'Well, if a builder can't see to his own roof, who can?'

George emerged from his back door, tightening his belt and springing his braces back to his shoulders as he came to greet them. He must have just risen from his after-dinner rest by the range when his wife alerted him of their arrival.

'Well, how be thee, then?' His good-natured face resembled nothing so much as a furrowed winter field with its grey stubble awaiting the plough. Effie wondered how he managed to chew his food with only five yellowed teeth visible and those inconveniently staggered in his gums.

'Pretty fair. How's t' work?'

'Fair ter middling. We been doing a biggish job ower t' Bradford these few weeks.' He smiled happily at them. 'But what can we do for thee?'

Jim glanced uneasily at Effie so she drew out the plan from her jacket pocket and unfolded it.

'We want a pond making, please, Mr Grinley. Here are the plans.'

'Ah – tha art in charge, missy, art tha?' grinned George kindly.

Effie smiled and spread the plans out on the bench smoothing the folds nervously with the palms of her hands.

'Are these figures feet, eh?'

'Yes, it's all in feet.'

'It's a fair sized pond this. Th'art tha grandfer's daughter – nay granddaughter – aren't tha? Always did things proud, the old man.'

'Yes. He and me made this plan last year and we … I do want

72

it just this way, if you can, Mr Grinley.' The last words were spoken appealingly.

'Why, course we can do it just that way, only it's going to cost a bit. I mean, just heaving the earth out of a hole that size is going to take a tidy bit of time.'

'That's all right,' said Effie eagerly. 'Grandpa left money especially for it. When could you start?'

George rubbed the back of his head and neck thoughtfully.

'Well, lass, we must finish this mill job, but that should be through next week. We mun't leave it till there's any risk o' frost. Maybe it would be best left till next year.'

'Oh, no. Please try to fit it in now,' pleaded Effie.

'Well, I'll come and see tomorrow then let you know what it will cost. Maybe tha'll decide another feller could do it cheaper, eh?' His eyes twinkled mischievously at Effie.

August came hot and dry and the garden luxuriated in summer fullness. The herbaceous border stood five feet high. White and purple laced dahlias shone out like catherine wheels from the lush green foliage. Flocks of marguerites floated white. Acid yellow potentillas, flame-coloured pentostemon and the pillarbox-red of the pelargoniums and tall lychnis reflected the relentless heat of the midday sun. Effie stood relishing the riot of life and colour; she closed her eyes and attempted to visualize this border in winter; low brown earth pricked by the grey bones and festooned with the white shrouds of this summer bounty, but the scene required an impossible flight of the imagination and Effie's attention was diverted by the intermittent sound of rough male voices from the side garden. An ill-understood feeling that her presence might be considered an intrusion on adult male work made her move quietly along the border to the tall fuchsia bushes at the edge of the side garden. There she curled up comfortably to watch. Three men were digging. A young man was naked to the waist, but the two middle-aged ones just had their coarse twill shirts unbuttoned above their belted and braced trousers. Their shirt

73

sleeves were rolled up untidily to their elbows. George Grinley rested on his spade to mop up the sweat that trickled down the furrows of his face, and then resumed digging. The artist in Effie was drawn to the naked back of the young man. He moved up and down, tossing each spadeful of soil on the rising heap with a graceful ease that emphasized the stiff movements of the older men. His bronzed shoulder muscles rippled as the spade was lifted from the hole and his lumbar muscles bulged as he drove the spade home again with his foot. Effie noted the almost poignant contrast between the ungainly gathering of the rough tweed trousers held to his hips by some hairy string and the smooth beauty of line as his waist widened upwards past the muscle-flecked ribs to the powerful shoulders. It would be a satisfying shape to view in repose upon the grass, but moving rhythmically in the act of digging it was consummately beautiful. He paused and turned sideways to rest an elbow on his spade butt. Effie wondered at the acuteness of her disappointment when she saw the affable coarseness of his features. The nose was too long and bulbous, the brow too recessive and jaw too large. She knew his face well but the unexpected beauty of his body had momentarily lifted him out of context, just as the winter would obliterate the summer beauty of the border. Life's delights are ephemeral. But Effie's thoughts were of the way nature discriminated against people and favoured plants. It never failed plants, or animals, for that matter. One might prefer one species to another but, in health, their perfect symmetry and correctness of form were indisputable. Alas that humans should be, by and large, ungainly – too fat, too thin, too loud, too coarse and usually ill-featured. They had always said that she was beautiful. Her mirror image seemed pleasing but maybe one can't judge one's own features? Maybe that young man looked in the mirror and was satisfied. Was he as critical of her face as she of his? Maybe he hadn't even noticed her – not more than just to doff his cap as he strode into the garden, spade on shoulder.

'Well, lads, see there's no idling because the gaffer's

watching!' George's bantering salute cut through Effie's reverie like a clean spade through clay. His sharp eyes had just alighted on her in the bushes and she rose guiltily on to her knees, blushing and laughing.

'We're getting on fair enough, en't we, eh?'

George indicated the foot-high posts marking the edges of the ponds. 'Ye see we began in this deep part and we've just reached where we start shelving off for yer shallower bit. Why didn't tha have it deep raight through, lass?' Effie was standing beside him on the hole edge.

'There's some plants as don't like it so deep. Some o' those French water lilies will only grow in two or three foot and there's even one that likes it one foot deep.' Effie spoke confidently, her composure restored by George's request for information. He regarded her respectfully.

'Well, I be d... blowed. Who'd have thought them water plants were so fussy? I allus thought all a water lily needed were water!'

Effie noticed with a twinge of returning discomposure that the young man was looking at her intently, brows puckered up in curiosity.

'You *have* got on fast, Mr Grinley,' she said quickly.

'Aye. No idling in this firm, even if it is a sight too hot for digging.' He stepped out of the hole and pulled a stoneware flagon out from the shade of a clump of marguerites under a rambling rose-bush. He unscrewed the cap and throwing back his head had a good drink, then carefully wiped the top with his earthy hand before passing it to the older man.

''Ere, Bill.' The young man climbed out and retrieved an enamelled milk pan from some shady grass.

'What tha got there, David?'

'Just me mam's cold tea. I finds it more freshening,' he muttered.

'I've a very distinct preference for beer ter cold tea,' laughed Bill as he wiped his mouth on the back of his arm. Effie's eyes were fixed, fascinated, on the undulations of David's belly as he gulped down his tea. The lithe muscular torso looked exactly like those of the Roman statues in the big book on classical sculptures in the library. They, of course, had beautiful small-featured faces – almost too pretty for men, really, and their genitalia were sometimes discreetly draped, or often naked, but very neat. She wondered whether male genitalia were as variable as faces ... but guiltily banished the thought from her mind as the three men prepared to resume digging. George gasped and grunted prodigiously as he scrambled back into the hole and the three figures began to stoop and straighten rhythmically again.

PART II

The Pond

CHAPTER ONE

The classroom was high and light and the teacher's voice rose and fell steadily '... the industrial revolution of the last century may have left the north of England with an inheritance of despoiled countryside and black mill towns but it did bring jobs and a sort of prosperity to country people who had been scraping a meagre living from the land and cottage industries ...' The contralto modulations faded as Effie's eyes dreamily lingered on the tall arched windows and then sought the distant moors lying deep purple and brown in the October sunshine. Their folds and crevices seemed to rise and fall lightly as if breathing – alive and wild. How the chains that fettered Effie's taut young body to this classroom chafed! How irrelevant was this history lesson! All that mattered was to be free among the reality of dark heather, russet bracken, broken earth and sparkling water. The curling becks sucked at the pebbles with a hollow gurgle as they trickled down rocky steps between heather-hung cliffs of peat to the main gully and then cascaded tumultuously down boulder falls into deep pebble-strewn pools. The vision was so vivid that Effie half rose from her seat. Her wooden ruler fell to the floor with a clatter that cut through her reverie like the crack of a gun.

'Elspeth Barrett, sit still!' Even Miss Grimshaw's voice sounded strident and Effie blushed, bewildered. The young woman looked at her intently for a moment and then the lesson bell sounded. Its jarring noise was immediately reinforced by a lusty slamming of desk lids and surge of conversation. Miss Grimshaw withdrew her questioning eyes from Effie's, deftly transferred her pile of books from desk top to arm crook and stepped briskly to the door. She was a study in controlled orderliness from the gleaming coil of dark hair at her neck, through the white starched blouse and trim belted waist to the neatly hosed black ankles, just visible beneath her flared skirt.

'Hey, Effie. Why did you jump up like that?' Susan demanded. Several faces turned in mischievous anticipation.

'Just thought I were somewhere else.' Effie raised her downcast eyes defensively, aware of her grammatical lapse. She still stooped, holding on to the desk top with the dark-eyed look of a cornered animal and the titters of delight welled up around her.

'Where, Effie, eh? Where did you think you *was*?' They teased relentlessly.

'Out on the moor by herself, I bet.'

'Do you really think she's by herself on those long walks she takes?'

'I reckon it's John Fletcher from St Julian's she meets up on those moors.'

'Arrh, yes ... She'm be a deep one, our Effie,' responded the class clown in broad dialect.

The girls chortled away happily and Effie did her best to smile nonchalantly. She envied her school mates their resilience. They didn't enjoy the confinement either, but they accepted its inevitability. Why couldn't she? Why this bitter insouciance as she craved for freedom? Why was indoors so oppressive to her? Could none of her friends understand the compulsion which drove her away as soon as she could escape?

In English yesterday, they had been 'reading-round-the-class'. The faltering voices had bored on flatly, avoiding any glimmer of expression which might have fanned on a tiny flame of dramatic appreciation. The elderly mistress sat sadly reconciled by many years' experience of such tedium but strangely, in the brief respite allowed for 'analysis', Effie found herself re-reading the passage. The beautiful young heroine fled from the bondage of domesticity and paternal protection, rejected the shelter of home and parents to throw herself upon the world and in particular into the uncertain solace of her lover's arms! Effie could not fully understand the impetus but if one substituted 'garden' or 'moors' for 'man', she could concede its possibility.

But who would really do such a thing? she wondered. Take Miss Grimshaw, young, pretty, full-bosomed, but so well ordered. Surely she could not gather up her skirt in one hand, Sutton's *English Industrial History* in the other and run – run past Miss Glover's room – out through the great wooden door – down the road and into the arms of ... a man; an ordinary, bewhiskered, betrousered man; the dark-haired young maths teacher at St Julian's perhaps? (His arched eyebrows and luxuriant moustache had innocently won him a certain notoriety at St Etheldreda's.)

No. Ridiculous fantasy! Inconceivable ... and yet, people *do* get married, have intimate and undiscussable physical relations and subsequently babies ... children. Even Miss Glover, the head mistress, must have had a mother and father!

Such a feat of imagination exhausted Effie and she returned to the drone of the flat voice, just audible above the foot shuffling, desk creaking and long sighs. The volume of these extraneous noises was expertly gauged to be just within the threshold of teacher-tolerance at that particular moment. Such corporate sensitivity encouraged the more discriminating teachers to hope that, sooner or later, they might be able to find a chink in the armour of apathy and creep in to deflect this integration from sheer nuisance into some creative achievement.

Effie's mind drifted back to her problem. How about our heritage of great English literature? What of Dorothea in *Middlemarch* and Catherine in *Wuthering Heights?* Could this all be founded upon a fantasy? Could these unfrivolous women really turn their backs upon propriety and security for the sake of a man? Read in a quiet corner of the school garden, these stories held such a ring of truth. They vibrated in sympathy with her own independent wildness. Of course, Jane Austen's heroines did not respond to any such unruly promptings. They lived decorously in hope until fortuitous circumstances delivered them to their beloved.

Mrs Saunders then fretted her way through forty minutes of maths. Her high-pitched, anxious voice worried through Effie's semi-consciousness like a puny wave pushing and drawing ineffectually at the shingle. To the class's inestimable relief the bell sounded and the desk lids slammed down to entomb another week's work. Black-buttoned shoes cascaded from each doorway, beating a frenzied tattoo upon the oak-setted corridors competing with the sound of laughter and muffled screams. The day girls and the weekly boarders discussed their home-going excitedly. Effie mutely yearned for Lily and Jim and the garden. They lay two lonely months away!

The North Yorkshire moors have a grandeur about their bleak isolation which offsets the prettiness of their wooded, water-worn vales, but Effie missed the comfort of the West Riding moortops that separate the chimney-studded valleys. It seemed as if a reservoir of nature lies upon the 'tops' as a refuge for the industry-ravaged people of the valleys and they regularly refresh themselves by walking and cycling out there each Sunday.

Effie avoided the knot of depressed termly boarders and took a circuitous route to her room, changed into her walking-out shoes, flung on a jacket and made her way unobtrusively to the back gate at the further end of the school grounds. The brown moors lay against the skyline screened by the naked branches of wind-turned beeches in the vicarage garden. She paused at the village shop to look in the window and gauge the extent of her hunger since she had no intention of being at tea. She opened the shop door hesitantly.

'Mrs Green ... please ... if I brought the 1½d down in the morning, first thing, could I have two buns?'

'Aye, lass. Don't tha forget though, and you be sure to remind that Miss Rose Carpenter as she owes me 6d, would tha? She said she'd bring it in last Saturday but she never come. I warrant she's forgot. Here's an apple for tha.'

'I've no money.'

'Nay, lass. They all be withering up and ought to be ate – but don't tha forget the 1½d and Miss Carpenter ... an' don't tha stay out on them moors too late, neither. There's been strange folk hereabout.'

'What like, Mrs Green?'

'Oh, just an old fellow with a beard – ginger, like. Didn't seem to know whether he were coming or going. He went up t'moor in the end.'

Effie thanked the stout shopkeeper and set off slowly down the road, savouring the freshly baked buns. They went all too quickly and, cramming the bag into her pocket, she bit into the apple and set off at a trot. A fresh breeze blew the scent of damp bracken and heather into her nostrils. The orange horizon was cut by grey cloud bars but, above these, the sky was clear, the orange merging into ochre, yellow and finally, the most translucent of pale turquoise greens. There was no boundary wall to the narrow gravelled road and her feet sank satisfactorily into the border of spongy turf that had been cropped short by the sheep. She soon turned off on a track barely distinguishable beneath the curving fronds of bracken, yellow and green. It crossed an area of burnt heather and Effie paused to admire the carpet of olive-green moss crowned by tiny rufus-capped fruits and the interposed areas of smooth emerald-green grass.

The light was beginning to fade as she descended into a concealed gully. She leapt lightly down from tussock to stone, exhilarating in the confidence of supple young limbs and the excitement of dusk. Is it possible that this feeling of restless adventure which urges some people out into the evening air harks back to a genetic fragment inherited from a primeval nocturnal hunting forebear; some tiny moon-eyed, spatulate-fingered lemur, perhaps? Effie's last downward leap landed her calf-deep in a sphagnum bog. The failing light had deceived her into expecting firm turf and she ruefully thought of the surreptitious washing and drying of shoes and stockings as she squelched on towards the beck. She paddled up and down but it was nowhere deep enough to wash her legs. She paused and sniffed. Wood smoke! No; it was gone again. She decided to work on up the gully to check for moor fires when she reached the top. Round the next bend, there was the whiff of smoke again. She stumbled on over the boulders and heather until she rounded a perfectly cyclopean hunk of gritstone and almost stepped into a small camp-fire. A rough face, its mouth drooping open in amazement, shone ruddily on the other side of the flames. A wide-brimmed felt hat of great age concealed its hair and eyes, but a bushy unkempt beard glowed red in the firelight.

Effie's first reaction was flight, but she only had time to quiver before the lower jaw rose and a rough voice said:

'Don't tha be frighted.'

'I'm not frightened,' said Effie haughtily.

The beard moved as if ruffled by a smile.

'Well, art tha a fairy, eh?' Effie smiled. 'I never seed anything as looked more like one!' The rufus beard and hat shook slowly from side to side.

'A bit too big, I should think,' said Effie.

'Maybe. But come and sit tha down and get warm.'

'I'm not cold but my shoes and stockings are rather wet. I trod in a bog, back there. Perhaps if I could dry them a bit they won't be noticed when I get back.'

'Aye, tha do that, lass. There are a pool in the beck just over yonder if tha wants to get t'muck out.' Effie retired to the beck, unclipped her stockings, rolled them off and rinsed out the worst of the black ooze. She returned to the fire and squatted down a good five feet from the man, eyeing him warily, but he didn't even look in her direction as he slowly filled an old droopy pipe.

'Tha hasn't any baccy, I suppose? Nay, tha wouldna have!'

Effie shook her head in confirmation of this deduction and

stretched her stockings over a stone pushed up close to the fire laying the buttoned boots open on each side of it.

'Tha hasn't any vittles, I suppose?' He evidently thought this more plausible and tilted his pipe towards her.

'Any what?'

'Any vittles. Tha knows – summat to eat or drink?'

'Oh, no. I'm awfully sorry. I had some buns from the shop but I ate them. Are you hungry?' He shook his head slowly.

'I had summat this morning at a farm.' Effie looked appalled.

'Won't you have anything else to eat today?'

'Nay. Nor tomorrow if I stays here, leastways.'

'Where are you going to sleep?'

''Ere,' he grunted, indicating the sheltered side of the stone.

'What if it rains?'

'Won't rain much.' He cast a look up at the clear sky. 'But it will be fair starvin'.' Effie's worried frown deepened.

'How long have you lived like this?'

'Don't raightly know – long time.'

Effie felt her stockings. 'These will be nearly dry by the time I get back.' She rose.

'Thanks a lot. I'll be back. I'll save some of my supper and come up very early in the morning. You'll be here won't you?' He nodded but kept his eyes fixed on the fire. She waited a moment, uncertain of the correct etiquette and then slipped off round the boulder and at a discreet distance put on her stockings and shoes.

CHAPTER TWO

Miss Grimshaw was sitting by Miss Glover's desk speaking of the number of new history books she would like for the following year. The old Head was parrying her gently by asking her to consider whether the book was sufficiently superior to the present author to justify the outlay since the textbook allowance for the year was already overspent. They agreed upon a compromise.

'How are you getting along with the girls? Do you find them cooperative? Any discipline problems?' Her small wrinkled face seemed confidently benign and very pink against her white wavy hair, but Miss Grimshaw pursed her lips carefully as she noted the shrewd twinkle in the tiny area of blue visible through the folded lids.

'No real problems, Miss Glover. None that I did not anticipate one would meet during the first few months of teaching. In fact I can almost name them all –' Her face suddenly broke into an engaging smile '– there is Mary Garrett in form 3b; Elisabeth Jenkins and her partner in crime, Susan Watson in 4a and, of course, little Letitia George in the first form.'

They both laughed.

'Well, none of those problems need cause you much concern. I am relieved to hear no other names mentioned because there are one or two who can be much more difficult.' Miss Grimshaw raised her brows interrogatively but the bird-like old lady did not intend to give her any damning information.

'There is one child who worries me a little ...', the young woman volunteered hesitantly. Miss Glover gave her a nod of encouragement.

'... that's Elspeth Barrett in 2a.'

'Is *she* difficult to manage?' asked the Head in surprise.

'N ... no.'

'Is her progress not good? It's always difficult to place these children from local schools into the correct forms when they first join us and she has only been here a term.' The old Head looked concerned.

'No. She is doing well enough in history, but I just have the impression that she is perhaps exceptional. I think she is a sensitive child and probably much more intelligent than her work indicates. We have spoken of her once or twice in the staff room and several others agree with me.'

Miss Glover nodded.

'Why is she not doing better then, I wonder?'

'I think she is not happy. I get the impression that very often it is only her body that is in the classroom. She seems to have an exceptional capacity for abstracting her mind, day-dreaming you know, but with much greater intensity than one usually sees.'

'This is the girl that Miss Ingrams met on the moors a good three miles from school the other evening, is it not?'

'Yes. I understand from her room-mate that she slips off to walk by herself whenever she can. I happened to look in at their room when I was on evening supervision duty,' explained Miss Grimshaw.

'And she was away then?'

'Well, yes – probably only for a short tine,' she rejoined defensively.

'And was that during the study period?'

'Er, yes.' The young woman shifted in her seat uncomfortably.

'Well, you know I try to allow the girls as much freedom as possible but the thought of one being out on the moors alone so far away frankly worries me. I *am* responsible for their physical wellbeing, after all.'

'I hadn't intended that you should restrict Effie's (that's

what the girls call her) freedom. I was just worried that she didn't seem to be settling into the school routine happily.'

'I shall think about this and perhaps speak to the child and some of the staff. Thank you very much for bringing it to my attention, Miss Grimshaw. You must realize that you younger mistresses may be accepted into the girls' confidence more easily than the more senior members of staff and this can be a very useful attribute when we have certain problems to solve.' The Head smiled dismissal in a kind but businesslike way.

CHAPTER THREE

The man on the moors had moved on to Barrow Hill. This was inconvenient for Effie since it was nearly two miles further than the beck. She didn't know what he did during the day but she thought he probably roamed about begging food from the moorside farms since he never seemed particularly hungry or to depend upon the small contribution she could scrounge from school. He had become restless after a few days at the rock by the beck and had been gone the following evening. She sat by the burnt-out fire and laid the two pieces of bread, the hard-boiled egg and the biscuit before her. Might as well eat it – after all, she was ravenously hungry. She hadn't had a full school meal for two or three days, and *they* were never quite satisfying, but as she lifted a piece of bread to her lips, she felt curiously guilty. Why? He had no claim to her food. He accepted it without a word of thanks. She ate the bread but still felt uncomfortable until she set off to search for him. It took two evenings, but then, up by the smugglers' track she caught a whiff of wood smoke and quickly ran her quarry to earth, with beaming triumph. He nodded his pipe at her compla- cently and accepted the handkerchief full of offerings as if he fully expected it. She was exasperated but could find no way of rebuking him within the non-verbal independent relationship they had so she picked up a stone and flung it violently at a boulder. He showed no response.

It took her three quarters of an hour to make the journey to the barrows at a brisk run. She only stayed to watch him eat. They rarely spoke to each other. In fact, she wondered at the amount of information that they had exchanged on the first evening. It would be totally dark by the time she set off to return and Susan had to wait at the back gate in order to unlock it and admit her since the gardener padlocked it at half past six each evening.

'Good Lord! Here you are at last. You're later than ever, Effie! I've been waiting half an hour. Where do you go? Why must you stay out so long? We'll be caught and then there'll be trouble,' scolded Susan. That evening he had gone again and Effie had carried out a fruitless search. She was tired and nervous.

'Oh, stop it, Susan. If I'm late tomorrow I'll tell you everything, I promise.'

She was late the next night. She had been searching country that was unfamiliar to her and had mistaken a track. She realized as she neared the back gate that Susan must have been waiting nearly an hour. Perhaps she would have given up and the gate would be locked. But no – it opened!

'Elspeth!' declared Miss Grimshaw's shocked voice. Effie's heart sank. She looked round for Susan.

'I have sent Susan to her room. I think you had better come to mine.'

There followed a long interrogation to which Effie responded in monosyllables or not at all. Miss Grimshaw's abundant patience wore thin and she dismissed the sullen girl with the threat that Miss Glover would certainly be told. Effie spent the next day miserably starting up each time the classroom door opened, but the summons to Miss Glover only came just before the end of afternoon school.

Effie crept along the passageway leading to the Head's room. This was the only part of the school which had carpet on the floor and that seemed to emphasize the sanctity of the forbidden part. She ran her tongue over her dry lips as she stood at the door and timidly knocked.

'Come in.' The little old lady did not look fearsome, in fact, not even awe-inspiring, but Effie closed the door behind her without turning away and felt her heart pounding in her chest.

'Come and sit here, Elspeth.' The voice was brisk but not unkind. 'I hear that Miss Grimshaw found you coming into the school grounds at half past seven yesterday evening?'

'Yes.'

'Where had you been?'

'Walking on the moors.'

'Do you often do this?'

'Yes, most evenings.'

'Why were you so late, yesterday?'

'I ... I was looking for someone.'

'Who?'

'An old man I met.'

'When did you meet him?'

'Last Thursday.'

'And you've met him each evening since?'

'No ... well, yes ... most evenings.'

'What was he doing?'

'He just lives out there.'

'On the moor?'

'Yes. I think he's a tramp.'

'What did you talk about?'

'Not ... very much ... He seemed to not have enough food.'

'Have you been taking him food?'

'Yes – just a bit.' Effie's heart sank. This would lead to a lot of trouble.

'I see.' Miss Glover moved some papers on her desk as she considered.

'Did it occur to you, Elspeth, that this man might have been

90

...' she searched for the best word, '... might have harmed you? Tramps may be violent men with a criminal record.'

'No. No, I am sure he wouldn't have done that.'

'What did he say to you?'

'Nothing much. He didn't talk much. He just asked if I could get him some food.'

'Did he thank you when you brought it to him?'

'No. He just ate it – in a sort of grateful way.'

'He must have been living a long way from school?'

'Yes. He moved about a bit. He was on Barrow Hill, Monday.'

'Barrow Hill! You've been a very foolish girl. Why did you do it?' Effie hung her head sullenly.

'I felt sorry for him, I suppose.'

Miss Glover sighed.

'Do you miss being away from home?'

'Yes.'

'What do you miss most?'

'The garden.'

'The garden! Have you a very nice one?'

'Oh, yes.' Her sullenness evaporated momentarily.

'Do you grow things in it?'

'Yes – well, I help Jim to. Jim's our gardener.'

'Would you like a little bit of garden here? It might be arranged.' Effie considered this doubtfully.

'It's not that I want to garden here, really. It wouldn't be quite the same. I mean ... our garden's very ...' How could she possibly explain?

'I should like to see it.' Effie looked up in surprise. 'Tell me about it.'

'Oh, well, it's large. There's an orchard and a shrubbery, and an alpine rockery ...' she looked up timidly, wondering whether Miss Glover was really interested.

'Yes. Go on. What plants are there on the rockery?'

'There's four – no, there's six different sorts of Dianthus,

91

and there's five gentians – one from Manchuria – and some Drabas and several different saxifrages.'

'You are a keen gardener, aren't you,' smiled Miss Glover. 'Do you know, my father was too, so I can understand how hard it is for you to be away from your garden.'

Effie looked at her in amazement. She had never expected sympathy.

'You think about that bit of garden I mentioned and if you think it would help you, come and see me and we shall arrange it. It will only be a tiny patch in the vegetable garden, you know. You won't really have room for a shrubbery; perhaps a very small alpine rockery – and you could bring some plants back with you after Christmas, eh?' Effie smiled.

'Yes – please – If you could. That would help a little bit.'

'Good. Now Elspeth – no more tramps. You may go for a *short* walk, but I should be happier if you took a friend.' She saw Effie's face cloud.

'Well, we all like to be alone sometimes – but will you promise me that you will go no further than the edge of the moor? Please, your firm promise?'

'Er … yes, I promise,' said Effie with downcast eyes.

'Right. Come to my room at nine o'clock on Saturday morning – and we shall go and see the gardener. I'll ask Miss Grimshaw to speak to him about it. You see we do want you to be happy here, Elspeth, because you must work hard and unhappy people can't do that.'

Effie rose to go.

'Thank you very much, Miss Glover. I'm sorry about the tramp.'

CHAPTER FOUR

At home the pond was shaping up. Jim and George stood in the late afternoon dullness surveying the newly rendered walls.

'Night be drawing in early this evening, it's so overcast. No fear o' frost tonight,' said George.

'Nay, but it mayn't be long. Can't depend on it at this time o' year. The sooner all the cementin's done and hard, the better, George.'

'Aye. It should be done by the end o' t' week.'

The two men stood in silence for a bit. Jim slowly packed his pipe.

'Miss Effie will be that looking forward t' seeing it,' he said.

'Aye. Does tha hear from her?'

'She allus writes a letter each week and it were two as I got last week. She seems desperate to get away from that school of hers.'

George half turned to look at the rugged old Dalesman. He had never heard him volunteer so much information at one go.

'It seems a shame, don't it. T'bairn would 'ave growed up and married a local lad and been perfectly happy. I'd have thought that were all John and Mary Barrett would have wanted for her?' queried George.

'She's a deep one. Got more of her grandfer's blood in her veins than theirs.'

'He were a right tartar and no mistake. I allus remember when I put young Jeff Ellerson (you know, Alfie's older lad) to do some wall-pointing for him. The lad were only beginning and weren't all that good but not so bad, tha know, neither. I sent a rule along of him but he didn't use it. He just trimmed off the lines freehand. Did old Mr Barrett raise a shindy about it? He had me down here that same evening. It were the lane wall over yonder,' George indicated. 'Fair rantin' he were!

'I said to him "You may have spoke to your millhands like that, Mr Barrett, but I'm me own maister and if you want me to do more work for you, you'd best keep a civil tongue in your head".'

'An' what did he say to that?'

'Oh, he came over more reasonable like and said in future I had better come mesen to do his jobs or send one of my experienced men.'

'Well, he were always pretty fair and the lass worshipped him.' Jim paused and puffed thoughtfully at his pipe, then a rare smile lifted the free edge of his mouth as he turned to confide to George.

'She still do, and I sometimes reckons she comforts herself with thinking of him being hereabouts!'

'Well, it were here that he died weren't it? Sitting just over there, weren't he?' George spoke uneasily, scrutinizing Jim's face, but the narrow eyes were veiled as they gazed across the pond. His head merely gave a slight lift of assent.

''Night, George. Must be getting on.' He moved away in the direction of the cottage. George shook his capped head and glanced apprehensively about the pond before turning homewards.

A few weeks later Jim was taking advantage of a mild spell to loosen the trampled soil round the edge of the completed ponds. He was trying to gauge the amount of lime mortar that had been trodden into the earth and deliberating about the plants that could be fairly set there.

'It'll be sour for that many years – I guess them rock roses or even the aubretia would be all right but there's no point in aputting in shrubs like them azaleas or magnolias – nay!' The sound of gravel scattering disturbed him but he had only time to straighten and half turn before he was nearly felled by the impact of a swirling mass of navy serge and long blonde hair powered by the deceptively slight frame of Effie. Her arms flung round his shoulder served to steady him a little but his fork flew out of his hand as a resounding kiss was planted on his stubbly cheek. He grasped her round the waist and held her away in a gesture of self-defence.

'Effie! Nay, lass!'

'Jim! You haven't changed at all.'

The animated face that shone appreciation at him *had* changed. It had assumed a pale elongated beauty enhanced by the flawless skin and fired by the forthright clarity of the grey-blue eyes generously framed by dark lashes. The lower of these were moist and clung to her slightly flushed cheeks.

'Miss Effie!'

'Don't call me "Miss", Jim!' She sounded hurt and quickly brushed her cheeks dry as she stooped to pick up his fork.

'Nay, but you've growed up such a lot!'

'Just a bit taller, that's all,' she replied defiantly.

At that moment Lily arrived fast, following a near-horizontal trajectory about three feet above the ground, hit Effie's hip with both forepaws – rebounded and jumped again to be engulfed by Effie's arms. Jim smiled down at the tousled head as Effie buried her moist face in the velvet softness of Lily's head with the ears held crumpled between her hands.

'She must have heard me talking to you, Jim,' came the muffled voice. Effie rose and Lily sat back and uttered one high-pitched hysterical bark.

'Oh, Lily love, you've got fatter!' – down on her knees again.

'How's Lettie?' she asked, casting an eye up to Jim.

'She is fine! I were just looking to see her leaping round the corner having broken out of her cage.'

They laughed delightedly and Effie extricated herself once more from Lily and looked over Jim's shoulder. She gave a gasp of excitement and bounded up the mound of earth to the main pond.

'Oh, it really is finished. Why don't you ever reply to my letters, Jim? I thought there must have been some problem. How shall we fill it – have you thought?'

'The hosepipe, I suppose.'

'Oh yes, of course. I wasn't thinking. I suddenly thought of the canal ...' Her voice trailed off and there was an awkward pause until she pulled herself together with a shake of her body.

'But will the tap water be all right? You know those fish Mr Kaye put in his new pond and they all died?'

'We won't put fish in till spring, lass. It will have all winter to work out the lime from the mortar and the water will be all right by then.'

'Ah, yes. But when can we put plants in? It would be best to have those well settled before the fish go in.'

Jim took a deep breath and endeavoured to repair his shattered composure. He surveyed the soil stolidly for a few moments and then turned towards the potting shed muttering.

'First things first, miss. I've got work to be doing.'

Effie's mouth opened with anguish but she stopped herself crying after him and watched his retreating back until her face relaxed into a smile. How many, many times had confrontations with Jim ended like this during her childhood! They used to leave her puzzled and upset but now she could understand something of the lonely independence which made these barriers necessary. She must wait patiently until after tea or even tomorrow morning before she could lay claim to his attention again. Lettie wouldn't really know she was back, anyway. She whistled for Lily was was careering round and round the lawn in wild ecstasy. How uncomplicated and comforting is the love of a dog!

Together they inspected the ponds carefully. The master one was D-shaped with the curved edge to the front. It was stepped to give a maximum depth of six feet extending from near the front to well beyond the centre. The terraces ran along the sides and back except for one mid-depth along the front. A narrow bridge with a low balustrade bisected it and led back between the two shallow ponds – each shaped as a quarter sector of a circle to complete a circular pond complex. On either side was

96

a crescentic wet bed for growing swamp plants and harbouring the amphibian progeny of the shallow ponds.

Effie doubtfully pondered the geometrical symmetry of the arrangement. It was precisely the plan they had made together – so long ago – no, not so long. The planning sprang vividly to mind. She could hear his voice. She could see her plump fingers holding the pencil, his coarse wrinkled hand with its short fingers gently commandeering the pencil and adjusting the shaky lines to strong even contours.

'Some folk might say it were a bit too nice and symmetrical, lass, but I've always been one for order meself and that's the way we want it, so that's the way it will be, eh?'

'Yes, that looks grand. When shall we make it?'

'We 'aven't put in how big it's to be yet.' He chuckled as he squeezed her shoulders and his eyes twinkled – penetrating, approving, and very, very blue...

She smiled happily. Yes, it was exactly as specified and therefore right. She sat on the low balustrade of the bridge and visualised the yellow flags, bulrushes, water forget-me-nots, giant hogweed and kingcups filling the bog gardens and clumped casually round the pond edges to obscure the low wall ... Water lilies, yellow and pink in the main pond – Potomagetum and crowfoot in the small ponds ... Water soldier, sweet rush. Perhaps they could start filling it tomorrow. It would probably take two or three days to fill ... Better not worry Jim today.

She and Lily must explore each inch of the beloved garden. It was so reassuring to find that the garden grew and progressed unerringly from season to season in her absence. Sometimes at school, as her mind escaped to wander along each border and bed, each turn in the mown grass paths between the roses and the irregular surfaces of the stone flags along the herbaceous border, a sudden terror gripped her that the garden was not an indestructible reality but a carefully created artifice that was as fragile as herself. She would then compel herself to remember exactly the late summer glory she had left; the high sunflowers, bedding asters, magenta sedum, early Michaelmas daisies and the ostentatious dahlias. The odd yellow leaf, the heavy morning dews and rosy flecking just visible on the apples had hinted at the approach of autumn. But the marguerite daisies had still blazed crisp as laundered sheets between the purple and pink phlox and the hydrangeas were covered with blooms from the palest pink and china blue to deep purple and indigo. It had been a good season for the hydrangeas. Grandpa would have been pleased for they had always been one of his favourites. Effie's tastes were less exotic; she particularly admired the clean curve of the montbretia spikes and the geometrical precision which set each dainty orange flower alternating up the angulated stem.

She darted from the pond and stopped abruptly on the slippery flagged path realizing with a shock that it was indeed winter and for the first time in her life she had missed a whole season; the gentle, golden harvesting season of summer-gone sadness; of opportunities which, if not now fruitful, were missed – unless, perhaps, another year was granted. Jim had gathered the apples and her father had picked the blackberries without her help. Jim, but not she, had watched the Michaelmas daisies bloom, lily-gilded with orange and amber butterflies on sunny afternoons. The marguerites and the phlox were now neat bundles of trimmed stalks and the montbretia at the edge of the shrubbery shrouded the ground like a tangle of auburn hair. Just here and there an aberrant shoot from the base of a near-dead foxglove bravely brandished a small flower as a reminder that it was only hibernation and not death that clutched at the heart of the garden. The laurels were glossy green, the aucubas spotted with gold and the holly berries gleamed red in their dark, prickly nests. These were the cheerful ghosts of Christmas yet to come. Next week she would pick branches and sprigs to intertwine in the carved banisters and balance precariously on top of the pictures and plate rack. She would put a big bunch of holly and some bronze chrysanthemums in Jim's parlour. He didn't like bits pushed here and there gathering dust and drying. The greenhouse! Of course – quick – off she ran, serge skirt billowing round her long black legs…

'More of t' stew, lass?' asked Jack Barrett kindly.

'They've never been feeding you proper – tha's that thin …' scolded Mary. '… and ter think o' the money they charge!'

'Well, it don't cost us nowt and she has got right tall. Maybe it'll take a bit of time o' time to fill her out again, like,' consoled her father.

'I'm sure I hope she don't get no taller – she's taller than me now.'

Effie sighed. Her mother's comprehension was, as ever, limited to the physical aspects of a thing and only the obvious ones at that. Her pat appraisal of people, plants and animals always irritated Effie.

'That Mrs Donnelly! She were out shopping in that big yeller straw hat with all them flowers stuck in – fresh flowers – not even them nice neat silk ones. It ent proper for a woman of her years …' 'Them giant thistles – I don't know why Woodgate don't pull them up. Just ugly great prickly weeds they are …' 'Them nasty starlings – I can't abide *them* with their ugly long beaks and the way they strut about…'

Her father was still trying to oil the grating wheels a little.

'She's talking a lot nicer now. They've taught her *that* at school.'

'Aye – not as I've heard her say a vast deal but it do seem better. Let's hope as they've taught her the manners to go with it!' Mary cast a baleful glance at her daughter.

Well, things didn't change in the house. The wittering was the same and so was the kitchen with its green distempered walls and profusion of brass knick-knacks on the mantel shelf above the range and the range itself, silkily black-leaded and warm. After the meal Effie curled herself up in front of it on the pegged rug. She picked at the inch-wide strips of wool fabric and remembered the garments from which they had come: Aunt Rosalie's old winter dress in dark blue stockinette!

'Have you heard from Aunt Rosalie lately?' asked Effie conversationally.

'Aye; she's fair ter middling. Had a bad cold and put her back out getting stuff out of the boiler,' replied her mother testily.

'She's allus got some grumble on,' John muttered.

'Aye. I'm amazed that she does much stuff in the boiler. She's always putting off doing her blankets and curtains because she says it wears her out too much and she's only got her own things to see to. She don't know she's alive, she don't.'

'Well, I just hope tha hasn't invited her over here.' Mary paused in the washing up and turned to face him, awkwardly wiping her raw sudsy hands on her linen apron.

'But what could I have done, John? After all, she is me own sister and she seemed so bad about it all I just wrote that if she wanted to spend Christmas here we'd be happy to have her and it would spare her back not having to do the dinner and such. She may not come – after all, she always says things don't suit her here proper.'

'Aye – cows *may* fly,' said Jack darkly. 'I'm always amazed how long she manages to put up with things not suiting her here. She's a proper martyr, she is.'

'Sh – sh! Not in front of t'bairn,' hissed Mary, tossing her head towards Effie who was silently examining the rug, but not missing a word. Aunt Rosalie with a bad back for Christmas! That really would mean an open-air time for her, but how about those long dark evenings? She couldn't spend them all at Jim's. They'd be wittering, anyway – all three of them. Ugh! She pulled viciously at a peg-strip and it tore off in her hand. She moved round to shield her knee from view and spread the strip out to examine. It was a bit of her grandfather's brown tweed trousers! She remembered the roughness of them against her bare legs as she sat on his knee. Yes, there were the flecks of bright red and yellow which her childish eyes had distinguished with some surprise.

'Aye, that be quite a fair tweed lass,' he said. 'Came from Bob Howarth's Mill over at Keighley, did that. Tweeds always have several different colour yarns in. That's what gives them their interest.'

Strange that the smell of the kitchen never changed and strange that it was quite different from the smell of Jim's scullery or Aunt Rosalie's kitchen or Mrs Wadsworth's. It seemed to have something of the smell of soap and burning wood and the coal scuttle, but all of these were in the other kitchens.

'Effie, do get up and change out of your school things. They must be washed and pressed and put away. Can't afford to go wearing them out at home. What a good thing I made a point of them being plenty big enough with you shooting up like this. I'll have to let the skirt down a bit already! Put on your yellow blouse with the old brown skirt, there's a good lass. Oh, and your clogs. I hope they're big enough still. I can't understand why you couldn't have taken them for your garden shoes at school.'

'Most of the girls have never worn clogs, Mother. Their fathers are doctors and clergymen and the like.'

'Ah, I see. Too high an' mighty to make use of summat that's serviceable and good.' Her mother's sarcastic note changed to one of concern as she looked round to search Effie's face. 'Do they look down on you, Effie, then?'

'N...no. They laughed at the way I spoke at the beginning but they've got use to it – partly – and I've come to talk more like them, I suppose.'

'So tha gets on all right dost tha, lass? Have you got friends like?'

'Not any special friends. No. But they're a nice lot mostly. There's one or two that are really stuck up but I don't take any notice of them. There's two girls share my room – Susan Mannering and Maisie Johnson. They're both nice. Maisie's really funny. She's always getting into trouble. She …' Her voice trailed off and the animated face became veiled as she recollected that the resiting of one end of the wash-room's clothes lines so that the corridor's more intimate undergarments were hanging across the top of the main stairway was unlikely to strike her mother as being very amusing. It certainly failed to impress Miss Morton in that way, too, but she didn't go to any great lengths to find the culprit, which was to her credit. Effie chuckled to herself and Mary nodded complacently. At least her worst fears had not been realized and Effie did seem a little less wild and unladylike.

'Get along with you, miss.'

There was no need at all for the economy in Effie's clothes; no need, in fact, for Mary to be cooking and cleaning. Old Jack had often told her to get a maid and even a housekeeper if she wanted to, but Mary found it necessary to be compulsively busy. She had been reared in the traditions of working-class Yorkshire people who held wealthy leisure in such distrust that she found it easier to ignore its possibility. She worked to defend her house-pride as her mother and grandmother had done and she even had the satisfaction that she could grumble about the iniquity of women's work with more justification than they, because her house was much larger.

CHAPTER FIVE

Early next morning Effie and Lily slipped into the potting shed. The raffia switch had an end-of-season spareness. Effie pulled out a wide strand, sniffed the grassy odour and then appreciatively filled her lungs with the most comforting smell she had ever known: the aroma of the potting shed! For her it exuded the confident security that many would find in a mother's bosom or a nursery. A fleeting streak of pale sunlight illuminated the muddy flecks on the windowpanes and the cobwebs in the corners. Inside, the shed was as orderly as ever. Tall towers of upturned flowerpots in graded sizes stood beneath the bench. Two pairs of shears, sharpened and greased, hung on nails on the wall beside the scythe and sickles and innumerable forks, broad-and narrow-tined, spades and shovels rested against the wall. On the window sill and shelf were ranged stone pots and glass jars, some with brushes in, tar and tape for sealing the fruit trees, and some containing potash, chalk, roofing tacks, staples and nails. Two pairs of secateurs – large and small – lay neatly beside Jim's precious pruning knife on the bench top. Effie thoughtfully laid the strand of raffia on the deeply grooved wood, lifted the pruning knife and carefully cut off a short length and then another, and another.

''Ere, now!' The gruff voice was loud and stern. 'What art tha doing with my pruning knife, eh?'

Effie's shoulders rose defensively as she recoiled in alarm. How could she be so absent-minded? Jim's precious, dangerous knife that she had been taught to hold in such awe!

'Oh, oh, sorry Jim. I weren't thinking – really – I – I just *wasn't* thinking what I was doing,' she enunciated carefully.

The old man grunted and replaced the knife firmly beside the secateurs.

'What are you doing today, Jim?' Her voice was sugary with appeasement.

'Plenty.'

Effie quietly sat down on an upturned box and Lily settled beside it leaning heavily against her thigh, her chin on Effie's knee and her warm soft ears in Effie's hands. They were reconciled to a long wait for the return of Jim's good humour. He busied himself with shifting seed trays from one side of the shed to the other, sorting out a tangled mess of green string into a neat ball and rolling up some strong pieces of wire netting. His face expressed such composure that it was hard to believe there was another soul anywhere near and an atmosphere of profound repose settled on the little stone building.

After many minutes Effie ventured to ask, 'Where shall we get the plants from?'

'Jacksons over at Pannal have got some water stuff – lilies and the like.'

'We want different sorts, white, pink and yellow. Do you know their names?'

'Amarillis is a good pink one.'

'How about the wild things for the bog garden?'

'There's them ponds along in the meadows between the canal and the river.'

'Oh, yes.' She jumped up gaily. 'Let's go there with some buckets. They won't have died back altogether yet. I know where the flags and bulrushes are.'

'I doubt whether we'll find the kingcups or forget-me-nots, though. Have to wait while spring,' said Jim.

'Let's get the big things now, though, and how about Jack Prescott? He said we could have some bits from his pond.'

'It isn't very big. We need a deal o' stuff for ours.'

'Can we start the hose going today?'

'Aye, we'd best do that first.' He grinned mischievously at her and strode out of the shed.

'Father! Jim and I want to get to Pannal to buy some lilies and things for the pond. Do you think we could borrow the pony cart from Mr and Mrs Hargreaves? We'd do it easy in half a day with that. – Perhaps you could come?' She added the conjecture as an afterthought to promote the borrowing of the cart. She rather hoped he wouldn't act on it in case Jim decided his own presence wasn't necessary. You could never tell with Jim. His unaccountable perversity of late sometimes seemed almost like childish pique.

Two days later the trio, foursome if one counted Lily, set off just after eight on a sunlit frosty morning. There was barely enough room in the little cart. Lily lay curled round on some

104

old sacks which Jim had put in for the plants. Jack said, 'I don't know where we put these plants. They'll be a fair size, won't they, Jim?'

Jim chewed his pipe stem meditatively.

'Aye, I reckon that dog'll have to run behind and our knees will be drawn up ter our chins. I could have gone over meself in the spring,' he grumbled.

'Yes, and I wanted to come too, as you well know, Jim. Anyway she'll enjoy running.'

'You watch how to speak to your elders, miss,' warned her father mildly. Effie beamed round, gaily unabashed.

'Just look at the frost on those old hogweed heads. They're sparkling! Will we go down Pool Bank?'

'Aye, but we'll have to walk. T'pony will be slipping all over as it is.'

'Bank' is a fine example of Yorkshire understatement. The view from its 300-foot-high edge was breathtaking. Wharfedale lay below them like a chequered patchwork in brown, ochre and pale straw. Dark walls bounded the blocks of colour and the river coiled lightly through the vale brushed by gold-fronded willows. Jim surveyed the view complacently.

'Well, can them North Yorkshire moors of thine come up to this, Miss Effie?'

'No – not quite. Mind, they *are* grand in a different sort of way though. They are right wild and dark on top with the heather but the lower parts with the little ghylls running down them have light turf and bracken that's a lovely russet colour just now. Very pretty – but it's good to be back here. You know, the girls at school think I live in one of them – those – back-to-backs. They keep saying silly things to me like "Is't trouble at t'mill, lass?" They think when I say I live between Leeds and Bradford that it's all black stone and no green! I wish they could just be standing here with us.' She shook her head gently and sighed in satisfaction.

'Why do you think it's so beautiful, Jim? – I mean, there's no-one else looking at it is there? Leastways – no folk that we can see – probably no-one bothering at all and if we hadn't come along this morning there would have been no-one to see it looking so – so gloriously beautiful. Whatever for?'

Jim slowly took his pipe from his mouth – opened it as if to speak and then replaced the pipe. Effie waited patiently, her eyes roving between him and the scenery. He suddenly removed his pipe again.

'It just be the way it is. 'Appen we think it's beautiful – well, that be grand for us. Many folks wouldn't give it a second glance and I think they're raight.'

'Oh, Jim,' indignantly, 'that's just because they've no soul – they can't see properly.'

'Nay – tha says it's beautiful, but that's just the way *you* 'appen to see it. It don't signify nothing to them fields and river and woods. It's just the way they grew and they give nothing for what *tha* thinks.' He spoke deliberately with no sign of emotion.

'No, I suppose not. We aren't really very important compared to real things like water and stone and trees.' She looked up pensively and Jim moved his pipe stem a little to smile at her.

'We'd best be getting on. Tha can look as tha walks.'

They climbed down from the cart and Jim slapped the shaggy brown rump to set the pony off stepping daintily down the hill. Her forehooves slipped harshly across the stone setts every few paces. Effie glanced at her father a little guiltily. She had quite forgotten about him, but he seemed happily unconcerned. That was one of the best things about him – he was so unobtrusive.

In the middle of the afternoon they were toiling back up the Bank again. In shady places the frost was still glistening white and above, the tree branches incised delicate patterns against the clear duck-egg-blue sky but a murky pinkness suffused the horizon and rose to merge with gathering tumulus clouds – gold and fawn.

'Weather's changing,' muttered Jim. 'Maybe snow afore morning!'

'We'll have to get these lilies in quickly in case a long freeze sets in,' said Effie.

'Aye, we will that.'

CHAPTER SIX

Aunt Rosalie arrived on Christmas Eve. She had come by train with a lot of Christmas parcels and Jack and Effie had met her at the station. They were having early tea in the parlour, which Effie and her mother had unshrouded the day before. Effie hated the small room with its impediment of furniture and its smell of musty disuse. It was allowed to remain free of dust sheets all summer after spring cleaning but just as its stiffened corpse was beginning to quicken and the open windows beginning to waft away the myrrhous odour of mothballs, 'back-end' cleaning overtook it and the superfluity of arm-chairs and sofas were once again enshrouded until Christmas.

'... And I had to change again at Keighley and what with carrying all them parcels and me bag and the jolting of the carriage – my poor, poor back were that bad I didn't think I should ever drag myself all the way from the station ...'

Every bit of 400 yards, thought Effie darkly. Her aunt's ample jowls quivered self-pityingly and her gargantuan thighs confined within her bright pink woollen dress bulged from the restricting pressure of the chair arms.

'Ah. Have another cup of tea, love,' soothed her sister.

'Ah, yes.' She took another large slice of apple pie proffered by Jack.

'This is a nice pie, Mary. You always had a way with the baking. I've been right off my victuals, you know. Just couldn't face nothing – toyed with a little of this and that but just had to force it down.' Effie and Jack exchanged glances. Rosalie's determination to eat must have been splendid for she hadn't lost an ounce.

Jack passed the mince pies and for the third time his offer was accepted with a sad, stoical smile. This large woman made him feel inadequate. She had such skill in intercepting fortune's slings and arrows so that she could be an object of constant compassion. It so exhausted those around her that they found themselves resenting her stolid inactivity but felt too guilty to withdraw their services. Effie's youth relieved her from obligation and Rosalie disliked her intensely for it.

'Well, how is the new school, Elspeth?'

'All right.'

'Is that all – Just "all right"! It should be better than that for all the money it's costing and your poor mother making and buying all those clothes. Are they nice girls there?'

'Yes.'

'You're certainly growing up. You should be a help to your mother. Do they teach you cookery and needlework?'

'Yes.'

'Well, no more running wild in the garden, eh? We must see you turn into a useful young woman.' Her florid face exuded jocularity but the insincerity of this emotion was betrayed by the malicious glitter in her shoe-button eyes.

Effie felt vicious. She willed the cup of tea to fall off the saucer, clutched in the plump beringed fingers. She hoped it would be really hot as it poured over the heaving mound of pink belly. If it had had more than the few inches to fall, it would probably have bounced. The corners of her mouth curled slightly. Rosalie eyed her suspiciously.

'I've not seen that big black dog. Has that gone?' Her parents turned apprehensively towards Effie.

'Do you mean Lily? No, she was in her kennel a little while ago,' Effie replied coldly and rose to go.

'Where are you off to?' asked Mary sharply.

Effie mumbled incoherently and left the room.

'It's a pity they haven't improved her manners at this school,' Rosalie retorted.

'She were a bit better,' said Mary defensively, 'and she's talking *much* better.'

'She hasn't given me much chance to judge that,' snapped Rosalie.

Effie picked some of the gold-spotted aucubas from the shrubbery and then some gold-bronze chrysanthemums from the greenhouse and carried them carefully to Jim's cottage.

He came to the door with a piece of bread in his mouth and reluctantly admitting her directed her to the scullery cupboard for a vase. She noticed his plate of bread and cheese and mug of tea on the fender as she walked through the parlour and regretted disturbing him, so she tarried in the scullery talking to Lettie. The guinea pig had become immensely fat since the summer and the once large head and ears seemed merely an indication of which direction to expect the sleek ginger hummock to move in. She burbled away complacently.

'Do you think Lettie's lonely, Jim?' called Effie.

'Nay. She's got a lettuce, en't she?' came the tart response.

Effie examined the dark round eyes for signs of emotional needs beyond that furnished by a lettuce, but convinced herself that there were probably none.

'Aunt Rosalie's come.'

'Ugh.'

'She's just as miserable as ever.'

'She don't come into the garden much as a rule.'

'No. You're lucky. Is there something I can help you with, Jim?' She was leaning against the scullery door frame, her lank fair hair in an untidy tangle on her shoulders.

Jim didn't answer. He was gazing into the fire with his elbows on his spread knees and his tea mug between his palms. Effie noticed for the first time that there was pink scalp visible through the thinning hair on his crown. She shuddered inwardly: mortality; loss; loneliness.

Christmas Day was gloriously sunny with clear blue skies. Effie looked wistfully down from her bedroom window. There was little prospect of getting into the garden at all today. She had unwrapped a pair of gloves from Aunt Rosalie, a school blouse from her mother and father, some wrapped boiled sweets, a coral necklace which she would not wear and a silver brooch in the shape of a small maple leaf. She rather liked this and still held it in her hand. It probably came from her grandmother's jewellery box which was kept locked in the cutlery and silver cupboard. She would keep it in the china pot of her dressing-table set. She regarded all jewellery as too frivolous to wear. Anything she liked would only drop off and be lost in garden or moorland foliage. How much better to invest one's visual delights in growing things.

She braced herself against the prospect of family breakfast, peeling vegetables, church, the muted hysteria of Christmas dinner preparations culminating in the carving of the turkey – was it adequately cooked? – were the vegetable dishes hot enough? – the gravy lumpy? – the Yorkshire puddings risen (these were eaten with the meat on this one meal of the year)? Then came the pudding. Was it as juicy as last year's – or the one before that? That part was unlikely to be enlivened by Aunt Rosalie's tooth chipping on a silver threepenny bit this year. One could only expect such diversions occasionally. They would have to content themselves with the account of how sensitive that tooth had been ever since – 'anything hot – or cold – or sweet, had set it so on edge ...'

Effie groaned inwardly. She could just see the edge of the cottage roof. How lucky Jim was to be utterly on his own. Would he cook himself a Christmas dinner? she wondered. Perhaps a small fowl given him by Mrs Murphy?

CHAPTER SEVEN

During that pleasant interval of 'no-man's-time' between the bustle of Christmas and the feverish make-believe of New Year, Effie, Lily and Jim plodded up to the canal. Jim carried a fork and spade and Effie a folded sack neatly tied with string. The weather had turned mild and the canal had thawed so that only the odd, partially submerged sheet of ice bore testimony to the pre-Christmas freeze. As they walked up the banking, they heard the loud crack of a boat whip and by the time they reached the towpath, a boat was coming on through the bridge.

'I wonder how far that has come?' said Effie.

'That's a Lancashire carrier. Tha can tell by the smartness of her. One of Outhwaite's boats from Wigan I should reckon.'

Jim proved right. The floral paintwork surrounding the company's name shone like a new wooden toy and the stocky, coarse-limbed horse was well shod and groomed. A small well-built man leant against the tiller spry in wide blue trousers and a loose blue smock.

'Good day to ye,' he called cheerily.

'T'aint bad. How's it at t'other end?' asked Jim waving westward.

'Had ter wait for the ice-breaker ter go through before we could get away on Monday.' He spoke with the flat nasal intonation of the other county.

'Let's see him to the lock,' said Effie; so they turned to the left and followed the round shaggy rump as it dipped from side to side in a leisurely but purposeful gait. Another boat was coming up through the lock, so the Outhwaite carrier had to wait at the tall post set on the bank.

'Why can't he go closer than this to wait?' asked Effie.

''Tis not done. There are a deal of ill-feeling if they go beyond t'post. Many's the fall-out I've seen with some pushing youngster trying to jump his turn. There may be four or five boats waiting sometimes and they'll all be in a rush to get to the warehouses to pick up some return loading. They be out o' pocket if they has to wait while next day for cargo.'

'What do they do if someone pushes in?'

'Ah well, they all shouts and more often than not it's one o' those rough Yorkshire boats on short-ply work with a young farm lad from up t'Dales who don't know what he's about and I've seen a couple of these Lancashire lads lay him out cold. Tha can understand it to some extent because it's their life. Most on 'em were near born on a boat and they know all the ins and outs o' t'job.'

The boatman jumped ashore with a clatter of clogs on the stone-flagged bank and adjusted the horse's towline. Effie watched with enhanced respect.

'Well, what be tha going to dig up?' he asked Jim.

'Just some wild water plants,' smiled Jim looking down at his boots diffidently.

'Wild water plants!' laughed the man. 'Tha can't put those in tha pot. I'll warrant ye be making for them cabbages and leeks down by Kirkstall one-rise.'

Effie laughed.

'No, we've got plenty of them in the garden. What do you cook on your boat? I don't suppose you have a garden?'

'Well now, I *have*, lass!' He winked and grinned. 'Just a little un up by the canal bank this side o' Wigan. Not all we folk live on our boats tha knows. We've a little settlement, like, cottages for when we're resting between trips.' Effie smiled encouragingly. 'But I wouldn't waste me garden on cabbages and the like. Nay – not when there's so many in them fields alongside the canal as no-one 'ud miss the odd half dozen. I grows them hybrid auriculas in mine.'

'Does tha! I heard ye was keen on them auriculas in

Lancashire. Don't ye have shows for them?' Jim's professional interest was roused.

'Aye. There were a grand one in the Corn Exchange at Liverpool last back-end. A lot of the lads went down to that. Beautiful blooms. I'd niver seen the like o' sich before. Old Harry Thorpe got a "second" and a "highly commended". He grows some nice ones. He's got one of Brown's boats from Nelson. You must have seen him down this way.'

'Is he the one that often has a young cripple lad with him?' asked Jim.

'Aye, that's Harry. T'lad's his nephew.'

A smart Liverpool boat emerged from the lock.

'Hallo, Jamie,' hailed the new boatman.

'How you doing, Nathan?'

'I've got a few ton o'coal. Could have fitted more in but stock were low. They said there'd be more coming in at Feversham's today, lad, if tha's interested.'

'Well, I'm fixed to pick up some mill machinery but if it stows well I may have a bit o' space. Thanks for tellin' me. Well, I must be off. Happy New Year to ye both!'

'Same to you,' chorused Effie and Jim as Jamie loosed the boat. 'Hold to!' he called to his horse.

'What does that mean?' Effie asked Jim.

'He's telling the horse ter take the strain of the rope steady and then that jerk's to set boat moving. See it's pulling over t'other way now to straighten the prow!'

'Goodness, they are well trained, aren't they?'

'Aye. Looks don't count over much. They pick 'em for their sense.'

They had turned and were walking back up the canal towards the round-arched road bridge.

'How long do their trips take, Jim?'

'Oh, four to five days each way if they make good time. A bit longer from Liverpool I guess.'

'They don't just live on vegetables they pick up by the canal do they?'

113

'Nay. They get provisions from the lock-keepers. Most o' the keepers' wives bake bread for them – quite a good business, but I warrant they buys no vegetables nor much meat, neither!'

'What do they do for meat, then?'

'Why, most on them is pretty good at the poaching business. They lay the odd trap and snare on the way down the canal and they empties them on the way back. If their families don't travel with them, they expect a few days' victualling when the boats get back.'

'Doesn't anyone mind?'

'Course they do. Many's the boatman as has found a policeman sitting by his snare when he's come to take it, but they're a quick-witted crowd. They usually think o' an excuse for popping into them woods.' Jim looked delicately aside and Effie smiled.

'Mind, they is good with t'whips too.'

'What, those long whips they crack at the horses' heels and let each other know that they are coming on through the bridge?'

'Aye. If they sees one o' them wild duck swimming ahead o' them and they needs a bit o' meat for the pot, they wait while it gets level with the prow, then one crack o' the whip and it finds it has three or four curls o' lash round its neck and it's hooked clean out o' the water and on to the deck before ...'

'... it can say "quack",' supplied Effie gaily.

'Aye. Just so,' smiled Jim.

CHAPTER EIGHT

Lily had indeed got fat, as Effie noticed on her return from school. After Christmas she was filling out visibly, day by day.

Jim shook his head despondently when Effie raised the subject.

'I rather afeared that this were likely ter 'appen.' Effie was a little exasperated by this defensive obliqueness.

'Do you think she is going to have puppies?' she demanded.

'Aye,' Jim capitulated.

'When?' Effie's face registered a conflict between happy excitement and anxiety.

'Next week, Ah reckons.'

'What *will* my mother and father say?' she groaned.

'They'll be fair put out with me,' responded Jim glumly.

'P'raps we needn't let them know very much about it! She could have them in the potting shed here.' Effie brightened up a bit.

'How about when they's bigger an' running all over?'

'Ah ... Do you think she'll have many?'

''Bout eight or ten.'

'Oh ... dear.' Effie's face fell again. She vividly remembered the traumas of Lily's puppyhood and that multiplied by ten was *not* the sort of thing her parents were likely to overlook. A gloomy silence settled on the potting shed. Lily looked appeasingly from one to the other and wagged her tail sadly, knowing that she was in some way connected with the reigning despondency. Effie patted her head consolingly.

'If she has them in here, Jim, we'll just mention it to them – Mother and Father, I mean – and I'll have time to go round and find homes for them before I go back to school, and they must go as soon as they are old enough.'

'Tha'll be hard pressed ter find homes for ten!'

'Do you know the father, Jim?'

'Almost certain Arthur Braithwaite's lurcher.'

'Oh, Lily, what a rough ugly old dog,' reproached Effie, but one glance at the worried black face made her relent. 'Never mind, love. You couldn't help it.'

It turned out not quite so bad. Lily had six puppies, two bitches and four dogs. Jim and Effie sat with her while they were born, one afternoon.

'Isn't it amazing, Jim?' Effie's face was aglow with excitement. 'Just like big black bubbles and there, inside, is a perfect fat pup.' She picked up a sleek plump body and gazed in delight at its blunt face, tiny black nose and wide pink mouth. The paws made swimming movements and the blind black head turned from side to side. 'It's just like that tiny shell tortoise with hinged legs and head I had for Christmas,' laughed Effie. 'Oh, you are adorable, all of you.' She gathered up another two in her lap and Lily licked them with maternal solicitude. Jim filled his pipe and watched and smiled. Maybe it was worth the trouble – however much it may amount to.

Effie was very nonchalant as she announced the happy event in the kitchen. Her father nodded darkly into his paper.

'We ent keepin' any,' said Mary promptly.

'Oh no, I'm going to find homes for them all before I go back to school.'

'Yer mother meant, they must be drowned,' Aunt Rosalie snapped.

'Of course not,' countered Effie.

'How many are there, anyway?' asked her father.

'Six.'

'Six! You mean to say you think yer mother'd have six puppies about the place?' asked Rosalie in mock amazement.

'They will live in the potting shed.'

'Ye can't have this – John will have to go straight and tell Woodgate to drown them,' Aunt Rosalie told Mary.

Mary looked at Effie's thunderous face. 'Maybe we could keep one or two if they stays in the potting shed,' she ventured.

'I'm keeping them all,' stated Effie firmly.

'You'll do as you're told, child,' snapped Rosalie.

'I will leave home and take the puppies and Lily with me.' Effie's voice rose in muted hysteria.

'Rosalie, please leave the bairn. She's upset,' pleaded John.

'Aren't *you* going to do anything?' screamed Rosalie.

116

John folded up his paper and looked helplessly first at his wife and then Rosalie, and then Effie's grim, set face.

'Aye.' He steeled his nerves. 'Ah think tha ought ter return home, Rosalie, and let us sort out our own troubles. There's nowt ter be gained from getting all upset. It'll likely make yer back bad again.' He added the last sentence in as conciliatory a tone as he could summon.

'Oh, yes. I'll do just that! No soul can accuse *me* of not knowing where I'm not wanted. I stand by my kin ready to advise and help but it is a thankless task. Them as 'asn't got the backbone to manage their own affairs proper ought to be grateful to any as is prepared to give good advice, but the world ent a fair place!' As she spoke she moved about gathering up her knitting needles, balls of wool, spectacle case and bag in an agitated way and then flounced out, shutting the door loudly behind her.

'Oh, John, tha's been and upset her proper now,' groaned Mary.

Effie slipped quietly out of the back door, grateful that her father had drawn the fire. Rosalie was prevailed upon to stay until the next day, but left then, still registering high indignation, and Mary's attack remained directed at John for the rest of the week, during which time the pups became established as a *fait accompli*.

Effie did find homes for all four dog pups and Jim reassured her that he would cope with the family and keep it out of her parents' way as well as he could. She was very sad to leave them at the end of the holidays and begged Jim to write a progress report every week. He did this after a fashion and each Thursday Effie would receive a laboriously written laconic note which she would read out to her room-mates after tea.

'... They are coming along champion and weigh about $1\frac{1}{2}$ lb. except the big dog that goes over two. All my flower pots are over and there seems no point in putting them back up. About eight are broke. They got the raffia down and ate a lot which did not suit them ...'

Susan and Maisie laughed uproariously but Effie's amusement was tempered by the thought of Jim's disordered potting shed.

Two weeks later '... They have got into the vegetable garden and messed up all the peas and beans but it don't matter as much as the kitchen rug what has its corner chewed off from when your mother left the door open while she were away shopping and I didn't notice that two of them wasn't with me ...'

Effie winced. Poor Jim. He must have to let them out of the potting shed now and try to watch over all six while he was working. If only she were home.

'... The dogs are now gone. They was only just six weeks but it is old enough and I couldn't do with no more trouble. Your mother is fair spare about the scratches on new paint and mess on carpet from when one got shut in the parlour ... I can't find no-one to have the bitches but I am going up to Airton next weekend and will take them with me. They seem quite intelligent and could make useful sheep dogs. If the way they finds mischief is anything to go by, they will be very clever dogs! ...'

Effie had one small solace at school. She had carried a box of precious rockery plants back with her and she made a tiny rockery in the corner of the vegetable garden. Her friends were highly amused and Effie's satisfaction was marred by the teasing she had to bear, but it did provide her with an excuse to be alone and out of doors and she daydreamed happily there, picturing her real garden at home.

By the time Effie returned at Easter, Jim and Lily had settled back into their old routines and no trace of the puppies remained, except one rounded corner on the pegged rug and her mother's bitter recriminations each time she noticed the damaged paintwork.

'I should love to have seen them before they went,' said Effie sadly.

'Tha can go up and see the big dog pup at George Smith's. He's shaping up quite well, George said t'other day.'

'How about the bitch pups?'

'Well, it weren't easy because them farmers usually raise their own dogs but I managed to persuade an old chap I used to help as a lad to have them on condition he could ...' Jim faltered awkwardly '... do as he thought fit if they wasn't no good.'

'You mean ... kill them?' Effie's eyes dilated.

'Well ... maybe he will find another home ...' Jim was not being honest and Effie knew it. She was silent for some time. After all, he had had all the trouble and done the best he could.

'Jim, are you going up to your sister's over Easter?'

'I had thought on it but I ent made no firm plans.'

'You've always said you'd take me up sometime. It would be good if we could go up and see how the pups are getting on.'

'Nay, it's a busy time in t'garden.'

'I'll help. I'll work really hard with you – before we go and when we get back. We'll manage everything.'

'How about your parents?' Jim's words came slower and slower as he parried her. Effie's impatience grew in proportion to her excitement as the thought of the trip.

'Jim! You've been promising to take me since I was five or six years old and you've always made excuses. There must be more room in the cottage now your nephews have left home. Your sister surely wouldn't mind, would she? I always thought she sounded a very nice person.'

This caught him in a weak spot.

'Aye, she is a very good woman and very welcoming.' He sighed deeply. 'You'll 'ave to see if it's all right by yer mother and then I'll write to her.'

Effie hopped from foot to foot gleefully, taking care to refrain from touching the dear stooping figure.

'Get out of my path. Tha will knock summat over and I'm fair set about with work.' Jim dismissed her grumpily.

CHAPTER NINE

Jim walked away from Skipton station, awkward in his best suit and leather shoes. He wore, or rather balanced, a bowler hat on his head since the incongruous nature of this accessory forbade it settling down happily enough to be 'worn'. He carried two cases and kept his eyes carefully averted from Effie who danced about him in an ecstasy of excitement. She was wearing her navy school skirt, stockings and button boots with a new sailor tunic and straw hat.

'Can't tha stop prancin' about an' walk sensible-like till we be out of town?'

'Sorry Jim, I've never been to Skipton before. Isn't the high street wide! Where's the castle?'

'Up at t'other end. Can't tha see them big round towers beside the church?'

'Oh, but it's very small. I thought it would be much bigger than that.'

'That's only the gateway. The rest is further back.'

'Oh! Can we go in and look?'

'Nay, but tha can walk up the Spring-cut and over the moat is a raight high cliff with the castle sort o' perched on top. It looks big enough from there!'

'Let's do that!'

'I s'pose so. Aye.' He smiled despite himself.

It was just turned four o'clock when they reached Airton. It was Jim's turn to curb his excitement.

'Well, there's t'green and there's t'cottage.'

'That one right in the middle? Is that really where Beryl lives?'

'Aye. Mrs Colston to you.'

'Yes, sorry. Look, there are stocks!'

'Aye, I know. I've played cricket by them often enough.' He was grinning broadly. 'The river's just down the lane by the mill. We'll see who can catch the most bullheads and I'll show thee the best place for crayfish.'

'Bullheads?'

'Them little fat fish with big heads an' short tails tha finds under stones. And trout – there's plenty up in the mill pond. We will borrow a rod and tha shall see.'

Effie flung out her arms and cavorted round Jim in delight. It had been a showery day but just now the sun was out, sparkling on the captive raindrops hanging in rows on the hedge twigs and the clump of daffodils by the half-opened cottage door. The pair reached the large paving slab at the threshold and paused shyly, but in a moment the door opened wide and their doubt was dispelled by the comfortably ample figure of Jim's sister Beryl. She beamed radiantly at them.

'Jim, lad!' They kissed cheeks. 'And Miss Effie!' Effie stepped forward to be engulfed in a bosomy embrace.

'I'm raight glad to see you, lass. We've been hoping Jim would bring thee up ever since tha grandpa passed away. He do talk so much about thee. Come upstairs to see tha room. Are't bringing her case up, lad? And then we'll mash some tea and have a bite to eat.'

Effie was overwhelmed. She had somehow pictured a feminine edition of Jim: tall, spare and taciturn, and this motherly, chattering figure was so much nicer. There was no awkwardness about what to say because there was no opportunity to do more than nod and shake one's head and smile and laugh. Effie's expression reassured Beryl about the comfort of their journey, their tiredness, the adequacy of the tiny bedroom ... Effie was charmed. The ceiling was a handsbreadth above her head and she had to kneel on the undulating polished floorboards to look out of the window. She gazed over the green and the mossy stone-slabbed rooftops to the tree-clad hillside across the little dale. The mill chimney and line of high square windows marked the course of the young Aire.

She hung her hat on the door peg, washed her face and hands in water from the ewer, brushed her hair and crept down the narrow wooden staircase, head held low to avoid the ceiling. The smell of home-baked bread and scones made her feel suddenly very hungry. The ample sitting-room table nearly filled the tiny room and, although only set for three, it groaned beneath a Yorkshire tea that would have victualled a small battalion. There was so great a variety of food that Effie could not register anything in particular except the golden trapezoid of sunlight glinting on knife and spoon and glowing on oven-warm baking, while a wisp of steamy breath from the teapot hung luminescently above.

'Come and sit tha down here, lass. Is thy tea all raight? – a little more milk, perhaps? – sugar? – one lump, so? Pass Miss Effie the scones and jam, Jim love. Aye, that's curd tart – ent tha ever tasted that? 'Tis made with buttermilk from t'farm, yonder. Aye, course I do all my own baking! There's no soul else to do it. It's grand to have some company to help eat it; I can't somehow get out of the habit o' baking for t' bairns. I allus seem to have more about than Jeffrey and meself can manage comfortable, like – and it's no good for my figure. I warrant I've got noticeably plumper since you were here last, eh, Jim? – Tha must have some wholemeal and lemon curd, lass. I did my bread this morning and them tarts and buns after lunch. Does tha like honey? That's local grown too!'

After tea Jim took Effie down to the river and they lifted stones to catch bullheads and crayfish. Effie was fascinated by the dippers. She had seen them occasionally on the canal but there were so many here.

'What do they catch when they jump in, Jim?'

'Oh – things on t'bottom – insects and the like. Tha can see them walking along the bottom turning up stones if tha's close enough. Mind, I allus wonder how they stay down because they must be that light. Maybe they hold on with their feet.'

Jim was so communicative. Effie smiled happily. For the first time she could just begin to imagine that he might once have been young. Perhaps as his enthusiasm for the scenes of his boyhood developed she might even manage to think of him as a boy – tomorrow, perhaps. She was too tired now and a wave of sweet contentment washed over her at the thought of the little bedroom with its tiny knee-high window. The river gurgled along timelessly, the wagtails tipped and dipped on the pebble strands and the pert brown dippers with their dapper white bib-fronts sat and watched.

Next morning Effie woke but dared not open her eyes until the river gurgle, the lark song and the distant bleat of sheep had convinced her that she was still, truly, at Airton. She opened one eye and saw the golden light shining through the floral print curtains. She opened the other to admire the pattern of cowslips, forget-me-nots and wild roses that adorned them and, sighing happily, slipped out of bed and crawled on all fours to draw them back. The sun was shining out of a blue sky on to the green and the mossy flagged roof tops and on to the stooping shepherd plodding along the narrow road from the bridge, with his dog at his heel. A ewe, grazing on the green with her lamb, lifted her head to look anxiously at the man. Effie could hear the sound of crockery and Beryl's voice downstairs.

After porridge and fried egg, a thick slice of home-cured bacon and golden toast and marmalade, Effie found herself skipping along surprisingly lightly at Jim's side.

'We'll go up to t'farm to see pups. They are shaping up grand.'

'Have you seen them?' asked Effie in surprise.

'Aye. Before tha had opened thine eyes! We country folk may be a bit slow but we make up for that by starting early. Bob Douthwaite were out checking his sheep at six o'clock when I reached him and I'll warrant that weren't his first job.'

'How big are they? Is he training them yet? How long before they're proper sheep dogs?'

'Hush. Tha shall see all in good time.'

They turned into the farmyard and were greeted by the two pups approaching appeasingly on their bellies, tails whipping feverishly and pink tongues flicking round their lips. They had lost their baby abandon and learnt the courtesy due to boss-dog man. Effie rubbed their proffered bellies reassuringly and they were soon leaping up at her. They were already as big as Lily and she giggled helplessly as she struggled to keep her balance and shield her face from the slavering tongues. Bob Douthwaite came to meet them. His age was indeterminate and as irrelevant as that of the fern-hung gritstone drinking trough which grew out of the nearby wall as naturally as the tangle of brambles above it. The oneness of man and nature in these moist soft dales was reassuring. Effie marvelled at the way the roughcast limestone cottages with their graded irregular stone roof slabs were so moss-grown and gently patronised by fern, bramble and St John's wort that they too seemed to have grown.

'Well, lass, how does tha think they are shaping up, eh?' He spoke slowly with the lilting dales' accent that has a distant root beside a Scandinavian lake or mountainside and the keen blue eyes bore further testimony to a distant Viking forebear. Any wandering fierceness which may have accompanied such an inheritance had long ago seeped away into the winter landscape of the dale.

'They've grown enormously! They seem a bit wild and silly for sheep dogs, though. Do you think they will learn all right?' She was striking bravely at the heart of her fears and waited anxiously for his reply. He looked into her face steadily, through narrowed eyes, and the corners of his mouth slowly drew out and up.

'Aye, I reckon they will. They are much like all pups o' that age but they'll sober up and learn easy – particular t'one there with the white patch at front.'

Effie laughed in relief as she stooped to pet the dogs and hide her face.

CHAPTER TEN

One afternoon the following August, Effie was weeding the front border when a carriage pulled into the drive. There was an older man and a young one with a heavy beard, sitting in it. Effie, puzzled, rose and went to meet them, fork in hand. She recognized old Mr Parker first and then the violet-blue eyes above the reddish-brown beard as William Parker's. She greeted them warmly.

'Well, how's tha grandpa, young lady?'

'I'm afraid ... he died the year before last ... only a day or two after you visited us, in fact.' It was an effort for Effie to keep her voice level, especially as she saw William wince.

'Eh lass, I am sorry! I hadn't heard,' said Mr Parker.

'Come and see the new ponds.'

'Nay, we shan't trouble tha.'

'It's no trouble. I should like you to see them. Do you remember you were going to tell us what to plant in them? We have put a few things in but there's a lot of room. I must get Jim – he's the gardener. I won't be a minute.' She spoke fast to conceal her feelings and then escaped, running away down the path.

'My, what a self-contained lass she is!' said Mr Parker.

'She must feel it more badly than she shows because they seemed very close, her and her grandpa,' responded William.

Jim shyly shook hands with the Parkers as they stood at the edge of the main pond.

'You really do things proud. It's going to look grand when the bog beds are planted up.'

'You do really think it's all right?' asked Effie earnestly. She was eager to be reassured that Grandpa was pleased with her efforts.

125

Mr Parker smiled down at her.

'It's amazing how you've got all this done since …' he hesitated, searching for a tactful expression '… last time we came. It's a grand job!'

'It took three fellows nigh four and a half weeks to get it dug out,' said Jim.

'What's the depth in the middle?'

'Seven to eight feet, shelving to five and then to two and just like you can see it at the edge.'

'Brick beneath the rendering?'

'Aye. And we ent had any trouble with leaks, so far.'

'A very nice job!'

'Do you grow water lilies in York?' asked Effie.

'Aye. We've got five varieties, haven't we, Will?'

'Seven, Father, counting the *albas*.'

'Hast tha got the big white one?' asked Jim.

'Yes, we can supply you with a nice basket of *Nymphaea alba*,' said William. 'It's a good vigorous grower in a deep pond.'

'What have you got for the middling depth, then?'

William looked towards his father in case he was monopolizing the advice.

'Well, how about these new French hybrids? There's *Fabiola*, a rich pink, with dark stamens. That's got a very long flowering season. Then there's *Marliacea* – that's a grand canary yellow,' said Mr Parker.

William touched Effie's shoulder.

'Come and see what I've got for you, young lady.'

Effie followed him, smiling.

'There! Just as I promised you. That's the very first one to be planted in a British garden.'

'Oh, how marvellous! What colour will it be?'

'A superb deep carmine. I saw this little group in full flower up at about 8,000 feet, in May.'

'What is its name?'

'At the moment I call it *Rhododendron barrettii*.' William

burst out laughing as Effie's eyes and mouth opened wide in astonished delight. 'But it's just possible it's already got a name. I sent off a flower to Kew but it didn't do so well this year. I expect the travelling set it back and maybe it doesn't like being potted. They want to see a good head of blossom before they'll confirm the new name, so you must nurture it well and next season we shall see.'

'What was it like in the Himalayas?'

'Glorious. The scenery is indescribable. The sheltered valleys on the lower slopes are incredibly prolific. There are glorious tall evergreen trees festooned with lianas and the sort of plants you see in conservatories – only much bigger – growing out from every nook and cranny and ledge. You would love it.'

'When are you off again?'

'Next February, I hope.'

'I do wish I could come.'

'Yes, so do I, but there is that awful school – or is it not so bad this year?'

'Worse, really. I go to a boarding school now and I'm only home in the holidays.'

'Oh dear! Cheer up! What does Effie stand for?'

'Elspeth!' Effie pulled a face.

'No. That's quite a nice name. It would be best for a special variety. I shall look out for a really beautiful colour variety of something when I go out again. Perhaps it will be a soft blue, like *your* eyes,' he teased.

Effie remembered his embarrassment last year when she innocently remarked on the colour of his eyes. He seemed so much more ebullient and confident now that it was difficult to think of him as the same person. But then, she had changed so much. She felt infinitely older than she did last year.

CHAPTER ELEVEN

Effie tended her tiny rockery at school for a couple of years. It served the function Miss Glover had hoped of providing a small anchorage for Effie's rebellious soul and, as the terms began to pass more quickly, she settled into a state of resignation. In December 1882 she sat in the Malton to York coach as it clattered towards its destination. The muddy horses steamed, but all Effie could see from inside were the flat wastes of harvested turnip and kale fields, dreary and wet through the spattered windows. Her grey eyes were veiled as she brooded upon the dissatisfactions of the term. It was with great reluctance that she had returned to school in the autumn, just after her eighteenth birthday, and she was determined to return no more. The summer examination results had been satisfactory but Miss Glover was still adamant that Elspeth could do much better if she applied herself properly. This term, Miss Glover had retired, to be replaced by a rather hard, efficient woman whom Effie distrusted. As she had guessed, the rôle of the sixth form was to put a final polish on the young ladies and the academic subjects had been relegated to make time for social studies, music, deportment and elocution. Effie had never regarded herself as a scholar but she realized now that even mathematics held a certain challenge that she could not find in deportment. She utterly despised the frivolity of rules for conducting oneself with decorum under a variety of complicated social situations.

It was dusk as they passed through the outskirts of the city and under the arch of Monk Bar to see the massive bulk of the Minster before them. At the foot of the steps leading up to the southern doorway Effie lowered the window and leant out to wonder once more at the immense solidarity of the old cathedral. They turned left and trotted down narrow streets flanked by Tudor shops gaily lit for Christmas. She would stay at the Black Swan tonight and tomorrow morning do her shopping before travelling on to Leeds. Her gloomy preoccupation was receding and the bustle of unloading her trunk and bag, tipping the coachman and engaging a porter to carry her luggage a few doors along to the inn, served to dispel it altogether. She was the only girl from the school on the coach and although the travel tutor had confirmed the hotel booking she still delivered her charge up to the coachman with misgiving. Effie, on the other hand, was relishing her independence. She sat before the log fire in the hall, pouring out a cup of tea and counting her blessings. The biggest was her grandfather's annuity which had increased and come entirely under own management upon her eighteenth birthday. Mr Jenkins was doubtful and her parents scandalized by this arrangement but the old man had insisted upon it in his will. He had sat in the office of Jenkins, Bailey and Jenkins as confident as a king, thrusting the stem of his pipe at Mr Jenkins to emphasize his point.

'At eighteen that lass will be able to manage her affairs all raight; you take it from me. It will give her a bit of independence at the time she needs it. No point in delivering that and her into a husband's hands at the age of twenty-one. Nay!

'Mind, Ah will be disappointed if she don't decide just what she will do about matrimony to suit her best, too.' He shook his head thoughtfully.

She might buy a dress and coat tomorrow. She only had her school coat and she was now sitting in her 'best' dress: a plain pale grey with darker grey binding at the throat and cuff. She liked it but maybe something a little fancier would be useful for Christmas? Her mother had already forwarded three party invitations to her. She had never been invited in her own right before and was doubtful whether she would accept these –

well, Mr and Mrs Cockcroft were well-meaning and might be hurt, so maybe she should go there. She just had an uneasy feeling that she had been invited on account of their son John whom she met occasionally over the years and remembered vaguely as a plump, ungainly and intensely shy boy maturing into an awkward, clumsy and intensely shy young man. A second invitation was from Maggie French who had never had much in common with Effie and had almost certainly even less now she was an over-sophisticated young lady. The third invitation was sheerly impudent. Effie had been introduced to Edward Carter at a Cockcroft tennis party in the summer. Later in the afternoon, she was sitting behind a bush idly watching the miniature rainbows playing on the spray of a lawn sprinkler and hoping she might be left out of the next set to save the chagrin of apologizing for missing nearly all the balls. She deplored wasting a perfectly beautiful summer afternoon in such a silly way.

A light tenor voice violated her refuge.

'My, what pretty babe-in-the-wood have we here? May I be permitted to join you?'

He had confidently thrown himself down on the grass beside her without so much as noticing the icy glare.

'What do you do with yourself, Miss Barrett? I have not met you at one of these sort of "do's" before!'

'No, I don't like playing tennis.'

'How about croquet? The Cockcrofts have some excellent croquet parties.'

'I don't play any ball games.'

'Oh, it only takes a little practice. I could teach you very quickly!' He smiled disarmingly.

'But I do not wish to learn. I consider I can spend my time very much better, thank you.'

Even now she blushed at the recollection of her anger when his handsome, blond face broke into uproarious laughter. She had jumped up, momentarily raising her racket, but quickly stepped aside and pulled the sprinkler lead so that the outer shower of drops caught his reclining figure.

'You little witch!' he cried, jumping up, but his mirth was undiminished …

Well, she didn't really want any part in this frivolity but she would surely be required to make a minimal contribution and so a slightly frivolous dress would be an advantage.

The next morning she set off in her dark school coat, her long hair loose, looking a full three years younger than her eighteen. She bought safe, useful presents for her mother and father, Aunt Rosalie, Mrs Wadsworth and Mrs Sugden. She spent a little longer purchasing some newly imported species tulip bulbs, a steel trowel and a rather beautiful cut-glass vase for Jim. The last proved rather an encumbrance with her two shopping bags and she wondered about returning to the hotel, but since it would mean retracing her steps to reach the dress shop she decided to struggle on and launched herself into the jostling surge of Christmas shoppers.

The junior assistant looked disdainfully at the dishevelled schoolgirl who tumbled into the gown shop showroom. She had dreaded this and almost turned to go when a middle-aged woman came from the back of the shop.

'Good morning, madam. Can I help you?'

Effie was momentarily crushed by the 'madam' but the woman had a kindly face so she raised her eyes and summoned a little confidence.

'I should like to see some dresses, please.'

'What sort of dress had madam in mind? We have day dresses on this rack and some evening dresses there. Is the dress for yourself?'

'Er, yes. I was thinking of something quite plain – that I could wear to a party,' explained Effie weakly.

The three assistants, although standing at a discreet distance, were evidently taking a keen interest in the encounter and exchanged arched glances at this contradictory order.

'Well, madam,' said the older woman doubtfully, 'one would usually consider an evening gown appropriate for a party.'

'Perhaps you could show me one or two, but I do prefer dresses that are quite plain.'

Effie looked round bewildered by the variety of gowns that were ranged upon all sides. A model stood on a plinth, resplendent in a many-tiered shell-pink gown of satin trimmed with tulle and pearls.

The supervisor followed Effie's eye and raised her brow interrogatively.

'Oh, no,' said Effie hastily. 'Nothing as elaborate as that!'

'Would madam like to remove her coat?'

The school coat was spirited away with the parcels by one of the assistants and the other two exchanged expressions of guarded approbation at the lithe shapely body demurely clad in grey. The sight clearly inspired their superior, who crisply called for several specified gowns to be brought. Effie selected two from these: a steel blue with softer grey-blue contrasts, and a sage green full-skirted one in water-figured taffeta prettily trimmed with cream lace. She held out the skirt of the blue one.

'I wonder if this will fit me?'

'Try it on, of course, madam. I will show you the fitting room.' Effie drew back in alarm but was swept away by the older woman.

She returned transformed. The supervisor fetched a hair brush and deftly arranged the pale tresses on Effie's shoulders.

'Of course madam can't judge properly until her hair is up. Perhaps you will allow me. Fetch some clips and pins, Miss Bates, please.'

'I always have my hair down,' protested Effie.

'Not with a low-cut evening gown!' The categorical statement firmly dismissed Effie's tendency to insubordination and her hair was gathered up into several loose coils on her head.

'Oh, lovely!' exclaimed the onlookers. Effie cast them a

severe glance, but they seemed absorbed in genuine admiration.

'Of course, the bodice is a little large but we can soon take care of that with a minor alteration.'

'The neck seems rather low, doesn't it?'

'Oh, no, madam! Not at all! We have many evening gowns cut *much* lower.' She raised her hand to send for one but Effie stopped her.

'I should like to try the green one on, please.'

Effie's return to the shop floor was almost triumphant. She looked in the mirror and her girlish uncertainty was transformed into secure confidence by the surprising apparition of a very beautiful young woman. She turned gracefully to study the side profile and back view, half conscious of the glowing admiration and ever-increasing respect of the watching girls. She was made slightly uneasy by the surprising satisfaction that she felt and she could not prevent the picture of Edward Carter's laughing face appearing before her as she imagined herself at his party in this dress with her hair braided up.

'This one fits well, does it not?'

'Perfectly! As if made for you, madam.'

'Good. I shall take it. How much is it?'

The huge sum was a test for Effie's newly acquired poise, but that just survived.

'Yes! I should also like to look at your winter coats, please.'

'How about the blue gown? We could have it ready for you by this evening.'

'Er, no. I am travelling to Leeds this afternoon, so I am afraid I can't wait.'

'Oh that is no problem, madam. We can send it tomorrow.'

'How much is it?'

'Five guineas. That is a very reasonable price but, of course, it has not quite the quality of the green gown. Bring madam the grey astrakhan coat to try.'

'I shall decide later about the blue dress.' Effie thought the grey astrakhan just a little too sophisticated at first, but its

133

tight-waisted elegance won the day after she had tried on several others.

'*Of course* people wear such coats in the morning and afternoon. It is just a smart walking-out model – not really evening wear at all. In fact, it suits madam so well, may I suggest that we pack up the old coat and you wear the new?'

Effie looked a little startled at the idea but quickly regained her composure.

'Why not! Yes, do that please and send the blue dress on to me.'

The two parcels were elegantly packed, the money paid and the address given.

'Madam has rather a lot of parcels to carry!'

'Oh, I shall manage. Would you put that one under my arm please. Be careful: it is breakable.' Effie glanced in the mirror.

'Oh, I still have your pins in my hair!'

'Do not worry, madam. You keep your hair that way. In fact,' the older woman edged closer for a final familiarity, 'all you need now, dear, is a nice pair of court shoes with a bit of a heel. I really should get those – in black or grey.'

They all ushered Effie out of the wide open door ceremoniously.

'We look forward to serving madam again,' called the supervisor.

The only problem that now presented itself was the incompatibility of the poise with the parcels. The pavement was still bustling with people and only three shops further on Effie's arms were beginning to ache.

'Excuse me, madam, but I wonder if I can be of any assistance? Maybe I could carry something for you since I am going in the same direction?'

Effie raised her eyes to the youthful face of the tall young man and resented the slightly patronizing smile.

'Oh, no, thank you very much. I can manage perfectly well. I haven't far to go.' His lips parted in protest but Effie turned away firmly. 'Thank you very much.'

She had barely turned the next corner when another young man passing in the opposite direction stopped her. His accent suggested a humbler origin than the first.

'You're all cluttered up, miss! Perhaps you would let me carry something for you?'

Effie's arms were aching and she felt more kindly disposed towards this honest good-natured face, but she was acutely aware that her first would-be helper was probably close behind and it would be too compromising to accept this offer.

'Oh no. Thank you very much. I can manage perfectly well and you are not even going in my direction!'

'That don't matter at all. I'd happily go in any direction with you!' he responded roguishly. Effie smiled in spite of herself.

'No, really.'

She moved on hoping he would detain her no longer since her arms were aching more every moment. One street further, she was recollecting that in her old school coat and straggling hair she would have put down all these parcels and sat to rest on the stone steps leading up to some offices, but the elegant coat and coiffeured hair made the idea too undignified to contemplate.

'You will excuse me, madam,' spoke a deep male voice, 'but I should be so much obliged if you would allow me to carry some of your parcels for you?'

Effie took one look at the well-bred face of a man in his early thirties and one back down the street but could see neither of the other volunteer carriers.

'Are you going in my direction? I am staying at the Black Swan.'

'Not at all out of my way, I do assure you.'

'Well, thank you very much.' Effie gratefully bundled all but the vase into his arms.

'I can take that one too.'

'It's breakable and I can manage it easily.'

'Oh dear! You think I might drop them all,' said the man with an expression of mock concern.

'No, I am sure you won't,' smiled Effie.

'You don't live in York, then?'

'No. I live near Leeds. I am going home this afternoon.'

'I suppose you prefer Garland's gown shop for your clothes.'

'I have never bought my own clothes before but it seems a good gown shop. I am on my way home from school and I have to come through York.'

The man nodded and smiled encouragingly at her.

'So those are the first two dresses you have ever bought, are they?' Effie was surprised he had noted his cargo in such detail.

'Just one dress and the coat I am wearing. That is my old coat in there.'

'Well, I must commend you upon your taste. You really look charming in that coat.' Effie felt a slight resentment that he should presume to take an interest in her personal concerns and was annoyed to find herself blushing and more annoyed to feel him noticing it. They walked the short distance to the inn in silence. She stopped to relieve him of his parcels but he insisted upon carrying them right in for her. She stepped forward to open the door but he held it open for her with his shoulder and the porter bustled up to help him with the parcels which they ranged on the low table by the hall fire.

'What can I get you, madam? Would you care for a hot drink?' asked the porter. He had addressed her as 'miss' the night before, she remembered.

'Yes, I should love a pot of tea, please,' she paused a moment and caught the man's eye. He didn't seem eager to be gone. 'Would you like some?' she asked hesitantly.

'Yes. That would be very nice, please.'

'A pot of tea for two, please.' She unbuttoned her coat and the man drew it off her shoulders, then removed his own and took them to the porter's room.

She noted his well-proportioned figure of average height and slightly less than average weight, and the smartness of his well-tailored suit and immaculate shoes. He returned to sit in a chair beside hers.

'My name is Cottingley – Ralph – please call me Ralph. What is yours?'

'Effie – Effie Barrett, actually.'

'"Effie" suits well.' He smiled a charming, intimate smile that made her battle with the colour rising to her cheeks again. She had never suffered this affliction before and had been scornful when her schoolmates recounted the horrors of uncontrollable blushing in male company.

'Tell me what colour your dress is.'

'It's a sort of sage green.'

'Is it an afternoon or an evening gown?'

'Oh, an evening one, I suppose, but not very elaborate – just some cream lace on the bodice.'

'I should love to see you in it if your dress taste is as good as your coat taste.'

She smiled politely and looked at the fire, hoping the tea would come soon to provide an impersonal diversion. It did and she poured out two cups.

'Is that enough milk?'

'Oh yes, just right.'

'Sugar?'

'Please – two medium-sized lumps. This is delightfully cosy, isn't it? I have not been here before but it has a good reputation. It used to be the main coaching inn in York, you know.'

'Do you live in York?'

'Oh yes – well, just outside at a little village called Heslington. I share a nice old house there with my mother, and I work in the city.'

'What is your work?' Effie inquired flatly in the interests of good manners only.

'I am a director at the Rowntree factory.' He said this with modest pride and even Effie realized that this must be a position of some prestige. He glanced at her through lowered lids to gauge what impression his information had made, but her youthful face was serenely veiled. He inhaled and pursed his lips slightly at the supreme perfection of her profile back-lit by the glowing logs. The coils of her hair gleamed golden and their soft random swathes made a fine contrast to the clear line of straight brow, delicately curved nose, full lips and firmly rounded chin.

Oh, for a photograph or painting to capture this sight, he thought.

'Well, we must have some lunch before you set off on your homeward journey. What time does your train leave?' he asked briskly.

Effie looked up in surprise.

'You have treated me to tea, I must treat you to lunch.' He made the statement sound beyond dispute.

'We shall lunch at The Albert. You'll enjoy it there; they serve an excellent selection of English and French cuisine.' Effie stood up helplessly only to find him helping her into her coat. He called the porter over.

'Will you please see that Miss Barrett's parcels are packed up together – be careful of the long narrow one, it is breakable – and brought to the station with her luggage. You have packed, Effie, haven't you?'

'Er, yes.'

'Brought to the station for a quarter past two for the Leeds train.' He slipped the man a tip which must have been a generous one judging by the alacrity of his departure.

The bewildered Effie was settled in a cab, handed out, dined with great extravagance and stowed on the train, all under the personal supervision of Mr Ralph Cottingley. Just before the train drew out he pressed a visiting card into her hand.

'Effie, you will write to me, won't you? Write and say when you can come over to York to have lunch or dinner with me. I shall be very disappointed if you don't. I shall have to come to Leeds to find you.' She nodded and smiled absently at him.

'Promise to write, Effie. Promise.'

'Yes, I will.' She hadn't brought herself to use his name yet.

Her mind was in such a turmoil that she could fix it on nothing as the train drew out into the countryside.

She felt an utterly different being from the schoolgirl of the morning. Could the innocent purchase of a dress and coat really change one's life potential to this extent? These men! All these three men rushing to help her – support her. She found it frighteningly unaccountable. One thing no-one had ever denied her was the capacity to be independent. They may have done their best to limit her independence but it had never been seriously disputed that she was her own master and would fight very hard for that doubtful privilege. Now, suddenly, she had seemed powerless to offer the smallest resistance to this overwhelming display of confident male dominance. She had not set eyes on the man before noon and yet she could not entirely resent those charming intimate smiles which seemed to disturb the most sacred recesses of mind and body and make her blush. What right had he to domineer and disturb her? None, but why had she not repulsed him? Because it would have been rude and have hurt his feelings in return for a charitable act; yes, quite reasonable but not quite the truth. She groped deeper. There was great comfort in these offers of support. Her arms were aching, she would prefer not to carry her own parcels; how delightfully idle to have one's coat removed and spirited away, every physical need identified and supplied without self-effort. Perhaps it was just laziness? Not altogether; there were elements of both these and the satisfaction of seeing in the mirror that she was beautiful and receiving the homage due, but there was some other ill-defined doubt as well.

Would Grandpa have approved of the way she had spent his 'brass' today? Again, the answers were confused.

'Aye, it's thine, lass. Tha spend it as tha wants.' She heard his dear, rough voice. But would he approve of the frivolity? Yes, he loved beautiful things; after all, some of those begonias he loved were the most frivolous of man-made objects –

interbred, sported, hybridized and greenhouse-cherished. He had enjoyed unconcealed pleasure in her own childish beauty and surely would now she was a woman. Was it not rather hard on the Susan Mannerings of this world, though? No-one had offered Effie assistance on her way to Garland's and no man would look twice at the short square figure and wrinkled splodgy visage of poor Susan, even arrayed in the most low-cut of evening dresses and the highest of evening court shoes. Mind, people like Susan *did* get married – for witness *she* existed and so did so many squat ungainly figures, both male and female that Effie knew. Many of them had hearts of gold, as the saying goes, and this must count for something, but Effie had not. Softer feelings towards her fellow men did not have much space in Effie's head and she had shown a minimal amount of encouragement to Ralph Cottingley, yet, if she were to write and say 'I shall be in York on Friday. Please marry me,' she was almost certain he would hand her out of the train fluttering the marriage certificate. He would probably have arranged for the lady at Garland's to select, alter and deliver a superb bridal gown to the grandest hotel in York. She giggled quietly at the thought. The elderly man sitting opposite her glanced in her direction and gave her a witheringly severe look as their eyes met.

Well, *that* should keep my vanity within bounds, thought Effie.

CHAPTER TWELVE

Christmas was much like many others: cold, wet weather, the garden dreary, and Aunt Rosalie. Jim was as taciturn as ever and positively grumpy on the receipt of his presents. Effie stood in the little parlour in an old woolly tunic holding aloft the glass vase resplendent with its burden of golden chrysanthemums and laurel. The well-cut patterns flashed blue and green in the firelight. It had cost a lot of money. Jim stood with kettle in one hand and poker in the other.

'Uh,' he grunted. 'I've got a vase in t'scullery!'

'I thought it would be nice to have a really good one. I bought it in York for you.'

'It's only the water that counts. T'old one holds plenty. Tha shouldn'a spend tha money on me.'

Effie stalked to the window sill and put the vase in the customary place with mock annoyance. He straightened slowly from putting the kettle on the hob and remained slightly stooped and old, eyes on the carpet, wondering whether he had really hurt her. With difficulty she controlled a passionate desire to rush over and hug him. She had not given in to this prompting since that first Christmas when she returned from school and they filled the pond. He had been disconcerted enough then; it was intolerable to even contemplate it now.

'I'm just mashing tea. Will tha have some?' The softness in his voice meant more to Effie than the most effusive 'thank you.'

'Oh, yes please, Jim.' She sat down on her old stool by the hearth. Jim called it his footstool but she had never seen him use it. She remembered with amusement how high off the ground it had seemed when she was two or three years old. Her knees were touching her chin now as she hugged them.

'This is grand, Jim. Just like old times. I think of sitting having tea with you when I am away at school, feeling low.'

'Does tha? Does't often feel low?'

'No, not often now. I've got used to being away, I expect. No, that's not true, I shall never get used to it. It just doesn't seem so bad. One can see the end of it when one's older. Each term used to seem so long.' He nodded. 'Do I seem to be away a long time to you?'

'Nay, tha's hardly gone when tha's back agin – but *that* be old age for thee. I was just thinking, seeing you there with them

141

flowers, that it were only last week that last Christmas were here.' They both chuckled.

'Is the pond all right? How about the leak?'

'Oh, that's bin bothersome. George Grimley came down and we siphoned some out and tried to seal it but it isn't raight yet. Must be a very small crack that gets made up until there's some wet weather then the extra flow clears it and the level starts falling again.'

'Some clay from the canal, perhaps?'

'Aye. I've got a fair idea where it is now so a bit o' clay built up from the bottom. It'll take a fair amount because the crack's some two foot up t'side.'

'We can do that after Christmas, if there's not a freeze set in.' They drank their tea in silence. Effie was remembering the sad sealing of ponds with canal clay many springs ago, and Jim probably was too.

Lily nudged Effie's arm to have her ears caressed.

The Cockcrofts' party was two days before Christmas. Effie wore her new blue dress and was much admired – verbally by the girls and older people and visually by the young men. John Cockcroft was not quite as shy as formerly and carried out the duties of junior host fairly efficiently but Effie couldn't help comparing his diffident demeanour unfavourably with Ralph Cottingley's aplomb. Edward Carter arrived late with a group of young bloods. They had been carol singing and were overfull of home-made wine, so they were rather boorish but also clannish which kept them out of the way. Edward detached himself once and sought out Effie.

'You haven't replied to my invitation, Miss Barrett. You *are* coming to my party in the New Year, I hope?'

'Well, I am not quite sure that I shall be able to ...'

'But you must. I shall take it as a personal slight if you do not. Please promise me now.' Effie smiled coolly.

'I shall if I am able to, I promise.'

He lowered his head and looked at her like a pleading little boy which softened her amazingly.

'I shall try to come,' she laughed.

'Good. I take that as a firm acceptance,' he laughed as he returned to his group.

Maggie French was also at the party and pressed Effie to come to hers. Effie thought she had mellowed a little over the last two years and graciously accepted the invitation, making an excuse for not replying earlier. Should she wear her green dress? It would be nice to wear a different dress for each party, but how about the third, should she decide at the last minute to go? It seemed illogical not to wear the green one but she found herself making excuses and considering the purchase of yet another dress in Leeds.

Another problem which she pushed to the back of her mind as unworthy of a prominent place but which continued to niggle, was the letter she had promised to Ralph Cottingley. In the end she purchased a rather large and tasteful Christmas card and inscribed it 'with best wishes from Elspeth Barrett. Thank you very much for your help and that sumptuous lunch.' It would never reach him in time for Christmas, but at least it was a gesture to quieten her conscience and did not carry her address which she would have to have revealed in a letter. Some days after Christmas she was disconcerted to receive a letter from him. It ran:

'Dear Effie,

Thank you for the card. I was very happy to receive it although a letter would have been better.

I find that I have business in Leeds and wonder if you would be so kind as to join me for lunch on either Tuesday January 8th or Wednesday 9th? We could conveniently meet at the Queen's Hotel at a quarter past twelve. Do bring a friend with you if you would prefer.

If the dates or arrangements I suggest are inconvenient please name some that would suit you better.

Should I not hear from you, I shall be at the Queen's Hotel at 12.15 pm on Tuesday 8th of January.

I do hope you will excuse my presumption in writing but York and Leeds are so far apart that it is difficult to call upon you without some kind of formal arrangement.

Yours very sincerely,

Ralph Cottingley.'

The letter was neatly written in a businesslike hand and the straightforward nature of the proposal accorded well with the impression Effie had of the man. She was puzzled how he had obtained her address until she remembered that the gown shop had it in order to send on the blue dress. He must have asked about her at Garlands! It seemed dubious practice for them to supply it to him but, of course, he must be a well-known business man in the city and his forceful nature would undoubtedly be difficult to counter. She could well imagine the consternation of the manageress and the speculations of the sales girls.

She could not decide how to reply. The answer should clearly be 'no', but he would come. He knew her address and would come. She could contrive to be out on January eighth but he would probably change the date of his visit. She knew enough of this man to know that he would not easily be thwarted in his intentions and he had the confidence of experience behind him. She vainly wondered about seeking advice. Her father? Her mother? No! Maggie French? She would certainly say 'yes' and excitedly offer to chaperone. After all it *was* rather exciting. Her real doubt was her capacity to stand up to this man. She had never doubted her self-reliance before and maybe it was only the initial speed of his attack that had disconcerted her? She had had time to think now. She tried to recall his face. He had well-groomed dark hair. He was not classically good-looking but attractive in a slightly rugged, charming way. She could remember these thoughts but could not visualize the face at all; neither the colour of his eyes nor the shape of his nose. She *would* like to see him again just to repair her shattered self-confidence.

She was sitting on the low parapet of the bridge over the pond.

'If in doubt – do nowt, lass.' The forceful tones of that dear, rough voice rang through her mind so vividly that she started and the envelope fell from her lap into the pond. She glanced round, wide-eyed, then bent down and fished out the letter.

She went to Leeds the day before Maggie's party and bought a creamy, lacy crinoline that would be suitable for a summer evening's formal occasion. She was slightly surprised at the rapidity with which her taste was changing. Two weeks ago in York she would have rejected this as being far too frilly. Her mother and Aunt Rosalie were with her and, to be honest, this was the dress which had charmed her mother. Aunt Rosalie declared it to be too fanciful by half and so low cut in the bodice she would be ashamed for a daughter of hers to seen by 'anysen' in it! Effie's lips tightened and she bought it forthwith, reassuring her vacillating mother that there were far lower bodices to be seen at the Cockcrofts' party. She was gratified by Aunt Rosalie's tongue-clucking glower which persisted all the way home in the cab and all evening until supper, when the priorities of eating redirected her thoughts.

Effie dressed for the party the following evening and quietly entered the kitchen in the midst of a heated argument between her mother and aunt upon the propriety and practicability of arranging a white veil to mask the lower part of the offending neckline. Her father noticed her before the adversaries and removed his pipe in surprised admiration. He had been reading his paper innocent of the subject of the argument.

'Ee, just stop tha wittering and look at our daughter, Mary, Rosalie! Ent she a sight for sore eyes. Fair beautiful!'

Rosalie looked at him witheringly, took a deep breath and sat down with her martyred expression. Mary looked at her daughter apprehensively at first and then with melting approval.

145

'Aye – it is a lovely dress an' she wears it so well. That bodice don't show too much do it, John?'

'Nay – not that I'd notice,' he rejoined uncomfortably, 'but you women folk knows best, I guess.'

'Who'd think she could look like this when she's messin' about in the garden in clogs and her muddy old raincoat!' Rosalie did not deign to reply.

The front door bell rang and Effie rose to follow her mother out. John Cockcroft had offered to escort her to the party. He stood waiting for her in the centre of the tiled hall beneath the chandelier and Mrs Barrett was well satisfied to see his bland plump face sag into an expression of enraptured awe as Effie advanced gracefully towards him. In a daze he took the evening cloak she proffered him and arranged it round her shoulders. He clumsily helped her into the carriage and spent the first half of the journey in speechless confusion. Effie eventually took pity on him and told him about the weather over Christmas, how windy it had been the past few days and of the weather Jim had forecast for the next week. This seemed to do him good and he was almost composed by the time they arrived. He relieved her of her cloak with a flourish that was quite gallant and she kindly insinuated her hand behind his rigid elbow to be properly escorted into the lounge. She could not help a slight thrill of gratification running through her as the conversation lulled and many eyes turned appraisingly in their direction. This stately room was connected to the large tiled hall by folding double doors so when the dancing began after supper, the couples could revolve back and forth between the two. Edward Carter arrived only a little late and quickly monopolized Effie to the chagrin of John, who felt he should have an escort's priority. Effie sensed this but felt that she had been kind to John long enough.

'Well, another beautiful gown on my babe-in-the-wood, eh? I really prefer this to the last I think.' He smiled meaningfully as he raised his eyes from her bosom.

'What confounded, charming cheek he has,' thought Effie.

146

Ralph Cottingley would never be so indelicate and yet she felt quite confident that she could cope with this bouncy youngster better than Ralph.

'Which will you wear to my party next week?'

'If I am able to come,' said Effie carefully, 'I shall wear neither.'

He raised his brows in exaggerated shock. Who had caught whom? 'I trust you mean to say that you have three new party gowns?'

Effie laughed wickedly. 'You will have to wait and see, won't you?'

They danced silently for a few minutes in mutual respect. His blond beauty struck Effie more forcibly in the sophistication of evening dress than it had in the rural surroundings of that summer afternoon – or maybe he was a little bit older? He had no awe of her and that gave him an attractive edge over the other young men she had met this evening. They met on equal terms which she found challenging and acceptable.

CHAPTER THIRTEEN

Effie woke late the next morning and began to search for the thread of dissatisfaction which had been running through her mind as she fell asleep. Yes, here it was – Ralph Cottingley; frivolity; artifice; beauty; new gowns; parties. Was this really what she wanted of life? She had never expected that such things would appeal to her but they had; for a time, anyway. Towards the end of last evening she had been standing in a group of girls – their hostess Maggie, Fanny Hawes, Christine Smith and two whom she didn't know. They were gossiping, giggling – about the usual sort of things she supposed – men, dresses and other parties – but Effie was not really one of them.

She was standing, gravely smiling, half aware of Edward's eye lighting on her from the other side of the room but her mind was somewhere above, looking down on the groups of people and the room as she grappled with this questioning dissatisfaction. A feeling of nausea overcame her and she hastened away to find John and tell him she would like to leave...

She got up and dressed and went downstairs but the feeling mounted to a pitch of foreboding despair as she opened the kitchen door. It was the twenty-eighth of December 1882; one of the few dates she remembered for the rest of her life. Mr Plaice the postman stood by the kitchen table, his mittened fingers grasping a wodge of letters. It was not uncommon for him to call in, particularly on cold winter days, for a chat and a cup of tea, but Effie sensed the threatening silence even before she noticed the grave expression on his face and her mother's and father's.

'Morning, Mr Plaice.'

'Morning, miss.'

'Is there some bad news?'

'Aye, there is.' He glanced questioningly at John.

'Bad do o'er at Bradford, lass,' said her father.

'What's happened?'

'Newland's Mill chimney collapsed at breakfast break,' supplied Plaice.

'What? This morning?'

'Aye. Eight o'clock or thereabouts.'

'How many people hurt?'

'They don't know yet, of course. But it's bad. They say there's near a hundred trapped under t'buildings.'

'It'll take a while to shift the wreckage, won't it?' said John.

'Aye, indeed. They've got fire engines. Our one's gone. That's how I got ter know, but it's the chaps they'll need – crowbars, pulley tackle and the like.'

'Oh, how terrible. Were there children working there?'

'Aye, bound ter be. There's allus a lot on the early shift because they aren't allowed ter work that late now.'

Effie shuddered and sat down at the table.

However she could feel responsible she didn't understand but the conviction that it would not have happened if her life had been less frivolous seemed inescapable. After all, the money that fuelled these parties came directly or indirectly from the toil of those men, women and children that were, at this moment, buried in agony under that rubble. They had started work at five and six o'clock that morning and had stopped for their breakfast at eight, while she was still sleeping away her dissipated life. The idleness she had inherited was thanks to the toil of countless people like them who had worked away their waking hours and many that should have been their sleeping hours and their childhood playing hours so that she might live like this.

'Well, I must be off. 'Bye, Mrs Barrett, 'bye, Mr Barrett.' He paused outside the door and spoke quietly to Mary.

'It seems to have upset thy lass. Maybe we shouldn't have told her.'

'Never tha mind – she were bound to hear. She ent easily upset as a rule.'

'Can we do anything, Father?'

'Nay, not as I can think of.'

'Will they need money for anything?'

'I expect there'll be some sort of collection made for the next of kin, later like.'

'Oh, God.'

'Tha mustn't take on so. It were none o' your doing.'

'I feel as if it were!'

The next afternoon, she was sitting in Jim's parlour with a mug of tea between her hands. They were each gazing at the glowing embers, he wondering why she had come and she bracing herself to ask the question.

'Have you heard how they are getting on at Newland's Mill?'

'Aye, I spoke to Arthur Bright this afternoon. His lad Frank were over with the fire engine yesterday morning.'

149

'What did he say?'

'He didn't get home while noon today – his hands all torn and bleeding with pulling the bricks and stone off. Daren't use picks for fear of hurting someone.'

'Did he work all night?'

'Aye, and they're hardly half through.'

Effie's face twisted in anguish.

'Can't more men work?'

'There ent room. But they're not short. They've got lights fixed up and teams organized now to take over as one lot tires.'

'How many people are in there still?'

'Well, it's difficult to be sure but they think there's something like forty folk not accounted for.'

'How many dead so far?'

'Frank said there were Lupton's warehouse made over to a mortuary and he'd seen twenty or thirty taken over. Bairns many of them but they got one lad out o' t'cellar unhurt this morning and he had been in there twenty-six hours!'

Effie bit her lip and there was a long silence.

'Did they know the chimney wasn't safe?'

'Aye. There's the terrible part of it. I remember a fellow from Bowling telling me five or six years ago as it weren't safe. Greenwoods wouldn't do nowt about it. It weren't raight when it were built. They had ter get engineers from Manchester in to straighten it a year or so after, owing to subsidence into coal mine workings underneath.'

'Won't Greenwoods be found responsible and have to compensate the relatives?'

'Maybe, but more likely not, the way things usually happen.'

'But it must be their fault!' fired Effie indignantly.

'Nay. 'Tis never owner's fault. 'Tis allus an accident that kills working folk – an act of God, like.' Effie looked up. She had never heard him speak so bitterly before.

'After all,' he continued after a pause, 'they was mending it. They had scaffolding up. Frank spoke to one of the men who were meant to be working on it. He said they had started the day before and there were such a strong wind got up early yesterday that they refused to go up.'

'So they knew it was dangerous – they could have stopped the mill.'

'Nay, that would mean stopping spinning machines making brass for something that might never happen!'

Effie shook her head miserably.

CHAPTER FOURTEEN

Despite her rising doubts, Effie did go to Edward's party the following week. John Cockcroft again offered to take her, but she told him that owing to another commitment she would not be able to arrive until late and it would be a pity for him to miss some of the party. It was just a ruse to prevent Edward thinking he had it all his own way. If he thought about her at all, he would think that she wasn't coming and then she could surprise him. 'What a shabby subterfuge,' commented her sensible self. John declared that he didn't at all mind missing part of the party and she must just mention a time that was convenient and he would be there for her.

'In fact,' he paused to rally confidence, 'the party will really not be worth being at until you arrive.' Effie smiled at him scornfully and he looked abjectly grateful, certain that his gallantry had been appreciated.

The Carters resided at Underwood Hall which was one of the most splendid establishments in the vicinity. A double drive branched from the shrubbery and curved up either side of a large steep lawn to converge beneath the castellated portico of the huge arched doorway. Swathes of evergreen with candles concealed amongst them decorated the porch and a line of chandeliers glittered above the black and white marble slabs of the hall floor. John was tremulous with nervousness and it was all the butler and two smartly clad maids could do to extricate him and Effie from their outer garments without John's long silk scarf tying all five of them into a helpless tangle. Effie tried to remain composed but ultimately started to giggle, which infected the youngest maid and earned her a severe reprimand from the butler.

At last they were fit to be ushered into the long ground-floor dining room which had been transformed into a ballroom for the occasion. Huge logs burned in the open fireplace and roses and evergreens trailed in elegant profusion from the plate rack above the dark oak panelling and among the branches of the superb chandeliers. Effie was resplendent, too, in the figured green taffeta which was much admired by the more discerning women. She had gathered up her long ash-blond hair into an informal chignon from which some curls escaped to tumble down the side of her neck. Her expression was radiantly mischievous after the diversion in the hall. Edward must have been waiting for her since he hurried through the dancing couples to her straight away and, without noticing poor John, made her a cursory bow and swept her away.

'Just as beautiful as ever, but I think I slightly preferred the white gown. It was prettier at the top,' he declared. Effie accepted this verdict with a cynically raised eyebrow which made him laugh.

'Do you know, I thought you weren't going to come. I am sure you were late on purpose, you little minx!'

'I have no need to dance with you. I could easily find a civil partner.'

'No, I'm sorry. I haven't really offended, have I?' He treated her to the sorry-little-boy look which worked again. 'Do you ride?'

'No, not really.'

'I was going hunting on Friday. I wondered if you hunted?'

'Oh, no, I can't ride well enough for that and I don't like the idea, anyway.'

'You are difficult to please, aren't you? No ball games, no hunting. I am very glad you like dancing.' She smiled. She had not realized until this moment how much she liked dancing.

'Do you enjoy walking?'

'Oh yes. On the moors you mean?'

'Yes. We shall go for a walk together on Thursday, shall we then?' She had absent-mindedly fallen right into this one. He quickly noted the fleeting wariness in her eyes.

'No – please don't think of an excuse. Do I really bore you so much?'

'Of course not. I shall be very happy to come – so long as it is a proper long walk. I walk miles and miles you know.'

'By yourself?'

'Yes, usually.'

'What a shame.'

'I enjoy it. I am not used to company really.' She realized too late that she had let fall her brash shield for a moment. His arm tightened round her waist drawing their bodies a little closer together.

'Supposing we started at the near edge of Rombalds moor and walked across to Ilkley for a late lunch? Would that be far enough?'

'Oh yes. That would do for a start. How should we get there?'

'I'll drive us in the pony chaise with Giles, the second groom, and he will take the chaise on to Ilkley to meet us. He will approve of that. It will give him two hours' drinking time at the Crown.'

She excused herself from his arms on the grounds of being out of breath. They had been dancing together for a long time and indecently closely for the last few minutes. She found the sensation surprisingly pleasant but she did not wish to feel compromised.

The following day she had to make a final decision about Ralph Cottingley. She took her writing case to the pond and sat huddled on the bridge. She had never consciously sought advice from that source before but so many were the times that her troubles had been solved there and the strange experience of the other morning had inspired her with even more faith.

She wrote:

'Dear Mr Cottingley,

Thank you very much for your kind invitation. I shall be delighted to meet you at the Queen's Hotel on Tuesday 8th of January at a quarter past twelve. I must join my mother and aunt for a shopping excursion at two o'clock but this should give us long enough to have lunch together.

Yours sincerely,

Effie Barrett.'

The shopping excursion was, of course, a fabrication in case she needed to escape and she might yet arrange it. Why did this man alarm her so much? She was not in the least troubled by the prospect of walking across Rombalds moor with Edward tomorrow. Her only concern was that he might walk depressingly slowly and she would have to keep waiting for him. This tried her patience beyond endurance and confirmed her preference for walking alone. However, it seemed unlikely considering his sporting activities and fine physique. This led her to recall the pleasurable sensation when he drew her body close to his – the soft resilient warmth against her belly. Many things lay before her to be experienced and understood and the spectre of Ralph Cottingley was perhaps a pure fabrication of her mind. Next Tuesday would prove him to be just a kind lonely man on the verge of middle age.

Thursday dawned foggy. Edward arrived in the chaise just after nine o'clock, and the sound of the wheels on the gravel brought Effie to the front door to meet him. For the first time the social implication of Edward's palatial home and many servants began to impinge upon Effie as she led him down the narrow hallway. Her childhood friends had been few and usually children from the nearby cottages who regarded Oakroyd as the grand house of the neighbourhood. She opened the kitchen door to reveal her mother's back, stooped over the sink and crossed by her linen apron straps, her father in his wicker chair reading and Aunt Rosalie knitting on the other side of the range. She tried to smile encouragingly at Edward and was upset to find a strangely rigid expression on his normally mobile face.

'Mother, Father, Aunt Rosalie. This is Mr Edward Carter.'

Mary turned from the sink sharply, pushing some straggly grey wisps back from her flushed face with her reddened sudsy fingers in an embarrassed manner. John stood up affably and grasped Edward's hand.

'You're right welcome, me lad – draw a chair up t'range.' Effie was certain the Yorkshire vowels were rounder and more emphatic than usual and there was no need to be quite as familiar as that.

'N-no thank you very much, sir. We want to get started early. There is so little light at this time of year.' Edward's good breeding had rescued him but Effie was saddened to see how ill at ease he was.

'We should not entertain young gentlemen in the kitchen, Elspeth!' Aunt Rosalie voice was high with shock.

'Nay, Effie, tha should have told us,' said Mary reproachfully.

'I did. I said we were walking on the moors, yesterday morning. We must be off as Edward says.'

'Does tha need a lunch pack?' asked Mary worriedly.

'Oh no thanks, Mother – we are having lunch out. Goodbye.'

'Goodbye, Mr and Mrs Barrett. Goodbye...'

'Miss Bradley,' supplied Effie shortly as she pushed him out of the kitchen. The view from the front door was imposing enough. The wide scrubbed stone steps led down to the immaculate gravel drive flanked by well-tended beds and lawns.

'You have a beautiful garden.' He didn't say 'Effie' as he normally would.

'Yes. We have a very good gardener.' He looked slightly relieved by this information. Should she apologize for the kitchen scene? Should she explain that her mother was a working Yorkshire woman who preferred to do most of the housework herself? No, she never had seen any reason to apologize for the way they lived and she didn't now. She was only upset by the disturbing effect it had had on Edward. He gathered his dispersed thoughts together.

'It is rather foggy. Do you think we should just go for a drive?'

'Oh, no. I know the moor well. We shan't get lost.'

'Well,' he said doubtfully, 'I have brought a compass and map in case you still wanted to go.' She smiled to herself. He would have been surprised if he had known her physical capability out in the open air, especially on those wide wild moors.

He helped her into the pony chaise and tucked a rug round her legs then took the reins from the groom who melted unobtrusively into the corner of the seat. Effie smiled at him.

'Is the fog as bad at Rawdon?'

'Aye, just about.'

'How many horses do you look after?'

'About twelve, countin' t'ponies.' Effie raised her brows in surprised interest but the groom awkwardly turned his head to the scenery. Was he shy, she wondered, or did he know his place as a gentleman's servant? She guessed the latter and it saddened her. Surely her life was the richer.

Edward seemed subdued. Effie chattered about the age of Hawksworth Hall, the pretty cottages in the village and the view across Tong valley to Baildon moor top, just rising clear of the fog. He seemed more himself after half an hour's walking. He didn't quite lag behind but he was clearly amazed at the rapidity of Effie's progress and her stamina. Over lunch at the Crescent Hotel he was nearly his old ebullient self but

Effie could detect a new restraint and although they passed the gate of his house he didn't suggest they call in but drove her straight home.

Effie was not surprised to hear nothing from Edward during the following days but a thread of disappointment hovered about his image. The square tanned face, neat nose, blond moustache and laughing mouth frequently rose into her mind and Tuesday crept ever nearer. She told her mother that she would hire a cab to go into Leeds shopping. Mary looked perturbed.

'I can't manage to come Tuesday, love. Maybe Rosalie will go with you.' Her mother seemed more affectionate and sympathetic towards her grown-up child.

'No, I shall be perfectly all right on my own, thank you. I shall be back by four o'clock.'

She was preparing to leave when the door bell sounded. She gathered up her hat and bag expecting the cabman but to her consternation Edward was standing on the step with a smart gig behind.

'Oh, you're just going out.'

'Yes, I was going into Leeds.' The cab drew into the drive at that moment.

'I shall be delighted to take you. You won't need that.'

'But it will be out of your way.'

'Not at all, I was going to let you choose where we should go, anyway.'

She wavered a moment and he took this as his cue to dismiss the cab – so she had no choice. His peremptory action and her agitation at a further complication to her day made her irritable.

'Really, Edward, you seem to be taking liberties with my arrangements.'

'But you will get there much faster in my gig. Have you looked at it? It is a belated Christmas present from my father.'

This genuine display of boyish excitement calmed her a little and she allowed herself to be wrapped up in the seat as she

157

pinned her tiny feathered cap in place. The gleaming coils of hair were caught up lightly on her crown as they had been in the dress shop. Their eyes met as he rose from tucking the rug about her.

'More beautiful than ever when annoyed,' he murmured. She looked sourly at him.

He unhooked the reins, cracked the whip and the showy bay cob stepped smartly off down the drive.

'You are my first passenger,' he called over his shoulder.

'I trust you are not too expensive?'

'Exorbitant! But you can walk home if you like. Are you going shopping?'

'Er, yes – and meeting a friend for lunch.' She thought he must be bound to notice the break in her voice as she said 'friend' but he did not question her. As they neared Leeds she wondered whether Ralph was already there and supposing he saw her arrive – still, it might be no bad thing if he did. It would establish that she was not the totally naive schoolgirl he may have thought her. But no sooner had the thought occurred than she was despising herself. They drove up Park Lane, past the Town Hall at a cracking pace with many heads turned to watch. Edward was very satisfied with the impression they were making. It was only eleven fifteen when they drew up outside a Briggate coffee shop.

'Well, where would madam care to be put down? Perhaps she has time for a cup of coffee?' He pulled off his cap in a gesture of deference and the wind ruffled his blond curls making him look very young and carefree.

'Yes,' said Effie recklessly, 'that would be very nice.' He walked the bay a few yards to the shop door, jumped down and beckoned to a boy to hold the reins. The youngster's round eyes took in the spanking new turnout and beamed enthusiastically.

'There you are … and sixpence when I come out. Just see there's no scratch on my gig, though.' Almost as an afterthought he handed Effie down. She stood back to examine her transport properly.

'Oh, yes. Very smart – and we came so fast, I was glad I had pinned my hat on properly.' He laughed complacently and opened the shop door for her.

'I am sorry I was grumpy to you. It has been much more fun than in a cab.'

'When will you be returning from your mission? Shall I wait for you?'

'Oh, no Edward. I really don't know exactly. I shall get a cab.'

CHAPTER FIFTEEN

She arrived at the Queen's at twenty past twelve and stepped towards the door suddenly agitated that she might not recognize him, but he came forward as soon as she emerged into the foyer. There was no outward trace of an ogre about him. In relief she scrutinized his face more carefully than she had done in York. Yes, kind, good-natured features and just irregular enough to grant him a rugged charm which was fortified by his soft deep voice and, yes – early thirties would be about right. He was smiling widely as he returned her scrutiny and only when their eyes met did she get a hint of that disturbing quality which had alarmed her.

'Effie! I am pleased to see you.'

'I wrote that I should come.'

'Yes, and I thought you would but I have been the victim of such shattered peace of mind since we last met.' That intimate eye smile – the rising blush. Effie looked away.

'I am sorry,' she said feebly.

If Edward had said such a thing, a cynical quip would have risen to her tongue in a moment.

He took her coat and revealed the neat navy dress, bodice and cuffs trimmed with white braid to lend a subtle sophistication.

'Have you bought any more gowns?' he asked as he led her to a seat.

'Yes – just one more evening one.'

'And have you worn all these dresses?'

'Yes, all three!' she laughed. 'I have been leading a gay life lately.'

'Do you enjoy that?' He was looking at her hard as if the answer was important to him.

Effie played with a ring on her finger while she considered.

'I have enjoyed these winter parties but they are the first I have been to and I suspect they are all similar and I shall soon tire of them.' The answer seemed to relieve him.

'So, you have met a lot of smart young men and they are all wanting to visit you, I expect?'

'No, not very many and they do not find my home particularly welcoming.' She could not resist the sour jibe but it would be enigmatic to him.

'Oh dear, what is wrong with your home?' he asked in a lighter tone.

'It would take much too long to explain, and be very boring.'

'Oh yes – do excuse me, Effie. I have been inconsiderately curious. Let's find something interesting to discuss. Would you like another glass of sherry?'

'No thank you – I feel quite light-headed already.'

'Right. We must go into the dining-room while you can still walk.' He took her hand to help her up, settled it in the crook of his arm and continued to hold it.

'We must get you to our table safely,' he joked.

He had evidently reserved a table, one of the best, in the window bay but set discreetly against the long brocade curtains. The head waiter danced attendance upon them summoning the wine list and the table waiter, who made a final adjustment to the position of selected pieces of cutlery. Effie wished she had not daydreamed through all of the deportment lessons. She felt utterly confused by the banks of forks, knives and spoons flanked by lines of glasses. He was watching her tenderly and when she raised her eyes said, 'What a silly lot of paraphernalia to eat a lunch with. I am almost wishing we had chosen sandwiches in a park.'

The meal was ordered and eaten using perhaps a third of the 'paraphernalia' and their conversation was inconsequential. Ralph did his best to banter lightly but there seemed to be something preying on his mind and Effie was ill at ease. 'I think it would be nice to have coffee in private, don't you?' He didn't wait for her answer but held her chair and an usher materialized to guide them upstairs to a private parlour with an armchair and sofa before a blazing fire.

'It is easier to relax in here, isn't it?' he said, handing her to the sofa. He ordered the drinks and sat down beside her. She reminded herself that it was really exciting and might become more so while her safety could not be seriously in jeopardy but she still remained apprehensive. The drinks arrived speedily and the door closed on their privacy.

'You seem nervous of me, Effie. I have not behaved badly have I?'

'No, of course not.'

'I am not pompous, awe-inspiring or ogreish, am I?'

'No, not at all,' she laughed.

'I am quite a lot older than you, of course. Does that make a difference?'

'No, I like older people usually.' He looked happily at her.

'You tell me why.'

'Why?'

'Why you are nervous of me?'

'I... I ... honestly don't know. I think it must be something to do with your efficiency.' He looked surprised and considered her suggestion. 'You mean you would be happier if I bumbled about – losing your property and forgetting to book a table and caused you a lot of inconvenience?'

'Well, no. It was just the way you took me over in York. I am used to being my own master,' persevered Effie bravely. His face broke into happy mirth. 'What! You really *preferred* struggling along with aching arms when you might have paid a passing lad twopence to follow you from shop to shop – or better still had the things delivered direct? You just aren't a very good manager.'

'No, I suppose I'm not,' conceded Effie laughing. 'I shall take your good advice next time I go shopping, though.'

'I should rather you took me.' The intimate smile – she struggled hard against it – but the inevitable blush followed.

He was leaning towards her, breathing rather fast. She leant away slightly.

'Effie?'

'Yes.'

'It is hard for me to make you understand what I want to say to you. Would you help me by trying to be very sympathetic? Can you imagine how lonely it is if you have a very good job – the sort where everyone does what you tell them without question and is always polite and all your friends assume you are too grand to need them any more? Can you imagine having no-one to confide one's deepest thoughts and feelings to?'

'Er, yes. I can imagine that it would be lonely.' There was a sort of magnetism about this man that she could not escape. He spoke with deep intensity and she responded with the same almost against her will. 'Then can you imagine living with someone whom you love very dearly and depend on utterly as your only confidant and support and losing that person suddenly …?' He put his hand over his eyes. Effie, deeply moved, laid hers on his shoulder. He shuddered, lowered his hands and gazed into her eyes, searching deeply for something.

'Effie,' he cried in anguish.

'Ralph – yes, I do understand that you are very lonely and

want me.' Her voice sounded cool and detached but within she was in an emotional turmoil.

He took her gently into his arms and brushed his lips over her face. She allowed him to but a hard cold voice within her said 'Do not give yourself to this man. Comfort him but he has no right to you. You are your own.'

'You are so beautiful, my darling child.'

He released her after a few moments and gazed at her downcast face.

'Effie, forgive me. I was carried away. I had no right to take advantage of you.'

She did not answer.

'Effie – you must like me a little or you would not have allowed me to embrace you? Perhaps you just felt sorry for me?'

She shook her head miserably.

'I must finish what I wanted to say else I shall be so wretchedly miserable as I have been ever since that age ago that we met. I am a rich man, securely rich. I can buy you anything you fancy. I can take you anywhere you want to go. We could travel the world together, if it would please you. We could live in the most beautiful house you could find and, above all, I can love you deeply – I already do and time would improve its depth. I do not want an answer. You are distressed, naturally. I would rather you said nothing – nothing at all. I am going to hire a cab and send you home. Oh, blast, you have to meet your mother and aunt?'

'No ... no I don't ... just send me home, please.' It seemed an abject response from one's own master – but there it was.

Three days later Effie sat on the balustrade of the bridge. She held her writing case again. It was not a decision that she had to make, it was just the composition of a letter that would wound no more than it must. She felt sincere pity for Ralph. She had never experienced deep love for a man of her own generation but she was certain that this feeling, disturbing as it might be, was not love. He had an undeniable magnetism for her but this was just alarming – the real emotion that he aroused in her was pity; which was surprising. After all, he was physically attractive in the most manly way and made love to her with great tenderness but she had remained comparatively unmoved by this, her first love affair.

'Dear Ralph,

Please do not consider me ungrateful because I am only too aware of the great compliment you have paid me with such an unconditional offer of your love and fortune. I cannot possibly accept for a variety of reasons which it would be pointless to explain.

I do so sincerely hope that you find someone who does justify such devotion but please choose carefully. I should hate you to be hurt any more.

Assuring you of my kindest thoughts,
Effie.'

She shook her head sadly. It was the best she could manage but how honest was this letter? She had sought long for that word 'unconditional' and now it sounded so hard and calculated. It was the word she had intended but it was not honest. One thing she had tried to tell Ralph, but he could not understand, was that his condition was too hard. He demanded – no he just assumed – immediately that she was waiting to be claimed. Just as he might pick a beautiful flower from his garden and place it in his buttonhole with the tacit assumption that it had been grown for that purpose – so he symbolically took her into his arms with her parcels. Many girls she knew would have willingly acquiesced – at first anyway – but the idea was utterly alien to her independent spirit.

Slowly she walked to the post box. She stayed her hand for a moment as it passed the letter through the opening and then reluctantly let it drop and turned thoughtfully away. Three paces on and her head rose higher; three more paces and she tossed her loose hair back, skipped lightly into the air and started to run fast – down the stone-setted lane – across the toll bridge, with as little thought to toll as she had ever had, and up to the canal bank. She paused then breathlessly to decide which direction held the most diversion and then set off at a rapid walk towards Rodley.

CHAPTER SIXTEEN

Spring came late. Effie's patience had worn thin during the dreary cold eternity between the snowdrops pushing through the ice-bound ground and the daffodils unfurling. Even the early species crocuses had only opened shortly before. Edward and she had had some good walks on Baildon and Rombalds and even up the delightful valley of the Washburn, but he seemed to be hunting or shooting three or four days a week and, despite his protestations, Effie would have no part in blood sports. She had ridden with him once but she was not sufficiently practised to be at ease on horseback and he had clearly found the exercise rather dull. Why teach her to ride if she wasn't going to hunt?

Ralph wrote almost weekly. At first he sought a change of heart and then a further meeting but Effie was adamant that neither could be. The letters were now composed of trivial news and thoughts – his diary, in fact, and Effie experienced a sad sinking feeling each time the envelope arrived. She chided herself. It was so small a duty to read a letter and pen a short affable acknowledgement, but it seemed to weigh heavily nonetheless. Her parents were intrigued by the regular York postmark which Effie told them was from a friend. They thought it must be a school friend but she was never forthcoming about the contents and the possibility that it was a man friend had passed through their minds. She lived in mild anxiety that he would arrive unannounced one day.

The other irksome complication to her life was John Cockcroft. He 'dropped in' as he was 'passing'. Effie could think of no good reason why he should be 'passing' so often. He remained incurably tongue-tied if they were alone together so she took him straight to the kitchen where, in direct contrast to Edward, he would chatter away to Mr and Mrs Barrett with comparative ease. To begin with Effie dutifully sat by with a look of alert interest on her face while her mind wandered far away. This, she felt, was one of the most valuable assets that her school education had endowed her with. During later visits she discovered that no-one seemed to notice if she slipped away and, latterly, as the spring gardening season set in, she merely rose from her knees and with trowel in muddy hand, took John on a very short tour of the garden.

'Look, John, those auriculas are in bud. They're a variety of Conqueror of Europe. It's a lovely dark velvety purple with a pale lemon stripe when it comes out.'

'Ah – how awfully nice.'

'The Daphne bush has been a picture this year. It has been in flower over three weeks but it's fading a bit now. You must have a look at the early daffodils along the wall in the orchard. They are full out!'

'Ah, very fine.'

The tour ended in the kitchen to the relief of both parties. Mary looked over her shoulder from the range.

'Ah, Mr Cockcroft! Lovely to see you again so soon. It brightens up my day having a little chat. My family's poor company. *He* just sits and reads and Effie's in the garden all the time.

'Do wash your hands, love, and we'll all have a mug of chocolate. The milk's just ready.'

'Oh Mother, it's not worth it; I'm going straight back. Just give me some in the old tin mug out here.'

'Nay lass. At least take tha clogs off and shut that door. It's getting fair starvin' in here,' cried Mary in exasperation.

John Cockcroft furtively surveyed the object of his admiration. It was impossible to imagine how that shapeless figure in the muddy garment was the same as the glittering princess who had floated up the hall to meet him that December evening. Well, folks aren't all the same thank goodness, and gardening was a harmless enough occupation. It showed she wasn't one of those featherbrained girls who insisted that a chap must be cracking clever jokes all the time else they would take no notice of him. Mind you, she didn't seem to be taking that much notice of him either, but he wouldn't mind starting to cultivate an interest in garden plants if that was all that was required.

As soon as John and her parents were happily chatting, Effie slipped back to her flower bed. It was against the eastern house wall and had a particular bindweed problem. At the beginning of each session, Effie dug and sifted the soil over and over through her hand fork picking out the white fleshy cylinders of root until she was certain that not one had been missed. Each summer the probing roots miraculously reappeared and by autumn some had managed to writhe to the nearby clumps of perennials and escape notice long enough to grow tall and strong. As she worked she daydreamed happily and pondered the strange truth that she was perfectly content to be alone sifting soil on her knees. She was certainly more content than she would be maintaining a laboured conversation with John or even sitting back on her heels to exchange sarcastic repartee with Edward.

PART III

The Canal

CHAPTER ONE

During her late teens, Effie's relationship with her parents had become more cordial. The main reason for this was that Mary knew her unruly daughter had grown up and what was done, was done. She had never had much influence over Effie and she could certainly have no more. The flow of potential suitors also appeased her and she could not but concede that the school had provided Effie with a sufficient veneer of gentility to satisfy the most aristocratic of the young men. Edward Carter, for instance, came from a very good family. Underwood House was quite a palace. But the foolish girl had put him off. Admittedly, there were reservations about the match on his family's side, so Effie said, but no-one could tell Mary that a young man would escort a girl anywhere he could persuade her to go for three years and not marry her if she were willing. And she seemed to actually enjoy his company! Then there was poor John Cockcroft. He was a nice lad! Nothing special to look at but right good-hearted and he doted on Effie. It must be coming up for five or six years that he had called nearly every week and would she have anything to do with him? No, not one bit of it, no encouragement. His parents were well off, second generation of a mill-owning family; homely people who just wanted to see their son happily settled. They even called one afternoon – Mr and Mrs Cockcroft. Mary gave them tea in the parlour. Effie had warned her in the morning they might come. If she had said the day before there might have been some good home baking, but no, the girl had 'forgotten to mention it' – so busy in the garden. It had even been difficult to persuade her to put on a decent dress. They had talked nice and comfortable about this and that and when Effie went to get more hot water for the tea they actually said what a lovely girl she was and how nice it would be if John and she ... Mary gave up. How many times had she said to Effie 'You ought to have that lad. He'd make you a right good husband, he would, and you'd never need for anything.' No, she'd toss her head and flounce off.

'You'll live to regret it, my girl. You're twenty-three. You'll find yourself a spinster with no chance one of these years.'

There *was* that older man. He rang the bell just after lunch one Wednesday, in the autumn. He was a proper gentleman with lovely manners and clothes. He drove up in a very smart phaeton. Effie said he came from York but she wouldn't say how he knew her. There were lots of letters she had with a York postmark. Well, she took him into the study. (The parlour had just been laid up for the winter.) They were talking there quite a time and then the carriage drove away and Effie just disappeared; must have gone up on to the canal to walk. She didn't come back until after dark and wouldn't talk about it. There weren't any more letters from York. Goodness knows what that was all about.

With each year that passed, Effie came to terms with life a little more – her own terms, of course. She could now see in perspective that eventful Christmas of 1882 which witnessed her brief celebration of being eighteen, beautiful and financially independent. She had been precipitated straight into the social demands of prenuptial gaiety and, if Ralph had had his way, it would have been indeed a brief celebration. Her tranquillity had been shattered and her day-to-day life had been disrupted by the demands of other people, which was just what she had left school to escape. She had innocently wondered whether her desires were those of her schoolfellows who seemed to find such social diversions so exhilarating. They were not, of course, and she should have known better, having lived with herself that long. The thing that amazed her was the speed and surety of the masculine response. It could not have been faster if she had just purchased a flag at

Garland's gown shop on which was emblazoned in large letters 'Here I am, eighteen and beautiful; marry me if you can!' The 'flags' still hung in her wardrobe. The cream one had been worn but once, the blue and green ones in alternation each Christmas to the Cockcrofts' family party which she attended reluctantly with her parents.

The other thing which surprised her was the prolonged nature of the havoc that this ill-considered action had wrought upon her life. Ralph had once called and had to be repulsed more firmly than ever. The faithful John still inflicted his company on her, albeit less frequently, and even Edward, now married with a baby son, dropped in for a racy chat occasionally. Effie ruefully remembered the brief but bitter pang of jealousy she had when John told her about Edward's engagement. He had watched her closely with as much feeling of malicious triumph as he was capable which, to his credit, was very little, but he had detected no outward sign of emotion on the cool face. Perhaps she lowered her eyelids a little abruptly but she was soon upbraiding herself with the reminder that she had only wanted Edward in the most superficial and physical of ways and had invariably parried his advances most discouragingly. Still, as he became older – they became older – his attraction for her deepened and their occasional encounters were gentler than they used to be. Perhaps it was only a sop to her injured pride but she felt he would probably hardly hesitate before accepting a compromising relationship with her. She wished she could hear some similar matrimonial news of Ralph. She never saw a York newspaper so it was unlikely news of him would reach her but until she knew he was safely married there was always a blemish on her peace of mind.

Such thoughts as these did not occupy Effie for long. Within a short time of being at home she had naturally slipped into a daily routine in the garden as a satellite to Jim's sun. Effie did not rise as early as he did and tended to feel a little delicate first thing so she joined him in the potting shed for a mug of tea about nine o'clock. He would already have been about for nearly four hours in the summer, breakfasted, done his bit of housework and made a start in the garden. This was the time when each indicated their plans for the day but Effie so intimately knew Jim's calendar and how it was influenced by the vagaries of the weather that there was little need for any communication beyond Jim's terse summary of the prevailing conditions.

'Fair chance this fine spell will hold for a day or two but t'soil's so sodden there's no good done turning it.'

'The late peas and carrots ought to go in but you dug enough for them last back-end, didn't you?'

'Aye, I'll just dibble them in gentle, like.'

'I'll put the sweet peas and asters and stock in, in the greenhouse. That begonia seed came yesterday – you know – those new fibrous rooted hybrids. I wonder how good they'll be in our northern clime. I had to order them from Merten's at London. I much prefer sticking to Backhouse's because they know what's all right up here. I've ordered those new alpine primulas from them. You know, the ones I showed you a picture of in *The Garden* that Mrs Webb was writing about. I'm looking forward to them coming.' Jim shook his head disapprovingly. All his working life he had been made a martyr to the growing of exotic plants which the Lord never intended should flourish in a Yorkshire garden. Just because they looked grand growing on an inaccessible mountain ledge in Tibet, where some crazy young fellow (not so young a lot of them, neither) had spent other folks' money getting to, didn't mean one was obliged to try growing them in gardens the length and breadth of the British Isles. Not that some of them didn't do surprisingly well; he had had to confess his surprise quite often, and most of them a right pretty sight too, but it still seemed to him to be interfering with nature.

It was William Parker who brought the primulas. Effie greeted him warmly.

'I was only saying to Jim yesterday that I wondered if you or your father might be able to bring my order.'

'Father died last February, I'm afraid.'

'Oh, Will. I *am* sorry.'

'It was very sudden. Better that way because he would have made a miserable invalid.'

'Yes. ... I expect you are busier than ever now.'

'Yes, unfortunately. I keep wanting to get off on a collecting trip but it's always a "particularly busy time" they say and that time never seems to come to an end.'

'The business must be doing well. I suppose that compensates a bit.'

'Yes. I shouldn't grumble but it's so *boring*. I'm not doing "proper" gardening like you, you know.'

Effie smiled. 'I thought *you* were the "proper" gardener!'

'Oh no. I am just a brass-bound professional. It's you who are the "proper" gardener, Effie. And you'd never believe the way those lower slopes of the Himalays call one back all the time. They are so incredibly beautiful. It is like being in a huge conservatory that goes on and on revealing more treasures each time one turns.'

'I wonder if I should like it,' pondered Effie. 'I get so much pleasure from the things I can grow outside here. It always seems a little bit like cheating to grow things under cover – all the time I mean.'

'But those mountain valleys aren't cheating. Everything is wild there,' said William indignantly.

'Of course! You must take me next time you go – but then maybe I shan't be satisfied in a Yorkshire garden any more.'

'I think you will. I shall write and tell you when to get ready. But why not come to visit my establishment? Come over to York for a day. Come and see our alpine greenhouse in May!'

As Effie thought about the light-hearted proposal to go collecting with William she began to realize how self-contained her little world had become. She hardly spoke to anyone except Jim and Mrs Sugden or her parents. Edward Carter and

John Cockcroft rarely came now and she had not heard from Ralph for nearly two years, fortunately. Her relationship with William had survived unchanged since her childhood. She always enjoyed his teasing good humour because he respected her plantsmanship and treated her fondly, but primarily as someone who shared his life's passion. She could not imagine the encumbrance of marriage ever entering his head and so he presented no threat to her independence. The lure of exotic plants and adventure had seemed attractive for a moment but, although he would write, she doubted if she would go with him. She was not yet confident that her world was robust enough to survive that and, anyway, she could not possibly leave Lily now.

CHAPTER TWO

'Jim, William has invited us to go over to York to see his greenhouses. He says May will be best for the alpines. Shall we go over for a day? We could go by the train. It only takes an hour.' Jim grunted and picked up his fork and hoe. It was a waste of breath making excuses. If she wanted him to go to York with her, go he would have to. He smiled gently to himself as he strode along the flagged path remembering that eventful trip to Leeds which led to the start of the pond and the pets. The pond was developing. It should look quite well established this season but Lily was near the end of her time. For the last few years she had barely left Effie's side and now Effie found herself pacing very slowly from one part of the garden to another for the sake of the stiff old bitch. She had started to drink rather a lot lately which worried Effie and now her belly seemed bloated and big although each bone of her spine showed through her skin.

'Jim?' Effie was seated on her customary box in the potting shed fondling the velvet ears and looking sadly at the old grey muzzle.

'Jim, Lily's drinking a lot lately. She's always thirsty and she seems thin on her back but her belly is so fat.'

'Aye, she's got dropsy.'

'Should I stop her from drinking so much?'

'Nay, there's nowt that tha can do. She ent in pain, is she?'

'No, I'm sure she's not. I wonder if the farrier could do something – or even Dr Smith?'

'Nay, nay lass. She's just old. People go the same and t'doctor comes and tells them not to do this and that, and take some pills and concoctions – foxglove and the like – but they all go the same way only it troubles them more.'

'You think it's better not to bother her?'

'Aye. That's the way I shall want it. I shan't want anyone fussing round trying to give me another week or two that I ent able to enjoy.'

'Yes, you're right, Jim.'

For the last few months of Lily's life Effie didn't walk further than the canal. They would rest at the lock chatting to Mrs Sugden and the boatmen. Effie knew most of the regulars by now.

'Hallo, Mr Pierce. You're back this way quickly!'

'Aye. It's fair surprised me, miss. The governor's got a lot o' mill machinery on order from Marshall's and since Mattie's coming home next week and I wanted to be back at Wigan, I said I'd fit in a quick run straight back.'

'Mattie's your youngest son in the army?'

'Aye, that's right, miss. He's a champion lad. Bit wild yer know – wouldn't come on to the boats before he'd seen summat o' the world. He's seen *that* right enough now, so maybe he'll settle down.'

'How long has he been away?'

'Three years come back-end. He's been out in India. He

177

were in the Lancashire Fusiliers! Edie, that's me wife, used to buy the newspaper every day to see what was happening to t'war but she can't read a letter and I aren't much better and none of the folks around could do it good enough for her so she used to take it down to the Yorkshire Penny Bank in t'town each afternoon and get one o' the banking gentlemen to read it for her.'

'Was there usually much news?'

'Well ... aye ... They usually used to say such and such a company were hengaged in a hencounter near ... (and then some Indian name what she forgot on the way home), and the casualties was slight.'

'It didn't tell you anything very useful about Mattie, then!'

'Oh, nay. But his mother dotes on him, I know one oughtn't to say it, but he's really been her favourite of them all – and the worst bother – and it made her feel she were doing something.'

Effie nodded gravely.

'Now I must be on. Jack there has just got his boat out of my path. If I can get Mattie to take to the boats for a bit, I'll bring him up to meet you. He's a grand lad and a regular ladies' man! You see you're here, lass.' He winked wickedly at her. Effie was pleased to hear the 'lass' – so much more comfortable than 'miss'.

Fred Pierce was as good as his word. He and Mattie brought a boat down a few weeks later. Effie wasn't around but Mrs Sugden said they'd send a message down in front of them next time. It was reported that a message sent along the canal from Liverpool or Leeds reached the other city faster than a fly-boat could. Mr Pierce and Mattie would be at the lock about lunchtime next day, Mrs Sugden told Effie. Effie laughed.

'Well, I suppose I must come just to please Fred Pierce.'

'I don't rightly know if tha should,' replied Mrs Sugden darkly. 'The lad looks right enough but I've heard tales ...'

'What sort of tales?'

178

'Oh, mayn't be true. Maybe just boat-gossip, but even his father says he's a wild one, don't he?'

'Don't you worry about me, Mrs Sugden. I can look after myself,' laughed Effie.

'Many's the lass that has said that and been proved wrong,' said Mrs Sugden sourly.

Effie walked home smiling. If the old lady only knew what adventures she had had and survived reasonably unscathed, she wouldn't be worrying about her meeting a young boatman probably as illiterate as his parents.

Effie and Lily strolled up to the canal next day about twelve o'clock and half an hour later Fred's boat came under the humped-back road bridge. Effie appraised the figure walking beside the horse as she went to meet them. He was smartly dressed in a conspicuously new blue waistcoat and the traditional wide-bottomed trousers. His white shirt sleeves were rolled up and a jaunty red neckerchief was tied to one side. He wore his curly brown hair quite long and the wind ruffled it across his straight forehead. Effie was immediately surprised by his slender build and height. (His father was short and stocky like most of the boat people.) His clear blue eyes were deep set and his delicately boned nose curved slightly to give him a dignity of mien which was engagingly contradicted by his humorous curved lips. Effie was quite taken aback. She could not conceive how Fred Pierce had procreated a son with such distinguished good looks, but she remained mistress of her thoughts enough to say saucily,

'Mr Mattie Pierce, I believe?' and hold out her hand.

'The bonny Miss Barrett!' he responded gravely but as he took her hand he smiled mischievously, his right lip lifting a little more than the left with an engaging asymmetry.

I could well believe some of Mrs Sugden's tales, thought Effie.

'I reckon Faither rather underestimated with his "raight bonny lass" tale, tha know.' He spoke in a soft deep voice as if to himself so Effie had to look up at his face to gauge the

179

nature of this remark. The expression of rapt admiration left her in no doubt.

How silly, she told herself. Fancy not knowing what to say to a young boatman, as if it mattered what I say, really. I must just be friendly in an off-hand way.

'Are you missing the army?'

'I were rather, this morning. Life on the cut's a bit much of a muchness usually, tha know.'

'Do you think you will stick it?'

'I shall give it a fair try – a year maybe. It isn't so easy to get a better job at the moment – not without training and I feel too restless for that.'

'Couldn't you have made a career in the army?'

'Aye, that I could. They wanted to make me a sergeant which ent at all bad at my age.' His voice sounded rather bitter. Effie raised her brows interrogatively.

'Well, would you have had me cold and dead now?' he asked her, laughing. 'That's how it would have likely been. The war was hotting up. More casualties every day. I didn't mind when I first went out, the hotter the action and the more there was of it, the better I liked it. But I suppose I've grown older. Had time to see what a lot being alive has to be said for it, like.' He put his head on one side and smiled challengingly at her.

'No, that seems very sensible. I don't approve of war and I always think how foolish of young men to rush out eagerly to get killed or badly injured, which might be worse.'

'I'm very glad to hear that. I thought you might tell me that I was an unpatriotic coward.' They laughed together, sharing his relief and the subtle compliment it implied.

'Here! Some of us has to get the day's work done yer know. Move yourselves out of my path so I can get t'horse free,' said his father. They had reached the lock and Mattie spun about, took the rope, made fast the boat and, with Effie's help, pushed the beam to close the top lock chamber. They leant against it chatting while the boat sank.

'So tha lives nearby?'

180

'Yes, just the other side of the river.' He nodded thoughtfully. She had been expecting she would need to make him feel at ease but he was completely master of the situation.

'Do you have many friends here about?'

'No, hardly any. I am afraid I am rather an unfriendly person.'

'I can't believe that.'

'No, really. I just enjoy being on my own.'

He smiled as if at a private joke and stooped to fondle Lily. 'She's getting on!'

'Yes, she's fourteen. How did you know she was a bitch?'

'By the expression on her face of course! No-one with any feeling for dogs can mistake that.'

'No?' queried Effie with interest.

'Nay!' he smiled. 'It's the way they behave too. Bitches are always more sort of soft and seeking. They never greet you all bouncy and their tails up like a dog does. They always look a bit as if they are expecting you might chide them. Same as women and men tha know!'

Effie smiled thoughtfully.

'I know just what you mean about dogs but I don't think I go about as if I'm expecting to be told off.'

'Nay? Maybe you're prouder than most but it's more concealed like with women, anyway.' He laughed at her surprised face and patted her shoulder in farewell.

'We should be back tomorrow teatime, all being well – shouldn't we, Father?'

'Aye. About then. We should get loaded quick with the two of us on the job, lad.'

'See you then, perhaps?' He cast her a slightly wistful smile as he leapt lightly aboard.

Effie usually managed to be at the lock when Mattie and Fred Pierce passed through. She often deceived herself into believing that she was too busy in the garden and wouldn't bother but somehow she felt the need for a change of scenery and

181

unaccountably found herself and Lily strolling up to the canal at about the appointed time. The last time that they went together, Effie realized with grief that it was almost too much for the old dog. She was panting hard and sat down frequently for a moment or two regarding Effie with such a beseeching apology. Mattie met them on the road just before the steep incline to the towpath. Effie looked up thankfully into his carefree face.

'Ah, there thou are,' he said happily. 'I thought Newlay three-rise was going to be disappointing for me today.' He noticed Effie's sad expression as he spoke.

'Poor old Lily's slowed up ent she?'

'Yes, she's not at all well, I'm afraid. She's thirsty all the time.' He bent down to fondle her sadly.

'Don't grieve too much about Lily, lass. She's had a right good life and it's got to end soon. She's got you and that's what matters to her. Promise me you'll bear up brave, lass?' He was looking up earnestly into her face still holding Lily's head between his hands.

'Y – yes, I promise; I'll try.' She gazed down at him abjectly. An expression of anguish floated over his face and he stood up, taking her by the shoulders and bending forward as if to kiss her forehead, but stopped short.

'Tha needs someone,' he said softly, shaking his head. 'I must catch Father up. We're coming back Thursday.'

Effie was not at the lock on Thursday because Lily had stopped eating and lay looking miserably sick. Each drink she took, she vomited back. Effie sat up that night stroking the soft skin that clung to the hard edges of her skull and moistening the inside of her dry lips with water. She hoped each time the patient brown eyes opened that she would not have long to suffer. Effie must have dozed off, for she was roused by Lily moving and found the old dog's legs stretched out rigidly in a final convulsion. She could see that the staring eyes were no longer aware and waited in anguish until the body was limp

182

and still. She sat silently for a long time, remembering the homeward journey from Leeds with the tiny warm bundle held tenderly inside her coat; the many, many scenes of war with her parents on Lily's behalf; the demented welcomes when she returned from school; the puppies and the years of undemanding companionship. As the grey sky began to lighten, she wrapped the black body in an old blanket and carried it downstairs to the front door, laid it down to draw the bolt, remembered a similar emotional exit nearly fifteen years ago, then took her burden to the potting shed where she bestowed a final quick kiss on the velvet ear and covered it up again.

Effie felt very much alone when she joined Jim at nine o'clock. As she expected, there was no sign of Lily. She sipped her tea in silence. Jim broke it.

'She didn't have to wait long.'

'No.'

'She's under the syringa near the walnut.'

'Oh good. I was thinking of there. Thank you very much, Jim.'

CHAPTER THREE

Although she had been up all night, Effie knew she would not sleep if she went to bed, so after the morning mug of tea she began to work in the garden. She could not settle to it. Strangely enough, it was not Lily that occupied her thoughts so much as Mattie. Her mourning for Lily had been effective. She had anticipated her death for several days and she had had the solitude of the small hours of that morning to relive their life together, to reaffirm that it had been happy and free from reproach; then she had wept a bit and closed that volume of the book. Lily was no more and Effie was alone except for Jim.

She remembered exactly the same intensity of loneliness after her grandfather died. She rose from her work and found Jim. She watched him hoe to loosen the earth where he had trodden to plant the beans. He knew she was there but could think of no adequate word of comfort so he just carried on hoeing. The easy regularity of the movement soothed Effie.

'Jim, I don't feel like working. I think I shall go for a long walk along the canal.'

'Aye. I'll tell tha mother and father.'

'Thanks, Jim. Tell them I shall be out all day. Tell them about Lily, please. They don't know.'

Stifling a sob she ran out of the garden as she was, in her old gardening coat and muddy clogs. As soon as she reached the canal bank she turned under the road bridge and stepped out briskly towards Rodley. Her clogs were comfortable so she had no regrets about those but the coat was very shabby and dirty – but whom would she meet that mattered? Well? For the first time it consciously occurred to her that somewhere, ten or twelve miles ahead, there must be Mattie. Her heart leapt. She had always fled to the canal to walk away life's tribulations and now it was blessed with the pleasant association of Mattie; it was her obvious refuge but she was certain she hadn't thought of finding him before that moment. She broke into a trot and by lunchtime she was passing through Saltaire. She began to feel a bit hungry and it occurred to her that she had no money. She stopped on the towpath by Sir Titus Salt's chapel and felt hopefully in her pockets: one empty seed packet screwed up, a muddy handkerchief, a slightly cleaner one and a hairpin. She smiled at the sorry collection in her hands. She could afford to be nonchalant about poverty because she had never known it and, fortunately, was never likely to. By two o'clock she was reaching the outskirts of Bingley. She had never been so far along the canal but she knew that just beyond, on the other side of the town, lay the famous five-rise locks, where boats could be held up for a couple of hours or more. She was eager to see Bingley five-rise for the first time and surely Mattie and

Fred would be there. Her pace quickened. The canal ran beside some mills and a steep wooded bank rose on the right-hand side and then, just beyond – the impressive rise of the locks. From a distance it looked as if the five gates were perched one on top of the other in a vertical tower. There were three boats waiting below but the Wigan one was not among them. She climbed the steeply stepped towpath in awe and scanned the boats at the top. One was drawing away upstream but it was not theirs. Quite a flotilla was waiting at the top post. Effie chose a smartly turned-out Liverpool boat.

'Have you passed Fred Pierce, please?'

'Aye, miss. He's just round t'field bend.' The man eyed her curiously. If it hadn't been for her accent, he'd have passed her off as a local farm lass but her face looked well-bred too. Strange!

She set off briskly and as she came round the bend there was the familiar red and green transome decoration.

'Mr Pierce; Mattie,' she called.

Mattie was walking with the horse. He turned, recognized her and exclaimed in surprise.

'Effie, lass!' He had never called her by her name before. He rapidly took in the details of the dishevelled figure running towards him, pale face, puffy eyes, shabby coat, clogs and windblown hair, and held out his arms in time to catch her.

'Oh, Mattie.'

'Is it Lily?' She broke into loud sobs so he pressed her head to his shoulder and stroked her tousled hair.

'Don't tha stop, Father,' he called over his shoulder, 'it's all right.'

'Yes, it's all right,' sang Effie's heart. 'It feels as right as anything ever has.' She wished that time would stand still and never start again. He gently lifted her chin and pulled his neckerchief off to dry her face.

'Is that better now, lass? Let's get off the towpath. It's uncomfortably like Piccadilly on a bank holiday.' She smiled up trustingly at him but her knees seemed to have given way.

He released her but she began to sink to the ground so he lifted her in his arms and scrambled down the banking, over a fence and along beside a stone wall until it bent round to conceal a corner of rough grass and brambles in the lee of a wood. He laid his burden down on some tussocky grass as lightly and tenderly as if it were a sleeping child. He knelt with her shoulders still in his arms and kissed each moist eye. She smiled up and he kissed her lips with mounting passion.

'Has tha walked all the way from Newlay?'

'Yes. I just wanted to get away and walk and then I remembered that I could perhaps catch you up.'

'And your clothes?'

'Oh yes. It's just what I garden in.' She searched his face anxiously. 'I must look a terrible mess. And my face – with crying.'

'Nay, lass, it don't matter one trifle to me. You're so beautiful. You're better like this. I feel I might stand a chance of having you.' They slowly kissed again, his lips gentle and soft then pressing harder to open her mouth and explore inside. She allowed him to and tasted the slightly metallic flavour of his saliva.

'When did Lily go?'

'Last night.' Her lips began to quiver.

'Nay, nay. Don't tha grieve. It was best like that. Have you been up all night?' She nodded.

'What have you had to eat?'

'Not much, I didn't feel like breakfast and I came away without any money.'

'Oh, love. No wonder you couldn't walk any more. What are we going to do with tha?' Effie shook her head as she smiled up at him.

'I'm perfectly happy. I just want to stay here with you.' He kissed her and held her close.

'I only wish we could. No troubles, no need of food or money or shelter.' He sighed deeply, shook his head and clenched his teeth so that his jaw muscles stood out, gazing at her in troubled love. She tried to smooth the lines of worry away with her fingertips and he held his head on one side and smiled in the asymmetrical way that charmed her.

'I wonder why your lip lifts more that side?' He shook his head. 'It always has.' He smiled teasingly to show even more of his white teeth. She kissed the offending lip. 'It fascinates me so much.'

'Aye? I can't think why, but I've been told that before,' he mused aloud. Effie experienced a sharp pang of jealousy. For some inexplicable reason, it had never crossed her mind that other women had lain in these arms but of course they must have … His father … 'a raight ladies' man' … Mrs Sugden … 'tales'.

'Nay lass. Don't tha look at me like that!' He was no longer smiling. He looked annoyed. 'It just slipped off my tongue and meant nothing in particular. I've never been really sweet on a girl – not deeply so, you understand, and I ent got a lass at the moment – except this one and she's very, very particular.' He ran his free hand over her face gently, moving her hair back from her forehead and exploring the crevices near her nostrils. They were rough hands and the broken bits of skin pricked but she relished his touch so much.

'But what *are* we going to do with tha, love? I just cannot decide, which is rare for me.' She let her head fall back so that she could see a line of dead cock's-foot grass heads and an umbel of Sweet Cecily engraved against the grey sky. She felt delightfully light and disembodied as if she could float in this irresponsible limbo of love for ever.

'Let's see if tha can walk.' He helped her up. She could stand now but felt very light-headed. He put his arm round her waist and they walked slowly across the field to a stile in the wall.

'Where are we going?' she asked as he lifted her down.

'There's a little farm along this path where Father gets eggs. They're good people. I knew them when I was a lad. They'll give us summat to eat and drink and when you feel stronger, we'll catch up Harry Ackroyd. He passed us just above five-rise so he'll be aiming to get to Dobson's Lock tonight, I reckon. Father would know for sure but I'm only green,' he explained with his smile. 'I'm sure he will arrange to get you home from there.' Effie clung to him in dismay.

'I want you to come, Mattie. Please don't leave me.'

'We'll see, lass. Let's get some victuals in us and think again after. I'm rare famished so I don't know how you must be.' They went on their way. A field before the farm, Mattie insisted that she walked unsupported.

'We don't want to make a bad impression on the Thomases, lass. They'd wonder about the like of me taking liberties with you, wouldn't they eh?' He grinned mischievously at her.

'I could always slap you when we got to the doorway.'

'I don't relish being slapped.' He felt his cheek reminiscently and noticed Effie's eyes flare up again and then be cajoled back to peace by his teasing smile.

Mr and Mrs Thomas welcomed them in, set them in the inglenook of the old farmhouse fireplace and overwhelmed them with tea, scones and home-made bread garnished with half-inch thick slices of ham and boiled eggs. Effie still felt strangely irresponsible and able to live from moment to moment in the most unusual way. She had not realized how hungry she was; the tea and food tasted better than she could ever remember and, as she ate, she looked across the table at Mattie's face – so infinitely dear to her. The dancing firelight made his eyes sparkle and his cheeks look warm and rough. He was keeping up a steady flow of pleasantries to their hosts. She didn't listen to what he said but just to the timbre of his soft deep voice and watched the profile of his nose and mouth change as he turned his head in the firelight. It was such an intelligent, lively face and so handsome.

He wondered what the Thomases thought of this strange visit. They had not seen him since he was a lad but they were sure to have heard frequently of his exploits from his father and the knowing look such folks often gave him made him wonder where else they had their information from. Effie's appearance was not easy to explain. He merely said she was a friend who had walked a long way and was not feeling very well and since she seemed disinclined to talk, perhaps they would think she was just a local girl. Whatever misgivings the Thomases may have had they kept to themselves and bade their uninvited guests the warmest of farewells, urging them to call again. Effie roused herself to thank them most sincerely for their hospitality and assure them that she felt so much better that she could safely make her journey home. Mattie seemed discomforted as she spoke. They set off towards Bingley, keeping to footpaths across the fields rather than the towpath. Effie realized that Mattie did not want them to be victims of the canal gossip and that disappointed her slightly because she had hoped he would be above caring. Still, she reminded herself, this was his life. It must be more important to him because he spent every day meeting these people. She was half regretting her protestations of renewed strength: she would have liked to have felt his arm supporting her again. She brushed against him as they walked and he took her hand, smiling tenderly down at her.

'I don't want to leave you and be all alone again, Mattie.'

'But tha must. As much as I should like it, we've nowhere to go together and my father needs me and your parents need you.'

'No they don't. They'll be worried when I'm not home but they don't *need* me. Only Jim does – leastways, I think he does. And Lily doesn't any more ...' Her voice faltered. He put his arms round her and kissed her cheek.

'Well, it ent that I don't want tha, love. I do, terribly strong, but it can't be.' Their eyes searched each other's.

How often had she heard these words? A simple proposition of mutual happiness stabbed and cast aside – '... it can't be ...' These words were spoken by people she loved, to reject the simple and obvious expedient she had proposed. There was Grandfather submitting to a social barrier as if he were powerless; Jim refusing to let her live in his cottage, and now

Mattie. Each time she knew they were acting in her own interest as they saw it but she was still sure that they did not see true. She and they were strong enough together to surmount mere social conventions.

Her mouth puckered with pain. This rejection seemed deeper and more devastating than the others. Mattie had suddenly and mysteriously filled every void in her body and soul. For the moment, the garden and Jim presented themselves to her as sacrificial objects which she would offer to him.

'It doesn't matter about my house, Mattie. I need you.' Surely he would appreciate this gesture of self-denial; of utter surrender? But his eyes did not melt tenderly. They were looking into her – no, through her – with an almost hard quality in their passionate intensity. She had glimpsed it before in Ralph's eyes and in Edward's. It was only her body that these men desired with an involuntary compulsion to which the sensitive complexity of her mind was irrelevant. Her knowledge of love and her experience led her to accept a man's procreative function as a biological fact to which women must acquiesce but it frightened her to see how utterly it enslaved Mattie. How it excluded any finer perception at a moment when she was preparing to commit her whole life to him. He seemed to have barely heard her words. His hands moved caressingly across her shoulders, spanned her waist, pressed her buttocks so that her pelvis was held tight to his. She felt awe at the size and hardness of his penis compressed between their bellies. He shut his eyes as if battling with his thoughts and then moved his hands to her shoulders and pushed her firmly away. His face had a look of anguish as he shook his head.

'Nay, love. Don't let me. I'm no good to you. You are playing Eve teasing me like this.'

'I am *not* teasing,' she pleaded. 'I meant it.'

'But tha's not thought it out.' His voice was still reproachful. Effie's spirit began to rise and, with growing indignation, she said, 'I don't say things I don't mean. I have just offered to leave everything for you and all you say is that.'

'But what would folks say? You're a lady and wealthy. They would say as it was me trying to better myself easy like.'

'And you would mind *so* much?' Effie's voice held a note of derision.

'Nay, Effie love. Try to understand me. I *am* proud but I could swallow that for you if that would make it right. But it wouldn't. I've seen more of the world than you have and if you can't see, you must take my word for it. We should not be happy. It ent as easy as that.'

The old familiar words and, fourteen years older, she still had to bow to them.

CHAPTER FOUR

The next three weeks dragged by wearily for Effie. As soon as she woke in the morning she thought of Mattie. She wondered what he was doing at that moment. Was he having breakfast in a little cottage kitchen and was his mother watching him fondly as he ate? Was he looking up to smile his dear wry smile at her? Perhaps he was on the boat with his father on their way down the canal. She walked up to chat with Mrs Sugden as naturally as she could contrive but there was never any message. Once, Effie had allowed herself to ask after Fred Pierce, just in case Mrs Sugden had let a message slip her mind. The stout old woman eyed her sharply.

'He may have slipped past but I ent noticed him and I ent heard no talk o' that son Mattie of his just lately, barring that he were seen with a farming lass up beyond Bingley five-rise a bit back. I wouldn't know what folks meant by "seen" but they said it meaningful like.' It may have been Effie's slight start that made Mrs Sugden look hard at her or it may have been her guilty conscience that made her imagine it.

High spring was breaking in the garden. There was now a profusion of different daffodils out but their sunny splendour seemed somehow tawdry to Effie this year. As she walked through the garden each day she would idly note the first species tulip to open, the earliest narcissus, a new alpine gentian but her old glowing enthusiasm for these things was gone as surely as Mattie had gone. Over the last few days, an unheralded conviction had settled on her that Mattie had left his father and the boat and would never come down the canal again. Her eyes lacked lustre and her appetite failed.

Mary was hanging up the washing in the garden when Jim walked up deferentially. Mary stopped in surprise with two pegs sticking out of her mouth.

'Morning, Mrs Barrett.'

'Morning, Jim.' He surveyed the muddy toecaps on his clogs.

'Miss Effie don't seem herself?'

'Nay, she don't seem right at all. I suppose it's the dog but fancy taking on so long.'

'I doubt if it's t'dog. I thought maybe she were ill?'

'Well, if she is she hadn't said nowt to me and I keep inquiring because she ent eating proper.'

Effie was pricking out some seedlings in the greenhouse the next morning when a boy of about twelve came up the drive. He saw her and walked over.

'I've a letter for Miss Barrett, please, miss.'

'I'm Miss Barrett,' said Effie in surprise.

'Aye!' he replied, smiling. He took off his knitted gloves and undid his jacket and fumbled about the inside pocket to pull out a pale blue envelope and hand it to her.

'Who gave it to you?'

'It were young Mr Pierce, boatman, you know.' Effie's heart leapt.

'W-what's your name?'

'Jerry Thomas.'

'Do you know Mr Pierce?'

'He comes to our farm for eggs, miss. Lot of the boat folk does.'

'Oh, do you live in that farm over near Bingley five-rise?'

'Aye, miss.' He smiled knowingly at her again and she guessed he had seen them together that teatime.

'He gave it to me yesterday because me dad told him we was coming over to Horsforth to pick up some ewes.'

'Is your father outside?'

'Nay, he dropped me at the top of the hill and said to meet him at Harry Raistrick's farm.'

'Well, thanks. You come round to the kitchen and I'll find you sixpence and some buns.'

'Ooh, thanks, miss.'

Effie saw him off and returned to the greenhouse, her hand clutching the letter in her pocket. It was not until she sat down on the wooden box that she realized she dare not open it. She drew it reluctantly out of her pocket trying to control her shaking hand. The handwriting was large and confident, sprawling as if hurriedly written.

'Miss E. Barrett'

'Oakroyd'.

With an effort she reached for her penknife lying by the raffia switch and cut open the seal, and slowly unfolded the page. Her heart was beating painfully.

'My dearest Effie,

I write this in haste against my better judgement.

I have been thinking of you every day – nay – every moment. I have been thinking that I was far too forward with you and it perhaps pains you to think of it now. I know that is the way it should be but it rails me so hard to feel you think badly of me when I was just carried away by my love for you and each day that passes makes you seem more dear to me.

I should tear this letter up now. If it reaches you, you must do so.

Please forgive me and grant that this hasty note has given me relief and I hope not pained you further. I promise you won't hear from me again.

Yours always,
Mattie.'

Effie jumped up, clasping the letter between both hands and pressing her lips to them in a gesture of happy ecstasy. Why, she didn't really know. The letter said nothing but that he loved her and was worried that she thought he had behaved badly. The impression Effie had of their last meeting was that he had every right to think that of her. In fact, he told her as much. But, he loved her still and the only thing that mattered was that they were apart. Her first impulse was to run up to Raistrick's farm and intercept the Thomases but what could they do? They might not see him again for weeks. What was he doing at their farm? He must have been with a boat but surely he would have continued to Leeds having got to this side of the Pennines. Why not send a message to her the old way? The thought that he might at any moment be passing along the canal bank distracted her. For the lack of any more constructive plan, she pushed the letter into her pocket and ran up to the canal. There was one boat coming up through the lock but it was an unkempt local boat carrying manure and turfs manned by a farm labourer. She waved to Mrs Sugden at the window and set off upstream feeling so unaccountably heady and light-hearted that she was barely aware of what she passed. The cool spring breeze ran through her hair and being like an intoxicating liquor. It must be that sort of feeling that makes the pale green shoots push through the winter earth and the buds burst and young leaves unfurl, she thought. She felt the same exhilaration as when the spring clouds blow across to briefly darken the sky and lighten the landscape with a flurry of hail. After a time she calmed down sufficiently to notice the origin of the boats she passed. She was seeking a Wigan-based boat. She guessed that Mattie would not approve of her seeking information but she could think of no other way of finding him and find him she must. Perhaps when she reached Apperley Bridge, they would not associate her with the usual stretch of canal. She would try to find a man she didn't know. Between Rodley and Dobson's Lock, she found what she wanted. The bright swathe of roses had 'Brown and Sons, Wigan' in bold three-dimensional blocked characters curved beneath it.

'Hallo.'

'Hallo, miss.'

'Nice sunny day.'

'Aye, grand for them as has time to enjoy it,' smiled the stout middle-aged boatman pacing up the path beside his horse. His wife held the up-curved tiller.

'Do you come from Wigan?'

'Aye, just below.'

'You'd know Fred Pierce then?'

'Aye.'

'Have you seen his boat recently?' He considered carefully.

'Nay, not on this trip.'

'How about his son?'

'Which one would that be? Tom who works the docks at Liverpool or Fred, his eldest?'

'No, the youngest one, Mattie.' A broad grin creased his face.

'Well ... I have heard tell a lot of young Mattie but they do say he seems to have settled since he came back from the army. In fact,' his face puckered up in an effort of recollection.

'Yes, what?' asked Effie eagerly.

'Ah reckon someone said t'other day he had changed his trade.' Effie's face fell.

'Aye, I remember now – only t'other week he got to be skipper on one of them horse-drawn fly-boats.'

'What, those express passenger ones?'

'Aye, that's it. They ply between Skipton and Liverpool, his firm. Take a lot of them immigrants from hereabouts on to the big liners at Liverpool. Can't see why they ups and goes so far away, myself. There may be more brass out there but, there again, there may not. At least we know our own devils here. Still, there's nowt so queer as folks.'

Effie sighed with relief. At each pause she had eagerly opened her mouth to guide him back to Mattie but he had ponderously continued.

'Will you see him on your way back?'

'Well, I may and on t'other hand I may not.' He saw the despairing expression on her face.

'If it's a message tha'd like taken, I daresay I can guarantee to get it delivered even if I don't actually see him myself.'

'That would be fine. I'll write him a note. Oh, have you got a piece of paper and a pencil?' He felt helplessly in his waistcoat pocket and then glanced lamely at the boat.

'Nay, I can't say as I have. We sign the lock toll but they allus has a pencil there for that job.'

If she could borrow a pencil she could write on the back of Mattie's letter but she was loath to let that go.

'Look, there's a cottage over the field. I'll go to see if I can borrow a pencil or pen and paper there and then I'll catch you up.'

'Right you are, miss. We can't stray far off t'cut,' he joked.

As she sped across the fields she wondered what she was going to write. The message had seemed simple enough – 'Mattie, nothing to forgive. I love you. I'm coming.' Practical arrangements for meeting seemed rather trivial but nevertheless essential. She could ask him where and when he could meet her but that meant two more messages and she couldn't wait.

'My dear Mattie,

Thankyou for your letter. I thought no such thing of you and am needing you desperately. I shall tell my parents that I have been asked to spend next weekend away and I shall be

196

at the Castle in Skipton on Saturday at two o'clock and I shall wait until you come or send a message.

All my love.

Effie.'

Effie folded and sealed the letter, wrote 'Mr Mattie Pierce' on the outside and thanked the woman at the cottage. She arrived back on the towpath and ran panting for half a mile or so until she caught up the boatman.

'There you are. I should be terribly grateful if you would see he gets that as soon as possible.' The man must have been deliberating upon his mission as he had walked and his jowly face was looking concerned.

''Ere, missy. I know it ent any o' my business – none at all – but I were just thinking how a young lady like you didn't want to take up with the likes of young Mattie Pierce – but then I don't know what's written in your letter and it ent any o' my business, anyways.' Effie felt like saying 'No – so you just mind what is,' but she mustn't be rude to her ungainly Eros.

'Why are the likes of Mattie Pierce so bad?' she asked. The boatman turned to appraise her slowly.

'I'm nay saying he's "bad". I'm just saying he's got himself into trouble once or twice – woman-trouble you know. They do say that were why he took off into the army sharpish like but there may be no truth in it. I daresay it's harder to keep clear of such when tha's blessed with a face and figure the lasses all fall sweet on.' He smiled impishly at Effie. 'They do say one's blessings may be disguised and that just goes to show what a blessing an ugly mug the like o' mine may be, eh? Though I found it difficult to think of it like that when I were younger.'

Effie laughed and bid him goodbye and not to forget her letter.

'Nay, rest assured, lass. It will be delivered and however unwise that may be, only tha and he will know!'

CHAPTER FIVE

Effie was at the Castle gate just after one o'clock. She had given a great deal of thought to what she should wear. She wanted to redeem her terribly forlorn appearance at their last meeting and yet he had assured her that he liked her best that way, out of kindness no doubt, but she had shied firmly away from looking too sophisticated and had left her hair loose. If she knew whether he would be wearing his working clothes or be in his best suit, it would help. She supposed that he must have a best suit – but maybe he had grown out of it these last three years and had not been able to afford to replace it yet. She yearned to have him in her care and indulged in delicious fantasies of how superb his mature but graceful figure would look when she took him to the best tailors in Leeds – or even London – and fitted him with the smartest of morning suits, afternoon and evening suits. She would be proud to be seen with him. Oh – what frivolous fantasies! Had her bitter experiences of eighteen taught her so little about life's priorities, after all? However could such a proud man enjoy being her plaything anyway? But she looked very comely herself as she paced impatiently round the paved approach to the arched gateway. She wore her grey waisted astrakhan coat and below the hem showed the skirt of a demure grey dress, high buttoned and trimmed in black. A small feathery black straw cap was set forwards on her head, slightly restraining her long ash-blonde hair.

From her vantage point she could look down the length of the wide High Street which was bustling with market-day activity. Stalls and booths, some with new, brightly coloured tarpaulin, lined each side, and a steady stream of gigs and chaises from nearby villages moved up and down between them. She knew he was unlikely to be there yet but a tiny quiver of disappointment ran through her as she scanned the unfamiliar faces passing by. She walked along to look at the nearby stalls, glancing hopefully towards the gateway every now and then. She bought some home-made fudge and treacle toffee with nuts in. She spoke to a jolly farmer's wife about her Wensleydale cheeses and bought a tiny one. She thought how her mother would like a stoneware casserole but hesitated to clutter herself up with parcels of that size. She hardly ever went shopping at home and it was a pleasant diversion to look at the wealth of attractive things that one could buy in a country market. There was basketwork from Craven and old men and women selling their knitting, socks, jerseys and cardigans. Some were even sitting on stools by their wares knitting away with one long needle held steady in a carved wooden sheath which fitted into their belts. She couldn't resist a heavy jersey for Jim and then there was Mattie of course. She glanced towards the Castle but there was no sign of him. She had never bought him a present! The idea delighted her and she set off to carry out a survey of all the hand-knitted waistcoats for sale. There were several she liked but she was finally oscillating between one in two shades of green with a little red and a blue and grey one while the tiny wrinkled old man who had made them sat imperturbably knitting. The blue went with his eyes and his working trousers, she decided.

'I'll take this one please.'

'Aye. Is t'size all right?'

'Oh, I hadn't thought of that.'

'Well, how big is he? Bigger than me, I reeckon?' He grinned gummily and Effie frowned.

'About as big as that gentleman.' She indicated the back of a man who had paused at the adjacent stall and who turned at that moment to find himself under the scrutiny of Effie and the tiny old man.

Effie smiled, embarrassed.

'We was just doing a bit of ready reckoning,' explained the

old man perkily. 'This lady's young man is just about your size, you see.'

Effie's composure was not improved by having assumptions about her private life aired publicly nor by the very plain features of the model she had inadvertently chosen. However, he seemed charmed and insisted upon unbuttoning his jacket for a cursory fitting. The old man was so tiny and bent that he couldn't reach to perform this office, so Effie had to conceal her exasperation as best she could and hold the garment up to his shoulders.

'By gum. He's a lucky fellow, ent he?' quipped the model. Effie smiled grimly.

'Yes, that will do nicely, thank you,' she said to the old man. 'And thank *you* very much, most kind,' smiling an icy dismissal to the model.

'Sure tha wouldn't have me stand in for him a bit longer – like to buy tha a cup of tea?' he asked smiling earnestly.

'Oh, no thank you,' simpered Effie. 'I am meeting him quite soon.' That seemed to discourage him at the cost of a little more privacy.

How do I manage to get in such a muddle as soon as I step out in some smart clothes? she wondered in annoyance. It must be as the boatman was saying the other day, I suppose, but it is difficult to imagine it being as hard for a man because women can't pick men up like they try to do to us. She walked back to the Castle gate engrossed in speculations on how a man could become as innocently embroiled in 'woman trouble' as she seemed able to in 'man trouble'. What, in fact, was the nature of the 'trouble'? The implication was far from being as innocent as her own. He was still not there. The church clock had struck two while she was involved in the waistcoat purchase. She settled down to wait patiently but could not stop anxiously scanning each approaching group of people. The church clock struck half past two. Perhaps the letter had not reached him. Perhaps the boatman's memory had been quite amiss and he had gone a long way away to find

200

new work. She lowered her eyes sadly and watched the shiny black toecaps of her elegant buttoned boots. Perhaps he was working – he surely would be – the boatmen had a hard life. He wouldn't be able to just leave his boat and come. She was certain he would get here sometime, somehow, but he would have to fit it in with his duties.

Whatever may have been said to his discredit there was never a suggestion of him failing in his duty to his parents, was there? He always seemed politely deferential to his father and they wouldn't offer to make him a sergeant in the army had it been otherwise. She raised her eyes happily and scanned the nearby crowd again. At three o'clock she decided to give him until a quarter past and then have a quick walk around the market stalls, keeping her eyes on the gates, of course. By a quarter to four she was back in her place again. If he *had* received the message, but couldn't come – he would surely send someone. He always had plenty of initiative. Surely he wouldn't leave her here for two hours if he could help it. The message could never have reached him. Hot tears of self-pity began forcing themselves through her downcast lids.

'What, he hasn't left tha waiting here on your own, 'as he?' said a man's voice. She looked up in surprise but it was only the model. Her spirits fell lower as she saw the intensely concerned expression on his shapeless face. She could not even be left in peace with her anguish.

'He won't be very long,' she said in a surprisingly confident voice.

'Sure you wouldn't like that cup o'tea? It's right nice in the Castle Tea Rooms just over there. You could watch for him.' For a moment she was almost tempted and then she realized the foolishness. How would she get rid of this man when he didn't come? She had now almost decided that he would not come.

'No thank you very much. It is most kind of you but I promised I would wait here.' She trusted he assumed that she had met her 'young man' who had subsequently left her for a

201

short time. It would be humiliating if he knew she had been waiting there in vain for over three hours. The clock had struck four. All the gaiety and attraction the market had held for her at one o'clock had vanished. She had no inclination to look or buy anything more. She sensed that the model would be keeping his eye on her, so as a passing group of people formed a shield she slipped into the churchyard and sat on a bench near the wall where she could watch the gates. Her mind was beginning to run to what she would do. How long could she wait? She said until he came – but there was clearly some reasonable limit. Where would she go? She had made no plans. She had plenty of money – she would go to the Red Lion hotel and take a room ... alone ... Oh – could she face a restless night tossing – turning – wondering where he was? Action of any sort was better than that. Perhaps there would be a late train back to Leeds? How late? How long should she wait? Her anxieties began to revolve again. There was a man standing looking at a stall. He was tall with an abundance of curly brown hair – how many times had she been caught out this afternoon and been appalled by the inadequacy of the subject of her mistake as he came closer? That man's figure was rather like, though – well proportioned – young but with a mature girth to his hips and shoulders. He still had his back to her. The awful disappointment would be when he turned. How foolish anyway to think that he would be looking at a market stall on his way to the Castle gates. He turned slowly, his head still lowered to look at the small thing he had just bought. He seemed sad. Effie rose and automatically gathered up her parcels with her eyes fixed on the distant figure. She went down the steps and began to walk up the street. He raised his head slowly and she began to run – no disappointment at all!

'Good God, Effie. What are you doing here?' His voice sounded deep and severe.

'Mattie! Oh, Mattie.' He didn't hold out his arms for her but stood, tall and aloof, looking elegant in a tweed Norfolk jacket and matching breeches.

Effie was bewildered. 'I ... I ... I've waited over three hours for you.'

'Where?' he demanded.

'The Castle gates – like I said in the letter.'

'The *Castle gates*!' He raised his brows. 'Oh, Effie. Just give me a moment. No. You just wrote "Castle" and I naturally thought you meant "The Castle" – you know – the public house by t'junction with Springs Branch cut.'

'Oh, Mattie – honestly – Am I likely to be familiar with public houses by the canal?'

'Well, I guess not – but I am, tha see. I'd even forgotten there was a castle here.' He put his arm round her appeasingly and smiled his slow wry smile. 'I'm terribly sorry, truly.'

They laughed as they held each other – tears ran down Effie's cheeks but she didn't know whether they were for happiness at finding him or remorse at the mistake.

'I'm sorry, Mattie. You must have been angry thinking I'd send that letter and not come. It wasn't so bad for me because I kept telling myself that you couldn't have got the message.'

'Aye, but I wouldn't have had tha waiting all that time for me. I'm right sure I'm not worth that, my darling.'

They made their way slowly to the churchyard and sat on a bench screened by some bushes and the lower branches of the limes.

'Do you still feel angry with me?'

'Nay, not one little bit. I couldn't have been feeling that black when you first saw me because I were buying this for you.' He drew a tissue-wrapped package from his pocket and held it out to her on the palm of his hand. She unwrapped a little black china dog – lying down with paws stretched out looking as much like Lily as a small cheap china ornament could.

'Oh, Mattie. And when you thought I hadn't come!'

'Well, I was angry but when I saw that, I thought of Lily straight away and I said to myself – Effie *would* come – look how she was with Lily. There must be a very good reason for her not being here – and all that time you were watching me. Do you believe people can make other people aware of them just by thinking?'

'Oh, if they can, you would have been so aware of me – for all these weeks and especially this afternoon.'

'Well, I reckon that proves it beyond any shadow o'doubt.' He kissed her gently and laughed.

'I've bought something for *you*.' It was not long ago that she had thought so sadly of opening that parcel but now she could be pleased and triumphant about it and forget the humiliation of the 'model'.

'Why, that's charming. That's a raight big present!' He looked at her in slight discomfort and Effie hugged and kissed him better. Just how foolish to dream that this proud man could live under the shelter of her wealth. He didn't need fine clothes, anyway. He had such natural dignity that he looked as confidently elegant in his cheap tweed suit as a lord in a Savile Row one.

'Tha looks so very beautiful I don't know how I dare sit here with tha in my arms. Your coat is so smart and that silly bit o' feather nonsense on tha head suits alarmingly well. Nay – it's thy beauty that shows thy clothes off, of course. I never did set eyes on a face as perfectly beautiful as thine.' His strict adherence to the old second-person pronouns made his words doubly eloquent to Effie. He smiled his charming, teasing smile and she kissed his raised lip and explored his creased cheeks lightly with her fingertips.

'You are devastatingly handsome too, you know?'

She was acutely aware as his smile broadened and his eyes flickered that many others had told him that but he was careful not to speak and she was careful to keep her eyes tender. After all it was by no means the first time that she had been told of her beauty by a man but it was the first time that she was intensely grateful for it.

'You've been here so long – where do you want to go now?'

She noticed again that he did not always speak in the broad dialect of the canal bank.

'It is so utterly different when you are here, Mattie. But perhaps we could go to the tearooms over there before they close. We won't stay long because it's better being alone, together.'

'Aye, 'tis that. 'Tis wonderful.' He kissed her passionately, and it was quite a few minutes before they were calm enough to move to the tearooms.

'Where are tha going tonight?' He was looking at her gravely. She had anticipated this question ever since she wrote the note but had decided that the answer could only be decided by the situation and it was still not clear what it should be. She played with her table mat and knife.

'Well, I am not going home. I can stay in a hotel, but ...' she raised her eyes to his face inquiringly. He wouldn't help her.

'But ... what?' he asked. She smiled gaily and placed her hands over his.

'But I really want to spend it with you and the place doesn't matter very much.'

'Oh – Effie.' He shook his head with the expression of painful conflict she had seen before.

'Has tha thought out all the implications o' that? Tha seems so young and innocent and I love tha so much – you *must not* depend on me, Effie. You do understand that, child?' He had raised his voice and was gazing almost savagely into her face. She caught the eye of the waitress looking curiously at them.

'Hush, Mattie. I am neither very young nor very innocent. I have never let a man make love to me –' she lowered her eyes '– not properly – you understand – but only because I have never loved a man enough to really want him to.'

'But tha does now?'

'Yes.'

'It hurts.' She raised her proud eyes defiantly.

'Only at first!'

'Aye.' He looked away from her, still intensely worried. 'It's tha I'm thinking of, Effie. Tha knows that – I wouldn't hurt tha for the world. I don't mean the pain – I mean your life.'

'I know and I want you, and I want you to enjoy being with me so you must just take my word for it and none of the responsibility. Will you promise me, Mattie? We can be very happy together and there's not much time. I'm only frightened I might miss some real happiness so I am prepared to be selfish and irresponsible and have you now rather than wait and lose you. Do you understand?'

'Nay. Thou art the strangest wench I ever found – but tha does seem to know th'own mind and I should be an ungrateful wretch not to go along with it wouldn't I?'

'Aye,' she declared with shining eyes. They squeezed each other's hands and rose to go.

'Where to, my mistress?' he inquired outside the door.

'Somewhere fairly comfortable and warm but as lonely as can be,' she smiled up confidently at him.

'My new boat is anchored half a mile upstream near Gargrave,' he volunteered.

'Comfortable?' she queried.

'A great big pile o'soft blankets and some bread and eggs and tea.' She laughed delightedly.

'You had it planned.'

'Nay! Did I suggest it before?'

'No – but do you always have a big pile of soft blankets on board?'

'A sailor should always be prepared,' he laughed.

CHAPTER SIX

Matthias Pierce was the new captain of the *Myrtle* which was one of the last horse-drawn packet boats belonging to the

Leeds and Liverpool Canal Company. She plied between Skipton, Wigan and Liverpool carrying passengers and small loads at the spanking pace of six miles an hour achieved by frequent changes of horses. The canal was still popular with a diminishing stream of immigrants who preferred to travel close to the remnants of their old life, packed into boxes and trunks, as they headed for the new. The other passengers were often shoppers from Wigan and all stops to Liverpool who spent a half day and night in the grand metropolis before returning home. The horse-drawn packets, however, were not popular with the day carriers because of the nuisance of passing and the arrogance of their skippers. Actually 'arrogance' was rarely the fair word. They were required to keep tight schedules and take meticulous care of boats and horses so they had to be paid accordingly and the job attracted the energetic and ambitious. Mattie was certainly both and he was already looking ahead to becoming skipper of one of the new steam fly-boats as he stood in his tweed suit in the company's Liverpool office.

'You're rather young for this job, Mr Pierce. Why did you leave the army?'

'I had only signed on for three years,' replied Mattie defensively.

'You didn't fancy signing on for more then?'

'Nay.' He raised his head and smiled challengingly. 'I preferred to stay alive.'

'Ah, I suppose that's reasonable.' The man smiled and Mattie knew he had the job.

'Mind now, lad. All our horses are sound and it's your business to see they stay that way. We give a month's notice of dismissal unless there's serious damage done and then tha's straight out. You understand?'

'Yes, sir. I understand.'

Mattie enjoyed the first few weeks immensely. He was already on good terms with the boat folk who respected his father and that helped day-to-day relations. He was a favourite with the lock-keepers, except perhaps the ones with teenage daughters.

'He do seem a polite enough young man but my mind will be a deal happier about Mattie Pierce once he's married,' declared the lock-keeper's wife at Gargrave.

'His sort don't get married too easy,' replied her husband. 'Who were that wench he had on his boat last week? The one with raight fair hair?'

'I don't know, but she were a rare bonny lass. Not from hereabouts. She talked proper too – well educated. I thought she must be a passenger but then she came back with him again.' His wife shook her head gloomily.

'Her parents will be grieving about that.'

They weren't particularly because they had no idea where she was. They were worried that Effie should go away for a weekend to an unspecified friend and then spend a week 'up the dales' a little later on but they no longer pretended to have any influence over her. Mary half hoped that there might be a man involved.

'Does tha think she could be with a man, Jack?'

'A man!' His honest face looked shocked. 'I hope she ent. She never seemed to like any, did she?'

'Well, there was that man from York.'

'She's a deep one, our Effie. It's no use our worrying.'

Jim was more concerned. He would sit shaking his head moodily at his range of an evening. 'She weren't herself for most of April – that low and depressed. It may have been t'dog but I doubt it.'

Effie hardly gave Oakroyd a thought that week. The only time she could remember such fulfilled happiness was the last few days with her grandfather. Mattie was so contented too. She watched him fondly as he leapt ashore to change the horses. He was sensitive with animals and took pleasure in knowing their individual ways.

'Right, Tom. I'm done. Stable this one for me, there's a good lad – we're running a bit late. Here's some baccy for tha.'

'Thanks. See tha on the way back, Matt. God bless – and tha lass.'

Effie waved, smiling. Mattie had given the young lad who worked with him a holiday and so Effie was an essential member of the crew, steering the boat while Mattie walked with the horse or went ahead to see to the lock. They were on their way down to Skipton now and as soon as the horse had steadied, Mattie was beside her at the tiller with his arm round her waist. They didn't talk much. They smiled contentedly at each other and watched the fields of grazing cattle slide by, the sun sparkle on the water, listened to the lap-lap of the water and the regular hoof thumps from the towpath and felt the reassuring warmth of each other's body. Effie wished they need not take people aboard but Mattie would soon begin to fidget and be only too happy to spring on to the quay to welcome their new cargo, check the passenger list, solve problems and reassure.

'Nay, Mrs Brown. He'll be right as rain. I've never had a bairn sick on my boat ... The liner? Well, I can't speak for that of course, but they do say tha don't feel much motion on them very big ones. Which are you on? Ah – aye – Well, she *is* a big one – safe as houses, you won't know you're on the water, I'll warrant.'

'Yes, Mr Pettifer? Well, I'm sure I stowed two. How many did you say? Nay, I'll check. We can't have tha setting off to the New World with a trunk astray right at t'beginning. Nay, no trouble.'

'Where's the Hemp family from Bradford? They were coming on the turnpike to Micklethwaite and boarding there. Whose boat were it? Oh, Mark Lawson's! That damn old cob of his will have gone lame – that will be the size of it. I'll wait a quarter of an hour, Harry. I daren't wait a moment longer. Send the lad down to see if they've reached the bend.'

'Art thou one of Harry Acroyd's sons too? I never realized, lad. Nay, I didn't have no time for fishing last Saturday. Well, we didn't do that well all afternoon the week before did we?

Aye, might have been better to have moved up there but I like the scenery by t'Castle!'

Effie smiled to herself. So that's how he waited for her. Men were different – even if he hadn't minded being seen waiting for her, he would have found the inactivity intolerable, whereas she could not have settled her distraught mind to any task that afternoon.

'So what held tha, Mark, eh? Just like I said. You'll have to get yourself a new nag. There's no way round it. That's the toughness of being a number one.'

Effie enjoyed the novelty of canal life. She had soon mastered the locks and took her turn to prepare them, walking briskly ahead swinging the windlass in her hand. The boat was travelling west towards the highest reach of the canal and the afternoon was fine as they floated quietly past the Anchor Inn at Salterforth and on towards Foulridge. Effie was quite excited at the prospect of the Tunnel passage after all the tales she had listened to on the canal bank as a child ...

'Nowt goes through Foulridge Tunnel baht ticket, tha know. Well, Ah don't tell truth! An old cow went through once. She must 'ave fallen in at one end and she just kept on swimming until they hauled her out at t'other, and chap at office said "Where's tha ticket?"'

They stopped at the Leeds and Liverpool Canal Company wharf and Effie saw the dark tunnel entrance beneath the bridge. It looked far from inviting. Mattie guessed her thoughts.

'You can walk over the top with the lad and horse if you like. It's only a mile. I must call in at the office.'

'Oh, no! I'll go through now. I've heard so much about "legging through the Pennines".'

'It ent much fun, miss,' said the legger. 'I sometimes think it would be no bad job to let them steamer tugs take over altogether. Mind, they'd still need us for the gunpowder for the Craven quarries, though. It ent at all healthy having a steam furnace over close to *that* cargo.'

Mattie laughed as he joined them.

'When will tha be changing to steam, Mr Pierce?'

'Not too long, I hope.'

He untied his six-foot-long legging plank from the side of the cabin and they lit the oil lamps on the front of the boat. Effie looked up dubiously at the cottage poised on the bridge and the stone terraces opposite.

'It must seem a bit precarious living perched up over the canal like that.'

'Nay, it's solid as rock, lass.'

The two men heaved on the towrope and, as the boat drifted into the tunnel, Effie glanced back, anxious not to be left alone, but they jumped aboard just in time and took up their positions on either side. The far end of the tunnel was visible as a tiny semicircle of white but it was impossible to gauge how far away it was. The beams of the boat lamps pierced two slender pencils of yellow through the unfathomable darkness and their light was reflected up off the disturbed water in an ever-changing play of bright ripples and crescents on the encrusted roof and walls of the tunnel. Effie had once been in a cave near Pateley Bridge and she recognized the pale cascades emanating from between the stones as percolating lime but sometimes the ripples of light momentarily caught a nebulous dark mass adhering to the roof, unidentifiable and horrid. The smell was dank and unclean and water dripped on her and rilled down the greasy walls. Effie shuddered and redirected her imagination to the many feet of rock and earth pressing down above, but that supplied little comfort. She had never experienced such a feeling of doom-ridden claustrophobia.

She rallied herself and became aware of the deep breathing of the two men as they lay, hips supported by the planks, moving their legs walking-fashion to push the boat forward, from the tunnel sides. The professional legger was not a young man and his frame was small and slight. He grunted rhythmically and Effie wondered how he could bear this hard toil in such loathsome surroundings.

At last the growing white semicircle allowed sufficient light into the tunnel to discern the details of the stonework and soon they thrust the boat out into the sunshine with sufficient momentum to carry it along between the high banks to the start of the towpath where the boy waited with the horse.

'There! Welcome to Lancashire, lass,' said Mattie in broad dialect. He was still lying on the deck as if reclining at ease on a lawn or carpet while he smiled gaily up at her.

'Don't you hate going through that tunnel?' she asked.

'Too busy legging to think, I guess. It would be much easier in a steamer, of course.'

'Suppose the engine broke down in the middle?'

'Tha'd drift out all right one way or the other. You see the water's flowing towards Liverpool now?'

'Why, yes! We really have gone over the top.'

'Aye,' joined in the legger, 'this is the summit pool. It usually flows this way because the locks are closer on this side.'

Mattie paid him and the lad, hooked the towrope to the horse and they continued happily on their way towards Barrowford.

There was just one regular note of discontent that marred the happy serenity of Effie's week on the canal. Mattie assumed that she would cook them an evening meal on the little stove. He would pick up bits of wood from the towpath and lock sides all day long so there would be quite a heap for her to stoke with. She had never lit a stove before but her failings in that respect were happily excused.

'Mattie! You'll have to do it for me. It just keeps on going out!' she cried in exasperation.

'Why has tha dabbed soot all over thy face? I prefer it without, tha know, love!' She pulled a face at him so he caught her and, holding her locked in one arm, bent over the side to dip his neckerchief in the water and splash her face clean.

'Mattie, you beast! It's all running down my neck.' He dried her tenderly, face, neck, breast, and kissed her, then got the stove going, but he was not so sympathetic about the food failures.

They tied up the boat some fields away from the stabling for privacy and he would leave her with the stove burning well to walk the horse up and settle it in. He took this duty seriously and polished the tackle even down to the brass bands on the turned ash swingletree that held the towrope clear of the hocks, before returning to the boat. He would spring aboard, declaring his hunger and then see Effie's worried face, as smutty as it had ever been.

'Stove-trouble, lass?'

'Well, not really – it's been going all right – too well, in fact!'

'I fancied I smelt burning down the towpath,' he would say grimly.

'I am sorry, Mattie. You see I am just not used to cooking! I've never done any!'

'Well, I'm as hungry as a hunter but I can't eat *this* now, can I? We'll cook some more eggs together and I'll show you again,' he would say, his voice carefully controlled.

'But there aren't any more.'

'Nay? But I brought you a dozen yesterday afternoon.'

'Well, this isn't my first try, Mat. The first two goes were worse than this. I had to drop them overboard ... I'm awfully sorry.'

'Oh, you can't be trying properly! I've had next to nowt all day long, skipping on and off t'boat – horses up – horses down – folks, luggage – I am really famished. I can't keep on without victualling. I wouldn't expect the horses to and I see they don't go without and you can't even fry me a couple of eggs.' She covered her face with her blackened hands and fled from the cabin.

'Effie, Effie, darling. Please – Let me touch you – I'm sorry. I shouldn't have railed at you. You are trying, I know you are. It's just that I'm so hungry – my temper is raw. Effie – please

213

– forgive me love – That's better – there – The soot doesn't matter. I can wash it off in the morning, love. I know how it must be to be in love with a chimney sweep now. No – sorry – I were only teasing. Oh, Effie, darling, come on in. I reckon I just have strength enough for one more thing – come on – Nay, I were teasing again – Forgive? I want thee; there is one thing th'art very good at without much practice, ent there? Oh, nay! Why don't I just stop wittering on. Effie, I love you. *I love you*. Does anything else matter?'

No, nothing else seemed to matter really. Effie found her happiness depending more on Mattie every day. So long as he was happy, she was. His happiness depended upon his work as well as her. In fact, she could never decide just how essential she was to it. He assured her constantly how important she was to him and she knew he believed it to be true but she was still aware that his energetic mind and body required constant employment. She could not deny herself the happy daydreams in which she pictured him living with her at Oakroyd, constantly by her side in the garden, walking together, talking together, rearing children together, but she knew in her heart of hearts that it could never be. The first obstacle was his pride, and maybe love *could* conquer that, but the horizons of the house and garden were too small for him – she would have to let him go or leave her beloved refuge to go with him.

They were alone on the boat for a short time again.

'Mat, love. How much do you like this job?'

'I'm very satisfied with it. More than I ever expected to be, you know!'

'Yes – I can see that, but how long will it satisfy you, do you think?'

'Just as long as you are here, my beautiful girl.'

'No, be serious, Mattie. Don't hug me so tight, it hurts.'

'I was being serious. I've never been so happy in my whole life as I have this week, love.'

'And me … but I can't stay. I must go home tomorrow.'

'Must?'

'Well, I can't just stay indefinitely, can I?'

'Nay – I suppose not ... Unless tha married me, Effie!' His face lit up as if the thought was quite new to him. 'Effie, my darling lass – *Would* tha do that?'

'I believe this is a proposal of marriage!' she enunciated in her best elocution voice.

'Indeed it is, madam. I will repeat it formally. Miss Barrett, will you do me the inestimable honour of consenting to be my wife?' She kissed his cheek delightedly.

'Tha hasn't answered!'

'Mattie! I seem to remember you accusing me of not thinking out the implications of our relationship not so long ago. I think this is the right time to do that. And I haven't properly and I am sure you haven't.'

'You are a strange wench! I still stick to my point that it might prove too late to *think*, love. You might find you're already very implicated – and you can't in all fairness blame me, can you?'

'No, of course not, Mattie, and I wouldn't dream of doing so. You know that, don't you? I'm not going to come to you and say "I'm having your baby – you'd better marry me".'

'Nay?' He looked so perplexed that Effie had to laugh and cuddle him.

'I have a shrewd suspicion that it might not be the first time that it had happened to you, either,' she said.

'You don't know any such thing!'

'No – don't be cross, Mat ... I was joking.'

'And anyway, I can't see the sense when I want you to marry me so bad. There would just be no need to be proud like that, would there?'

'It wouldn't be being proud, darling. It would be a matter of choosing between living my life and living yours.'

'Aye. I can see that this is no use to the likes of you. I didn't realize why you were asking me how long I should like it. But I *am* satisfied with it and there is nowt else I can do for the moment and I thought you had made your choice that Saturday and it were for me.' His tone was sad and bitter.

'Mattie, don't be like that. You'll break my heart.'

'I'm not sure you have one – not a proper woman's one, else you wouldn't talk this way.' She was silent. Could he be right? No, God only knew how deeply she loved him … and yet … she was not prepared to sacrifice Jim and the garden, now. She had been once, and if he had accepted her then, she would have abided by it. This week had taught her a lot about life. On the credit side was the utter fulfilment of reciprocated love, but then such fulfilment only lasted a relatively short time and in between was a gentle happiness in which life's various demands, like working and eating, still carried on. The debit side stipulated that in order to enjoy the other, one of the partnership had to sacrifice independence. If one was capable of supreme selflessness or, perhaps, if one's independence was not very valuable, then this might be happily done; but could Effie do it?

No! She could so clearly see the chafe. Mattie would give his love and protection freely but he would not happily swallow his pride and would not consider leaving his work for her although he would expect her to do both these things if she loved him. This was the custom in a man's world and only she seemed to consider it unfair.

They had nearly reached the quay. Mattie squeezed her shoulders.

'Don't tha grieve, lass. We'll sort it out tonight.'

Yes, thought Effie bitterly. We'll sort it out in a man's way, tonight.

CHAPTER SEVEN

Home seemed strange without Lily. Effie could stride about the garden at her own pace again. She could flit up to the canal as easily as a pigeon but she would have so eagerly forgone this freedom to win back the adoring dark face framed by the appeasing, pendulous ears. She squatted on the parapet of the tiny bridge tossing some breadcrumbs into the water. The gold, orange and olive shapes rose smoothly – hiccoughed and turned downwards skirling the surface with their backs and tails. Her loneliness and inward strife seemed to lessen here. The longer she stayed the lighter her troubled mind became until, at last, it joined the disembodied spirit of the water garden and began contentedly to appraise the straight strong spears of the bulrush shoots, the pendulous young flowers on the sedge, the first yellow, tawny-lined flags unfurling, the sky-blue forget-me-nots and the ecclesiastical purity of the floating crowfoot flowers with their cherub-haired stamens.

The character of the garden was changing subtly as the eye of its latest protector took effect. Rather than a formal ode to bright colours and orderliness which had marked the days of old Jack Barrett, it was becoming freer and wilder. It was still tightly guided by the hands of Jim and Effie – but their effect was subtly concealed. The annual beds surrounding the rose garden were tending to lose their geometrical symmetry and the outer edges often curved across the grass paths, to merge with the herbaceous border.

They no longer carried the seasonal pageants of crocuses, primulas and tulip; salvias, lobelia and pelargonium; pansy, wallflower and daisy as they used to, but more unusual perennials began to appear. There were the dainty yellow pagodas of Erythronium in the spring, Peruvian lilies and erigeron in the summer and autumnal sedum, crocus and cyclamen. Effie was tentative at first when she suggested a change to Jim, but to her surprise, he rarely raised an objection unless it was to point out a practical problem which she had overlooked. His job was to manage the day-to-day, season-to-season work of the garden in order to achieve the effect required by the governor. The design was not his business and between the time of Jack's death and Effie's return, he had made very few changes. The exotica were not replaced as they succumbed, the salvias and zinnias were not so evident in the annual beds but the overall pattern was little altered. He was happy that Effie was now experienced enough to take command. If anything, he naturally tended towards the informal flower gardens of the last century himself and so their aesthetic feelings for the garden concurred well.

'Jim, don't let's plant zinnias at all this year. I know Grandpa liked them but they are terribly stiff and their colours are crude – I've never liked them not even when I was small. After all, there's lots of things for him in the garden still.'

'Aye.' Jim's voice was unusually lively and he cast her a rare challenging look and smile.

He didn't open his mouth but she could hear his playful question, 'Does he still care, then?' This was something that could not have passed between them in her youth when even the mention of her grandfather's name made her lip quiver.

'Yes,' she replied to the unspoken challenge. 'We'll always grow his real favourites, the tulips and the hydrangeas and the fancy fuchsias.'

Jim nodded. 'I can't say I ever cared for them salvias over much, neither.'

'No. There's something really miserable about that bright red and green. Strange. It must be the sort of red because the *Lychnis chalcedonica* aren't like that at all yet they're bright red. It must need that touch of orange to make it a cheerful colour.'

Effie sighed as she pushed a piece of gravel into the pond with her toe. There was a momentary flurry of gold and then peace settled upon the watery glades of olive green. She felt sick in an undefined sort of way. She could well guess why but she was reluctant to acknowledge the certainty of her 'implication'. She and Mattie had parted bitterly five weeks ago and had not been in touch since. She missed him terribly. She fell asleep with the end of her pillow clasped to her bosom each night, the upper part, on which her head rested, was often damp from her yearning, but the lonely anguish did not torment her as it had those weeks between falling in love and possessing him. She thought of him often, but she knew where he was and what he was doing, now. She knew that her life *could* continue without him and to include him meant a personal sacrifice which she was not prepared to make. Unless she could see her way clear to making a firm proposal one way or the other there was no point in seeing him, but how she yearned to rest in his arms; to see him smile tenderly down at her – his raised lip – his white teeth; to feel the reassuring strength of his firm body. Only here, by the pond, could she view the situation with sensible detachment. A baby? Well it would be his – that could not be bad. After all, it was a part of him which could be happily fitted into the confines of her heart and garden and not come between herself and Jim. Her mother and father? That was a more awkward issue. They would take it very badly. She could never expect them to understand or even accept such a situation. Aunt Rosalie? Her lip curled gleefully. Why, it was almost worth it; she could hardly imagine the delicious depths of horror and shock it would provoke in that ample bosom. Mrs Sugden? She would guess! That hurt Effie's pride, rather ... 'just a young boatman, probaly as illiterate as his parents' ...

'Many's the lass as has said that and bin proved wrong' ... Oh well, there it was and did Effie regret the amazing revelation of Mattie? No, not for one pride-chilling moment did she regret Mattie. Had he proved more amenable to her desires he would have been that much less appealing to her heart.

Away from the pond her thoughts were in a turmoil. Indecision and pride prevented her from seeing him and she guessed that the same reason accounted for the absence of a message from him but, surely, when it had always been she who had sought him, he could swallow his pride just sufficiently to come to her for once. How much did he think of her as he busied himself with the boat and horses and passengers? Was *he* lonely at night? Perhaps another girl . . . the thought made her wince . . . Surely not. Not after that week together and the deep sincerity of his love-making – surely she meant more to him than that. She had seen the way the boatmen's and lock-keepers' daughters had looked at him – even the susceptible passengers and the lady in the carriage at Gargrave Lock had followed him through lowered eyelashes. Of course she had noticed this with all the surety of her woman's instinct and it had made her proud. That gleam of envy in their eyes had been directed at her and he had not seemed to notice any of it. It was this conflict between the way Mattie seemed to her and the things she suspected of his life before, that worried her. All her reason told her that there is no smoke without fire; that a young man as conspicuously attractive as Mattie must have had his choice of women, and yet any allusion to these things only provoked his anger. He was so ready to dismiss them as irrelevant to his love for her and she was so ready to believe him – But should she? Well, if she had no intention of claiming him, what did it matter? He could not remain celibate for the rest of his life . . . Oh, but it hurt! Why did he not come?

At last a letter with a Skipton postmark arrived.

'My Darling Effie,

How are you?

I have been waiting to hear but there has been no message. I wonder if you have sent me one that has gone astray? I am missing you so much and can only remember our parting with sorrow. I didn't mean some of the things I said, I spoke in anger because I couldn't understand you, my love. I still can't but perhaps you can make me. It is difficult for me to get away except on a Sunday but if you want me to come, give a message to Mark Lawson who will be through Newlay three-rise about lunchtime Wednesday and it will certainly reach me by Saturday. Do please make the message very plain and write clearly.

Effie, my darling, beautiful girl, the memory of you teases me all the time – especially at night, alone. I do need thee.

Your ever loving

Mattie.'

Effie's heart sang as she read the letter but then, what could she reply? Where could they be alone if he came here? What was there to say? She would put him into a difficult position. He would plead with her to marry him and that she could not do, but the temptation would be so great.

'My darling Mattie,

Thank you for your letter. I have not sent a message because there seems to be nothing to say except that I miss you terribly. I am sorry, too, that we parted as we did. There are things which I must sort out with myself before we meet again. I do not trust myself to do what is best for us at the moment. My thoughts are in such a turmoil and all I know clearly is that I love you terribly.

Your loving

Effie.'

Mattie read with disappointment. He was sure Effie would have wanted him to go to her on Sunday or even have come to him again. He should have felt relief that there was obviously no baby to be reckoned with but he was disconcerted to realize that he had been hoping that this contingency would drive her back to him and he was sad at that news, too.

Several more weeks passed. Effie felt miserably sick each morning and as time passed the feeling lasted longer. Mary worried about her daughter's pallor and lack of appetite.

'I think I will call Dr Smith in, John.'

'Eh?'

'Oh, do put tha newspaper down a moment. Effie's ill, tha know. She hasn't eaten any breakfast these three or four weeks and she looks that pale.'

'What do she say?'

'Nothing, of course – Says she won't see him if he comes. I don't know what to do.'

'She don't seem that bad. She is out in the garden all day as usual.'

'Aye. I'll leave it a while maybe. I don't know what to do. What with her and the housework getting on top o' me. We ought ter move and that's a fact, John. I've said so this many year and we don't get no younger. There's no sense to us living in a big place like this.'

'How about her?'

'Oh, I don't know. If only she'd get married we could leave her to see to it. But I don't believe she will. I don't believe she'll ever take a man. She's too proud to bend and make a doormat of herself like one has to.'

John raised his brows quizzically but didn't feel the injustice strongly enough to invite the sharp edge of her tongue.

'She'd never leave the garden,' he said.

Jim watched Effie toying with her morning mug of tea in the potting shed, shook his head and moved his feet in a gesture of depression.

'What's the matter, Jim?' He turned away, shaking his head again.

'You worrying about me, too?' asked Effie sullenly.

'Aye.'

'I should like to tell you what's wrong, Jim, in case it affects your plans at all.'

'Why should it?'

'Well, I just don't know how it might upset you. That's what's been bothering me most, lately.' She kept her eyes resolutely fixed on the bottom of her mug.

'Is it that bad?'

'It's all a matter of opinion.'

'Tha should know mine after all this time.' He sounded dour. Effie wished he had said 'lass'. Was it possible that he knew? No, how could he? He knew nothing of Mattie. For God's sake get on – he had to know sometime and she would rather it was she who chose to tell him. Suppose he was really shocked ... suppose – suppose he left her ...

'Jim,' she blurted out, 'I'm going to have a baby.'

'Aye?' His voice sounded gentler – almost relieved.

'Did you know?'

'Aye – well, not for sure, of course.'

'What are you going to do?'

He was filling his pipe and carefully completed the task before he looked up. 'There's not a great deal I can do, is there, lass?'

She felt like hugging him, but recollected in time to prevent herself.

'Then – you won't leave me, Jim?'

'Nay – not unless tha wants me to.'

'Oh, God – of course not, Jim. I shall need you because Mother and Father must go ... and anyway ... you know I shall need you, Jim,' she finished lamely.

'Tha aren't going to marry, then?'

'No. He asked me to but I won't.' Jim took his pipe from his mouth and turned to look at her.

'He do know then?'

'No. He wanted me to marry him before.' Jim shook his head despondently.

'It ent none o' my business ...'

'But what, Jim? I don't mind you asking.'

'Don't tha love him?'

'Oh yes. Very deeply.' Jim sighed but asked no more although the gathering silence indicated that he hoped she might make the situation clearer.

'You probably won't be able to understand any more than he can but getting married is not the right thing for me, Jim. I shouldn't be happy and so neither would he.

'He's a very fine man – one of the best. You would like him.' The old man shook his head, bemused, but seemed a little happier.

'Ah only hope tha knows what tha is doing.'

CHAPTER EIGHT

Aunt Rosalie came to stay in the autumn. She usually came for a couple of weeks in the summer but this year John had firmly, very firmly for him, told Mary he would rather she didn't. It was now October and Mary sat in her wicker chair by the kitchen range with her glasses askew and Rosalie's latest letter in her hand.

'John, there's this letter from Rosalie.'

'Mm – ah – yes. Is she all right?'

'No. She's still grieved about us not asking her for the summer and her back's been bad again and I should like to have her here because she always do know what to do.'

'What to do about what?'

'Well, I ent said anything to you because I weren't sure but doesn't tha notice anything about Effie?' Her face was haggard with worry as she looked at her husband. He looked back in surprise.

'Nay – nothing bad. I were only thinking this morning how bonny she were looking. She seems to have snapped out of that upset in the summer right well.'

'Yes, but she's getting big.'

'Aye – she may have put on a bit o' weight and all the better for it. You were allus saying she were too thin.'

'Nay, John – I mean about the belly. I do believe she's with bairn.' He dropped his paper and snatched off his spectacles in horror.

'Nay, Mary. What's tha saying?'

'I'm not right certain, John. She are always in them old gardening clothes – but I saw her cross the lawn today an' she had her jacket off because it were warm, and I'm sure she is.'

'I can't believe it. We would have known – she would have said summat.'

'Nay – she's allus been so close. She'd be too proud to say.' Mary spoke with bitterness.

'It all figures when tha thinks about it. She were off for that weekend and then that week at the beginning of May and then she were clearly feeling sick of a morning. It all figures, John. Remember how ill I felt with her and then it all wore off until near the end? I don't know what to do. I need Rosalie – she's allus got ideas – sensible like?'

'Sensible like my foot, and Effie can't abide her.'

'I don't think we've any need to consider Effie's finer feelings under the circumstances.'

'Tha's not certain.'

'Well, there's no harm done then is there? I won't say anything to Rosalie till she gets here.'

John shook his head despairingly. If there had to be trouble he couldn't see the sense in amplifying it. He dreaded to think of Effie's reaction to Rosalie's interference if Mary was right. Surely she wasn't. Effie had no time for men. She was only interested in dogs and plants and Jim. Jim! God. He rubbed his hand across his face. There was poison in that idea. He had always revered Effie, in his quiet way, as one of the fighters, the earth-inheritors, like his father. Something that he could never be and never understand but worthy of respect. The common

225

carnality implicit in Mary's suspicion shattered his respect for his daughter.

Not many evenings later, Rosalie sat with them by the range, knitting. There seemed to be an oppressive intensity about whatever she did. John found himself unable to concentrate on his book. His eyes kept moving from the page to the podgy beringed fingers which thrust the sharp metal needle through the wool and jerked it back, flung a noose of wool around it, clicked it against its partner and probed viciously into the stitch again. He watched fascinated by the violence inherent in this occupation usually associated with feminine domesticity. Mary's and Effie's eyes were unaccountably fixed on Rosalie's knitting too, and lurking unease hovered over the hearthside.

'The conversation don't seem that stimulating do it?' remarked Rosalie acidly. 'I might just as well be on me own at home for the sake o' the company.' Effie shifted and cleared her throat. Rosalie looked at her sharply.

'Ha, for a moment I thought you was going to tell us something of interest, Elspeth.'

'Well, I could I suppose,' said Effie capriciously.

'Well then – do that – we be all ears.' Rosalie's voice was heavy with sarcasm and John gripped the arms of his Windsor chair in dread.

'I'm going to have a baby in January.'

The needles' click stopped dead. There was the sound of caught breath and then stark silence. John noticed with a shock that Effie was smiling.

'Is this a joke, child?' snapped Rosalie.

'No,' smiled Effie.

'Mary, what is this? Is the girl teasing me?'

Mary looked intensely uncomfortable.

'It is true then?' she asked timidly. Effie arched her brows and raised her head in assent.

'Did tha know this, Mary?' demanded her sister.

'Nay, Rosalie – I knew she weren't feeling well earlier in the summer and I just wondered lately, but ...'

'Why didn't tha write to me?' stormed Rosalie.

'Well, I didn't know till now, did I?' Effie watched the fire serenely. It had to be done sometime and this seemed as good a way as any – and *such* satisfaction in baiting Aunt Rosalie. She had played right into her hands.

'What's tha going to do?' demanded Rosalie of Effie.

'Nothing much,' replied Effie coolly. Rosalie stood up snorting with emotion.

'This is the most disgusting thing I've ever heard. She is enjoying humiliating us!' Her voice rose in pitch and John covered his ears and eyes in despair.

'Rosalie, try to calm yourself, love,' cajoled Mary. 'It's too late at night to get so upset. Let's all go to bed and discuss it in the morning.'

'Don't you care, Mary? Your only daughter. If I've said it once, I've said it a dozen times – you've spoilt that bairn. Letting her run wild in the garden – never took her in hand, and now look.'

Tears of exasperation began to pour down her inflamed face. They ran in little rivulets between the blotched, puffy lobes of flesh.

'Oh, Rosalie, don't take on so. John! Come and help her up the stairs. Can't you see how shaky she's gone.' John rose with a punch-drunk expression and shambled out of the door after them.

Effie sighed. Fortunately she had learnt never to feel sorry for herself a long time ago so the sigh was one of relief for another hurdle taken and not self-pity. She moved down on to the thick pegged rug, opened the damper on the range and put another log on. She would not have been surprised if the three had gone to bed since it was nearly ten o'clock, but her father returned in a few minutes and sat down awkwardly in his chair. Effie could feel the constraint of his embarrassment and was wondering how to break the silence when he spoke.

'Don't tha take on, lass, will tha? It ent the first time it's happened to a wench and it won't be the last. Don't take no notice of Rosalie.'

'Ha – have you ever known me do that?' Her voice sounded so brittle and hard to his shattered nerves. His hand went up to shield his face again.

'Oh, sorry, Father,' she said gently. 'I've had time to get used to the idea and I don't care but it must be a shock for you.' He shook his head miserably.

'I can't think how you came to do it, lass. *You* of all people. Were it an accident, like?'

'No, Father.'

'I mean, I'd better do summat, hadn't I? I'd better go an' see him.' Effie couldn't help smiling.

'No, certainly not. There's nothing to be done. It was my fault entirely and I've no regrets really.'

John felt guilty at the immense relief he felt and looked at her helplessly.

'Be he married?'

'No.'

'Do I know him?'

'No.' She smiled and put her hand on his knee.

'Father, don't worry. You know me – I will manage all right. There is just one thing I should like and that is for you and Mother to buy a little cottage somewhere – like she's always wanted – and move out as soon as you can. I shall be champion on my own and she couldn't bear to stay and I couldn't bear to have her. You do understand, Father, don't you?'

'But who'd look after you, Eff?'

She shrugged her shoulders. 'Mrs Wadsworth can come in to do the housework still. I don't need much.' Effie hadn't actually thought about it. She remembered the cooking failures on the boat and wondered how long it would take her to learn. She would have to look after the baby properly too. She gazed at the fire with rising consternation. Perhaps her mother was less dispensable than she had imagined. No; she could cope – necessity was the mother of invention. She would soon learn all that was necessary.

The next morning when Effie woke it took a few moments for her to identify the foreboding depression which lingered from her last waking thoughts.

Oh – Aunt Rosalie and Mother. She wished the confrontation had been extended last night so she didn't have to face it this morning. They had slept on it – maybe the first emotion had played itself out. How would they react; what line would they take? She sighed and turned over. Better to go down late and allow them time to confer and decide.

By ten o'clock she felt stronger. In fact, as she stood with her hand on the knob of the kitchen door, she felt a sense of exhilaration. 'How very adolescent,' commented her maturer part. 'How superficial to find the abrasion of human ties entertaining.'

She opened the door. Her mother was not at the sink as usual but sitting at the scrubbed pine table facing Rosalie and her father between them. The almost untouched porridge and the toast were pushed away to the further side of the table. Ha, still in conference, thought Effie.

'Good morning,' she said lightly.

'G'morning,' mumbled her father. 'Hmff,' snorted Rosalie. Her mother's face registered timid apprehension, pleading, fear and despair in conflicting succession. Effie sat down opposite her father and began to sort out the discarded bowls and plates, stacking them in the middle of the table to leave herself a clean plate and knife, then took some toast and began buttering it.

Rosalie was visibly swelling with indignation as this went on and soon could contain herself no longer.

'Look at her,' she exploded. 'Cool as a cucumber. Sits herself down next to *me* and gets on with her breakfast when we've been that distressed we couldn't touch a morsel. She

don't care. She's a common strumpet. If she were my girl I ...
I'd ... throw her out!'

'Oh, Rosalie, don't,' wailed Mary. 'You ent got no bairns.
You don't know how it feels.'

'And my, how grateful I am I ent, if this is what they do after
you've strived and strained from the very first for them. Just
look how bad you were before she were born – an' when she
were born – an' when she were such a difficult, disobedient
bairn ...' Rosalie gasped to a standstill.

'Effie, this really is true ent it? You don't seem ter care?'
Mary pleaded helplessly.

'I wouldn't tell you for a joke, whatever Aunt Rosalie may
think.' Effie took a bite of her toast and marmalade.

'Oh, what ever are we going to do?'

'Well, Mother. You know you were only saying the other
day how much you'd like a little cottage up off Town Street.
That's what you ought to do. You and Father buy that and
move straight away. Speak to Mr Jenkins; he'll get in touch
with the agents and they'll find you one easily enough and he'll
see to the money. It shouldn't be difficult.'

'How about you?'

'I shall be perfectly all right. Mrs Wadsworth can come in a
bit more often. I don't need much.'

'But the new bairn. What will tha do with that?'

'I shall probably get a woman to come in while it's small,
who knows what to do.'

'Ha! She talks as if people will come running to her, don't
she? Don't you realize, miss, that respectable folk won't want
ter know. Get a woman in, eh? I know the only sort o' woman
that's likely ter be. How about Mrs Wadsworth? You can't
expect her to – to – compromise herself by looking after the
likes of you. You haven't thought about *that*, have you?'

Effie hadn't – not in that light and she felt an unpleasant
sinking feeling in her chest. She mastered her equanimity as
quickly as she could. The old woman had a poisonous tongue.
It could not be as bad as that. Mrs Wadsworth was kind – but

– her family – maybe there would be pressure there? Maybe she should not expect it? There would always be someone who didn't know the family who would be pleased of a job ... Oh, how unpleasant to have strangers around the place.

'And,' resumed Aunt Rosalie, 'there's Jim Woodgate ent there? Just imagine her living on her own here with him. Just think how the tongues will wag, eh. He won't stand for that!'

Rosalie finished with a note of triumph as her screwed-up eyes saw the expression of stark blankness pass across the girl's face.

Jim – God – Jim. Should she tell him to go? No – she couldn't. The price of this baby suddenly seemed prohibitively expensive. She lowered her head to escape the jubilant eyes. Rosalie had won her point. Effie summoned her fleeing spirit desperately. Jim knew!

'Then, will you leave me, Jim?'

'Nay, not unless tha wants me to.' Was that his faithful sacrifice? Had he realized then that his honour and reputation were in jeopardy? She had no right to allow that.

'... not unless tha wants me to.' Had she missed his tactful way of asking for dismissal and selfishly interpreted it as an unquestioning commitment?

'Yes, tha would do well to dwell on some facts o' life, miss, even tho' it be overlate. Tha's niver faced ...'

Effie leapt to her feet, jarring the table so that the crockery clattered.

'I don't know why you are here. You have no right to be here. This is my house and I did not ask you to come and neither did I ask for the benefit of your poisonous tongue. You had better leave as soon as possible. When my parents have their own home it is their business whether you visit them but I don't ever want to see you in mine again.'

The four were all on their feet. Effie turned and swept out of the back door into the garden.

CHAPTER NINE

When Effie swept into the garden, the momentum of her anger carried her on her accustomed path to the potting shed but she slowed down as it came into view. She could not face Jim until she had thought about this terrible dilemma. She was in such a turmoil of dismay that she was unaware of where her legs carried her until Mrs Sugden's cheery voice called a greeting from the door of the lock-keeper's cottage and Effie found herself leaning against the bar of the upper lock gate in her skirt and knitted jacket. She self-consciously drew the jacket across to make sure it covered the two linked safetypins which held her old navy skirt across her ever-increasing waist.

''Tis a grand day for t' back-end, ent it?'

'Yes, grand,' agreed Effie, noticing for the first time the sunlight sparkling on the water and brightening the last russet leaves on the oaks across the lock.

'Tha seems sad this morning. Why don't tha get a puppy? It's a long time since Lily went and life has to go on tha know. She wouldn't have wanted tha to be lonely like this would she, now?'

Effie smiled and lowered her face to hide the tears that welled up into her eyes. What a strange thing was human emotion. She had felt so viciously angry some minutes ago that she might have killed Aunt Rosalie without remorse and now a few words of kind concern had reduced her to tearful helplessness.

'I've just got some tea mashing, lass. Come on in and have a cup. It will do me good to have a chat – t'canal's been so quiet this past few days. I ent seen hardly a soul to have a good natter to.' Effie followed her in reluctantly and sat down quickly by the little kitchen table. If Mrs Sugden noticed, her real secret would be out. Still, why worry – there was no keeping it much longer. It was just a pity that not only Mrs Sugden would know what she wished to conceal. Perhaps she should confide and ask her to keep it to herself. Effie reviewed the plump kindly face and opened her mouth – then closed it again. Mrs Sugden was the local link in the canal news-system and it seemed an unwarranted and probably hopeless constraint to put on her apart from the gall to Effie's pride. Connived secrets do not suit haughty spirits.

Mrs Sugden seemed unaware of Effie's shape. She prattled on contentedly.

'I think I may give this work up, tha know. Our Jeremy could manage. The bairns are old enough not ter be too daft with the water. Our Meg, that be his wife tha know, wouldn't consider it early on. I were always telling her that it weren't the canal folks as got themselves drowned. Some bairns are born on them boats and all the lock-keepers up and down the canal and it's rare for one o'theirs to fall in even. They're brought up with it tha see. But I suppose she were right. Still it's been a hard life for me since his father went and I don't get no younger.'

Effie nodded sympathetically. After all, Mrs Sugden had no proof. She had never seen them together. If tales of Effie's week on the boat above Skipton had percolated down to her, it would only be surmise and the obvious delicacy of the situation might curb even Mrs Sugden's tongue.

'Well, I must be going, Mrs Sugden. Thank you very much for the tea.'

Effie spent a miserable two days working in the garden, carefully avoiding Jim, and as far as she could, her parents. The only comfort was that Aunt Rosalie departed with uncharacteristic speed on the day of the scene.

The following Sunday morning Jim was away paying a weekend visit to Airton and her parents were at church, so Effie was feeling a little more at peace as she sat on the parapet of the bridge. Her chin rested in her hands as she surveyed the aquatic scene beneath her. In desperation for clothing to cover her relentlessly expanding body she had unpicked the waist-band of a smart nut-brown satin skirt and inexpertly cobbled the generous gathers back so that it held up over her belly. Her long blonde hair fell loose over a turquoise jacket with silk embroidery, selected for being sufficiently long to conceal the skirt top. It was not at all the modest garb that she usually favoured but the effect was charming; doubly so, reflected in the water. Mattie stood, partly hidden by a blue juniper bush. It was the first time he had seen the house and garden and to see Effie sitting there in fine clothing so much mistress of all she surveyed made her seem sadly remote to him. After watching her quietly for a few moments, however, his heart was bursting with joy, admiration and a pride he hardly dared to acknow-ledge. He sighed deeply and stepped out on to the grass. Effie turned quickly and froze, hardly believing her eyes. He put his head a little to one side and slowly smiled, his right lip lifting and cheeks creasing.

'Mattie!' She rose and sped into his arms.

'Effie, darling! ... But, God, what is this? Why didn't you tell me?' She drew him to her again and buried her weeping face in his shoulder.

'So this is what the message meant,' he muttered grimly.

'What message, Mattie?' she sobbed.

'Didn't you ask Mrs Sugden to send for me?'

'No – no – honestly – Oh, Mattie, it's Mrs Sugden – she must have noticed. I would *never* have sent for you.' She had drawn away from him and stood with her chin raised and an expression of injured pride on her tear-stained face.

'Oh, Effie, don't look so, lass. Tha should have sent for me before. There were no mention of this in your letter. I were almost disappointed – and then no message all t' summer ...' He faltered under the haughty gaze of her blue eyes and frowning brow.

'No, Mattie. I decided that I should not tell you since there is nothing to be done. It is all my responsibility and not yours.

I made that quite plain and I am not even particularly upset – except just these last few days.' She lowered her eyes and her lip quivered despite her resolve.

'Darling, please let me hold you. It's been such a shock and I were so overjoyed to see you again.' She took his hand and led him down to the potting shed, closed and bolted the door, then sank into his arms.

'Haven't you missed me, Effie?'

'Oh, Mattie, so terribly much.'

'You've such a grand house and garden here. I suppose I can understand that much.'

'It's not what you think, my darling. It's not that I think I'm too grand for you. You must know me better than that?'

'I don't know what to think, love. Would you have never let me know and had the baby on your own?'

'I shall, now.'

'Effie. Tha can'st!'

'Well, what do you want me to do?'

'Come and marry me, of course.' She smiled ruefully up at him. His pleading, anguished face smote her heart and they kissed tenderly.

'Effie, I love tha – more than anything in t'world.'

'That's not really true, Mattie.'

'It is.'

'No, it's just that we're upset and in each other's arms.'

He shook his head despairingly. 'Please come with me.'

'Where to?'

'I – I ent had time to think it out – Home, I suppose, for the moment. It's not a grand place like this, of course – it's tiny, but my ma and pa will make you right welcome ... and my brothers ... Oh, I can see the hopelessness ...' He turned away from her, shielding his face with his hand.

'Mattie, darling. It isn't that I'm too proud, honestly. It's not like that at all. Let me think a bit ...' He turned back with a look of hope.

'No, don't hold me, love. Stay there. I'm lost once I'm in

your arms. Nothing seems to matter and I can't think sensibly.' A glimmer of confidence returned to his face.

It was an awful dilemma. She was overjoyed to see him but Mrs Sugden had not done the right thing. Nothing was changed but Mattie's peace of mind and he should not have known. She had almost reconciled herself to never seeing him again. She stalwartly resisted the overwhelming temptation to seek his arms. No! She must think this out. There was the terrible burden of Jim. Could Rosalie be right? Perhaps she should go. Perhaps if she returned later with the baby it would not matter so much. Perhaps she might somehow manage to reconcile their lives. She looked at Mattie. His handsome face was more composed and confident. Had she not just confessed that she was helpless in his arms? Surely that was all she needed and the baby must seal her dependence on him. He couldn't believe that she wouldn't marry him. Effie read all this and a tinge of bitterness crept into her soul. He had not suggested that he stay here with *her*. The thought had never crossed his mind. He had left his boat for the day and felt happily satisfied that by this token he would claim that he loved her more than anything in the world.

No, she would not ask him to leave his work and come to her. She had explored this possibility so many times and always rejected it. Unless he proposed it and convinced her that he understood his commitment, it was an impossible solution. He would be unhappy and threaten the delicate thread which made her life meaningful. The exact nature of this thread was difficult for her to grasp but it was intricately woven through the garden, pond, Grandpa, Jim and herself and Mattie's warp could only lay itself passively beside the others. But this left her little choice. Could she bear to say farewell to him; to send him away bound to forget her – and find someone else? And Jim! Oh, God!

'All right, Mattie. I will come with you,' she said slowly, 'but only if you promise not to press me into marrying yet. Will that upset your parents too much?' He took her in his arms.

'Mattie – sh – stop a moment. Mattie, I mean it. Will you promise me?'

'I'll promise you anything, my love.' She shook her head sadly. She must go with him hopefully, prepared to make his happiness her only concern, to fit in with *his* life and turn her back upon her own. He would never even understand what it cost her.

CHAPTER TEN

Effie laid down the wet mop, took the pail of grubby water in both hands and wearily swung it out through the doorway, down the three yards of flagged path and sluiced it into the canal. A late golden leaf from a poplar and an empty bottle floated past on the oily water which was thick with coaldust and algae. She turned back to appraise the tiny terrace house, stone built and sturdy but hardly big enough for three people let alone the six it housed at the moment. The orange and black chequered tiles in the tiny hall shone damply clean – and so they should. It was only three o'clock and she had been asked to wash them twice that day and might yet do it again before nightfall.

Mattie's mother appeared in the hallway – short, plump and agitated.

'Oh, tha shouldn't 'ave emptied the bucket, lass. Tha'll be doing thaself a mischief. I said I'd see to it.'

She was at her wits' end what to do with the girl. It wasn't good for her to sit moping and she didn't like to have her wandering about advertising her condition – at least – not until they were married. It would be hard enough to bear then. She couldn't understand why they weren't but she had to be satisfied with Mattie's curt explanation of official uncooperativeness and delays with the banns and such. She had always doted on the lad, perhaps she *had* spoiled him a bit, but she was paying the price now and although Effie *was* a beautiful girl she was 'too cold and offish' – not really uppish – she *were* trying her best – but tha couldn't be comfortable with her. She didn't say much and didn't seem able to sew – or knit – perhaps not even cook (a dreadful thought – how would she look after Mattie and a bairn when they had a place of their own?). Mattie weren't much help. He were very close about her – just asked his mother to look after her and not ask her to do too much in the kitchen. Why? Now if she couldn't cope proper shouldn't she learn fast? His father knew a lot more about her than he'd say. Each time she asked him he just shook his head and said 'it were a rum do'. Well, she must make t'best of it – but the girl just weren't the sort that you could sit and chatter to about the baby and things – nice and natural like.

Effie had written to her parents and Jim explaining that she was staying with friends until after the birth of the baby. John thought they should find out where she was, but the preparation for moving soon engulfed him. Mary wept tears of guilt and remorse but before long allowed her innermost feeling of relief and the pressures of the new cottage to allay her feelings. Jim remained upset and worried. He felt Effie's departure was out of character and he wondered what had prompted it. He guessed she must be with the father of her child, but what little he knew of that relationship, he mistrusted.

Mattie got home nearly every night. Only his drawn face and utter physical exhaustion told Effie what it cost him. During the summer he had worked out his swift apprenticeship with the horse-packet and now skippered a steamer between Wigan and Liverpool. He was only earning a little more since he had had to replace the boy with a 'chap' that knew a bit more about engines than he did himself. The wage was good by canal standards. A young fellow living at home could manage quite handsomely on that but not to rent a place and keep a wife and bairn. Perhaps he could get his own boat – then another – a fleet of his own would be grand ... but that takes capital.

Mattie's two brothers were austerely polite to Effie. She was acutely aware of the constraint that had settled on teatime in the little dining room since she arrived. She was not and could never be one of the family – it was no good pretending otherwise – but what about Mattie? His presence there never ceased to amaze her. Here was a comfortable little family of short, sturdily built boat people – snub-nosed, stout and simple who accepted Mattie as one of themselves and yet, physically and mentally, he might have just strolled down off Mount Olympus. Effie had already noticed the canal dialect that he used for work and home, while to her he spoke in a noticeably more cultivated way. Although he never attempted to disguise his northern origin she was sure he could, had he had the mind to.

He came home a little earlier than usual that day so he and his father, who had just returned from several days 'over t' Leeds', ate their tea together. Effie dried the dishes and listened.

'How's t' steamer trade then, lad?'

'Not bad. I picked up fourteen folk not counting t' bairns off t' pier this morning. I left the cut at Burscough tonight and got a lift back. T'engine's been going grand the last few days. I reckon we've fixed that trouble with the leak.'

'Steamers may be very useful for tunnels and fetching a turn of speed if they're working all right but they'll niver push out t' horses. You don't have ter have the knowledge of them engines for horses.'

'Nay, but they don't go lame and drown themselves in t' cut and get indigestion because some scoundrel's given 'em bad hay, do they?'

'All this dashing about makes for ill-feeling, too, frightening the horses and making big bow waves – it's getting more like sea-sailing on t' canal these days.'

'Go on, Father! There were enough ill-feeling on t'cut

239

without the steamers. How about Eddy Jackson and Piper Morris, eh?'

'Aye. Has tha heard the latest round?' The old man's face became animated.

'Not since Piper left t' lock empty because he knew Eddy were just behind him over at Gargrave.'

'Well, they were both heading t' Leeds and they put up at Kildwick overnight. Eddy put his horse in at Jim Phipps and Piper stabled his by Brown's garage and when he went to get it out about seven next morning, there were no gear ter be seen. He thought someone must have shifted it a bit and he couldn't see in the dark so he went for a lamp but when he came back, there were only bridle – collar, swingletree and tow all gone!

'Well, he were that spare – then he thought of old Eddy and stormed round to Jim's and found he had already set off so off he went up the towpath swearing like a trooper and there, 'bout two miles along, just before the turn, was his gear – all lying on the grass by the towpath!'

'What a rotten trick! I suppose it must have been Eddy. He ent t' only one that Piper's fallen out with.'

'Must have been. You see they was both heading for Marshall's wharf for some machinery and there weren't likely to be two full boat loads so they was sort of racing each other knowing t' last one would have to go round to get summat else to fill in with and that would set him back a day.'

'I'd like to be around when they met up at Marshall's.'

'Aye, I ent heard about that yet but it's more than likely I shall.'

Father and son shook their heads and chuckled. Effie couldn't make much out of the story. What on earth was this precious swingletree?

'It be the wooden bar as keeps the towline clear of the horses' hocks. They can't join t'horse on to t' boat without collar and swingletree,' explained Fred.

'It will take me a long time to make a good boatman's wife, I think, Mr Pierce.'

'Well, tha weren't born to it, were thou,' he replied gently.

'It must be difficult getting used to managing in that tiny little cabin.'

'Aye, it's better to have a cottage especially when bairns are small. We've always had this place.' Effie noted the pride in the old man's voice. She had been thinking how meagre this lodging was and it was so much better than these people might have been obliged to live in that they were proud of it. The living room was an enlarged edition of a boat cabin and Mrs Pierce kept it polished and bright as a new penny. Every inch of the wall was covered by ribbon-laced plates from sea-side resorts around England, horn and wooden spoons, brightly shining brass ash trays and knick-knacks of all sorts. On each end of the mantelpiece were proudly set a pair of Staffordshire figures mounted on apologetically feeble little horses. A couchant Staffordshire lion stared sternly into the room from the centre and between these three figures were ranged an enormous variety of little porcelain pieces, thimbles and bells. Even the lace curtains draping the window had bright ribbons threaded through them.

'Ah,' said Mattie. 'Look, those are a pair of swingletrees crossed on t' wall above t' fireplace. They're just for show with all that copper and brass on them.'

'Aye, I draw the line at washing and polishing tack and keepin' bobbins on traces smart and painted. I wouldn't want to be polishing all that metal as well,' laughed Mr Pierce.

'How about those beautiful woven string belts?'

'Ah, now lass. One of them – that on the left – were my grandfather's and t'other were my father's, Mattie's grandfather yer know. And we wear them sometimes, don't we, lad?'

'Aye, Dad.'

'In fact, young lady – you ought to see that young man of yours really dressed up proper. Like you was for young Bertha Gibson's wedding last Easter, eh lad?'

Mattie smiled gently at his father and cast Effie a diffident glance. It said plainer than words, 'These folk of mine are

241

proud to see me a boatman but that can mean nothing to you and nor should it. I'm sorry but there it is.'

'In fact', said Mr Pierce, 'I think we need a cheer-up. This Saturday night there's a do on t' pier down town outside The Boat. Why don't we all get dressed up proper and go down to join them? It's for Eva and Len Shield's eldest daughter who's just got betrothed to a lad at Nelson.'

'Would tha like that, Effie?' asked Mattie doubtfully.

Effie hesitated. 'How about your mother?'

'She loves them do's. Loves getting all smartened up,' declared Mr Pierce enthusiastically.

Mattie understood Effie's doubts better.

'It'll be dark and at this time o' year you need to be well wrapped up.'

'Yes, that would be nice. What sort of things go on?'

'Oh – they'll be drinking beer, of course, a-plenty, and there'll be Jonathon Oates with his fiddle – maybe his son too and there's usually someone (Morris, maybe, if he's still in one piece) with a whistle and the lads and lasses dance – in their best clogs yer know. It makes a champion clatter all in time to the music.' Fred Pierce was so excited now that it would be difficult to disappoint him.

About seven o'clock the following Saturday Mattie went upstairs and forbade Effie to go up until he came down. Both string belts were missing from the wall and Mrs Pierce was busy at the mirror pinning on her best straw hat. During the day she wore the traditional boatwoman's bonnet poked out round her face and with a shoulder-length quilted skirt, to protect from wind and rain, but now she had her best full blue cambric skirt on and a small hand-made lace apron so only her best straw hat would do.

'Hasn't tha got a bonnet to wear, lass?' she asked kindly.

Effie had not brought very much with her but she had a little straw bonnet.

'I have a small one with blue ribbons down the back.'

'Well, put that on. We must have you looking your best.

242

Tha'll wear tha long cloak, won't you?' She asked this question a little anxiously and could never quite decide whether the informal 'tha' was appropriate for Effie as a member of the family or whether it should be the less familiar 'you'.

Mattie's father surged into the room resplendent in gleaming white shirt gathered at the wrists and neck into hand-embroidered bands. Over it he wore his best blue waistcoat ablaze with multicolour embroidery and his grandfather's five-inch-wide string belt secured with leather straps and polished brass buckles. The two women gave a gasp of admiration.

'Oh, magnificent,' said Effie. Mrs Pierce lovingly dusted off some invisible hairs from his shoulders and chest.

'There! Every stitch I did with me own hand,' she announced.

'Really! It must have taken ages!'

'Nay – one summer – the first we was married. I spent a lot of time on the boat – before our Freddy came – and I did it between locks. One always gets a great deal done between Gargrave and Kildwick, don't one, eh?'

'Because there are no locks,' explained Effie quite proud of her canalmanship.

'Aye – Thou wait till tha sees Mattie, now.'

In he stepped – not so ebullient as his father, his eyes fixed on Effie.

'Oh!' she exclaimed inadequately. He smiled slowly, quizzically, wondering what she really thought.

His was not so much a shirt as a full-sleeved blouse with a lace ruffle at the throat and wide bands of white herringbone embroidery on the cuffs. His waistcoat was pale blue embroidered in white and grey. His abundant brown curls gleamed with brushing and his blue eyes had a violet depth as they gazed questioningly at her from his bronzed manly face. The combination of foppery and virility unsettled her.

'Oh, Mattie. You look overwhelming. Who made *your* shirt and waistcoat?'

'I made his shirt. I always like those right full sleeves on a young man,' said his mother lovingly. She clearly hadn't made his waistcoat and Mattie volunteered no information so Effie guessed, bitterly, that some young female hand had. She remembered, too, that she had never seen him wear the knitted waistcoat she had bought in Skipton for him.

'Don't be too long, you two,' called Mr and Mrs Pierce as they left. Effie pinned on her little navy straw bonnet with the long blue ribbons and Mattie held her so their heads and shoulders were framed in the mirror together. 'Mr and Mrs Pierce, boatfolk, eh?' he murmured in her ear. She smiled sadly.

'Come on, lass. We're going to enjoy ourselves aren't we? Or does tha not want to be seen with me dressed up in this nonsense?'

'Oh, Mattie, you look wonderful. You look so – so handsome and yet – that lace and embroidery look like those gentlemen highwaymen must have done – when they stole the hearts of the pretty young lady coach passengers as well as their jewellery.'

'Well I suppose I am. A water-highwayman!'

They laughed and kissed passionately and for a few hours it seemed as if everything was possible.

CHAPTER ELEVEN

A day or so later the crowded confinement seemed unendurable to Effie. There were only two bedrooms. Mattie and Effie slept pressed together in a three-quarter bed that Mattie had slept in so long alone that it sagged in the middle and they were constantly rolling on to each other. In normal times they might have borne up but Effie found it difficult to get comfortable with her troublesome burden now and Mattie was so exhausted at the end of each day she hated waking him up to move.

'I'm sorry, love – I've got pins and needles in my arm and you're lying on it. We can't go on like this, Mattie. It's no good; there just isn't room for me here.'

'Shsh – you'll wake our Jack.'

'But Mattie –'

'I'm tired, love. I'll have to get up soon. Can't we talk about it tomorrow?'

'How can we? We're never on our own and you're so tired when you get in. What are we going to do? I can't go on. I have tried, honestly.'

'I'm saving up hard, Effie – give me a bit more time and when the baby's born I'll have somewhere fixed up.'

'Mattie?'

'Yes.'

'Mattie, would you let me buy us a little cottage near here somewhere?'

'It's for me to get *tha* a place to live,' he said sternly.

'We could live on your boat for a bit.'

'Nay, there's no room. T'cabin's tiny and I need the chap for t'engine.'

'Can't you save your wittering for the day?' moaned Jack.

'Sorry, Jack,' said Mattie. Effie sighed despondently. Her foot was numb and the baby was kicking violently.

Mattie stroked her hair a few moments before he fell asleep.

Two days later Mattie announced over his late supper that he had the chance of a five-day trip which he ought to take because of the money. Mr and Mrs Pierce recommended it.

'You go, lad. She'll be fine here – won't tha, lass?'

Effie hung her head as Mattie looked darkly at her.

'Shall we go for a stroll, Effie?' he asked.

'Yes – let me get my cloak.'

'I must do this trip, Effie – it's important for the money just now. Tha can see that, can't tha?'

245

'No, Mattie. I can't stay here – and definitely not without you.'

'It's only five days.'

'No. You know perfectly well that if you weren't so proud we shouldn't need the money.'

'I'm never living off you.'

'And why not? I've tried – I've done my very best to live your life and it won't do. All I am proposing is to get a place where we can live together.'

'It isn't only the money. I like the job.'

'I'm not asking you to give anything up for me except a little bit of independence.'

'That "little bit of independence" means a great deal to me!'

'It's no good. I told you it was no good. How I wish Mrs Sugden hadn't sent for you.'

'Of course, she shouldn't have needed to send for me. Tha should have done, and we certainly can't go on like this. It ent fair to Mother and Father – we must get married. I saw the vicar about it last week so there won't be any delay. We'll do it when I get back.'

'I am *not* getting married.'

'You must. Don't be so childish, Effie. You can't have the bairn out of wedlock.'

Effie's chin was raised. If there had been light enough Mattie would have seen her blue eyes blazing but she said nothing, and he interpreted this as acquiescence. He put his arm round her shoulder to guide her back to the cottage and felt her body resisting him but she had five days to come round, he thought.

She went upstairs to bed as soon as they reached home and he spoke quietly to his mother in the kitchen.

'Effie's a bit upset but she'll come round all right I expect.'

'Aye, lad. Don't tha worry about her. It's only five days and I'll look after her. How about t' wedding?'

'As soon as I get back.'

'Oh – I must start baking. Shall I see about the chapel hall for a little do after?'

'I'm not sure Effie'd like that. You talk it over with her.'

Early next morning Mattie kissed Effie's cheek as she lay sleeping, and crept away.

Effie rose later and packed her few belongings into her bag. She checked her purse and found enough to get back to Leeds but little more. She sat on the bed gazing bleakly out of the little window to the terrace roof tops the other side of the back. Where could she go? Skipton? To a hotel? Not enough money. She might write to Mr Jenkins and get some sent perhaps. She couldn't have a baby in a hotel. She needed someone. Airton? Beryl! Her hope sprang up – Beryl was so kind and comfortable. She would know how to arrange it. There was no time to write, she would simply have to go.

Mattie's mother was perplexed.

'It's all right, Mrs Pierce. You see I have quite a lot of money so there is no need for me to marry Mattie and you must be able to see it wouldn't work. We don't get on well enough together.' Effie winced at this untruth. 'You must tell Mattie that I have gone to stay with friends and I don't want to see him again.'

'I suppose your friends have a lot of money too?'

'Oh, yes. I shall be very well looked after.'

'I know our cottage ent very special except to us.' She was weeping now.

'Oh, Mrs Pierce, you have been very kind to me but you haven't got room.'

'Nay – it ent very grand.'

'It's not that. But I shouldn't be able to make Mattie really happy would I? You know I wouldn't don't you?'

'I weren't happy about it but it weren't my business – not that I don't dote on him but they allus said I spoilt him. I don't know what to do. He'll be that angry with me when he gets home,' the old lady sobbed. Effie patted her shoulder.

'No he won't. Look, here's a letter I've written explaining everything. Just give it to him.'

'I must come to the station with thee and carry t' bag.'

'There's no need.'

'Oh, I must – Please let me do that for tha. He will blame me.'

'No he won't ... but come if it makes you feel better.'

Effie got off the train at Giggleswick and walked through Settle. She had been worried whether she could walk all the way to Airton but trudging up on the moors she felt fit and strong. The sharp peaty air blew through her hair and brought colour to her cheeks. The dry russet bracken rattled and sang and her anxiety melted away leaving her feeling as wild and free as the curlews that wheeled, mewing, off the stone walls, as she reached them. From the top of Malham Cove she looked down on to the infant Aire and followed its meandering boulder-strewn way through the chequered fields to merge with the misty woods. Somewhere out there, just beyond the horizon, this young river matured and rolled evenly past her beloved garden and there she too would return in due course. Twilight was gathering as she stood timidly on the edge of the village green. A warm light shone through the orange curtains of the little living room. She remembered the table creaking beneath a gargantuan Yorkshire tea. There was also a cooler light shining through the green curtains of one of the bedrooms. Misgivings began to rise in her breast. What would Jim think of her arriving unannounced in this condition? Perhaps it was the last thing he would wish his sister to know and she was not protecting him at all.

She turned away from the door hesitantly. Maybe she would think this over more. She put her bag down by the stocks and, drawing the cloak tighter about her against the frosty evening chill, she began to walk, engrossed in her problem. She stepped across the stone stile on the further side of the bridge and sat down on the step slab. The river burbled along timelessly and two grazing sheep drew gradually nearer. The rising moon sparkled on the frosty grass. The sheep cropped rhythmically and the silhouettes of the naked ash trees seemed engraved on the luminous sky. The scene was breathtaking. So brittle and detached. Of what consequence were her petty problems? Of what consequence was she in this still, timeless beauty of sky, stone, tree and river?

Clog steps came down the steep hill from the farm and crossed the bridge. A moment later, a shaggy black and white form leapt noiselessly on to the wall by the stile. The sheep started and Effie caught her breath. It was one of the pups – she was certain.

'Lily's pup?' she murmured to it and it jumped lightly down, crouching appeasingly to lick her hand. She buried her face in the soft neck and yearned for its mother. If Lily were here, she would not feel so desperately lonely. Mr Douthwaite whistled and the dog disengaged itself and leapt back over the stile leaving Effie alone again. She felt suddenly tired. She would ask Beryl if she could stay just one night. Maybe she would be able to talk to her, unburden her problems and perhaps even ask her if she knew how Jim really felt.

As soon as Beryl opened the door, Effie knew her hopes would not be realized. The matronly figure seemed hunched up and withdrawn. There was no sign of that cheery welcoming embrace she remembered from the Easter long ago.

'What can I do for tha?' asked the strained voice.

'It's Effie Barrett – do you remember, Mrs Colston?'

'Oh, my dear, I never recognized you in the dark – do come in. Whatever brings you here so late?'

'I'll … I'll explain – it's rather complicated.'

'Oh dear, this is a poor welcome, t' fire's nearly out and I haven't had the mind to bake for this many a day.'

'Please don't worry. I just wondered if I could stay the night perhaps? I'm on my way to Skipton.'

'Tha's always welcome but it's not a cheerful house just now.'

'Why? What's wrong?' In the light of the oil lamp Effie could confirm her first impression. Beryl's face was sunken and gaunt and her body not so buxom as it once was. She cast her eyes up towards the room above.

'It's Jeffrey! He's been that poorly for nigh on six weeks now and not himself for a time before that. I tried to think it were just getting on made him a bit feeble like but I blame myself now. If I'd taken him to doctor then, maybe it wouldn't have been too late.'

'It can't be too late, surely. Lots of people are ill for that long but they get better in the end.'

'Nay. Doctor came this morning. He didn't say it out straight like but it were plain enough. He ent got much longer.' She sat on the edge of the table and put her hand to her forehead.

'There. Just come and sit down. You look terribly tired. Maybe it isn't as bad as you think.'

'Aye, I must be tired. I ent undressed these two nights. Oh, there he is coughing again. I expect he's slipped down off t' piller.' She started towards the stairs.

'May I come? Will he mind?'

'Nay, lass. He'd love to see you. He were only talking about that Easter last night and what a grand time we had.' She smiled a ghost of her old smile.

As soon as Effie saw Jeffrey she knew she couldn't comfort Beryl. He had been a large, strongly made man but he lay so wasted and the skin was stretched tightly over his temples, transparent to the fine blue veins. He smiled, showing much more of his teeth than he used to.

'Well, who would have thought it. It were only last night we was talking about Jim's fairy lass weren't it, Beryl?'

'Aye.'

'We had great times together that Easter didn't we? Dost remember the picnic along the river, lass, when tha slipped on t' stones catching bullheads and we had ter bring tha back dripping wet?'

'Oh yes, it was the best holiday I ever had. I always think so warmly of Airton and the cottage and you two.'

250

'Aye. It *is* a warm place. It's always been the most comfortable place in t' world ent it, Beryl?'

Beryl bowed her head unable to answer.

For the second time that evening Effie had to concede that her problem wasn't that important. She let Beryl make some tea and made her eat some too and insisted that she would sit with Jeffrey while Beryl slept a little. The old lady was reluctant but Effie was forceful and when Jeffrey began to reminisce gently about old times, with Effie listening enthralled to the tales of their Airton childhood, of the strange remote lad Jim had been and how he seemed able to make the ailing sheep and dogs better just by being with them, she crept to bed and didn't wake until the sun was rising. Effie was still at her post having dozed a little each time Jeffrey did and she felt surprisingly robust after a little breakfast. Beryl seemed calmer after her rest.

'Jim was up here the other weekend, wasn't he?'

'Aye, it were a comfort having him even though it were so short a time.'

'He hadn't told me about Jeffrey.'

'Well, he didn't know how bad it were till he came. Didn't he say nowt when he got back?'

'Well, no – he couldn't because I went away that Sunday so I haven't seen him.'

'I'm right glad to see you looking so bonny because when we asked about you we got the impression he were worried about you too.'

'Did he say why?'

Beryl averted her eyes uncomfortably. 'Nay; but he's always that close.'

'I wonder what I should do. I could stay and help you if I could be of any use but perhaps you would rather have Jim and I think my parents will have moved out so he won't feel he can leave the place till I get back.'

'Your parents moved? Will t' be on your own then?'

'Yes. My mother's always found the house too big. They've bought a little cottage at the top end of the town.'

'Well, love – tha has been very good to us already. It is such a comfort just being able to share troubles with someone ent it? And I did need that good sleep. Tha stay just as long as tha's mind to. I don't know how long it will be. Jim has seen Jeffrey now.'

'Shall we write to Jim to come up as soon as he can and I'll stay till he comes?'

'That would be best I think.'

Effie stayed for three days and then made her way to Skipton in the late afternoon so that there would be a bed for Jim when he arrived and she could catch an early morning train back to Leeds. She hadn't enough money to go to the Red Lion so she put up at a modest 'family' hotel near the station. Her back room looked out over the canal close to the wharf where Mattie had gaily welcomed aboard his passengers that sunny May which seemed half a lifetime away. She was just finishing her breakfast in the little parlour when she heard a familiar voice; a man's; deep and confident.

'Miss Barrett? Why yes, sir. Mrs Barrett is in the parlour. Who shall I say?' But the announcement was not necessary as Ralph Cottingley strode into the room.

'Effie! I've found you at last! What *are* you doing here?'

Effie had risen from her chair in alarm and opened her mouth but no sound came.

'Oh, Effie!' She blushed crimson.

The proprietor and his wife were now in the room, wide-eyed in anticipation.

Effie could say nothing and even Ralph seemed disconcerted.

'You must come with me to the inn, at once. Shall I send up for your things?'

'No, I can get them,' answered Effie helplessly.

'I shall get a cab.'

Effie was once more in Ralph's power. At the inn he

explained how he had called at Oakroyd to find Jim alone and worried about where Effie was. He, Ralph, had set about finding her in considerable alarm but had had no success until her letter arrived from Airton when he and Jim set off immediately only to find she had slipped away yet again.

Jim had clearly not explained her condition to him and he seemed shocked and restrained. Effie condemned herself for allowing him to take her to the inn but even after all these years, she found his masterfulness impossible to resist. She was not embarrassed; she did not care what anyone but Jim felt, but she was a little remorseful as she watched the painful conflict of emotions pass across Ralph's face.

'Why did you call to see me?' she asked.

'It is difficult to explain now – you see, I didn't know ...'

'No, how could you?'

'I ... I ... well, I shall be perfectly honest, Effie. Perhaps more honest than I had planned to be.'

'Yes – please – do go on.'

He began to speak rapidly, as if to relieve his agitation.

'I have met a lady – an older woman, in fact a little older than myself. She is a widow and we have been friends, nothing more, for two and a half years. We get on well and ... well, you know I am a lonely man. It seemed sensible that we should marry. But when I was on the verge of asking her, I just couldn't bring myself to do it, because of you. You have been in my thoughts almost incessantly all these years, Effie, and suddenly I realized I could not ask another woman to marry me until I had made sure that you were absolutely out of my reach. So, on the spur of the moment, I set out to find you. Mr Woodgate didn't tell me you were married, you see. He just spoke as if you were living on your own ...'

He paused awkwardly, but Effie didn't help him.

'You are married, of course?' he asked timidly.

'Well ...' Effie battled with her honesty. 'No ... no!'

He passed his hand over his face. Effie's malicious streak

murmured to her, 'Well, there, Ralph. Fancy a situation that you can't cope with.'

'Oh, Effie!' he blurted out at last. 'Effie, however did it happen? Who is this man?' He was white with indignation. Effie sighed. How she wished she could get away. She felt a deep revulsion for him and yet she couldn't bring herself to really hurt him.

'What do you want me to do about it? I do wish you would confide in me. God knows how wretched you have made me all these years.'

'I am sorry. I certainly didn't mean to, but this is *my* business, Ralph. There is nothing you can do.'

He interlinked his fingers and straightened his arms in silent anguish. After a painfully long interval, he said carefully,

'Effie, will you marry me? I shall stand by everything I said when I asked you that question before.'

'Oh!' groaned Effie. Why could he not leave her alone? Hadn't she enough trouble?

A glimmer of hope crept into Ralph's eyes.

'I should look after you. You would want for nothing. I think I might even come to accept your child as my own, given time. You can have no doubt about my feelings for you now, can you?'

'No. You're very kind, but ...'

'But? Please, please, Effie.'

'No, Ralph. I cannot marry you.'

'Why not?'

'I do not love you.'

'Perhaps in time ..?'

'Please take me home.'

The Red Lion is a fine Tudor coaching inn. Its mullioned windows have looked out upon many a flurry of stage-coach arrivals and departures and elegantly turned-out chaises and fours and colourful hunting meets. It still offered high-quality hospitality for those who could afford it although they generally travelled by train and hansom cab. Ralph had hired the smartest cab Skipton had to take them to the station and he now appeared protectively ushering Effie out through the arched doorway. Mattie stood watching in his working clothes, legs apart, fists clenched, an agony of conflicting emotions sweeping his face.

On his return home, his mother had told him Effie had taken a ticket to Giggleswick so he had guessed her destination and set off straight away first to Airton and then on to Skipton, in a state of deep remorse. His mother had tried to dissuade him. She told him about the rich friends who would be looking after Effie. He thought it most likely a white lie to calm his mother, but then Effie had never spoken to him about her friends and relatives. Of course, in his egoistic pride he had never inquired, he thought bitterly.

Effie had not yet seen him. Ralph helped her tenderly into the cab and climbed in beside her. The porter had put down the two small bags and returned to the inn and the cabman was adjusting the horse's harness.

'Just put those bags on to the luggage rack, my good man,' Ralph called to Mattie.

Unthinkingly, Mattie stooped to lift them, his eyes fixed on Effie. She saw him through the window and froze. The expression of bitter anguish on his face seared into her heart. She dazedly leant forward to open the door as he reached up the bags but, before she could move, Ralph tossed him a coin and the cab drew smartly away, leaving Mattie stunned.

CHAPTER TWELVE

When they reached home, Effie was still very distressed by the irony and humiliation of Ralph's and Mattie's meeting. Ralph thought it was due to her condition and his entreaties. They were sitting in the study.

'How can you possibly live here alone in your condition?'

'I shall manage perfectly well. There is a woman who comes in each day.'

'What about your mother?'

'My aunt has told her that she should consider me a deep disgrace so I am sure she would rather not come back here, and I should certainly prefer her not to.'

'Effie, my child, you have no idea of the task you are undertaking. You cannot have this child and rear it without a husband. You are too innocent to realize the degradation and the demands of the position. You will need to arrange for a midwife and a nurse. Supposing it is a boy! How will you be able to guide and control him and see to his education? ... Of course, it's not your fault. I only wish I could discover the bas... rogue that got you into this terrible situation!'

Ralph faltered. He was disconcerted to see that his harsh words had not reduced Effie to the pathetic, weeping girl he had anticipated, but instead, she had risen to her feet, her frame and face blazing with passionate anger. She didn't even address him by name.

'You know nothing about this "terrible situation". I am not an innocent child. Fortunately, because my grandfather made a great deal of money and left it to me, I can behave exactly as I like. There are very few people whose opinion I care about and they are not my aunt, my mother, or even you. You are utterly mistaken in thinking I am the victim of a "rogue", but since I had decided not to see him again, I must be a little in your debt. You have undoubtedly accomplished *that* for me, although you have no idea how you did it!' She finished in bitterness rather than anger.

Poor Ralph! Fostered by Effie's uneasy fear of domination, he had been wistfully savouring his vision of an innocent young beauty, soft and dependent, whom he could protect from the harshness of the world. Suddenly he found that his

Effie existed no more, perhaps had never existed outside his own mind. Only her beauty was real.

He sat rigidly, gripping the chair arms, his downcast eyes unseeing. The tables had turned abruptly. Effie paced the room impatiently.

'I am sorry, Ralph. You see how you have always misunderstood me. The best thing is to utterly forget me and marry your lady friend. I should never mention me to her ... I'll tell the cabman that you're ready.'

He rose mechanically as she went out to the kitchen and then allowed her to escort him out to the cab.

'Goodbye. I hope you will be happy at last,' she said.

Ralph's face was still dazed with bereavement as he raised his hand. 'Goodbye.'

At last Effie was alone and at home. With immense relief she set off to see how the garden was. The potting shed was locked but she quickly found the key which hung on a particular twig in the amply concealing laurel bush nearby. Her box was not as comfortable as it used to be. She had to accommodate her belly between her knees somehow, but the fleeting thought of sitting on Jim's stool was quickly dismissed.

The altercation with Ralph had done her good. It had buoyed up her sinking self-confidence, but even now the one unresolved doubt began to creep back. Jim! How did he really feel? Supposing ... a new thought harassed her ... after Jeffrey's death, Jim were to move back to Airton to keep Beryl company? The possibility became a conviction and Effie left the shed, head bowed and quite different from the confident figure that had entered a few moments before. She walked inevitably to the pond.

After all these years of companionship, would he leave her at a time like this? Was it conceivable that he could be deeply shocked by what she had done? Had there ever been an occasion when she had needed his support – the pond or Lily or the pups – that he had let her down?

'No. No. No.' The answers came back clear and certain.

'He has to live, and tha pays him. It's allus useful stuff, is brass. It makes life easier.'

'Yes,' mused Effie, 'that is what Grandpa said, but he couldn't have said the first bit then, could he? Anyway, the important thing is that there is nothing to worry about.'

She rose happily from the balustrade and returned to the house to write a letter to Jim. She asked him to remain with Beryl and arranged for his pay to be sent to him. That, at least, had got Jim out of harm's way for the moment.

There was a letter waiting from William upbraiding her for not visiting the nurseries in May and being out when he called in November. He would certainly be setting off for India in March. If she felt she could face the journey, particularly the overland trek to the mountains, she was very welcome to accompany him. There were quite reasonable hotels along the route and the weather should not be desperately hot, he said. He made a rough estimate of the cost of the trip.

Effie read his letter with mixed feelings. She felt she might have gone but for this baby. Perhaps it would not live. Perhaps *she* would not. It was the first time she had thought of that. She would like to see William. His happy straightforward nature was reassuring, but how could she possibly see him? Suppose he called in! What would his reaction be? Shock, or just the detachment of a bachelor? She could not decide. He would call sometime. What answer could she write? She decided not to write at all for the moment.

Mrs Wadsworth was coming in each morning, but Effie noticed that her manner seemed a bit strained. One morning a few days after Effie's return she tapped on the study door.

'Come in,' called Effie cheerily.

'Please, Miss Barrett, I can't manage the time to come no more.' She paused awkwardly.

'You see, it's Mr Wadsworth ... he ain't been too good lately and ... Tha'll be able to find someone else all right, won't tha?'

Effie looked worried.

'Do you know someone else who would come?' she asked.

'Well, not just now like … I could ask Mrs Smith up Featherbank Lane – but I don't know.'

Mrs Smith did not come and after a few days Effie reluctantly called to see Mrs Wadsworth. Her husband answered the door curtly. He looked in good health. His wife was distressed – No, Mrs Smith was too busy – the only thing she could think of was a young girl from Bramley.

The girl arrived at Oakroyd the next day – she was only seventeen but looked older. Her hair was dull and ill-cared for, her blouse grubby and she was clearly six to seven months pregnant. Effie regarded her bitterly. She could no longer doubt the reason for Mrs Wadsworth's defection. Effie thanked her for coming and sent her away with ten shillings for her trouble.

What was she to do? Mrs Sugden might help her. Effie had not been up to the canal for two months and she didn't wish Mattie to be summoned again. Pride had prevented her from telling her mother about Mrs Wadsworth and she knew Aunt Rosalie had come to 'settle them in' so there could be no help from that quarter. Well, the housework was not important, but the baby! She had no idea who the local midwife was, so she wrote a letter to Dr Smith asking him to arrange for her to call.

She proved to be a brusque, ill-natured-looking woman called Mrs Wright whom Effie immediately disliked.

'Well, Mrs Barrett, I see you'll be needing me soon.'

'Miss Barrett. I am not married.'

'Oh.' Her professionally jovial manner changed abruptly.

'I normally only supervise confinements for married ladies.'

'What do the others do?' asked Effie malevolently.

'Well, there is St Mary's – the nuns do take some but they are usually Roman Catholic girls, you know.'

'… and otherwise?'

'The workhouse, of course, but that would be hardly fitting…'

'No. Thank you very much. I'm sorry I troubled you.'

'Perhaps, under special circumstances, ma'am.' She smiled and moved her handbag meaningfully.

'No, do not worry. I am sure I shall be able to arrange something,' said Effie haughtily.

CHAPTER THIRTEEN

Two days later Effie sat miserably in her father's old chair. She shivered; the range had gone out again. She rocked forward awkwardly on to her knees and began to pick out the unburnt coal.

Could Ralph be right?

'Oh, Mattie, Mattie!'

She pulled herself to her feet, put on her cloak and walked up to the canal. She tapped on Mrs Sugden's door.

The old lady drew back in horror when she saw Effie.

God! Surely I have not really deserved this, thought Effie miserably.

'C…come in.'

'No – don't worry – I just wondered if you could get a message to Mr Pierce for me, please?'

'Oh, my. Oh dear … Do come in.'

She didn't say 'lass' as she used to. Effie stepped hesitantly into the living room.

'There, sit tha down and I'll get thee a cup of tea.'

Effie felt too cold and weary to protest. She had never seen Mrs Sugden as distraught. Her hand was shaking so much the tea shuttered off the caddy spoon all over the range top.

'Has tha not heard about Mr Pierce?'

'No, I've been away until last week.'

'Oh my. Oh dear.'

'Is there anything wrong?'

'Aye! But I don't raightly know how to say it.'

Effie's face became ashen.

'Just tell me, please.'

Mrs Sugden bit her lip and looked fixedly at her handkerchief in her clenched hands as she began to speak slowly.

'Young Mr Pierce, Mattie, tha know, were in t'Angel at Saltersgate Saturday night last. He were drinkingg fit to drown himself...' She caught her breath and continued more rapidly.

'... he could allus do justice to a glass of ale or two, but then he could hold it all right they say, but he must have had summat on his mind, I guess, because he were in a bad state there on t'Saturday before, too...'

'Go on. Go on,' cried Effie desperately.

'Well, someone took up with him and he hit him and there were a bit of a brawl and they put him out of the public bar and he got into his boat and some of the fellows tried to stop him but he wouldn't listen and off he went up towards the tunnel ... and ... and ... well, only t'boat came out. It were floating empty at Barrowford end on Sunday morning.'

'Have they found him?'

'Aye – dragged tunnel all day Sunday, an' brought him up in the afternoon.'

Effie's head dropped to the table on her arms.

Two hours later Effie, stunned and pale, was sitting on the edge of her bed with her cloak drawn round her and a candle guttering on the dressing table. She had the little black china dog in her hand and her eyes gazed vacantly ahead as memories flitted disjointedly across her mind ... Dear Lily! ... The tall young man bending over the market stall and her rising joy as she became sure it was Mattie ... and now – this is all she had – a little figure of a recumbent black dog...

Not quite all – a discomfort in the very centre of her belly

261

identified itself as a pain and surged upwards in her consciousness until she was obliged to grip the edge of the bedstead and gasp, then it steadily subsided again. She didn't care! The greater the pain, the greater her penance for Mattie. It no longer mattered how this baby was born or even if it was born at all. All that she cared about had gone. Was that the pain coming again? Good.

Sometime later she heard the back door bell ringing. She ignored it but it persisted, so she eventually rose and picked up the candle. She had to stop in the kitchen and grasp the table as another pain overwhelmed her. The person at the door must have seen the light because the knob turned and in stepped Dr Smith. He soberly noted Effie's anguished face and the cold range.

'Who's looking after you?' he asked in his curt, Scottish brogue.

'N...no-one at the moment.'

'Didn't the midwife come?'

'Yes, but she didn't want to see to me.'

'How much did you offer her?'

'I didn't like her.'

'I see. Well, she'll come all right for six pounds and she's competent. You haven't much choice, have you?'

Effie compressed her lips in annoyance.

His manner was brutally to the point but she knew too well how right he was and his directness had recalled her to the fight.

'The first thing to do is to get someone here to make the place ready, and quickly too. I suppose you have nothing prepared?'

'No. It wasn't due for two or three weeks.'

His face softened slightly.

'You can never depend on babies to arrive at the right moment. I had better get your mother, hadn't I?'

'No – no – please don't,' begged Effie. 'There's a girl up Bramley Town Street. Martha Watts – I'm not sure of her address. I don't think she'll know much about it but if you told her what to do...'

'Watts? – Watts! Ah yes. She *should* know what to do. There's been enough bairns born in that household of late. Her sister's had two in the past fifteen months. I'll drive up the hill and fetch her straight away – but you make other arrangements as soon as you can. Martha's habits in the kitchen won't be up to standard. make her wash her hands *twice* before she deals with the baby or the food.'

Effie groaned. Dr Smith continued to speak briskly as he moved towards the door.

'Get some paper and wood for the range and the bedroom. Martha will see to lighting them when she comes. Get six clean sheets – the oldest you can find ... Four pans of water ... soap ...'

Mrs Wright delivered Effie of a baby boy early next morning. He was small but vigorous and his mother was suffering only from exhaustion.

'There, ain't he a grand little lad?'

Effie viewed the tiny contorted features with apathy verging on distaste.

'There – after a good sleep tha'll be raight pleased with him,' said Mrs Wright soothingly as she tucked in the bed covers.

Dishevelled Martha bore the small bundle away and Effie tried to rouse herself. Oh, surely the midwife would have seen the girl was clean. She relinquished responsibility and closed her eyes.

CHAPTER FOURTEEN

Effie's sleep did not make the baby seem any dearer. The sight of the little creature caused her such pangs of bitterness and remorse that she fed it as quickly as possible and passed it back to Martha, who seemed to become more fond of the mite each day. Mary Barrett called to see them. She didn't stay long, probably because she had come without Rosalie's approval, but Effie was amazed by the look of devoted rapture that transformed her face as she held the babe in her arms.

'Eh – there. We must start knitting some things for the wee little man, mustn't we?' she cooed.

Effie tossed and fretted in her bed. Her life had reached a slough of despondency from which she could contemplate no future. Even thoughts of the garden did not console her. She was certain that Jim would not return to his job and her lack of maternal affection for the baby made her feel guilty. After five days her room became so unbearably oppressive that she got up and dressed despite Martha's dire predictions of 'womb-dropping' and kindred afflictions. She felt very weak as she made her way downstairs and walked unsteadily to the tool shed. As she reached the door she couldn't stifle the irrational hope that Jim would be there but, of course, the hut was empty. Effie sank down on her box. Even her old sanctuary had an air of forlorn neglect. It had never been without Jim for so long since it was built.

She crouched miserably for a long time savouring the memories of the morning mug of tea, Jim on his stool and Lily warm against her side. After a bit she noticed a plantsman's catalogue she had given Jim earlier in the season, trying to arouse his interest in some new hybrid lilies. She rose and reached it down off the shelf.

Ah – there was a white plant label stuck in as a bookmark at the fruit tree selection and five large ticks against the list of varieties. They had discussed replacing some of the older trees in the orchard. He must have made a start. She stepped towards the door, half intending to go and see, but the enervating apathy overwhelmed her.

What did it matter, anyway?

Faint steps sounded on the garden path. They were coming closer. Jim's? No, too fast and light. The door opened and William Parker's bearded face appeared.

'Ah, there you are!' he said happily as he stepped inside. 'Effie! You're not well.' She smiled wanly at him.

'I'm getting better, I think.'

'What's happened? Who's that girl in the kitchen? Where are your parents?'

'Oh, Will. So much has happened, I don't know what to tell you.'

'Why can't you tell me everything? I'm not in a hurry.' He drew a seed-box out from under the bench and set it on edge as a seat.

'You might never come to see me again.' She caught her breath in a half sob.

William gazed at her searchingly and reached out to take one of her hands, which was cold and trembling.

'I can't think of any terrible thing you could have done which would stop me coming to see you after all this time,' he said gently.

'Have you thought of everything, I wonder?'

'I think so. Tell me the very worst thing first.'

'I've just had a baby and I'm not married.' She couldn't bring herself to look up at him, but the pressure on her hand didn't change.

'Well, I suppose that has been terrible for you, but it doesn't affect *me* one jot I mean it's not even as if it's my baby, is it, Eff, you silly!'

He shook her hand to make her look up into his smiling face, which he tried to keep as carefree as usual.

She took his other hand and pressed them both to her lips as she began to sob.

'That's ... that's the nicest thing anyone has said to me for months.'

'Oh, Effie. Pull yourself together, girl. The worst must be over. I've heard people say that women who've just had babies can get very low. You'll feel better as you get stronger. When was it born?'

'Last Thursday.'

'Shouldn't you be in bed?'

'I couldn't stand being inside any longer.'

'Isn't your mother here?'

'No. I didn't want her to be. Oh, you can't think how dreadful it's been.'

'Effie, love! ... Can I ask you just one more question?'

'Of course. It's wonderful having you here talking to me,' she sobbed.

'What's happened to the baby's father?' She squeezed his hands together in anguish.

'He's dead. He was drowned in the canal last week.'

'Oh, God!'

'He wanted me to marry him but I felt I couldn't do it. Oh, Will, if I had he would still be alive. How can I ever forget that? How can I?'

'I don't know what words of comfort I can give you because I don't know all about it but I think, just for the moment, you must try to put it out of your head and get better. He would have wanted you to look after the baby well, wouldn't he?'

'Yes, I suppose so.'

'Is it a boy or a girl?'

'A boy.'

'Is he well?'

'Yes, I think so.'

'You're cold and trembling. You must go back to bed and

rest and, if you'd like me to, perhaps I can sit and have a cup of tea with you. Where's old Jim Woodgate, by the way?'

'Oh, that's worrying me so much as well, Will.'

'Come on. Tell me all about that over a cup of tea.' He helped her to her feet and supported her back to the house.

Effie felt a little better after William's visit. He was sure Jim would return. 'Why shouldn't he? He's your gardener and even if idle tongues did wag – would he know, or care?'

Effie was not convinced. Jim had always observed the demands of social respectability very exactly and now there was Beryl on her own who would not want to leave Airton and her sons.

The next day she got up again and collected the fish food from the potting shed. Seeing it yesterday reminded her that no-one would have fed the fish since Jim left, and the weather had been mild. She made her way to the pond and moved carefully along the bridge to sit on the balustrade. The first flakes of food to reach the water acted as a dinner gong and a rare smile stretched Effie's lips as she saw the orange, yellow and piebald shapes come sliding towards her from every part of the pond. As she watched them skirl and jostle beneath her, her spirit began to lighten. She raised her eyes to the russet bulrush heads and began to visualize their ribbony leaves long and green rising out of the summer jungle of watermint. The vision became so vivid she could even smell the damp tangy odour of mud and mint as the early spring sunshine began to warm the pond and she could see the golden fleur-de-lys shapes of the young walnut leaves, but for a moment, the tree stood alone. There was no pond, only a wicker chair in which an old man sagged as he watched a child digging, backlit by the hazy spring sunshine. Grandpa was speaking. She strained to listen. '... useful stuff is brass. It makes it possible to live how you want and do what you want...' The voice faded off and then returned deeper and clearer, '... raight grand to see tha back in thy garden, lass.' That was not Grandpa's voice. She turned.

'Jim!'

There he stood on the grass by the pond, grinning broadly at her. He didn't look as if he had spoken. She felt confused and light-headed. Was he real? Yes, and cradled against his coat was a tiny black puppy – the image of ... No, it couldn't be.

'Lily!' Effie had somehow reached him. He put out his hand to steady her.

'Nay, not quite. Lily's granddaughter!' laughed Jim.

'For me?'

'Aye. Of course.' He put the pup into her arms. The soft velvety skin round its neat curved nose wrinkled as the delicate pink tongue explored her fingers.

'Have you come back to stay, Jim?' Effie asked the question expressionlessly, her eyes on the pup.

'Aye. Of course.'

She buried her face in the small warm body and began to sob. Jim shifted awkwardly but knew he could not withdraw his support else she would crumple to the ground.

'Nay lass. Don't tha grieve so. Is the bairn all right?'

'Yes, yes,' gasped Effie brokenly. She suddenly realized that in her emotional confusion she was thinking that the pup was the baby. They *must* both be loved.

'Would you like to see him?'

'Aye, of course!'

CHAPTER FIFTEEN

The baby was called John, and he soon grew into a sturdy toddler with curly brown hair, keen blue eyes and well-moulded features. He would stand particularly erect with his head back and a little to one side and smile at his mother. If she was about to scold him for some misdemeanour her annoyance melted at once and she would hold out her hand with a sad smile playing across her pursed lips.

'She's spoiling that bairn terrible, John! I've never heard her say a severe word to him,' said Mary.

But Johnny was not spoilt because, by that strange quirk of heredity to leap-frog a generation, he was a contented, unadventurous little fellow; good-natured and placid. He happily followed Effie and Jim about the garden, fetching and carrying for them but only mildy appreciative of the flowers they grew. When he was six, Effie suggested they should make a garden for him, not by the pond which held some anxiety for her now but at the other side of the house. She was looking forward to reliving the rapture of that first spring sowing but, although he helped her, he wasn't particularly eager to see his plants grow – only to share her pleasure, and so it was as he grew older.

Effie and Jim had soon settled back into their daily routine and Johnny joined them. If they found a job for him to do, he was contented, especially if it was to help his mother, the most beautiful and accomplished person in the horizons of his small world. If there was nothing for him to do, he played happily nearby. As time passed and he became stronger, there was more gardening work, particularly as Jim's back became stiff and painful. Jim never complained but it tore Effie's heart to see him digging with such stilted movements and frequent rests. It contrasted so sadly to his old rhythmic fluency. When he needed to pick something up off the ground, he paused and then slowly bent from the knees with a straight back. There was little she could do to help since he resented being 'moithered' over and gardening was his life but she tried to arrange the heavier work so that she and Johnny could deal with it and directed Jim to the greenhouse and potting shed jobs, which also spared him the worst rigours of the weather. He was now about seventy-four years old and Effie sadly detected a reversal of the old anxiety in their relationship. The shadow which had darkened periods of her youth had been the

269

dread of Jim leaving *her*; now she realized that the old man was worried that she didn't need him any longer.

One March morning they sat as usual, Jim on his stool-throne, Effie on her box and Johnny on a smaller one. The eight-year-old was quiet and serious, as became the junior member of the team. His feet were firmly planted apart, elbows on knees, mug between hands in the traditional stance. Jim seemed withdrawn so Effie opened the daily review for him.

'Well, it's a raw, damp day I'm afraid.'

'Aye.'

'We ought to get the vegetable bed turned once before seeding. Do you think it's too wet?'

'Nay, there's been a brisk wind since Sunday. Shouldn't be that sticky. I suppose I must get on with it,' he sighed.

'No, Jim. You pot-up the runner beans and start pricking out the seedlings. Johnny and I'll dig – eh, lad?'

'Yes,' he responded enthusiastically. 'Can I have the big fork, Eff?'

'Hm ... how about the big-little fork – I think that would be about right.'

'Yes – this one? That's the one I meant!' His mother nodded and smiled, but Jim still looked gloomy.

'I enjoy digging, Jim. You know I do but you hardly ever let me do it,' Effie said with mock sulkiness.

'I'm getting too old for this job. Tha will have to get thaself another gardener.'

'Nonsense, Jim. You'll never be too old. There's a lot more to gardening than being able to do a bit of digging and planting. Anyone can do that if they're told when and where to do it. The important part is *knowing*.'

She spoke with animated conviction to carry the old man along but he was not so easily swayed.

'Nay. Ah'm worn out,' he said curtly.

'Jim. You're being perverse. Do you honestly think I could do with some stranger in the garden after all these years? You make me cross being so gloomy when there's still so much you

270

can do better than me and you've got so much knowledge that only years of experience can give.'

'An' if I makes tha cross as well ...' There was a glimmer of humour in his voice now and Effie knew she was winning this round.

'I think what we need is a lad just left school, to help with some of the heavy work and get trained. I'll call in and ask Miss Robinson about it. We do need an intelligent, cheerful sort of person. It would be better to do without than have someone who didn't fit in.'

'Aye, tha's got enough gloom about already.'

'Oh, *Jim*! Stop it – do! You don't really take my wittering seriously do you?'

She tossed a tangle of tow at him playfully and Johnny laughed and jumped up and down.

'Now mind that! I had to wheedle that out of old Jock McIntyre, t'plumber.'

'What's it for?'

'Ter seal, guttering fallpipe; holds t'pitch together,' he said, sounding quite his old active self.

'Oh,' murmured Effie happily.

William Parker called in to see Effie and Jim quite frequently now. He was always planning his next collecting trip, but since his father's death he was needed in the York nursery and found it difficult to get away. He would often stay several hours, delighted to see how most of the treasures he had brought back for Effie were thriving, taking cuttings and helping to plan new areas for planting and protecting exotic plants. Johnny enjoyed his visits immensely since he was always ready to tease and romp and never came without a gift.

'Ah-ha, young man. What do you mean, "What have you got?" I've got this very handsome auricula for your mother. You take it along to her. Mind! Be very careful of it – and I'll see if I can find some old bit or piece in my pockets for you, eh?'

271

They walked along to the greenhouse together and found Effie busy there.

'Oh, William! How lovely to see you! Oh my! For me? Really? Isn't this Marquis of Anglesey?'

'Yes. I got old Ferguson, you know the chap that helped me on my first trip, to bring it up from Isaac Emmerton's when he came to look at our stock last week.'

'It must have cost a lot!'

'Trade price, of course – but he didn't go home empty-handed.'

'It's a fine big plant and just look at that velvety texture and the beautiful saffron eye! Thank you very much.'

'My goodness. I've found this little box in my pocket! I wonder who I got that for?' puzzled William.

'I think it might have been for me,' suggested Johnny, not quite sure whether he was being teased.

'I wonder! Well, you look and see what's in it.'

Johnny had soon unpacked a miniature fire engine and rushed away gleefully to show Jim.

'Come and look at the new rockery. I had old George Grinley send some fellows down last month with three massive bits of bed rock that they'd dug out up the hill where they're building.'

'My, you still do things on a grand scale, don't you?' said William admiringly.

'It's a good opportunity. They will have to get out some more hunks like this. I'm just wondering about extending round there, through an angle. What do you think about the light, though?'

'If you swing it right round to make a crescent, this end will be screened from the early morning sun, which will be an advantage. It can do a lot of damage on a frosty morning, thawing the plants out too quickly. What do *you* think about all this, Mr Woodgate?'

'Umph! Where I were bred, we spent our days moving rocks off the ground, not dragging them back on!'

William laughed. 'And that was somewhere up the Dales on the limestone, I'll warrant.'

'Aye. Upper Airedale,' smiled Jim.

'You wait till we've got it planted up, then you'll like it. How about some of those Swiss alpines of Mrs Webb's, Effie?'

'Oh. Yes. I've just been reading about those in *The Floral World*. Do you think they'd survive here?'

'Some would. The *Soldanella* and some of the primulas and fritillarias are tricky, but they'd be all right in the conservatory.'

'Mmm. The only problem is space. We really need a bigger one.'

'Well, let's get the new rockery finished and then we could think about extending your conservatory, perhaps. It would be fantastic for me to have indoor space for the special stuff I bring back. We have to concentrate on the things that propagate well for the firm and there's constant carping about me using greenhouse space for exotics that aren't vigorous enough to earn their keep.'

'The best thing would be to pull down the old one and build a completely new elegant one – like the tropical house at Kew!'

'Have you been there?' laughed William.

'No, but I should love to.'

'It's gigantic, Effie! You could cover half your garden with it.'

'Truly?'

'Yes! You come down to London with me next month and we'll go to Kew. I must go down and get some collecting orders from Veitch and Loddyes and perhaps Salter's, then they'll have to let me off my leash at York. I'll get away in the back-end.'

'Where will you go? The Himalayas again?'

'Yes, I think so. Unless I could get to Japan, of course. That would be fascinating.'

'I envy you.'

'Come with me?'

'Who'd look after the garden and Johnny?'

William smiled at her order of priorities. 'Well, come to London, anyway.'

'Yes, I should love to, please. Write me a letter about the plans.'

CHAPTER SIXTEEN

The gardening lads came and went, some good, some indifferent, but none of them stopped long. There was a constant supply of jobs in the mills and engineering works and these proved more attractive to the youngsters than the solitary, weather-worn lot of a gardener.

'You'd think there might have been one lad among them that would have made a gardener, wouldn't you, Jim?'

'Nay. The younger ones aren't like they used to be. We was glad to take any steady job with a living wage and stick to it when I were young. There's too much brass about for the youngsters these days.'

'I don't think that matters so much. I think that some people are born with a love of nature so that the only thing that always gives them deep satisfaction is seeing things growing and living. You know, the individual colour and shape of plants, the scenery and the effect of the weather and season and time of day? I honestly thought one of these lads would bound to have been that sort and when he got the chance he would have soon realized the satisfaction of the job. You were born in the real country, of course, Jim, but you understood plants and animals when you were very young, didn't you?'

'Did I?'

'Yes, of course. Jeffrey told me all about it. About the pig at the farm that would wait to farrow until you got there and the sick farm dogs you cured and the ewe that had the bad lambing and the farrier said would die.'

Jim smiled and nodded, drawing deeply on his pipe.

'What's farrowing?' asked Johnny.

'When the pig has babies. They have twelve or fifteen, you know,' answered Effie.

'All at once?'

'Aye. That old sow used to have twenty regular and it were a full-time job seeing the little ones got their nourishment.'

Johnny looked impressed. He was a handsome lad of eleven, nearly twelve, and beginning to look so disconcertingly like his father that Effie caught her breath sometimes when he turned his head suddenly and smiled at her. Occasionally she thought how much Edie and Fred Pierce would like to see him and toyed with the idea of a trip to Wigan but the associations of the place were too sad for her.

'I don't think you ought to bother getting another gardening chap. I can do a bit each afternoon when I get back from school and there's the weekends and holidays.'

'Well, that's nice of you, dear, but I always feel that it's just work to you and you don't get that much satisfaction from it and there's your homework to think of, too.'

Johnny smiled wryly.

'I don't mind at all, Eff, honestly!' She shook her head remonstratively. 'I think we must have another lad, but I shall be very pleased of your help too.'

Johnny was as good as his word. He worked steadily at the straightforward heavy jobs and Effie and a new lad did the rest. Jim spent more and more time in front of his range in the cottage, still rising early but only walking slowly round the garden with his stick. He seemed reassured that all Effie wanted was that he should end his days peacefully in the cottage and advise on the day-to-day problems that arose. Their relationship was rather like wood and screw which the years steadily drove closer and deeper and each depth reached a deeper intimacy.

The ritual of nine o'clock tea in the potting shed continued but Effie was in front of the cottage range after lunch and tea most days and Jim would talk at length about his life and thoughts in a way that he had never done before.

'I wonder what will happen to the garden when Johnny leaves home?'

'I don't know. I wonder too. Perhaps he will carry on living here. I think he will. He has always done what he thought I wanted but I should hate to be one of those mothers who's dreadfully possessive about her son. Do you think I could be, Jim?'

'Nay. Not for a moment. That's one thing tha's never been – not even about tha man.'

Effie looked up, surprised. Jim had never referred to Mattie once since the annunciation in the potting shed twelve years ago.

'Do you think I should have been?'

'I didn't know him and tha did.'

'Yes, it was terribly hard to make that decision – not to try to bring him here, you know, but it was right. I have never really doubted that except for a little while when I heard what had happened to him.'

'What did happen to him?'

'Oh, he was accidentally drowned in the canal.'

'Nay, lass! It's late to say it but I am deeply sorry.'

'It's a long time ago but I can see him so vividly. It must be because Johnny's so similar. He looks awfully like him, not quite so handsome and his right lip doesn't lift when he smiles, like his father's did, and he's not so much alive somehow. His father was sparkling with energy and vitality – that's what made it so difficult to imagine him being dead when I hadn't even seen him, you know.'

'Aye, I've known folk a bit like that. Two, anyway,' he smiled at Effie.

'Oddly, one of my regrets is that you never met him. You didn't, did you, Jim? He must have called at the cottage at

Airton looking for me, just after you got there, when Jeffrey was dying.'

'Aye, but I were out walking. Beryl spoke to him and she were raight impressed.'

'Was she? What did she say?'

Jim spoke slowly, carefully recalling his sister's words.

'She said, he were a tall, straight bonny lad and very respectful and had a very lively, charming manner about him.'

Effie smiled at her hands, folded about her handkerchief in her lap.

'When Johnny gets married, perhaps he will have a child who will be a gardener. If you think about it, there was Grandpa but not Father, and then me but not Johnny. Do you think things could turn out as neatly as that?'

'Nay. It's verging on coincidence, I reckon. Still, tha can never tell.'

The new conservatory was nearing completion. It was three years since Effie's visit to London with William. She had been enchanted by the tropical houses at Kew and returned home determined to have a conservatory large enough to take a small palm or two, orchids and other epiphytes divided off from a cool alpine house. William had insisted that he should put some of his own capital into the building so that he could grow plants for himself rather than the firm, but as Effie's ambitions took flight the costs soared until William's contribution seemed to be shrinking into insignificance.

They sat in the study one summer afternoon with several plans spread out on the table.

'I am beginning to feel so thankful you are not one of my partners in the business, Effie. We should be racing downhill towards bankruptcy at an alarming speed.'

'Oh, come, Will! "If a job's worth doing, it's worth doing well" and we don't want to be falling out over whose plants can be grown because there's not enough room, do we? Furthermore, I want you to come in here when you've just been told

277

you can't go to India for another six months and be able to feel it's almost as good. That's the only time you're grumpy.'

'Well, I guess I should be complimented that you are prepared to pay so much to keep a crusty old bachelor like me good-humoured.'

'Yes, neither of us is getting any younger. You know, I really am going to go collecting with you on the next trip. I must not discover any excuses or, at any rate, you must *not* accept them, Will. Johnny will be perfectly all right here with Martha and Jane.'

'Yes, it is amazing how that girl has come on. Do you know, I was quite shocked when I called just after Johnny was born. She looked such a slattern and her condition seemed to make it even worse.'

'A few days earlier and you would have found two of us!' said Effie bitterly.

'Effie, don't. It's past and over. You know what you promised me. I'm sorry … I shouldn't have brought it up.'

'No – my fault, Will. You're right. Martha is a really good friend to me. She was so grateful when I let her have her baby here, but what else could I do? Dr Smith tried to persuade me not to, but she had looked after me and Johnny so well in her way and now I couldn't manage without her, and Johnny and Jane are company for each other. Mind you, she has several admirers – well, two anyway. Quite nice young men. I ought to encourage her to marry, I suppose, but I feel a bit selfish.'

'Perhaps she could carry on living here. If the fellow she chose was right it could be very useful. Jim can't carry on much longer.'

'Oh, Will! That is something else I try not to think about. Whatever I just said – I cannot possibly go to India and leave Jim now.'

William remembered that it was Lily that stopped her joining him the first time he invited her, but he steered their thoughts firmly back to the conservatory plans.

'It's the break in the spanning arch to give us the extra ten feet of height at the centre which is so expensive, Eff. Do we really need it twenty-five feet high?'

'That's not a very big palm tree!'

'No ... I don't know why I try to talk you out of this megalomania. It's in the blood. You inherited it from old Jack Barrett.'

CHAPTER SEVENTEEN

As Jim became more homebound Effie spent longer and longer at the little cottage.

'Dost tha remember wanting to come and live here when tha were a bairn?'

'Oh, yes. That was the first rejection I had and it made me sad for ages.'

'Nay – did it? I thought tha would have forgotten quickly. Anyway, tha's almost managed it now, eh?'

Effie laughed.

'It's the cosiest place I've ever known, you know, sitting here in front of the range on my stool, with you smoking in your chair. I think the potting shed is perhaps the most *secure* place but this is the cosiest and the pond is always the place to go to when one is in a dilemma.'

'Aye?'

'Yes. Don't you go there to think things out, Jim?'

'Maybe,' he replied.

He was seventy-eight when he died after a short illness. Almost his last words to Effie were 'Dost tha remember what I said when Lily were poorly?'

'About not wanting people fussing round getting doctors?'

'Aye.'

279

'Yes, I remember all right, Jim.'

Effie wanted Jim's funeral to be a small family affair in sympathy with his solitary shyness, but she had to let Martha have her way about the tea. 'Tha *must* bury him with ham!' Martha insisted indignantly, and this meant using the parlour. She laid out a fine spread of pickles with home-baked bread, curd tarts and cakes about the generous joint of boiled ham.

The undertaker laid out Jim incongruously in the bay window and Effie miserably dreaded the afternoon.

William arrived early looking uncharacteristically smart and sombre. He embraced Effie tenderly.

'Well, Eff. Here is the end of an era.'

'Yes,' agreed Effie abjectly.

'And the start of a new one, of course!' This platitude seemed unworthy of a reply but she was grateful he was there to help her through the ordeal of the afternoon. Beryl was too upset to come but her two sons were there and old Mr Douthwaite from the farm at Airton braved the journey with them. Even Mrs Sugden came, crippled though she was with arthritis. George Grinley and his sons were there and Martha and her new husband Joe, who had moved into Oakroyd, and Effie's father completed the group.

Mr Slater, the undertaker, arrived with a fine pair of Belgian blacks drawing the hearse.

'You must ask him and the carriage drivers in for a drink,' prompted William.

Effie carried out this duty mechanically, and the cortège left.

She tried not to listen to the service and the bits she did hear seemed so inappropriately trite that she managed to maintain a brave face. It was gusty and showery in the cemetery so they didn't linger long after the interment, but when they returned to Oakroyd the sun began to shine and the sheltered garden seemed quite warm, although it was only late March.

William caught Effie's arm to help her out of the carriage.

'Why don't we carry the table out here, Eff? That blessed

service seemed so far removed from Jim's brave life let's wave him off in his garden. We may not be able to be merry but let's eat on his lawn surrounded by his flowerbeds. I think he would have been happier with these daffs and narcissus than that heap of cut greenhouse blooms we've left in the cemetery.'

'Oh yes, Will. Let's.'

William must have made a joke to Beryl's sons and Joe because the four men were laughing as they struggled down the front steps with the heavy mahogany table. Martha darted round them steadying first one plate and then another. Some of the older men followed with chairs and then Martha and Effie with the teapot, jugs and cups and saucers. This bustle of activity relieved the tension amazingly and the plates were passed round amid animated conversation. Effie moved round to visit each little group in turn.

Mrs Sugden was holding court from a large armchair.

'... Aye! And Miss Effie would only be five or six. Then, when her grandpa went, Mr Woodgate used to come up with her. *He* understood the canal goings-on as if he were born on t'cut. Does tha remember old Jethro Higgins's horse, lass? He – though I think it were really a she, if me memory serves me raight – were a rare intelligent beast. I've heard Jim Woodgate say to Jethro "Ah don't know why tha bothers ter come, lad. If tha stayed at home in Wigan that horse would manage the trip all right."'

Mr Douthwaite was talking to Mr Barrett and William.

'... dost tha know – that old sow used ter wait ter farrow while Jim came to t'farm. He were three years younger than me but he knew a deal more about animals' ways and about the wild countryside, too. Even t'old fellows used to ask Jim's advice. He were a rare good fisherman in his youth, too.'

He turned and noticed Effie.

'Well, how did that pup shape up, miss?'

'Fine, but she can't compare with her grandmother, of course.'

'Nay! Jim said that ... what was her name ... Daisy?'

'No. Lily.'

'Aye. He said Lily were a rare grand bitch. Mind, her daughter that mothered that pup were a champion, too. I've had none better.'

George Grinley was the first to take his leave. He grasped Effie's hand warmly. 'Take good care of thysen, miss. I know a lad that tha can train up. Young Jamie Cooper from West End. I've known him since he were a little chap and he's only sixteen now but I think tha'll find he's got the makings of a good gardener. Should I ask him to call?'

'Oh yes. Please do, Mr Grinley.'

'Good! And fifty years hence maybe he'll know nearly as much as old Jim, eh?'

'Maybe, but probably not,' smiled Effie.

'Aye. He were a grand fellow, and like my dad used to say, "deep waters run quiet and gentle".'

When everyone had gone, Effie and William strolled to the pond and stood gazing into the water. Effie broke the silence.

'Do you know, Will, I almost enjoyed that – at least the last part. I was dreading it all so much and then you had that brilliant idea to be in the garden. I am sure that was just how Jim would have wanted it, although he wouldn't have been there himself even if he could have been. He was much too shy.'

'I reckon he was watching us all from over here, though – just peering through that berberis there,' smiled William.

'Yes, I can almost believe that. Do you know I am never lonely by this pond. When Grandpa died I was certain he was here and I've sort of grown up feeling that there was something very special about this part of the garden. Something very comforting.'

'This garden is their memorial. They would want no better one. Their cherished garden on the verge of spring! It's a pity you won't see it all this year, but I think old Jack and Jim will.'

'Why won't I see it all?'

'Because we sail for India next week.'

'*We*?'

'Yes, Effie. Here is your ticket.' He took out his wallet and sorted out the ticket to give her. 'Liverpool-Calcutta return. Outward journey on the S. S. *Maharajah*.'

'Will! But I can't!'

'No excuses accepted, remember? And there's that colossal conservatory to fill. I wasn't being pedantic when I said this was the start of a new era.'

Belva Plain

– the best-loved bestseller –

Evergreen

The tempestuous story of Anna Friedman, the beautiful, penniless Jewish girl who arrives in New York from Poland at the turn of the century and survives to become the matriarch of a powerful dynasty.

Random Winds

The poignant story of a family of doctors – Dr Farrell, the old-fashioned country doctor who dies penniless and exhausted, his son Martin who becomes a famous brain surgeon but is haunted by his forbidden love for a woman, and Martin's daughter Claire, headstrong and modern, whose troubled romance provides a bitter-sweet ending.

Eden Burning

A romantic saga set against the backdrop of New York, Paris and the Caribbean. The island of St Felice holds many secrets, one of which is the secret of the passionate moment of abandon that threatened to destroy the life of beautiful Teresa Francis. A story of violence, political upheaval and clandestine love.

Crescent City

Miriam Raphael leaves the ghettoes of Europe to become a belle of New Orleans. Trapped in a bad marriage she begins a turbulent, forbidden love affair with dangerous, attractive André Perrin. But the horrors of the Civil War sweep away the old splendour, and Miriam must rebuild her own and her family's life from the ashes.

FONTANA PAPERBACKS

Victoria Holt

The supreme writer of the 'gothic' romance, a
compulsive storyteller whose gripping novels of
the darker face of love have thrilled millions all
over the world.

THE CURSE OF THE KINGS
THE DEVIL ON HORSEBACK
THE HOUSE OF A THOUSAND LANTERNS
KING OF THE CASTLE
KIRKLAND REVELS
THE LEGEND OF THE SEVENTH VIRGIN
LORD OF THE FAR ISLAND
MENFREYA
MISTRESS OF MELLYN
MY ENEMY THE QUEEN
THE PRIDE OF THE PEACOCK
THE SECRET WOMAN
THE SHADOW OF THE LYNX
THE SHIVERING SANDS
THE SPRING OF THE TIGER
THE JUDAS KISS
THE DEMON LOVER
THE TIME OF THE HUNTER'S MOON
THE LANDOWER LEGACY

and others

FONTANA PAPERBACKS

Catherine Gaskin

'Catherine Gaskin is one of the few big talents now engaged in writing historical romance.'

Daily Express

'A born story-teller.' *Sunday Mirror*

THE SUMMER OF THE SPANISH WOMAN
ALL ELSE IS FOLLY
BLAKE'S REACH
DAUGHTER OF THE HOUSE
EDGE OF GLASS
A FALCON FOR A QUEEN
THE FILE ON DEVLIN
FIONA
THE PROPERTY OF A GENTLEMAN
SARA DANE
THE TILSIT INHERITANCE
FAMILY AFFAIRS
CORPORATION WIFE
I KNOW MY LOVE
THE LYNMARA LEGACY
PROMISES

FONTANA PAPERBACKS

Book Tokens

**Give them
the pleasure of choosing**

Book Tokens can be bought
and exchanged at most
bookshops.

Fontana Paperbacks: Fiction

Fontana is a leading paperback publisher of both non-fiction, popular and academic, and fiction. Below are some recent fiction titles.

- ☐ THE ROSE STONE Teresa Crane £2.95
- ☐ THE DANCING MEN Duncan Kyle £2.50
- ☐ AN EXCESS OF LOVE Cathy Cash Spellman £3.50
- ☐ THE ANVIL CHORUS Shane Stevens £2.95
- ☐ A SONG TWICE OVER Brenda Jagger £3.50
- ☐ SHELL GAME Douglas Terman £2.95
- ☐ FAMILY TRUTHS Syrell Leahy £2.95
- ☐ ROUGH JUSTICE Jerry Oster £2.50
- ☐ ANOTHER DOOR OPENS Lee Mackenzie £2.25
- ☐ THE MONEY STONES Ian St James £2.95
- ☐ THE BAD AND THE BEAUTIFUL Vera Cowie £2.95
- ☐ RAMAGE'S CHALLENGE Dudley Pope £2.95
- ☐ THE ROAD TO UNDERFALL Mike Jefferies £2.95

You can buy Fontana paperbacks at your local bookshop or newsagent. Or you can order them from Fontana Paperbacks, Cash Sales Department, Box 29, Douglas, Isle of Man. Please send a cheque, postal or money order (not currency) worth the purchase price plus 22p per book for postage (maximum postage required is £3.00 for orders within the UK).

NAME (Block letters) _____

ADDRESS _____

_____

_____

While every effort is made to keep prices low, it is sometimes necessary to increase them at short notice. Fontana Paperbacks reserve the right to show new retail prices on covers which may differ from those previously advertised in the text or elsewhere.